P

Through

"Kim Vogel Sawyer paints a picture of redemption and forgiveness in not one but many lives in *Through the Deep Waters*. Just as weary travelers found comfort in Mr. Harvey's hotels, readers will find comfort in this wrenching tale of one woman's shameful past and one man's struggle to look beyond her indiscretions and accept the woman she has become—a woman redeemed by grace. Ms. Sawyer's historically accurate novels tug the strings of the heart while giving hope to those who feel unworthy."

> —PAM HILLMAN, author of *Claiming Mariah*

"Kim Vogel Sawyer's careful attention to detail and heartfelt writing make her one of the industry's favorites."

> —LORI COPELAND, author of *The Healer's Touch*

"Kim Vogel Sawyer has crafted an emotion-packed novel about two damaged souls whose faith and courage ultimately come shining through. Readers will root for Dinah and Amos to overcome the wounds of their troubled pasts in order to find love and hope for the future. With its vividly rendered settings and well-rounded characters, this lovely story is sure to please Ms. Sawyer's many fans."

> —DOROTHY LOVE, author of *Carolina Gold*

Through the Deep Waters

BOOKS BY KIM VOGEL SAWYER

Echoes of Mercy
Just as I Am
The Grace That Leads Us Home
What Once Was Lost

Through the Deep Waters

Kim Vogel Sawyer

A NOVEL

WATERBROOK
PRESS

THROUGH THE DEEP WATERS
PUBLISHED BY WATERBROOK PRESS
12265 Oracle Boulevard, Suite 200
Colorado Springs, Colorado 80921

All Scripture quotations are taken from the King James Version.

This book is a work of fiction that includes some historical characters and facts. Details that cannot be historically verified are products of the author's imagination.

Trade Paperback ISBN 978-0-307-73129-6
eBook ISBN 978-0-307-73130-2

Copyright © 2014 by Kim Vogel Sawyer

Cover design by Kelly L. Howard; photography: girl by Kelly L. Howard; background by Danita Delimont

Published in the United States by WaterBrook Multnomah, an imprint of the Crown Publishing Group, a division of Random House LLC, New York, a Penguin Random House Company.

WATERBROOK and its deer colophon are registered trademarks of Random House LLC.

Library of Congress Cataloging-in-Publication Data
Sawyer, Kim Vogel.
    Through the deep waters : a novel / Kim Vogel Sawyer.
        p. cm.
    ISBN 978-0-307-73129-6 (pbk.) — ISBN 978-0-307-73130-2 1. Single women—Fiction. I. Title.
    PS3619.A97T47 2014
    813'.6—dc23

                                        2013045097

Printed in the United States of America
2014—First Edition

10 9 8 7 6 5 4 3 2 1

For those who feel broken inside,
with prayers for you to discover healing
through the precious touch of Jesus

And he said unto her, Daughter,
be of good comfort:
thy faith hath made thee whole.

—LUKE 8:48

Chapter 1

Chicago, Illinois, 1883
Dinah

inah Hubley curled her arms around the coal bucket, hunched her shoulders to make herself as small as possible, and then made a dash for the kitchen. The odors of stale tobacco, unwashed bodies, and stout whiskey assaulted her nose. Each time she made this trek through the waiting room, she tried to hold her breath—the smell made her want to give back her meager lunch. But weaving between the haphazard arrangement of mismatched sofas and chairs all draped with lounging men took longer than her lungs could last. So she sucked air through her clenched teeth and did her best to make it all the way through the room without being stopped.

No such luck. A man reached out from one of the overstuffed chairs and snaked his arm around her waist.

Dinah released a yelp as the man tugged her backward across the chair's armrest and into his lap. Lumps of coal spilled over the bucket's rim and left black marks on the bodice of her faded calico dress. But she was worried about something more than her only dress being soiled.

Keeping her grip on the bucket, she pushed against the man's chest with her elbow. He held tight and laughed against her cheek. "Hey, what's your hurry, darlin'? Stay here an' let ol' Max enjoy you for a bit." He nuzzled his nose into the nape of her neck, chortling. "I always did like gals with brown hair. Brings me to mind of a coon dog I had when I was a young start."

His foul breath made bile rise in her throat. She rasped, "Let me go, mister, please? I have to get the coal to the cook."

Max plucked the bucket from her arms and held it toward a lanky man who'd sauntered near. "Take the coal to the kitchen for this little gal, Jamie. Free her up for some time with me."

Jamie took the bucket and set it aside. Then he caught Dinah's arm and gave such a yank, she feared her arm would be wrenched from its socket. She didn't lose her arm, but the drunken man in the chair lost his grip. Her feet met the floor. She would have stumbled had Jamie not kept hold, and a thread of gratitude wove its way through her breast.

She regained her footing and offered the man a timid smile. "Th-thank you, mister."

Jamie's eyes glittered. Dinah knew that look. She tried to wriggle loose, but his fingers bit hard while his thumb rubbed up and down the tender flesh on the back of her arm. Shivers attacked her frame. He leaned down, his whiskered face leering. "How about ya show me instead of tellin' me? Gimme a kiss." He puckered up.

Dinah crunched her eyes closed. Her stomach rolled and gorge filled her throat.

A voice intruded. "Jamie Fenway, if you want to keep coming around here and making use of my girls, you'd better let loose of that one."

Relief sagged Dinah's legs when she realized the proprietress of the Yellow Parrot had entered the room.

The man released Dinah with an insolent shove, sending her straight against Miss Flo's ample front. Barrel-shaped and as strong as most men, the woman didn't even flinch. She took hold of Dinah's upper arms, set her upright, then turned her kohl-enhanced glare on Jamie and Max. "How many times do I have to tell you no free sampling, fellas? Everything you want is waiting upstairs, but until you've paid, you keep your hands, your lips, and whatever else you think you might be tempted to use to yourself."

The men waiting their turns with Miss Flo's girls laughed uproariously. One of them wisecracked, "Besides, Jamie, that one you grabbed on to ain't hardly worth stealin' a pinch. If she was a striped bass, I'd throw her back!" More guffaws and sniggers rang.

Jamie's slit-eyed gaze traveled up and down Dinah's frame. "Even the smallest fish tastes plenty good when it's fresh."

Dinah hugged herself, wishing she could shrink away to nothing.

Miss Flo grabbed a handful of Dinah's hair and gave a harsh yank. "What are you doing carting coal through the waiting room, anyway? I don't want that mess in my parlor."

A few smudges of coal dust would hardly be noticed among the years' accumulation of tobacco stains and muddy prints on the worn carpet. But Dinah ducked her head and mumbled meekly, "I'm sorry, Miss Flo."

"I know you're sorry, but that doesn't answer my question." Miss Flo's voice was as sharp as the teacher's—the one who berated Dinah for wearing the same dress to school every day and checked her head for lice in front of the whole class. "We've got a back door to the kitchen. Why didn't you use it?"

Dinah winced and stood as still as she could to keep her hair from being pulled from her scalp. "I couldn't get in through the back. The door's blocked."

"By what?"

Miss Flo's newest girl, Trudy, liked to meet one of the deputies on the back stoop. He was so tall Trudy had to stand on the stoop for their lips to meet. The image of them pressed so tight together not even a piece of paper could come between them was seared into Dinah's memory. But she wouldn't tattle. It was bad enough she had to listen to the taunts in school and on the streets of town. She wouldn't set herself up for belittling under the only roof she'd ever called home.

When Dinah didn't answer, Miss Flo growled and released her hair with another vicious yank. "Get that coal out of here."

Dinah bent over to grab the handle of the discarded bucket.

Miss Flo kicked her in the rear end, knocking her on her face. "And don't let me see you traipsing through this room again. Next time I might not be around to stop the men from taking their pleasure from you." She stepped over Dinah, the full layers of her bold-yellow skirt rustling. "All right, fellas, how about some music while you wait?" Men cheered and whistled. Miss Flo, her smile wide, plopped onto the upright piano's round stool and began thumping out a raucous tune. Drunken voices raised in song.

Dinah scrambled to her feet, grabbed the coal bucket, and raced from the room. She darted straight to the coal box in the corner and leaned against the wall, panting. So close… Jamie'd come so close to claiming her lips. She covered her mouth with trembling fingers as Miss Flo's warning screamed through her mind. The proprietress often screeched idle threats in Dinah's direction, but this one was real. The older she got, the more likely it became that the men who flocked to the Yellow Parrot after sundown seven days a week would see her as more than Untamable Tori's unfortunate accident.

The cook, a hulk of a man with a bald head and forearms the size of hams, glanced in Dinah's direction. "You gonna dump that coal in the hopper or just stand there hugging the bucket?"

Dinah gave a start. "S-sorry, Rueben." She tipped the bucket and dumped the coal into its holding tank. Black dust sifted upward. Some of the black bits were sucked up inside her nose. She dropped the dented bucket with a clatter and turned to cough into her cupped hands.

Rueben stirred a wooden spoon through a pot on the massive cast-iron Marvel range. The rich smell of rum rose. Another cabinet pudding in the making—Tori's favorite. For years Dinah had suspected Rueben was sweet on her mother, and when Dinah had been much younger, she harbored the whimsical idea that he might be her father. But when she asked him, hoping she'd finally get to call somebody Pa, he laughed so hard she scuttled away in embarrassment. Now, at the wise age of sixteen, she realized the question of her paternity would never be answered. Not with Tori's occupation being what it was.

Dinah inched toward the stove where the scent of the pudding's sauce would be stronger. The smell of rum on someone's breath turned her stomach, but somehow when rum was blended with cream and sugar, it became delightful. She leaned in, and Rueben grinned knowingly.

"Wantin' a sniff, are you?"

Everyone who called the Yellow Parrot home and everyone who visited knew better than to disturb Rueben when he was cooking. He considered preparing tasty dishes an art, and he tolerated no intrusion on his concentration. But he'd never sent Dinah away. She nodded.

"Well, tip on in here, then."

She put her face over the pot's opening. Steam wisped around her chin, filling her nostrils with the sweet, rich aroma. The foul smells from the parlor drifted away, and Dinah released a sigh of satisfaction.

"All right, move back now. I need to dump this over the sponge cake an' get it in the oven if it's gonna be done by suppertime."

Suppertime at the Yellow Parrot was served well after midnight. More often than not, Dinah was asleep by then and didn't have any supper. But Rueben always put a filled plate in the stove's hob for her breakfast. Rueben poured the thick sauce over chunks of sponge cake dotted with chopped figs and currants. She licked her lips. "What else are you fixing besides the pudding?"

"Got a leg of lamb with cherry sauce slow bakin' in the oven out back. I tucked in some whole sweet potatoes studded with cloves, too—I'll mash 'em with pecans and cinnamon."

Dinah's mouth watered.

"Plannin' to steam a batch of brussels sprouts and fix up a cream sauce to pour over 'em to kill the smell. You know how your ma pinches her nose when I fix those things. But she always gobbles them up anyway." He shrugged. "Nothin' much." Rueben moved to the washbasin and began trimming the thick stems from the brussels sprouts with a flick of a paring knife.

She should go upstairs. Her duties for the day were done, and unlike Miss Flo's girls, she didn't have the luxury of sleeping until noon. But instead, Dinah perched on a stool in the corner and watched Rueben work. She preferred the kitchen to any other room in the stately old house outside of town that Miss Flo had turned into a place of business. The good smells, the warm stove, the clean-scrubbed floor and work counters—Rueben wouldn't allow even a speck of dirt to mar his domain—provided her truest sense of "home." Until Rueben told her to get on up to her room, she'd stay.

Rueben sent a brief frown in her direction. "I heard the commotion in the parlor."

He had? "I didn't do anything wrong."

"You were in there durin' working hours. That's wrong."

Dinah's face flamed.

Rueben tucked the pudding into the oven, closed the door as gently as a mother placing a blanket on her sleeping newborn, then faced her. He put his beefy hands on his hips. Although he didn't scowl, his huge presence was intimidating enough. "I know why you used the front door instead of the back. I'm gonna tell Flo she needs to keep a tighter rein on Trudy. But that don't excuse you. You've gotta defend yourself, Dinah. You ain't a little girl anymore."

Dinah cringed, recalling the way Max's hand had roved across her rib cage. Although not as buxom as her mother's, her chest strained against the tight bodice of her one calico dress. She was womanly now. And in a place like this, being womanly was an invitation.

He went on in the same blunt tone—not kind, not harsh, but matter-of-fact—as if Dinah should already know these things. "If you want to carry coal through the back door, then you need to tell whoever's in the way to step aside. If you don't want somebody pestering you, then you need to come right out and tell 'em to leave you alone. If you don't want to stay in a brothel, then you need to pack a bag an' move on."

Dinah's jaw fell slack. She'd never had the courage to stand up to the sniggering schoolboys or snooty girls who taunted her. How could Rueben expect her to be brave enough to set out on her own? He'd lost his senses. "Where would I go? What would I do?"

He sauntered to the oak secretary where he planned his meals and made shopping lists. He pulled down the drop door that formed a desktop and reached into one of the cubbies. When he turned, he held a scrap of newsprint that he laid flat against the desk's scarred surface. "C'mere."

On quivering legs, Dinah obeyed.

He tapped one sausage-sized finger on the paper. "Read this."

She leaned over the desk. The dim light made it difficult for her to make out the print, but she read slowly, painstakingly, reciting it word for word inside her head. *"Wanted: Young women 18 to 30 years of age, of good moral* *character, attractive, and intelligent, to waitress in Harvey Eating Houses on the Santa Fe in the West. Wages: $17.50 per month with room and board. Liberal tips customary. Experience not necessary. Write Fred Harvey, Union Depot, Kansas City, Missouri."*

The reading complete, she hunkered into herself, deeply stung. Didn't Miss Flo call her an ugly duckling? Didn't the teacher at school remind her on the days she managed to attend classes she should just stay away because she'd never amount to anything? She was neither attractive nor intelligent and everyone knew it. Why would Rueben—the one person who'd been kind to her—tease her this way?

He bumped her shoulder. "What'd you think?"

She set her jaw and refused to answer.

He caught her chin between his thumb and finger and raised her face. "There's your chance. Write to this Fred Harvey. Get yourself outta here."

Rueben had chided her to speak up and say what she thought. She jerked her chin free of his grasp and spouted, "He won't take me! I'm— I'm—" She couldn't bring herself to repeat the hurtful words people had thrown at her all her life. So she said, "I'm only sixteen."

He snorted. "You won't be sixteen forever. An' with hotels an' restaurants poppin' up along the railroad line all the way to California, he'll be needing waitresses for a good long while." He folded the advertisement and pressed it into Dinah's palm. "Keep that. Write to him when your eighteenth birthday's past. Because, girlie, sure as my pudding'll come out of that oven browned just right and tastin' like heaven, if you stay here, you're gonna end up bein' one of Flo's girls." He curled his hand around hers, his big fingers strong yet tender. "Wouldn't you rather be one of Harvey's girls?"

Chapter 2

Dinah

*W*ouldn't *you rather be one of Harvey's girls?"* Over the next weeks as Dinah browsed the markets and filled shopping lists for Rueben, she thought about becoming one of Harvey's girls. When she washed the soiled linens and ironed the working girls' fancy robes and underthings, she imagined being one of Harvey's girls. As she sat at the desk in the back corner of the schoolroom completing lessons, she daydreamed about becoming one of Harvey's girls. Late at night in her attic bedroom, listening to the noises coming from the rooms below, she longed to become one of Harvey's girls.

Toward the end of May, school ended for the season. Although she'd passed the exams, she didn't attend the graduation ceremony to receive her eighth-grade certificate. If only she could be like the other students who walked across the teacher's platform and received the rolled document tied with a crisp black ribbon! But she'd look the fool, being so much older than the others who were privileged to attend daily rather than hit or miss. And she had no one who would attend, smile with pride from the audience, and offer congratulations afterward. Thus, participating in the ceremony for which she'd worked so long and hard held little joy.

Her seventeenth birthday arrived the first day of June. Rueben prepared her favorites for lunch—glazed ham with scalloped potatoes and steamed green beans seasoned well with bacon and onion—and baked her a spice cake with a half inch of fluffy vanilla cream between each of the three moist layers. All of Flo's girls trooped downstairs and partook of her birthday treat, but they fussed about eating such a heavy midday meal in place of their customary noon breakfast. They didn't sing to her, and no one gave her a present. Everyone else's lack of attention made Dinah appreciate Rueben's gesture all the more. She thanked him over and over for his kindness until he told her, "Hush now. You're embarrassing me."

When the girls shuffled back upstairs for a few hours of rest and quiet before the men began storming the doors, she offered to help clean up the mess. But Miss Flo looped elbows with her and tugged her away from the table.

"No dish washin' on your birthday. Come into the parlor with me instead."

Dinah caught a glimpse of Rueben's brows descending in a scowl, but Miss Flo ushered her out of the dining room so quickly she didn't have a chance to explore the reason for it. Miss Flo aimed Dinah for the bay window where two brocade chairs were crunched close together beneath heavy draperies. It would be a cheerful spot if the curtains were ever separated to let the sun pour in.

Miss Flo pointed to one chair, and Dinah sat while the proprietress flopped into the other with a loud *whish* from her silk skirts. Miss Flo folded her hands in her lap, crossed her legs with another wild rustling of skirts, and smiled— the warmest smile she'd ever aimed at Dinah. "Well now, seventeen, are you?"

"Yes, ma'am."

"And as unsullied as new-fallen snow..."

An uneasy feeling wriggled through Dinah's belly. "Ma'am?"

Miss Flo barked a short laugh. "Oh, I was just thinkin' how different you are from the girls upstairs. Them all bein' so...experienced. You're something of an oddity in a place like this, Dinah." Her well-rouged cheeks and kohl-darkened eyes gave her a hard appearance, yet Dinah believed she caught a hint of envy in the woman's expression. "By the time I was your age, I'd been workin' for over two years. Young but old already. This work will make you old fast. All you gotta do is look at your ma to see how this work ages a person."

Yes, Tori appeared much older than her thirty-nine years. She applied kohl to her eyes and bold rouge to her lips and cheeks, powdered her pale face, and dyed her hair with India ink—all attempts to look youthful. But nothing hid the truth. The woman who'd been known as Untamable Tori to the men of Chicago for the past twenty years was worn out.

Dinah's chest constricted. "I know."

"And she's sick, too."

Miss Flo spoke so flippantly Dinah wasn't sure she'd heard correctly. She crunched her brow. "What?"

"Sick. She's sick." Miss Flo examined her long fingernails, then picked at a loose cuticle. "It happens in this business if you ain't careful." She raised one brow and aimed a knowing look at Dinah. "An' considerin' that you came to be, we both know Tori ain't careful."

She'd noticed Tori's drop in weight and the dark circles under her eyes, but she'd just thought her ma was tired. "She's with child?"

Miss Flo rolled her eyes. "She's *sick*, I said."

Then Dinah understood. Twice before she'd watched one of Flo's girls succumb to a sickness that turned her skin yellow and made her waste away to nothing. And now the sickness had its hold on Tori. Dinah folded her arms across her ribs and held tight as fear and worry attacked.

Miss Flo lifted one shoulder in a shrug. "She didn't want me to tell you, but I figured you have a right to know. She is your ma, after all."

Dinah had never been allowed to call Tori by anything other than her name—she always claimed the men wouldn't be interested in her anymore if they knew she had a child. The few times she'd slipped and said "Ma" or "Mama," Tori had slapped her hard, so Dinah learned not to say the terms out loud. But inwardly she'd called her mother by the affectionate titles and longed for the day they'd leave this place and become a real mother and daughter. Another dream that would never come true.

Tears stung. She forced her voice past her tight throat. "Is there anything you can do?"

Miss Flo shook her head. The feathers she wore in her streaky black-and-gray hair gently waved, as if offering a sweet farewell. But there would be nothing sweet about Tori's passing—not if she had the same sickness as those other girls. "Not a thing. In fact, I ought to make her leave. Another week or two and she won't be able to work anymore. And you know everyone has to earn their keep around here."

In all of Dinah's lifetime, Tori had never set foot outside the confines of the Yellow Parrot. She rarely even ventured into the yard. Tori would die of fright if told to leave. Dinah clutched the carved armrests to keep herself in the chair. "But you can't send her away!"

"Well, I can't have her fillin' a room meant for moneymakin'." Miss Flo glared at Dinah. "This is a business, not a charity or a poor farm. If she can't earn, she can't stay."

No poor farm would take in a soiled dove. No charity house would extend a kind hand to someone who'd sold herself to men. Dinah's heart beat fast and hard. Panic made her dizzy. The girls of the Yellow Parrot were trapped here like birds in a cage. She hung her head, helplessness sweeping over her with the force of floodwaters breaking through a dam.

"But maybe…"

Dinah jerked her gaze at Miss Flo. The woman was smiling again. Sweetly. Invitingly. Whatever idea she had to keep Tori from being tossed onto the street, Dinah would listen.

"I could let your mama stay here through her last days. It would be hard on her, wouldn't it, to be sent off somewhere to die all alone? So I could put a bed for her in the attic, let her live out her final days under the roof where she's been sheltered an' fed all these years."

Hope ignited in Dinah's chest.

"I could do that if you'll give me, say, twenty-five dollars."

The hope fizzled and died.

"See, I figure with her bein' sick, she won't eat much. Accordin' to the doctor, she ain't gonna last even another three months, so I figure twenty-five dollars'll cover the rest of her life."

Dinah sagged in resignation. "I don't have twenty-five dollars."

The woman's gaze narrowed, her smile changing to a knowing smirk. "You could earn it."

Oh, no…

Miss Flo leaned forward, bringing her rouge-brightened face close to Dinah's. "I know a man—a rich businessman who doesn't visit the brothels. He has very specific…wants. And he pays well."

No, no, no...

"For settin' it up with him an' providing a room, I'd need to take my standard half. But your share would be fifty dollars, Dinah." Miss Flo's tone became wheedling. "Twenty-five to give for your ma's keep, an' twenty-five to use for yourself any way you please. A new dress—two or three, even. Some new shoes an' stockings an' hair ribbons. All kinds of things. Fifty dollars is more than most people earn in a whole month, an' you could make it just like that." She snapped her fingers and Dinah jumped. Miss Flo reached across the short distance between the chairs and took Dinah's hand. Her cold fingers squeezed, squeezed, squeezed. "I'll get it arranged. Yes?"

Dinah's ears rang. One line from the advertisement she'd memorized screamed through her mind: *"...of good moral character."* She'd given up on so many dreams—having a father, a mother, a home. Could she let her dream of becoming one of Harvey's girls die, too?

She yanked her hand from the woman's grip and leaped to her feet. "I'll find another way to take care of Tori!" She turned and raced for the stairs.

Miss Flo's mocking voice trailed after her. "No pay, no stay—for either of you. Remember that."

Every day during the month of June, Dinah set out in search of a job. She spoke to shop owners, café owners, clinic directors, and business office receptionists. She offered to mop floors, to scour pots, to wash linens or scrub aprons, to deliver messages—no job was too menial. And in every case when she answered the simple question, "Where do you live?" she was sent away with a firmly stated, "We don't need your kind around here."

After weeks of fruitless searching, she came to a grim realization. Her eighth-grade certificate, so slowly and painfully won, didn't matter. Her willingness to work hard at whatever task she was given didn't matter. By association, Dinah was tainted—trapped in the same cage that held her mother captive. She'd never find a decent job. Not in this city. And to get out of the city would take money.

With the summer sun waiting until late to creep over the horizon, the working hours at the Yellow Parrot moved forward. The customers preferred to visit under the cover of darkness. Dinah had always found it ironic that men who so eagerly and unashamedly forked over their dollars to Miss Flo didn't want to be seen coming or going. As summer descended, the most booming business took place between ten and midnight, with a few stragglers sticking around until two or three in the morning until Miss Flo finally gave them the boot.

On the last day of June, Dinah managed to stay awake until the very last man clomped off the porch, straddled his horse, and moseyed toward home. She waited until the girls had eaten their supper and returned to their rooms. She waited a little longer, until all murmuring and bedspring squeaking had hushed. Then she crept down the narrow enclosed stairway from the attic to the second floor and entered her mother's room.

Scant moonlight filtered through a slit in the heavy curtains and fell like a pale thread across Tori's sleeping face. For a moment Dinah hesitated. Despite her illness, Tori had worked tonight. She had to or Miss Flo would send her away. Her sagging skin and slack mouth proved her exhaustion. Maybe Dinah shouldn't disturb her. But by morning the others would be awake and would possibly overhear. And Dinah needed this conversation to remain private.

Drawing in a breath of fortification, she leaned forward and shook Tori's shoulder. "Tori? Tori, wake up."

Tori snuffled and slapped at Dinah's hand.

Dinah shook her again, more forcefully this time.

Slowly Tori's eyelids rose. Her bleary gaze settled on Dinah's face, and she scowled. "What're you doin', pesterin' me? Get outta here. Lemme sleep." She started to roll over.

Dinah caught her mother's arm, holding her in place. "You can sleep in a minute. I need to talk to you. It's important."

With a grunt, Tori wrenched her arm free. "What's so blamed important it can't wait until morning?"

After easing onto the edge of the bed, Dinah clutched her hands together and whispered, "You." She swallowed. "I know you're sick, Ma."

Tori's face pinched into a horrible grimace. "I told her not to say nothin' to you. An' don't call me Ma."

"I can call you Ma now. Nobody's around to hear. I needed to know about you being sick. You should've told me." Even as she chided her mother, Dinah realized the pointlessness. She and Tori had never talked—not the way she imagined mothers and daughters were supposed to talk, sharing secrets and laughs and concerns. Mothers and daughters were supposed to look out for each other. They might have failed in every other sense, but maybe they could do at least one thing right. "Miss Flo says if you can't work, you can't stay here anymore."

"Stingy old biddy." Bitterness tinged Tori's weak voice. "All these years I stayed, lettin' her get rich off me, an' now she's ready to put me out like some dried-up milk cow. She don't know the meaning of loyalty."

"I want to help you."

A soft snort left Tori's throat. "You got a cure up your sleeve?"

Dinah hung her head. "I can't make you well. But I...I want to take care of you. I can't let Miss Flo send you away. Not when there's a way to let you stay here."

A glimmer of hope appeared in Tori's purple-smudged eyes. "How?"

Why couldn't life be like the stories in the fairy-tales book Rueben had given her one year for Christmas, where a knight rode to the castle and rescued the distressed maiden from the dungeon? No knight would help her or her ma. Dinah had to depend on herself. "If I give Miss Flo some money, she'll let you stay. Until you..." She couldn't make herself say the word *die*.

"Where are you gettin' money?"

Dinah forced a glib shrug. "I found a way."

For long seconds, Tori stared at her through mere slits. "I wanted to get rid of you when I found out you were comin'. There're ways, you know."

Chills rolled through Dinah, as if her blood had turned to ice water.

"But I'd already done so much wrong, an' doin' away with you wouldn't fix none of it. So I went ahead an' brung you into the world. Brung you into this…this *den of iniquity*. An' over an' over I've wished I'd done different way back then. Wished I'd not brought you here at all."

Realization bloomed. Tori didn't regret Dinah's birth because she hated her, but because she hated the life into which she'd been born. Which meant her ma cared. Cared about *her*. The ice in her veins turned liquid and warm. Tears filled her eyes, and they pooled in Tori's eyes as well.

Tori continued brokenly. "Now here you are, a woman grown, offerin' to take care of me when I never in all your life did nothin' to take care of you." One tear rolled down her sunken cheek. "I don't deserve any kindness, Dinah. I don't deserve bein' cared for."

The rejections she'd faced over the past days, the past months, the past years swirled up like a giant whirlpool and threatened to topple Dinah from the edge of the bed. Even if she was just the illegitimate child of a prostitute, she'd deserved to be treated better. And even if Tori had sold her body to men to make a living, she didn't deserve to die alone on the streets. Why couldn't those high-and-mighty people in town turn up their noses at the men who paid the dollars instead of saving all their disgust for the women who pocketed the coins? Things sure were backward in the world.

She smoothed the tousled, dry strands of hair on her mother's head. "You deserve to be cared for, Ma, an' I'll see to it you are. You'll die warm in a bed instead of cold on a street."

Dinah returned to her room so her mother could sleep. She dropped into her tiny bed, resigned but also resolute. Tori would enjoy one small good in a whole host of bads. And Miss Flo said Dinah could use the money to buy anything she wanted. She'd use her twenty-five dollars to buy a train ticket and take herself to Mr. Harvey. So far away from Chicago nobody'd know where she'd been or what she'd done to earn her freedom. She'd be one of Harvey's girls, and nobody would look down his or her nose at Dinah ever again.

Chapter 3

Dinah

*D*inah perched on the end of the hotel room bed, where Miss Flo had directed her to sit. The woman, her face crunched in concentration, arranged Dinah's skirt just so and finger-combed her hair into a fluffy veil that tumbled across her shoulders. Then she stepped back, gave her a frowning examination, and finally nodded. "You'll do." She aimed her finger at Dinah's nose. "Stay right there so he'll see you when he comes in the door. He'll be here soon."

Dinah licked her dry lips. "What should I say to him?"

Miss Flo laughed. "He ain't comin' for conversation, Dinah."

Embarrassment heated her face. She hunkered low.

Hard fingers gripped her chin and yanked her upright. "Don't pull into a burrow like a scared rabbit."

Miss Flo's makeup caked in the lines of her mouth and eyes, drawing attention to every wrinkle. Dinah was glad she hadn't been told to paint her face. Up close, it looked terrible. The woman pinched Dinah's chin hard, as if she'd read Dinah's thoughts, before releasing her and moving toward the door to the adjoining room. "Just sit there, like I told you, and wait." She glanced back, her face impassive. "There's no reason to be scared. It's nothing, really, for the female. He'll do it all. You just do what he says, an' everything'll be fine." She swept through the doorway and clicked the door closed behind her.

And Dinah was alone. The gentleman coming was too fine to make use of one of the rooms at the Yellow Parrot so he'd rented a hotel room uptown. She'd never imagined being in anything so luxurious. A large gilt mirror on the wall reflected ceiling-to-floor damask draperies and an enormous four-poster brass bed with a lacy canopy. The thick mattress wore a silk cover of deepest green—dark as fir needles. Dinah cringed, imagining how she must look in the midst of such beauty. Like a thistle in a rose garden.

She folded her hands on the lap of her dress—her familiar blue-flowered calico—and crossed her bare feet. She'd wondered if she would have to wear one of the bawdy costumes the other girls wore for greeting the men, but Miss Flo said her everyday dress was best for this man. Dinah had been relieved. She felt like herself in this simple frock, even if it was faded and too tight in some places. Dressed like this, she didn't feel like a harlot. But she supposed even if she didn't dress like one, she was one. Miss Flo had waved the money—a fanned display of crisp bills—in excitement when the appointment was set. She hadn't given Dinah her half yet. She'd get it later. Afterward.

Nausea attacked. Could she do this? She swallowed. She had to do it. For Ma. To get out of this place. One time. Only one time. She could do it one time.

She stared at the raised paneled door. *"He'll be here soon,"* Miss Flo had said. If Dinah's heart didn't settle down, she might be dead by the time he arrived. She never felt such a thud and thump in her chest. Every muscle in her body was tight and aching, too. How had her mother borne this awful anticipation, night after night for years on end? Maybe she couldn't do this…

A scrape-click sounded—a key in the lock. Dinah pressed her palms against the cool silk bedspread and held her breath. The door eased open on silent hinges, and a long, trouser-covered leg slipped through. Dinah, her chest aching to hold its lungful of air, slid her gaze from the trouser leg to the buttoned vest and open suit coat, to the crisp white collar, and finally to the goateed face of a distinguished-looking gentleman.

Her breath whooshed out. He looked so different from the rough men who visited the Yellow Parrot. Clean shaven. Well dressed. Sophisticated. Even, she dared to reflect, fatherly with his nickel-colored, slicked-back hair and top hat held in his gloved hand. Her deepest apprehensions melted as she took in his appearance.

When he spotted her, a smile lifted the corners of his mouth, and Dinah found herself offering a timorous smile in reply. He tossed his hat onto the nearby dresser, took off his gloves, and closed the door with a sharp snap. Then he slipped his thumbs into the little pockets of his vest and gave her a thorough appraisal from her bare toes to her hair. His gaze seemed to linger on the thick, wavy tresses.

Should she have tied it back? She self-consciously reached to toss the strands over her shoulder.

"Don't."

Dinah froze with her fingers caught in the heavy strands.

"Leave it alone."

Miss Flo had told her to do what he said, so she lowered her hand to her lap and linked her fingers together again.

He removed his jacket and tossed it carelessly next to his hat. Then he began unbuttoning his vest. Little by little, the vest opened to reveal a white shirt straining against a well-filled belly. "Flo told me you were a pretty little thing."

Dinah gave a start. She had? She'd always called Dinah homely.

"She was right."

Heat filled Dinah's cheeks. Miss Flo had told her she didn't need to speak, but according to the deportment lessons at school, she should acknowledge his comment. "Th-thank you, sir."

He chuckled. "And polite, too." He tugged off the vest and sent it flying. It landed on the jacket and then fell to the floor. He left it there. He took a step toward her, his gold-flecked brown eyes pinned on her face. "I think we're going to get along just fine, Diana."

"Dinah."

"Dinah. Of course." He reached out with one hand and caught the trailing end of a strand of her hair. Slowly, he wound the freshly washed length around his finger, inching closer with each turn. Dinah sat as still as a mouse, hands in her lap, heart hammering. His trousers brushed her knees, sending a prickle down her spine. When his knuckle touched her temple, he arched one brow and gave her a pensive look. "Are you as innocent as Flo proclaimed?"

Unsure of what he'd been told, Dinah didn't know how to answer. She lifted her shoulders in an uncertain shrug.

He tugged on the strand of hair, and she tipped her head in response. Without warning, he planted his mouth over hers. His lips hadn't looked hard beneath his neatly trimmed mustache, but they felt hard. Demanding. Bruising. She tried to draw back, but his grip on her hair prevented her from moving. She whimpered.

He straightened as abruptly as he'd leaned in and released her hair with an impatient yank.

She touched one hand to her sore mouth and the other to her stinging temple. She blinked back tears.

He gazed at her, satisfaction glowing in his eyes. "Completely unspoiled." He tugged the shirttails from his waistband and began unbuttoning his shirt, the motions jerky and eager. "You'll be worth every penny of that two hundred dollars."

Two hundred? Dinah pulled in a startled breath and looked toward the adjoining door. Miss Flo had lied to her about the money. Other things the woman had said played through Dinah's memory. *"It's nothing, really, for the female… You just do what he says, and everything'll be fine."* Had she lied about all that, too?

She bolted to her feet, determined to fetch Miss Flo, but the man caught her arm.

"What are you doing?"

She strained to free herself. "I…I need to talk to Miss Flo."

With amazing ease, he lifted her and threw her onto the bed with the same indifference as he'd used when tossing his clothes aside. "You don't need Flo. I'll show you what to do."

Dinah scrambled for the edge. "No. I want Miss Flo."

His gaze hardened. "I don't give a fig what you want." He gave her a vicious shove that sent her backward. Her skirt flew up, and his gaze fell to her exposed limbs and ruffled underthings. His eyes glittered in a far-too-familiar manner. Had she really thought him a gentleman? He was no different than

Jamie or Max or any of the others who'd sent lecherous looks her way in the past year.

Dinah quickly shifted to a seated position and pushed her skirts down until they covered her ankles. Her ears rang. Her head throbbed. Her heart pounded so hard her chest felt ready to explode. "Please get Miss Flo. She's in the room next door. I don't want to do this."

"Shut up." He reached for her bodice.

His fingertips connecting with her collarbone ignited waves of shame and fear and revulsion. Dinah pushed his hands away and began to cry. "Please... Let me talk to Miss Flo."

"Didn't I tell you to shut up?"

She pulled as much air as possible into her heaving lungs and bellowed, "Miss Flo!"

He swung his palm against her cheek with a resounding smack. The force sent her flat against the mattress again. She yelped, and he silenced any further sound by clamping his hand over her mouth. The soft edge of his palm blocked her nostrils. She couldn't breathe. Panic thundered through her veins. His face loomed over hers, his expression forbidding. "This can be easy or hard. Do what I say, and it will be easy. Keep fighting me and..."

He didn't finish the threat, but he didn't need to. Her throbbing cheek communicated his meaning. And she needed air. Stars were dancing behind her eyes. She bobbed her head slightly. A smile reappeared on his face, and he moved his hand. Dinah sucked in a long, shuddering breath.

"Good girl." He patted her face on the same spot he'd slapped. She bit her lip to keep from whimpering. He slipped his fingers beneath her collar. With one fierce jerk, he tore open the bodice all the way to her waist.

She shivered as nausea rolled through her stomach. She was going to be sick. If he slapped her for talking, he'd surely beat her senseless if she dared to vomit. Dinah crunched her eyes closed. This was a dream. Only a dream... A nightmare, yes, but not real. It couldn't be real.

Over the next hour she learned Miss Flo wasn't the only liar. Dinah had lied to herself—it was real, not a nightmare. And he'd lied, too. There was nothing *easy* about what he did to her. When he finished, he made use of the water in the pitcher, dressed, and left without a word.

She lay on the soiled mattress, curled in a discarded ball, for nearly another hour before she found the courage to unfold her sore, aching body. Bruises dotted her wrists. More decorated her thighs. Warm, silent tears rolled down her cheeks as she haltingly gathered the torn remnants of her dress, petticoats, and chemise.

As she eased herself up with her wadded clothing in her arms, she caught a glimpse in the mirror of a pale face wearing a pinkish-purple smudge on the cheekbone and surrounded by a mass of tangled hair. She blinked twice in confusion. Was that truly her? She took two stumbling steps closer and stared hard at the image. Yes, her own face—and yet a stranger's face—peered back at her.

She dropped her clothes, covered her face with her palms, and burst into loud, pain-filled sobs. Her entire body convulsed with the force of her crying, but the torrent of tears did nothing to wash away the pain and degradation of the past hours.

A door latch clicked, footsteps approached, and someone slipped something warm and soft around her bare shoulders. Hands guided her to the bed and eased her onto its edge. Then fingers caught her bruised wrists and pulled them downward. Despite the thick robe covering her nakedness, chills shook Dinah's frame. She looked at Miss Flo, who stood before her. Tears veiled her eyes, making the woman's image waver, but she heard clearly her calm, unconcerned statement.

"I've ordered a tub an' hot water. You'll feel better after you've soaked a bit an' had a good wash."

Dinah might have foolishly believed such a statement earlier, but her innocence had been shattered. That man—that so-called *gentleman*—had left his imprint on her soul just as he'd left his mark on her face. She'd never be clean. She'd never feel better. She touched her bruised cheek with her trembling fingers and grated out, "Liar."

She expected Miss Flo's anger, but instead the woman laughed. She kicked at the pile of clothes on the floor. "I'm glad I thought to bring another dress. You're gonna need it."

Dinah swiped the tears from her face with her wrists, then hunkered into the robe. "I don't want your dress." She didn't even want the promised money. But she'd take it. She hated how much she needed it. She hated herself for how much she needed it.

Miss Flo balled her hands on her hips. "Well, you can't leave here in the altogether. So you'll have to take it whether you want it or not." She sighed and plopped down next to Dinah. "Listen, honey, take it from someone who knows. It'll never hurt like this again. But there's only one first time. That's why you gotta get as much as you can from it." She reached out as if to pat Dinah's knee, but Dinah jerked away. Miss Flo sighed again and rose. "I'll go hurry them up with that tub. Just wait there." She left the room.

Naked and so sore it hurt to breathe, Dinah had no choice but to wait. One of Miss Flo's comments returned to haunt her. *"There's only one first time."* She found no reassurance—if it were even true—that it would never hurt like this again, but it mattered little compared to the realization now collapsing her heart.

Her entire life she'd envied the children who went home to a mother and father, who fought and shared and played with brothers and sisters. She'd dreamed of the day she would grow up, marry, have children, and be part of such a family herself. Why hadn't she stopped to think about the future, being courted, giving herself to her husband on her marriage bed?

"There's only one first time." She had just sacrificed something she could never get back. No decent man would want her now.

Chapter 4

Florence, Kansas
Amos

mos Ackerman ducked beneath the straggling branches of the scrub oak growing next to the chicken yard and shook his head at the Leghorn hen sitting as pretty as a queen on her throne on a low branch. "What is it you're doing up there?"

The chicken tipped its head and blinked one round black eye.

"All the nice roosting boxes I built for you and your friends, and you think you need to sit in a tree?"

It clucked as if defending itself.

Amos laughed. "Is that so, huh? Well, I don't think I believe a word of it." He lifted the chicken from its roosting spot, ignoring its indignant *cluck-cluck-cluck* and wing flapping, and placed it gently on the ground. "Go on now. Keep your feet on the ground where they belong." The chicken joined the other feathered fowl pecking in the yard, and Amos chuckled at its continued complaining squawk.

He stood for a moment beneath the tree's skinny branches and observed his flock. Four dozen in all—snowy Leghorns with rosy combs that flopped to the side as if too lazy to stand upright. They were sassy birds, chattering to one another as they foraged among the clumps of grass for tasty morsels. Pride filled his chest. Would he ever have imagined owning such a fine bunch of chickens? No, never. But Ma always said God gifted His children beyond their deserving, and Amos Ackerman's chicken farm proved it.

A prayer left his heart, his talking to God as instinctive as breathing.

Thank You, my dear Lord and Savior, for my home and the means of providing for myself.

Bending forward to avoid catching his hat on the tree's prickly branches, he moved into the sunshine. The mid-July sun burned hot overhead, and he hurried across the yard to the barn where its deep shadows would offer a cool respite. He'd learned to swing his good leg twice as far as the bad one to make up for his stiff hip, giving him an awkward but effective gait.

The Leghorns had scattered from him in nervousness the first time he moved among them, but over their weeks together they'd grown accustomed to his hitching means of walking and now pecked, unconcerned and trusting, around his feet. He had lots of reasons to like the birds—their willingness to forage for food, their easy acceptance of the roosting house, their consistent delivery of eggs each day that would let him make a decent living—but he liked them most because they didn't shy away from him.

He reached the barn, and two curious hens darted ahead of him to poke their beaks against the dark earth floor. He stepped past them and made his way to the straw-lined wagon where he'd placed the morning's eggs in with the previous two days' bounty. Admiring the washed, smooth orbs, he smiled. Twelve-dozen eggs in three days' worth of laying. When the salesman in Hutchinson had told him the birds would each lay an egg up to 360 days a year, Amos had been skeptical. Almost an egg a day? But so far, the man's words had proven true.

Of course, the hens were tricky about it, laying an egg in twenty-five-hour cycles and only when the sun shone. So his egg retrieval had to change every day according to the hens' schedule. There'd be fewer eggs in the wintertime, too, with the shorter days. But even so, he was happy with his choice of the Leghorns. They were certainly the best egg-laying chickens a man could own.

He fingered the eggs, thinking. At twenty cents per dozen, with four dozen hens laying, he could make eighty cents a day. If he doubled his flock, then he could make a dollar and sixty cents a day. A dollar and sixty cents times 360 days came to—

With a wry chuckle, he stopped himself. He sent a grin in the direction of the two hens. "What now, am I counting eggs before you even lay them? I should know better."

He took hold of the handle of his wagon and headed for the barn door. The wagon was nothing more than a child's toy, but it worked for transporting his eggs into town. He'd spent every one of his carefully saved pennies plus the money Pa had given him—what Pa called an early inheritance—to buy the farm and chickens, so he couldn't afford a horse to get his eggs to those who would buy them. But it was less than two miles into Florence. Even with his bum hip, he could make it. Hadn't the Lord been good to lead him to a farmstead close enough to town for him to walk? *Thank You, dear Lord.*

The wooden wheels moaned like rusty hinges, and the pair of chickens scattered, clucking in alarm when he pulled the little cart from the barn. "Now, now, you are fine. It's only noise. It can't harm you."

Without warning, words he'd heard in the past taunted his memory. His mother always quoted the rhyme about sticks and stones breaking his bones but words not hurting. Ma had been right about most things but not that.

Words did hurt, and even remembering them hurt.

But he was far from those who had tormented him, so he pushed aside the remembrances and addressed the chickens once more. "Be good and stay on the ground. No flying up in trees. I'll be back soon."

He headed down the dirt road, his wagon squeaking behind him. Was it foolish to talk to chickens? Most people would probably think so, but sometimes a man needed to say things out loud. There wasn't anyone else around to listen. His heavy boots scuffed up dust, but the Kansas wind whisked it away. He watched his long shadow stretch toward the scrubby brush alongside the road, and a hint of melancholy struck. If only the shadow were another person walking with him.

"Now that I'm settled," he said to his shadow, "I should get myself a dog. A dog could walk to town with me." Maybe he could even get two—one to go with him and one to stay behind and keep watch over the chickens. Not that he worried much about predators during daylight hours. Even so, extra precaution wouldn't be foolish. He'd ask in town about litters of puppies.

Some dogs chased chickens, he knew, but they could be trained not to do so. His pa had trained their dog by hanging a dead chicken around its neck and then beating it. Afterward, the dog had been afraid of chickens, but it had also been afraid of Pa. So Amos wouldn't train his dogs in such a heartless manner. He wouldn't want his dogs skulking away from him in fear.

He paused, checked to be sure the eggs weren't bouncing together, switched hands on the handle, then set off again. Yes, it would be nice to have a dog or two to sit beside the table when he ate his meals or to trot along with him when he did his chores. He'd look less silly talking to a dog than to the chickens. Dogs were good companions.

But even better than a dog would be a wife.

Sweat dribbled into his eyes, and he winced. He yanked off his hat, cleared the moisture from his forehead with his shirt sleeve, then tied the handkerchief he always carried in his pocket around his head to catch any other dribbles. He settled the hat over the bandanna. It was a tight fit but it worked. He moved forward, the sun heating his head and shoulders, a breeze teasing his cheeks, and his thoughts carrying him to places he tried not to go.

He'd turned twenty-four in mid-January. By the time his older brothers had reached twenty-four years, they were already married with a youngster or two underfoot. Although the Good Book advised against covetousness, he envied his brothers. Partly because they had families, and partly because they had two healthy legs that enabled them to walk behind a plow and cultivate the soil, just as Pa had done before them. Pa was proud of his strapping farmer sons. Another reason to envy his brothers.

They'd been astounded when he said he intended to raise chickens. He'd only be squandering his money, they told him. Chickens stunk, they said. Chickens were messy. Chickens attracted foxes and coyotes and hawks, and he'd never be able to raise enough of them on his own to make a living. Recalling their bold statements, he even envied their surety—Titus and John were confident men, so unlike Amos.

But maybe he had some confidence after all because he'd spouted at them,

"Wait and see. I will be a successful chicken farmer." Then he'd gone ahead and bought the farm and chicks despite his brothers' dire predictions. And things weren't going so bad for him.

People in town bought his eggs. He even sold a few, at a reduced price, to the local grocer. If that big, fancy hotel run by Mr. Fred Harvey started buying his eggs instead of having them brought in on the railroad, he'd be set. He squared his shoulders and felt a smile growing. Wasn't it fine to prove his brothers wrong? To show his pa he was still capable of taking care of himself even with his bum leg? And if he showed himself capable of making a living, then maybe—*It's possible, God, isn't it? I don't want to be alone my whole life long*—he'd find a lady who didn't mind his gimpy gait and crooked hip.

He reached the edge of Florence and stopped at the first house, where the missus had said she'd take a dozen eggs twice a week. She answered the door on his first knock. A bright smile burst across her round face.

"Good morning, Mr. Ackerman! I was hoping you'd be by today. I need to bake a birthday cake for my youngest grandchild—he turns three tomorrow—and I'm all out of eggs."

"Do you need more than a dozen?" Amos couldn't resist bragging, "I have plenty."

She held out her apron skirt to form a pouch, laughing as she did so. "How about two dozen today, then?"

"Yes, ma'am." Amos loaded her apron, careful to place the eggs so the shells wouldn't crack. He counted out twenty-four and then waited while she went inside to unload her apron and fetch his payment. He cringed when she returned with a fifty-cent piece pinched between her fingers. "I'm sorry, ma'am. I came here first, and I don't have any change."

"No need to worry." She pushed the coin at him. "You just keep it."

He held up both hands in protest. "Oh no, ma'am! I can't take a whole fifty cents from you."

"That's what I would pay the grocer for two dozen eggs, and Mr. Root doesn't deliver them to my doorstep."

"But—"

A mock scowl marred her face. "Didn't your ma teach you not to argue with your elders?"

Amos chuckled self-consciously and ducked his head. His ma had taught him that and a whole lot more. He pocketed the coin, then met the woman's gaze. "Thank you, ma'am. And tell that grandson of yours happy birthday."

Her smile returned. "I will. Good day, Mr. Ackerman."

The woman's kindness warmed his insides as much as the sun overhead warmed his outsides. Amos continued his trek through town, knocking on doors, accepting refusals as politely as he accepted coins in exchange for eggs. By the time he reached Root's Grocer, only twelve eggs remained nestled in the straw. The owner took them and gave Amos fifteen cents, which Amos requested be placed on his account. Then he used up that credit plus a little more by buying cornmeal, a half pound of sugar, coffee, beans, and a side of bacon.

He bade Mr. Root farewell, loaded his wagon with his purchases, and turned his feet toward home. But then he paused at the edge of the boardwalk. The steep-pitched roof of the three-story turret on the Clifton Hotel peeked above the treetops, capturing his attention. Selling his eggs to individuals was fine and good, but if he wanted to fulfill his dreams of expanding his business—adding more chickens to his flock for eggs and also for meat—he needed to sell to something bigger. And the Clifton Hotel, the townsfolk of Florence boasted, was the biggest hotel in all of Kansas.

The Santa Fe railroad that had brought him to town carried passengers through Florence every day of the week. When the train stopped for watering, those passengers marched up to the lunch counter or entered the dining room to partake of the hotel's offerings. Word had it, up to a hundred people enjoyed a meal in the hotel each day. Which meant the cook needed eggs. Lots of eggs. Would they let Amos provide them?

Temptation to head over to the hotel and ask to speak to the manager made his feet itch. But then he glanced down the length of his dusty bibbed overalls to the toes of his scuffed boots. When a man pursued a business deal, he shouldn't be dressed in his work clothes. Besides, he'd sold every last egg from his wagon. The manager and cook would want to see the quality of his eggs—their size and color—before making a decision.

A distant whistle cut through the air, alerting him that another train would pull into the station soon. At the same time, his stomach rumbled. Dinnertime already. He needed to get back to his farm. Giving the wagon's handle a tug, he bounced the wooden box from the boardwalk and headed for home.

As he followed the dirt road out of town, he made his plans. Tonight he'd fill his big tin tub and take a bath. With store-bought soap so he'd smell extra good. Then in the morning, after he gathered the eggs, he'd put on his Sunday suit and take the fresh eggs in to the hotel. Anticipation coiled through his stomach, making him wish he could leap in the air and kick his heels together in excitement, the way he'd done before the accident stole the ability from him. But even if his legs couldn't leap, his heart could. It beat an eager thrum the whole way back to his farm.

Because tomorrow, his dreams very well could come true.

Chapter 5

Kansas City, Kansas
Dinah

I'm very sorry, Miss Hubley, but Mr. Harvey's stipulations for servers are quite clear. You must be eighteen years of age to apply for a position as waitress in one of the restaurants."

Dinah slunk low in the tapestry chair on the far side of the interviewer's desk. With her fistful of money, she'd purchased decent clothing and train tickets. Then she secured an interview with the Harvey House representative and traveled the distance from Chicago to Kansas City, all in pursuit of a dream. Hadn't she learned by now dreaming was a useless waste of time? Of course she had, but at Rueben's encouragement she'd found the courage to climb into the boat of hope. Mrs. Walters's statement poked a hole in the boat's bottom, and Dinah sank with it.

Why hadn't she lied about her age? She'd already given a false address and blatantly misled the Harvey representative concerning her moral character. She'd claimed herself an orphan, which might not be true—Tori'd been buried two days ago, but Dinah didn't know if her father, whoever he was, still lived. So many mistruths had slipped from her lips, but when asked her age, she baldly gave an honest answer. Perhaps there was some small droplet of decency still left within her dry, barren soul. But what had her honesty accomplished? Rejection. A bitter taste filled her mouth.

Mrs. Walters's face pursed in sympathy. "Don't be so downtrodden, Miss Hubley. Your eighteenth birthday will come in a year's time, and you can apply then for a waitressing position."

Tiredness, frustration, helplessness rose up in one mighty wave. "What am

I to do until then? I can't go back—there's nothing there for me. I came all this way for a job so I could take care of myself. I'm almost out of money." She'd have had a tidy sum if she hadn't purchased a burial plot in one of the city's nicest cemeteries, a fine pine casket, and a carved granite headstone. But she couldn't bear to place her mother in an unmarked grave in the potter's field no matter how Rueben chided her for spending her money on the dead rather than the living.

She blinked back tears and finished. "Please, won't you let me train to become one of Mr. Harvey's servers? I won't tell anyone I'm only seventeen."

The woman's eyebrows descended. "We must be forthright with Mr. Harvey, Miss Hubley." Her expression softened. "But if you're open to other positions…"

The draining hope dared to puddle. "Other positions?"

Mrs. Walters began ruffling through a stack of papers on her desk. Her face lit up and she lifted one small sheet. "Would you be willing to go to Florence?"

The name sent a jolt through Dinah's middle. She looked frantically right and left, as if Miss Flo might materialize from the wood paneling.

Mrs. Walters continued, seemingly unaware of Dinah's inner turmoil. "The Clifton Hotel in Florence, Kansas—Mr. Harvey's only hotel—has need of a chambermaid."

Slowly Dinah's frozen mind thawed enough to process the interviewer's words. Florence was the name of a town. In Kansas. Far from Chicago. "You said…chambermaid?"

"Yes. You would be responsible for cleaning the hotel rooms after guests have departed. The job includes a room and meals as well as uniforms and sixteen dollars a month. Might this interest you?"

A chambermaid. Cleaning other people's messes. Wasn't that what she'd been doing at the Yellow Parrot since she was big enough to wield a broom? A lump of cynicism tried to fill her throat, but she pushed it down. At least she'd be part of Mr. Harvey's staff. And next year, after her birthday, she could apply again to become a server.

Dinah offered a hesitant nod. "I am interested, but I don't have much money. What does a train ticket cost to get to…" She didn't want to say the name *Florence*.

A smile tipped up the woman's lips. "If you accept the position, I will arrange transport for you." She glanced at the stately grandfather clock in the corner. "As a matter of fact, I believe we can get you to the station for the evening train, and you could be in Florence by morning."

She paused, gazing at Dinah with expectation. "Shall I send a telegram to the manager at the Clifton Hotel, informing him the position for chambermaid has been filled?"

Dinah closed her eyes. Becoming a chambermaid hadn't been her plan, but at least she'd be sheltered, fed, and clothed. She'd be far from Chicago where the stigma of the Yellow Parrot couldn't touch her. She'd be working for Mr. Harvey, perhaps earning his respect, and have the chance to become a server when she turned eighteen.

"Miss Hubley?"

Dinah popped her eyes open.

"If I'm to reach the manager with a telegram today, I need an answer."

Dinah drew in a big breath and blew it out. *Florence, Kansas…* Could she live in a town with the same name as the woman who'd callously arranged to steal her innocence? But what other choice did she have? Resigned, she nodded. "Yes, ma'am. I'll go."

Florence, Kansas
Amos

Amos cradled the basket of eggs against his ribs and made his way up the paved walkway dividing the front garden of the Clifton Hotel into identical halves. Although he'd seen them before, he couldn't resist pausing to admire the pair of ornate fountains sending up water in a crystal stream. Something inside his chest seemed to flutter. A man who could afford such elaborate trappings in the yard of his business would have the money to buy eggs. He only needed the manager to take a liking to him and his Leghorns' creamy-white eggs.

As he stepped onto the porch, lifting his good leg first and pulling the lame one behind him, a ruckus greeted his ears. He peeked through the big glass window into the dining room. Such activity! The chairs around all six tables held guests, and waitresses in long black dresses with starched white aprons bustled here and there, bringing out plates of food. He drew back.

In his eagerness to show his eggs to the manager, he'd forgotten the morning train carried passengers hungry for breakfast. He peeked in the window again, shaking his head. Such a dolt! No one would talk to him with all those people wanting their food. Well, then, he would wait. Twenty minutes—that was the length of time the engineer needed to fill the train's tank with water. Not much time at all.

Tucking the basket, which he'd covered with a red-checked square of cloth to make it look more presentable, under his arm, he aimed himself for the gazebo corner of the rambling porch. White-painted wicker chairs invited guests to sit and relax. Guilt tried to nibble at him—he wasn't a guest, so should he make use of those chairs?—but in the end the ache in his hip from the long walk overrode any worry. He needed to sit.

He moved beneath the octagon roof, sighing as the shade from the lilac bushes growing alongside the railing touched him. His dark wool suit was too warm for this weather, but he owned no other. Underneath, he felt sticky from sweat, and he hoped the scented soap from last night's bath hadn't worn off already. He chose a chair near the hotel's lapped siding and sank down, placing the basket of eggs in his lap.

Only then did he notice he wasn't alone. On a chair in the deepest shade from the lilacs, a girl slept with her feet tucked up underneath her. Her hands, the palms pressed together and resting against the chair's rolled armrest, formed a pillow for her cheek. A few strands of her light-brown hair had worked loose from her simple braid and swayed gently against her jaw as the Kansas breeze teased its way through the thick bushes. How peaceful she looked. He couldn't help smiling at the picture she created.

But he'd startle her if she awakened and found him sitting there staring at her. He should find someplace else to wait. One hand gripping his basket, he used the other to push himself out of the chair. As his weight left the seat, the chair tipped up on two legs, then descended with a hollow thump against the floorboards.

The girl leaped up so quickly Amos thought she might sail over the railing and into the lilacs. Round eyes as delicately blue as the larkspur growing in Ma's garden back home stared at him in obvious fright. She clutched her fingers together at her waist, and her bodice lifted and fell with frantic puffs of breath. Her face had lost all color. If she fainted, he would catch her. But first he'd better put down his eggs.

When he bent to place the basket on the chair, the girl gasped and covered her mouth with both hands. "Wh-what are you going to do?"

His eggs safely set aside, he straightened and gave the girl a curious look. Because her hands were over her mouth, he couldn't be certain he'd heard her correctly. "Did you ask what I'm going to do?"

She nodded, still hiding the lower half of her face—an appealing face, Amos noted—heart shaped with high cheekbones and thick-lashed eyes.

He chuckled and gestured to his little basket. "Well, I hope I am going to sell my eggs to the hotel's manager."

Her wide-eyed gaze zipped to the basket and then back to him. Slowly she lowered her hands. "Oh." Her shoulders wilted, and she eased back into the chair.

Amos heaved a prayer of gratitude that he wouldn't have to catch her after all. He'd never held a girl before, and his hands went moist just thinking of doing so now.

The train whistle blasted, the sound piercingly shrill so close. Both he and the girl winced. Guests spilled out of the hotel and headed across the street to the loading platform, their clamoring voices nearly as loud as the whistle had been. In a few more minutes, he'd be able to take his eggs inside and show them to the manager. But he needed to do something else first.

He hitched two steps closer to the girl—one wide stride, one shorter one.

She shrank back, her blue eyes sparking with distrust. He stopped. "I want to say I'm sorry for scaring you. I didn't see you there until I'd already sat down, or I would have left you alone to sleep." From the look of her pale face, purple-smudged eyes, and trembling limbs, she needed a good long rest.

Sympathy twined through his chest followed by a host of questions. Why was she sleeping on the hotel porch? Was she old enough to travel alone? She didn't appear to be, so where were her parents? Why was she so skittish? Her reaction to his approach brought back painful reminders of his family's dog slinking away in fear from Pa. He swallowed and asked, very kindly, "Will you forgive me?"

She stared at him, her brow puckering as if she were confused. Her rosy lips parted, closed, then parted again. Her answer sighed out, so soft he might have imagined it. "Yes."

Amos smiled, more relieved than he could explain. "Good. Good." He picked up his basket of eggs and started for the dining room. His feet on the floorboards made an odd *bump-clunk,* his bad leg falling heavier than the other.

"Mister?"

The girl's timid voice stopped him. He looked over his shoulder.

She was pointing at his hip. Her cheeks wore bright splashes of pink. "What...broke you?"

Heat rushed to his face. The question was tactless, yet her tone held no rancor. He sensed she didn't intend to insult him, so he decided to answer. "A wagon wheel rolled over me when I was eleven."

"Oh..."

Her expression held such deep dismay he wanted to assure her. "It was a long time ago. It doesn't bother me anymore." Well, it did, both in physical pain and embarrassment, although not as much as it had in the beginning. But he didn't need to tell her all that. To his relief, a small smile appeared on her face. "Good-bye now, miss." He plodded the remaining distance to the front doors and started inside. But before he crossed the threshold, he glanced at the girl.

She still sat in the chair but with her hands braced on the armrests, leaning forward a little. Tense. Alert. Like a prairie dog keeping watch for a preying hawk. His heart turned over. She'd asked what had broken him. An unexpected question formed in his mind.

What had broken her?

Chapter 6

Dinah

inah waited until the man with the basket of eggs entered the dining room. Then she flopped back into the chair with a sigh of relief. Had she really fallen asleep out here in the open? What a foolish thing to do. Anyone could have sneaked up on her—and someone did!

When the chair legs crashed against the floor, she'd been certain he was coming after her. In her sleepiness, his dark suit, combed-back hair, and solid form had too closely resembled another man. But then he spoke kindly. And then he limped. And then he asked her forgiveness.

She shook her head in wonder. He'd only frightened her, but he asked for her forgiveness. He hadn't even sneaked a look at her chest—she knew because she watched his eyes. He behaved respectfully, speaking to her gently while keeping his eyes and hands to himself. No, he hadn't been anything like the men who visited the brothel or the man who'd hurt her.

Even so, she needed to be careful.

Now wide awake, she contemplated going inside. She'd tried to go in earlier when the train cars emptied of passengers, but the man at the desk asked if she was eating, and when she said no, he sent her away before she could explain. Now that everyone was gone, she should let the manager know his new chambermaid had arrived. But she didn't move.

The man with the eggs was in there, talking to the manager. She didn't want to disrupt their conversation. Mostly she didn't want to see the man again. He must think her a complete ninny, the way she'd behaved. She hated feeling so jumpy inside, always fearful. The egg man said he'd gotten hurt a long time ago and it hardly bothered him anymore. Would she be able to make the same claim someday?

The sound of footsteps—uneven ones—reached her ears. She hunkered low in the chair and peeked over the high back. Sure enough, the egg man was leaving. She tried to see his face. If he looked happy, she'd know he'd sold his eggs. But he held the basket upright in the curve of his arm. If it was empty, he wouldn't have a reason to carry it up against his ribs. So he must not have sold them.

Unexpectedly, anger boiled in her middle. He'd looked so eager, saying he hoped the manager would buy his eggs. Would a cook need eggs? Of course he would—Rueben had arranged for daily delivery of eggs at the Yellow Parrot. So why had the manager said no? She watched the man stride away in his funny big step–little step way. If she had a house and a kitchen, she'd chase after him and buy some eggs to make up for the manager's refusal, even if it took every penny she had left in her pocket. It wasn't fair. Life wasn't fair.

"May I help you?"

The voice startled her so badly she yelped. She bounced up from the chair and turned to find herself being scrutinized by a short, wiry, gray-haired man wearing round, thick spectacles on the end of his nose.

The man's heavy gray brows descended in a scowl. "Are you a guest here at the Clifton?"

Dinah shook her head. "No, sir. I was hired to be the new chambermaid."

His expression remained dour. "You're Miss Dinah Hubley?"

"Yes, sir."

"What are you doing out here on the porch, then? The telegram Mrs. Walters sent yesterday afternoon indicated you'd be arriving on the morning train. The morning train's already come and gone, and you haven't checked in with me."

So this must be the hotel manager. The past days had been fraught with difficulties—standing firm against Miss Flo's wheedling to stay and take her mother's place, handling Tori's death and burial, traveling to Kansas City, being sent to Florence to clean rooms rather than serve diners… And now she was being scolded when she'd only done what the man at the desk inside had told her to do, which was to go away. Added to that, the manager had refused to buy the nice man's eggs.

"What was wrong with the eggs?"

The manager blinked twice, his pale-brown eyes huge behind the thick lenses. "I beg your pardon?"

Why did it matter to her whether the hotel bought the man's eggs or not? Because he'd asked her forgiveness, that was why. No one—not even Rueben, who'd scolded her severely for going to the hotel room before admitting he was really angry at Miss Flo, not at her—had ever asked her forgiveness before. But how could she explain her interest to the manager? Dinah sighed. "Never mind."

The man harrumphed. "Well, Miss Hubley, I am Mr. Irwin, the dining room manager and staff supervisor. I assume you have a bag somewhere?" He seemed to search the area.

What few items she owned she'd stuffed into a woven satchel. She retrieved it from its spot beside the chair where she'd slept. "Yes, sir."

"Very well, then. Come with me." He turned and moved across the porch floor with hardly a sound, his frame so slight. Dinah followed, observing how sprightly he moved for an older man—much more so than the egg man, who was no doubt decades younger. But Mr. Irwin hadn't been run over by a wagon wheel when he was eleven.

She pushed aside thoughts of the egg man and trailed Mr. Irwin past a pair of closed doors where guests had been sitting a half hour ago, past a lunch counter where the smell of bacon and yeasty bread still lingered, and then up a narrow flight of enclosed stairs that emptied into a long hallway well lit by gas lamps on both sides. He led her to the last door on the left and pointed to the number six painted in gold on the center panel.

"You will share this room with our other chambermaid. She's working right now so I will introduce the two of you later. Her name is Ruthie Mead— a fine young woman. She's been employed here at the Clifton for more than a year and will be able to explain the cleaning procedures to you. Since you traveled all night, Mrs. Walters recommended allowing you today to rest and begin your duties tomorrow." He didn't seem very happy about letting her rest. He pulled a key from his pocket, unlocked the door, then handed the key to her. "Don't lose that."

Dinah curled her fist around the brass key and stepped over the threshold. She dropped her bag on the carpeted floor and glanced at her new home. Although cheery with lace curtains at the windows and flowered paper on the walls, the room was barely large enough to hold the double iron bed, wardrobe, bureau, dressing table, and washstand. She would share this small space with someone else? When the interviewer had mentioned room and board, Dinah envisioned a room of her own. Another expectation dashed.

"Come to my office this afternoon after you've had a chance to rest a bit and we'll find uniforms to fit you. While employed by the Clifton, you're to wear a uniform at all times, even when away from the hotel. You represent the Clifton and will conduct yourself with decorum or risk dismissal." The man's scowl never faded.

Trepidation tiptoed across her scalp. Was he still angry about finding her on the porch, or did he disapprove of her for some other reason?

"We also expect our employees to be tidy, so if one uniform becomes soiled, you need to change it immediately. Take your soiled items to the basement washroom. Laundresses are always on duty and will see to your needs, so there's no excuse not to have a clean uniform at your disposal at all times."

Accustomed to doing her own wash, Dinah silently celebrated this piece of news.

"Now, Miss Hubley, I must return to my office. At noon feel free to sit at the counter and order a plate. I'll alert the lunch-counter staff of your arrival." He turned and departed.

Dinah closed the door, paused for a moment, and then turned the lock. The other chambermaid should already have a key, but she didn't want anyone else walking in on her unannounced. It took only a few minutes to put away her belongings. With the money Miss Flo had given her, Dinah had purchased three simple calico dresses—one of which she now wore—shoes, stockings, and underclothes. She'd always gotten by with little and could continue to do so. Something had to stay the same after everything that had changed.

She started to stretch out on the bed for a nap—she'd hardly slept on the rocking train last night. But the bed was made so neatly—the sheets pulled taut and the bright patchwork quilt centered perfectly on the mattress—she hated to muss it. And she couldn't determine which side the other chambermaid had already claimed. So instead of lying down on the bed, she settled herself on the floor in the corner behind the wardrobe, rested her head against the wall, and promptly fell asleep.

Ruthie

Ruthie Mead hummed as she made her way to the staff's sleeping quarters. Despite having been hard at work for nearly five hours already, her steps were light, her spirits high. Today the new chambermaid would arrive! She couldn't wait to meet her new friend. For she was certain she and the new girl would become fast friends, just as she and Phoebe had been.

For a moment, sadness descended. Ruthie missed the former chambermaid. The past week of cleaning rooms on her own had been so lonely. But she didn't begrudge Phoebe's decision to marry her beau and take care of her own little house instead of hotel rooms. Someday Ruthie hoped to have the same chance for marriage, when God deemed it time, but for now she could pay her own way and even share with Mama and Papa every month. Papa's preacher salary barely stretched to cover the family's needs. How it pleased her to help. *Thank You, dear Lord!*

She kept her key hanging on a chain around her neck where she wouldn't lose it. She eased the chain from beneath her uniform bodice and bent forward to unlock the door. Still humming "Bringing in the Sheaves," one of Papa's favorites and hers, too, because it skipped happily along the notes rather than slogging, she stepped into the room and aimed herself for the wardrobe, where her fresh aprons waited.

But her humming abruptly stopped when she nearly stumbled over a satchel lying at the foot of the bed—evidence that indeed the new chambermaid had arrived. She searched the room for other indications of another's presence, and she spotted a pair of legs stretching across the short expanse of floor between the edge of the wardrobe and the bed. Stifling a giggle, Ruthie rounded the bed and crouched next to the stocking-covered legs and pair of black boots with the feet lying slack so the toes pointed in opposite directions.

Leaning forward a bit, she peered into the corner. The giggle she'd pushed down moments ago found its way from her throat, and the girl asleep in the corner opened her eyes with a start. Ruthie stuck out her hand. "Hello there. I'm Ruthie. You must be the new chambermaid. But what are you doing there in the corner?" She tittered and couldn't resist teasing. "When my little brothers are hiding in a corner, it's because they've done something wrong and they don't want Mama or Papa to find them. Have you done something wrong?"

The girl scrambled upright with a flurry of ruffly petticoats and calico skirts, but she remained pressed into the narrow slice of space behind the wardrobe and watched Ruthie with wary blue eyes. She didn't speak.

Ruthie straightened, uncertain how to proceed. Such a peculiar girl… "You *are* the new chambermaid, aren't you?" Maybe this girl had sneaked in and really was hiding. Two months ago a man had managed to hide out for two days in the hotel without paying a dime. The sheriff arrested him for loitering. Ruthie hoped she wouldn't have to turn this girl in as a loiterer.

The girl gave a slow nod.

Relieved, Ruthie smiled. "What's your name?"

"D-Dinah."

"Dinah! Your name is Dinah?" Ruthie could hardly believe it. "Why, my little sister—she's five and is the cutest little girl you've ever seen—is named Dinah June. I was named for my grandmother, but my mama is Leah and my papa is Jacob, and they said they had to have a little girl named Dinah since the Leah and Jacob of the Bible had one. They had five boys before they had another girl—my mama and papa, I mean, not the Bible people—and they were so happy when God blessed them with little Dinah."

The chambermaid Dinah was staring at Ruthie in complete confusion.

Ruthie laughed. "I'm sorry. My folks scold me all the time about talking too much, but I can't seem to help myself. My head is full of ideas and thoughts, and my mouth is never reluctant to share them." She caught Dinah's hand and gave a light tug. "Come on out of the corner. There's no need to hide."

The new girl stepped out of the shadowy space. She pulled her hand from Ruthie's grasp and put it behind her back, as if protecting it. "I'm not hiding." Her tone held a hint of defensiveness.

"I didn't intend to insult. But I've never found anyone sleeping in a corner that way, although a missionary to China visited our church one time and said he slept on the floor while he lived in the foreign country." While Ruthie talked, she slipped off the apron, which she'd stained by spilling a bit of leftover tea from a cup left in one of the rooms, and retrieved a fresh one from the wardrobe. "I'd make a terrible missionary because I much prefer sleeping in a bed. Don't you?"

"It's your bed. I didn't want to muck it up."

Ruthie pulled the clean apron over her black dress and tied the strings behind her back. She smiled broadly, eager to put Dinah at ease. So taciturn, she was! "Don't be silly. It's *our* bed now." Dinah didn't speak a word. Her expression remained sour. Ruthie blew out a light breath and tried a different approach. "So where are you from, Dinah?"

For a brief moment, Dinah ducked her head, her forehead crinkling into rows as crooked as the ones Seth carved in Mama's garden with a hoe. "Chicago."

Ruthie squealed. "You came all the way from Chicago? Mr. Irwin said you'd arrive by train today, but he didn't tell me you'd be coming from a big city. I've never even visited a big city. You'll have to tell me all about it."

The furrows in Dinah's forehead deepened.

Uneasiness squeezed the excitement from Ruthie's chest. "B-but only if you want to." Mercy, she'd never stammered in nervousness before. Not around strangers or customers or even bashful people. But something about this girl left her floundering. She forced another smile. "Well, I only came up to change my apron. We're to stay fresh and tidy at all times—I'm sure Mr. Irwin told you. Now that I'm presentable again, I'll"—she eased toward the door—"get back to work."

She paused with her hand on the knob, obliged to be friendly enough for two people since Dinah seemed lacking in cordiality. "It's nearly lunchtime. I take my noon meal at the counter downstairs. If you join me there, I'll introduce you to some of the other staff—the ones who aren't busy serving in the dining room. They'll have to wait until evening to get acquainted with you. Mr. Harvey wants us to become like family, so they'll all be eager to meet you. Do you want to join me at lunchtime?"

An odd look flittered across the girl's face—a mixture of longing and fear. She offered a hesitant nod.

"Good! I'll see you in a bit, then. Enjoy your rest, Dinah." Ruthie clicked the door closed behind her and headed for the stairs. An image of Dinah's unsmiling face filled her memory. Oh, such a solemn girl. She might have a hard time living with this one. But hadn't Papa taught her to never let someone else's behavior dictate her own? She would do as the apostle Paul instructed the Colossians—she would put on mercy, kindness, meekness, and patience.

As she trotted down the stairs, holding her skirt high to keep from tripping, she consoled herself with the thought that Dinah was probably only tired from her trip—all the way from Chicago!—and feeling a bit out of place in her new surroundings. In a few days, they would be as comfortable together as she and Phoebe had been. Her smile returned. Of course they would.

Chapter 7

Amos

mos counted his money again, but the amount remained the same. He shifted his gaze from the carefully stacked coins on his table to the single window of his little house. The beautiful colors of the sunset had already faded from the sky, leaving a smudgy gray expanse in its place. He'd never liked this time of day—no sun shining but not yet any stars to blink overhead. The depressing view added to the memory of the hotel manager's words brought a wave of defeat.

"Four dozen eggs a day? Mr. Ackerman, our kitchen staff requires three times that number on a daily basis. I'll not deny your eggs seem of highest quality, but you can't possibly meet our needs with such a small flock of chickens. Now, if you were to triple or even quadruple your flock, then I would most likely purchase your eggs. But not until then."

All the walk home, Amos had pondered how to increase his flock to meet Mr. Irwin's demands. While scattering grain for the birds, working in his garden, and repairing the fence, he'd continued to think and pray. Now, sitting at his supper table with the meager contents of his money jar glinting in the lamplight, he gathered the conclusions he'd reached.

He had space for a bigger flock on his land. He'd need a bigger chicken house, but he could tear down the two sheds on the back edge of his property and use the lumber to expand the current chicken house. Fortunately his arms and back were still strong even if his damaged leg slowed his progress. If he bartered with the neighboring farmer to clear a bit more of his land, he could increase his corn crop for feed. He didn't mind working longer and harder to take care of a bigger flock.

But how to get the bigger flock? Chicks cost money. He shifted his attention to the stacked coins again. Mr. Irwin said to triple or quadruple his number of birds, but to even double his flock would cost more than what he had. His shoulders sagged. A sigh wheezed from his lungs. "You've blessed me in so many ways with this house and land and barn. I'm grateful for what You've given, and I don't want to be a complainer like the Israelites who could never be satisfied with what You gave them, but…"

He swallowed. Should he even express a "but" to the One who'd already given him so much? Then he decided to go ahead. The Almighty God knew his thoughts anyway, so he wouldn't surprise Him when he spoke them aloud. He turned his face to the ceiling. "But with forty-eight chickens I'll never have enough money for what I really want."

Tightness built in his chest. The chickens weren't his biggest dream. Becoming a family man like his brothers was his biggest dream. But he couldn't have one without the other. "Is it too much to ask for a bigger flock? I'll be an honest farmer, Lord. I'll continue to tithe—I won't be selfish with the profits. I'm not asking for a fancy house or a new carriage or even a hip that doesn't pain me when I walk. I can make do with little. But, dear Lord, can't I please have what Titus and John have? Can't I have a wife and children?"

He rose and plodded to the bucket of water he'd brought in earlier. He heated a pan of water on the stove, poured it into a basin with a little lye soap, then scrubbed the few items he'd used when preparing and eating his supper. As he set the clean plate in its place on the sideboard, an idea struck with such force he dropped the fork. It clattered against the wooden floor, its *ting-ting-ting!* matching the wild clamor in his chest.

He slapped his forehead and laughed aloud. "What a fool I must be not to see the answer!" He looked up, shaking his head and grinning at the ceiling beams as if God's face were there instead. "Thank You, Lord, for opening my feeble mind."

He hurried back to the table, doing a double hop on his good leg in his eagerness, and separated out the fifty-cent piece from the other coins. As he dropped the pennies, nickels, dimes, and quarters into the jar, he laughed again. Why hadn't he thought of it earlier and saved himself some worry? If he bought a rooster or maybe even two, his eggs would be fertilized. He could leave behind a few eggs each day for the chickens to hatch. Then when the chicks were hatched, he'd let the pullets grow up to lay eggs, and the roosters could be butchered, bartered, or sold.

As he reached to set the money jar on its high shelf, he caught a glimpse of the night sky outside his window. Black velvet had replaced the dingy gray, and stars winked white. He sent a silent prayer of thankfulness to the One behind the stars. Yes, it would take longer, raising his own chicks to expand his flock, but did he have to be in a hurry? Mr. Irwin hadn't said, "Come back next week or I can't work with you at all." So Amos could be patient. His dream was worth waiting for.

Dinah

While Ruthie visited the outhouse, Dinah scrambled into her nightclothes and dove beneath the covers. The open window allowed in a breeze, but even so the room was stifling. The lightweight quilt might as well have been a stack of wool blankets. She'd rather lay uncovered on top of the cotton sheet. If she had a room to herself, that was exactly what she'd do. But sharing a room meant having someone—someone she hardly knew—see her in her nightgown. She couldn't bring herself to let anyone, not even someone as harmless as Ruthie, see her dressed so scantily.

After being issued uniforms from Mr. Irwin, she'd followed Ruthie and observed the cleanup practices Mr. Harvey required. The man was a stickler for cleanliness, much more so than Miss Flo. The beautifully decorated rooms reminded her of the one in the hotel where she'd met the gentleman, and she hadn't wanted to enter them. But Ruthie had laughingly ushered her over the thresholds, teasing that she couldn't very well clean from the hallway.

As Ruthie demonstrated the required cleaning practices, she told Dinah about Mr. Harvey's wife traveling all the way to Europe to purchase linens and furniture for the rooms. Listening to Ruthie blather on and on had helped chase away the ghosts haunting her mind. By the end of the day, she'd made a silent vow to forget the only other hotel she'd visited and concentrate on doing exactly what was needed to please Mr. Harvey.

In addition to showing her the ropes, as Ruthie had put it, the outgoing chambermaid introduced her to the other staff members. Everyone—the cook, the kitchen helpers, the busboys, and the waitresses—welcomed her into the Clifton family, just as Ruthie said they would. Dinah swiped at a trickle of sweat easing along her temple as she tried to recall their names. If she was going to live and work with these people every day, she needed to be a part of them. But their easy acceptance, instead of pleasing her, left her on edge. She wished she could understand why.

The doorknob rattled and Ruthie breezed into the room. Dinah had never met anyone who moved with such grace. Did the girl's feet even touch the floor? And how could she be so cheerful at this hour after working all day? Ruthie hummed—Dinah had discovered if Ruthie wasn't talking, she was humming—as she removed her dressing gown and hung it on a hook behind the door. She glided around the end of the bed, and Dinah expected her to extinguish the lamp and fall onto the mattress. Instead, she paused at her side of the bed and smiled at Dinah.

"You're tucked in already. Have you finished praying?"

Dinah searched her memory. She recalled being instructed on how to dust, sweep, wash the pitchers and bowls, strip and remake beds, and fluff pillows. But she didn't recall anything about praying. She shook her head.

"Well, you're welcome to join me if you like. God's ears are capable of listening to two of us at once." Ruthie dropped to her knees beside the bed. Only her head and shoulders showed above the high mattress. She pressed her folded hands beneath her chin and closed her eyes. "Dear God—"

Clutching the covers to her chest, Dinah sat up and stared at the other girl. "What are you doing?"

Ruthie's eyes popped open. She looked as dumbfounded as Dinah felt. "I'm praying. I always pray before I go to bed. Don't you?"

Before going to bed, Dinah had always willed the noises from down below to stop so she could sleep. She shook her head.

"Do you pray in the morning, then?"

Dinah scowled. "I don't pray."

Ruthie's eyes flew wide. She gripped handfuls of the quilt as if she needed an anchor. "Not at all?"

"No."

"But, Dinah, you have to talk to God every day." Ruthie sounded so dismayed Dinah experienced a rush of guilt she didn't understand. "If you want Him to bless you, you have to make time for Him."

Dinah flopped back against her pillows, jerking the quilt as she went. Ruthie lost her grip on the fabric. She didn't know who this God was, but she'd never been blessed. Was it because she hadn't made time for Him? She pushed the thought aside. If there was a God who gave blessings, He didn't bestow them on girls raised in brothels.

Ruthie continued to stare at Dinah with sad eyes. Dinah rolled over so she wouldn't have to see her. "Do whatever it is you're doing so we can turn out the lamp and go to sleep. We'll miss the ten o'clock curfew if you don't hurry."

For long seconds silence hung in the room. Then Ruthie's soft voice carried to Dinah's ears. "Dear God, thank You for another day to work hard and earn my keep. Thank You for giving me the strength to finish my tasks. Help me always do my best and bring You glory. Be with Mama and Papa, Seth, Jonah, Noah, Timothy, Joseph, and little Dinah June. Bless them and keep them safe." She prayed for each of the staff members by name, asking for various things, including healing for the dishwasher's husband. "And, dear God, thank You for bringing Dinah to the Clifton Hotel."

Dinah's heart skipped a beat. Eyes wide open and unblinking, she held her breath and waited to hear what Ruthie would say next.

"Help her to feel right at home. Let us become good friends. Please give us a good night's rest and let us awaken fresh and ready to do Your will tomorrow. In Your Son's name I pray, amen."

A slight creak followed by a looming shadow on the wall let Dinah know Ruthie had risen from her knees. The light flickered, and then Ruthie's shadow was swallowed up by darkness. The mattress shifted, and a soft sigh sounded from behind Dinah, along with muffled rustling as Ruthie apparently wriggled into a comfortable position.

Dinah's chest ached, and she released her long-held breath. She stared unseeing at the wall, tired but too tense to rest, and listened to the nighttime sounds of her new home. Wind whispered through the window. The curtains gently swished against the windowsill. A night bird called. In the room next door, a bedspring popped and someone coughed.

Ruthie whispered, "Good night, Dinah. Sleep well."

A lump filled Dinah's throat. Occasionally she'd paused outside her mother's door and called, "Good night." Tori had always hollered, "Go to bed already!" No one, not even Rueben, had wished her a good night. And no one had ever prayed for her. She should say, "Good night, Ruthie." Or "Thank you, Ruthie." But an unwelcome emotion writhed through her middle, and her tight throat refused to release the words.

Dinah blinked back tears. Why couldn't she be more like Ruthie? Open. Happy. Kind. Comfortable with herself. She recognized the feeling holding her captive. Envy. After several more seconds, another sigh wafted from Ruthie's side of the bed. Soon deep breaths let Dinah know the other girl had fallen asleep. But Dinah lay awake, her mind playing over her first day in Florence, Kansas. She remembered the egg man apologizing for startling her. Mr. Irwin scolding her. The smiles and welcomes from the staff members of the hotel. And she remembered Ruthie's prayer.

She'd watched the other girls at school huddling together at recess to chatter and laugh, sometimes flirting with the boys. They never invited her into their circle, though. She'd longed for a friend, and the idea of having one now created a deep ache in the center of her chest. But she wouldn't be friends with

Ruthie. If she opened herself up to this girl—if she told her where she'd been and the things she'd done—Ruthie would run away in shock. And Dinah would be crushed. So even though Ruthie had prayed for them to be good friends, Dinah would make sure it didn't happen.

She was here to work. To impress Mr. Harvey. To become one of his girls. Maybe then she would be worthy of forming friendships.

Chapter 8

Dinah

After only three days of working at the Clifton Hotel, Dinah settled into an easy routine. Rise early, wash, twist her hair into a coil, don her black dress and full-length white pinafore apron, then join others in the staff dining room off the kitchen to eat a delicious breakfast. Mr. Gindough, the hotel chef, cooked as well as Rueben, but she wouldn't tell her friend so in the letter she planned to send as soon as she had time to sit down and write.

After eating, she collected fresh linens from the laundry room, retrieved her basket of cleaning items from the closet, and went to work. Even cleaning the rooms followed a pattern. First strip and remake the bed, then wash the pitcher and bowl, dust or scrub every surface depending on what it needed, sweep the floor, and dispose of rubbish.

When every room was clean and ready for the next guest, she remained in the chambermaids' small sitting room near the front desk and listened for what Ruthie called the "beckon-me bell," which meant one of the guests had need of something—a cup of tea, an extra pillow, a newspaper… She never knew what might be requested, but she was expected to respond quickly and adequately. She did her best not to disappoint the guests or Mr. Irwin.

And she did her best to hold herself aloof from the other staff members, which proved to be the most difficult of the tasks. After a lifetime of people turning up their noses at her, she now lived among a group who seemed too willing to accept her unquestioningly. Their friendliness ignited a deep desire to be part of them, but oddly it also frightened her. She wanted to join in the chatter at the lunch counter, to tease with the busboys and blush at the flirtatious comments the railroad men threw at the girls the way the others did. They were all so relaxed and unfettered and carefree.

But the years of living in the Yellow Parrot had stolen the carefree from her. When the busboys teased or the railroad men flirted, Dinah's insides rolled. When the girls formed a talkative circle, whether laughing or serious, Dinah tensed. She didn't know how to lightheartedly chat or tease or flirt. As much as she wanted to belong, she knew she didn't. Because she wasn't like them. So she kept her distance, fearful she'd accidentally share the secrets of her past and let everyone know just how different she really was.

On Saturday, rather than eating her turkey sandwich at the counter with the others, she took her plate to the chambermaids' sitting room. The pale blue-and-green-striped wallpaper, white wicker chairs, and clusters of potted plants filling the corners gave the little windowless room an airy, porch-like feel. Dinah appreciated the Harveys for making every part of the hotel and restaurant—even the parts only occupied by staff—cheery and comfortable. She sat in one of the chairs, draped a napkin across the skirt of her pinafore, and then placed the plate in her lap.

As she lifted the thick sandwich to her mouth, Ruthie entered the room. Ruthie held a plate in one hand and a glass of frothy milk in the other. As usual, she was humming a merry tune. When she spotted Dinah, she smiled and plopped into the second chair.

"I wondered where you'd gone. I hope I'm not intruding, but the counter was too noisy for me today. A host of men from the town came in, all excited about a cow auction, and their loud voices gave me a headache."

How could Ruthie look so happy if she had a headache? Although curious, Dinah didn't ask. Ruthie set the glass of milk on the ridiculously tiny table between the chairs and lowered her plate to her lap. She bowed her head and closed her eyes, just as she did at bedtime. Dinah watched out of the corner of her eye, wondering about Ruthie's strange habit of praying. She'd noticed several others following the same practice in the breakfast room. She considered pretending to pray just so she wouldn't be left out, but closing her eyes while others had their eyes open made her feel as though they were all staring at her. So she didn't do it.

Ruthie picked up her sandwich and took a bite. "Mmm. I'm glad there was enough turkey left from yesterday's dinner to have sandwiches today. Mr. Gindough makes the best turkey. So moist, and with just the right seasonings. I hate to say it's better than my mama's turkey, but it really is." She took another bite, chewed, and swallowed. After a sip of milk, she aimed a grin at Dinah. "Did your mother bake turkey as good as this?"

Dinah flicked a crumb from her lips with her finger, nearly laughing as she tried to imagine Tori wrestling a turkey into a roasting pan. "Um…no."

Ruthie giggled as if Dinah had said something clever. "Even if this turkey is better, I bet Mr. Gindough can't bake gingerbread as good as Mama's. Her gingerbread is the best thing I've ever eaten. Last month she baked a whole gingerbread cake just for me, and I was completely selfish and didn't share one bit with anybody." She paused to take another bite of her sandwich, then followed it with another dainty sip of milk. "What's your favorite food your ma makes?"

Dinah's stomach trembled. She didn't want to answer. She didn't want to answer with the truth. She opened her mouth, fully intending to tell a lie, but something else spilled out. "My mother didn't cook. Rueben did."

"Who is Rueben?" Ruthie seemed genuinely interested.

Rueben was her only friend. But she couldn't say so. "Our cook."

"Oh my." Ruthie lowered her sandwich and stared at Dinah. "You had a cook in your house? Your family must be wealthy."

Dinah released a little snort. If only Ruthie knew how wrong she was. She set the remaining half of her sandwich aside and rose. "I'm going to go get myself a glass of milk. I think I'll get a piece of pie, too. Do you want one?"

Ruthie sat, silent and staring, as if dazed.

What had stricken the always-jabbering girl silent? Dinah frowned. "Ruthie, do you want a piece of pie?"

Ruthie gave a little jolt. "Pie? Oh. Yes. If there's a piece of cherry remaining, I would like one. Thank you."

Dinah hurried out, relieved to have left the conversation behind. Odd how the simplest topic, such as favorite foods, led to divulging parts of her past. She'd have to try even harder to discourage Ruthie from asking so many questions. It wouldn't be easy—Ruthie was so talkative she even muttered in her sleep. But somehow Dinah would find a way to discourage the girl. She couldn't let anyone know where she'd lived before coming to Florence. Not if she intended to be a waitress when she turned eighteen.

Ruthie

Ruthie gazed after Dinah, marveling. A cook in her house! She'd never known anyone who'd employed their own cook. She would never have guessed Dinah came from such extravagant means. Her clothes, although obviously new, didn't hint at money. Her speech—what little she said!—didn't reflect a cultured upbringing. Her willingness to work as a chambermaid also seemed in opposition to the expected attitude of someone who'd been raised with servants to see to her needs. If she'd thought Dinah a puzzle before, her befuddlement increased a hundredfold with this new bit of information.

She finished her sandwich, playing back over every minute since she'd discovered Dinah asleep in the corner behind the wardrobe. Despite her best efforts, Ruthie hadn't been able to draw Dinah into a meaningful conversation. Dinah had also snubbed the others' attempts at friendliness. She'd reasoned with herself that Dinah was bashful, was tired, was striving to adjust to her new surroundings. Could it be she was—Ruthie cringed even contemplating such a thing—snobbish? After all, even Papa preached it was harder for a rich man to enter into the kingdom of God than for a camel to pass through the eye of a needle. Ruthie had seen a camel once—a big, lumbering beast—in a circus. The sight had brought the reality of the scripture to life. Dinah's seeming disdain of speaking to God in prayer could very well represent the biblical reference.

Ruthie nibbled her thumbnail, suddenly worried. Could she live with someone who was snobbish? Bashfulness could be overcome. Tiredness would fade. Time would bring familiarity. But she knew no cure for snobbishness. The thought of being treated with indifference every day for weeks on end did not sit well. She closed her eyes and tried to imagine enjoying leisurely activities while someone else performed the rudimentary tasks in her home. Despite her active imagination, the pictures refused to form.

On the tail of worry came another unpleasant emotion: jealousy. Papa worked so hard, but his small monthly stipend, lovingly offered by their congregation, didn't allow for extravagance of any kind. Now that Ruthie lived in the Clifton Hotel, Mama had no help with cleaning or cooking or sewing. Somehow it didn't seem fair that her kind, loving parents had to labor while Dinah's parents apparently paid others to labor for them. Jealousy was wrong. A verse in Proverbs said envy was the rottenness of one's bones. Ruthie didn't want her bones to rot, but at that moment she would have given almost anything to trade places with Dinah's family for one day and let her family enjoy a little luxury and leisure.

Approaching footsteps pulled Ruthie from her reverie. She looked up as Dinah entered the room with two saucers of oozing cherry pie slices balanced on one arm, the way the servers carried several plates at once, and a glass of milk in her other hand. Dinah dipped her knees to set her milk on the little table without upsetting the saucers. Ruthie got a glimpse of the slices of pie. One was significantly larger than the other. Someone must have taken a sliver from one of the pieces rather than eating an entire slice. Dinah lifted the saucer bearing the larger slice first, and Ruthie expected her to place it next to her glass of milk. But instead she held it out to Ruthie. Ruthie blinked twice, startled. Wouldn't a wealthy person keep the best for herself?

The jealous feeling whisked away as guilt swept in. She'd been thinking ill of Dinah, and she was wrong to do so. Papa and Mama would be mortified if they knew. *Forgive me, Lord, for my uncharitable thoughts.* She shook her head. "No, you take that one."

Dinah's brow crinkled. The same strange combination of desire and defeat danced across her expression. She opened her mouth to speak, but then without a word she plopped the saucer containing the larger slice on top of the crumb-laden plate in Ruthie's lap. She returned to her chair, lifted her fork, and began to eat the pie. But no enjoyment showed on her face.

Ruthie took up a bite as well, but she couldn't find pleasure in the juicy cherries or flaky crust. Somehow she had to make amends for the ugly thoughts she'd entertained. Even if she was right—even if Dinah was snobbish—it didn't give Ruthie the right to disparage her whether inwardly or openly. What could she do to ease her conscience? She gasped.

Dinah gasped, too, nearly dropping her fork.

Ruthie reached across the little table to touch Dinah's elbow. "Tomorrow is Sunday. Mr. Irwin allows us an hour's break midmorning. Papa changed the time of worship at the chapel where he serves as minister to accommodate the employees here at the Clifton. Would you go to worship with me? I want to introduce you to Mama and Papa, little Dinah, and the boys." She almost forgot to breathe she was so eager for Dinah's acceptance.

A scowl tensed Dinah's face. "Why?"

Ruthie drew back. "Why…what?"

"Why do you want me to meet your family?"

Ruthie tittered. She couldn't confess she was trying to make up for thinking derogatory thoughts about her roommate. "Because we're friends." But were they? She'd been so certain she and Dinah would grow as close as she and Phoebe had been. But if Dinah came from an affluent background, she'd always be different from Phoebe. And different from Ruthie. Maybe they'd never be friends.

Dinah stared at her. Her stunned expression showed her disbelief.

Ruthie hung her head as another tentacle of guilt wrapped itself around her. Had she really invited Dinah to church to appease her own conscience? What of Dinah's soul? The girl obviously had no relationship with God. If Jesus's statement about rich men entering heaven was true—and of course Jesus didn't lie!—then Dinah needed to hear Papa's preaching. She needed to hear how much God loved her.

Ruthie reached for Dinah again, but the girl drew back, avoiding Ruthie's fingers. She sighed. "Dinah, may I be honest with you?"

She offered a hesitant nod even though her eyes flashed denial.

Ruthie gathered her courage, then spoke in a rush before she lost her nerve. "I want you to come to church with me to meet my family because I want them to know who my new roommate is, but mostly I want you to come because I love God very much and God loves you very much and I think the two of you need to become acquainted. The best place to get to know Him is in church. So will you come?"

Dinah set her lips in a firm line. Her body seemed to tremble. With rage? disdain? discomfort? Ruthie didn't know, but her heart ached as she witnessed the turmoil shuddering its way through Dinah's slight frame.

A bell rang.

Both girls looked toward the doorway. Then they looked at each other. Ruthie started to set her plate aside to see to the guest's need, but Dinah leaped up first.

"I'll get it. Enjoy your pie." Dinah dashed out the door as if demons chased her.

Chapter 9

Dinah

W as she really doing this? Dinah climbed into the back of the two-bench buggy Mr. Irwin made available to businessmen who came to town. All night she'd wrestled with herself, bouncing back and forth between wanting to go to church with Ruthie and not wanting to go. She'd often walked past an ornate church building in Chicago. Its enormous stained-glass window of a man in a flowing robe with his arms outstretched had beckoned to her. But when she asked Tori about visiting the building, her mother laughed and said the holier-than-thou people would chase her out if she dared to darken their doorway. Dinah hadn't known what "holier than thou" meant, but the way Tori spit the words let her know it wasn't a good thing. So Dinah had stayed away.

But now here she was, planning to enter a church for the first time in her life. Because Ruthie said she would meet God there. Because Ruthie said God loved her very much. The very thought drew Dinah in with the same intensity as the image formed by pieces of colored glass. Would this Kansas church be filled with holier-than-thou people who would chase her away like the one in Chicago, or would they let her in so she could meet God?

One of the busboys, Dean, had been assigned the duty of transporting the girls to church. He sat proudly in the front holding the reins. Ruthie clambered up beside Dinah, followed by two of the servers, Lyla and Minnie. The remaining two servers, Matilda and Amelia, shared the front seat with the busboy.

Dean flicked a glance into the back, and a grin climbed his cheek. "You look as snug as cigars in a new box back there."

Minnie slapped his shoulder. "You shouldn't be talking about cigars, Dean Muller!"

"She's right," Ruthie added, her lips pursed up as if she'd tasted something sour. "Cigars don't make for nice Sunday morning talk."

He laughed, his dimples flashing. "I didn't invite you to smoke one. No need to get yourself in a dither."

Ruthie frowned, but Minnie hid her smile behind her fingers and giggled. She fluttered her lashes at Dean, the way the girls at Miss Flo's used to do to entice the men to choose them. Dinah's breakfast curdled in her stomach.

"Are you staying for service, Dean?" Lyla asked.

Dean shook his head, nearly dislodging his cap. He tugged it a little lower on his forehead. "Coming back here and sleeping during our break. Me an' the other fellas stayed out too late last night. Missed our curfew." He touched his finger to his lips, as if swearing the girls to secrecy, and waggled his brows. "But my, the party at the opera house was grand! I danced with at least a dozen girls."

Amelia nudged Dean with her elbow. "Stop yapping. We'll miss the service altogether if we don't get going."

"All right, all right." Dean flicked the reins, and the horses strained against the rigging. In moments, they'd bumped across the railroad tracks and were heading through the center of town.

Dinah's side, pressed against the iron frame of the seat, ached. Even though Minnie sat on the edge of the seat rather than against the back, Dinah was wedged so tightly between the seat and Ruthie's hip they might not be able to free themselves when they reached church. Why had she agreed to go, anyway? Curiosity, partly. But mostly some strange inner longing to discover for herself if what Ruthie had said about God loving her was true. An image of the beautiful church in Chicago filled her mind, and a little chill spread across her limbs despite the summer sun shining down. If God lived in such a place, and He loved her, could that mean she wasn't as worthless as she'd always believed?

Perspiration trickled from her temple down to her chin, but with her arm locked against Ruthie's, she couldn't reach up to wipe it away. So she turned her face toward the breeze and allowed the hot wind to dry the dribble of sweat. She kept her face angled outward until Dean drew the horses to a halt.

Ruthie said in her cheery voice, "We're here, Dinah. Let's go!"

Dinah turned to look, and if she hadn't been wedged into the seat, she might have fallen out of the buggy in shock. This tiny white clapboard building with clear-paned windows and a set of slanting wooden risers climbing to the single door was a church? *This* was where God lived? She'd expected so much more.

Dean had hopped out and was assisting the girls from the buggy. Other people, presumably coming to attend the service, walked across the sparse yard toward the porch. Ruthie waved to each of them, and as the girls alighted, they formed a little group and shook the road dust from their uniforms. But Dinah remained on the seat, staring at the sad-looking little building. Why had she allowed her hopes to grow so high? Of course any God who loved her wouldn't reside in a fine, beautiful, towering building with bright-colored windows. He'd be in a ramshackle place. As ramshackle as her sorry life.

"You coming out, Dinah?" Dean stood with his hand out, ready to help her.

His reaching hand got tangled up with the remembrance of the outstretched hands on the beautiful window in Chicago, and even though she'd fully intended to return to the hotel, she found herself placing her palm in his.

He helped her down, then hopped back onto the driver's seat. "I'll pick you girls up at eleven." He brought down the reins, and the horses carried the buggy away.

The four servers in their matching uniforms hurried to the church and went inside. Ruthie started to follow, but then she stopped and looked back at Dinah. She giggled, returned, and caught Dinah's elbow. "Come on in. They won't bite."

With Ruthie tugging at her arm, Dinah found the ability to move forward, but although her feet headed toward the church, inwardly she strained away. She'd hoped—so hoped—to find something of beauty here. Something bigger and better and *purer* than what she carried inside. Her gaze drifted to

the building's roofline. There wasn't even a cross to signify this was a church.
Tears stung. How could anything of worth be housed within such a plain
shell?

They reached the stairs and Dinah dug in her heels, bringing Ruthie to a
stop. "Wait."

Ruthie shot her an impatient look. "What is it? Service is due to start. We
need to go in."

Music—not from a resonant organ like she'd heard in Chicago, but pro-
duced by disharmonious voices—drifted from the open door. Dinah cringed.
"I…I don't think I can."

Ruthie was staring at her with her normally smiling lips set in a disapproving frown. "I don't want to be rude, truly I don't, and especially not on the
Lord's day, but if you're refusing to go inside because my papa's church doesn't
meet with your rich standards, then I'll have to be very frank with you and say
it hurts my feelings."

Her *rich* standards? "It isn't that. It's…" But what could she say? If she
confessed the building too closely resembled her own less-than-beautiful life,
she would not only insult Ruthie, but she'd share a hint of the past she wanted
to keep buried. Why did everything have to disappoint her? She lowered her
head and caught a glimpse of the little black book Ruthie carried. She'd seen
similar books held by others entering the church. She pointed weakly at the
book. "I don't have one of those."

Ruthie's eyes widened. Then her face pinched in regret. She squeezed Dinah's elbow. "Is that all?" She guided Dinah up the first step. "You don't need
to worry. Not everyone has a Bible to bring to church, and Papa reads the
Scripture out loud." Another tug, and Dinah moved up another riser. "I'll
share mine with you, all right?" One more tug and they reached the door.
"Hurry now—they're almost finished with singing and Papa will begin to
speak."

Ruthie hurried Dinah through a narrow entry that extended in both directions. Nails pounded into the walls served as simple hooks. No wraps or
jackets hung on any of the nails, but men's hats hid a half dozen from view. The

people were standing as they sang, and Ruthie led Dinah straight up the center
aisle between the groups. Dinah felt curious gazes aimed at her, and she kept
her head low, watching the toes of her shoes cross the wide pine planks all the
way to the front. At least she could hide behind her uniform, which gave her a
small measure of comfort in these strange surroundings.

Ruthie pulled Dinah into the first row on the right side of the room. A
man wearing a black suit, his mouth open wide in song, stood at the front on a
slightly raised platform. Dinah was so close that if she reached out with her
foot, her toes would tap the wooden edge of the platform. The man glanced in
her direction, and even as he continued to sing, a smile lifted the corners of his
lips. Dinah blinked in recognition. The man had Ruthie's smile.

She focused on the words being sung with gusto. "Rapture, praise, and
endless worship will be our sweet portion there." The song ended with a series
of wheezing breaths.

The man at the front, Ruthie's father, aimed a beaming smile across the
gathered people. "Wonderful singing this morning! Aren't we all so grateful to
have a friend in Jesus? To know He bears our burdens and hears us when we
pray?"

A chorus of *amen*s rang behind Dinah, startling her.

"To have the assurance of eternity with Him?" Ruthie's father boomed.

More, heartier *amen*s exploded.

"Amen, indeed!" Ruthie's father waved his arms. "Bow your heads, folks,
and let's talk to Him now in prayer."

With shuffling feet and soft murmurs, those gathered in the church followed Mr. Mead's instruction. All except Dinah. While Ruthie's father offered
a lengthy, big-voiced prayer from the front and everyone else listened, she took
advantage of the moment to give the room a thorough perusal.

Although the church's interior was far from the opulent beauty she'd expected, it held a simple charm that smoothed the edges of her unease. White
plastered walls gleamed in the sunshine pouring through the clear glass windows. A small, battered table on the corner of the front platform held a Mason
jar filled with fragrant wildflowers. Against the plain backdrop, the flowers

seemed brighter than any Dinah had ever seen. A thick book lay open at the base of the jar. A few green leaves dipped low as if reading the exposed words. The breeze easing in from the doors open at both the front and the back of the church rustled the book's pages, and Dinah experienced the strange sensation to step near and see what they had to say.

"Amen," Mr. Mead said, and everyone raised their heads.

In one accord, the people seated themselves on the benches. Ruthie pulled Dinah down next to her, then kept hold of her arm. Dinah gently extracted it. As she did so, she caught sight of those lined up on Ruthie's other side. Several children—a little girl with spirals of strawberry-colored hair and five boys of various ages, all with close-cropped hair of reddish-blond the same shade as Ruthie's—tipped forward slightly to look directly at her. Apparently Ruthie had led her to the same bench where her family sat. She shouldn't be here at the front with Ruthie's family as if she belonged.

Ruthie's father picked up the book from the little table and held it in his broad palm the way a mother might cradle the head of her newborn child. "If you have a Bible with you, turn with me to the book of Isaiah, the twenty-sixth chapter, beginning with verse two." He began reading aloud, his voice so full and rich it bounced from the ceiling beams and downward again. The little row of faces turned forward, gazing at their father attentively.

Although the words Mr. Mead read were beautifully crafted and delivered with intensity, Dinah wished he'd have the people stand up and sing another off-key hymn. If they were standing, she might be able to sneak her way to the back bench. Sitting here in the front, she felt like an interloper. Was everyone behind her looking at her, wondering why she sat with the preacher's family? She fidgeted, her body itching with discomfort. Surely they'd sing again, wouldn't they? As soon as they did, she'd move. Or could she? She hadn't looked to see if there was an open space in the back.

As surreptitiously as possible, she shifted to send a glance toward the benches farthest from the platform. And her gaze landed on a familiar face. The egg man, who'd frightened her and then asked her forgiveness for having done so, sat next to the center aisle on the very back bench. For the first time that morning, for reasons she couldn't begin to explain, her stiff muscles began to relax.

The man's face turned slightly, and he caught her looking at him. For a moment his brows descended, as if he was confused, but then a smile bloomed on his square, honest face. With a movement so slight she might have imagined it, he bobbed his head in a simple hello.

Beside her, Ruthie cleared her throat softly. Dinah's face flamed. She jerked her gaze forward and kept it there the remainder of the service. She tried to listen to Ruthie's father—his full-throated voice and enthusiastic delivery commanded attention—but her thoughts drifted repeatedly to the very back bench where the egg man sat. It was ridiculous, but knowing he was there made her feel less like an intruder.

"That concludes our service for today." Mr. Mead closed the Bible with a gentle snap and set it aside. He turned a smile on Ruthie and then Dinah. "It seems my daughter has brought a guest. Ruthie, would you like to introduce your friend so we can all get to know her?"

Dinah's mouth went dry.

"Yes, I would." Ruthie bounced up, beaming. She pulled on Dinah's arm, forcing her to rise. Dinah stood on quivering legs, facing the Mason jar of flowers, while Ruthie turned to look at those gathered in the room. "This is Dinah Hubley, who came to Florence all the way from Chicago, Illinois. She's the new chambermaid at the Clifton." Ruthie looked at her expectantly. Dinah pretended to ignore her.

Mr. Mead chuckled. "Miss Hubley, would you mind turning around so our congregation can properly greet you?"

Dinah didn't want to turn around. She didn't want to see all those eyes looking at her. But she had little choice. Drawing in a breath, she turned a slow circle and faced the small crowd. Light applause broke out across the room along with several politely uttered hellos and welcomes. Unnerved by the attention, she sought the one familiar face among a sea of strangers. But to her surprise, the spot where the egg man had been sitting was empty.

Chapter 10

Dinah

inah stood with the others and listened while the congregation sang one more song—one about Christian soldiers marching to war—and then Mr. Mead dismissed them with another boisterous but short prayer. The moment he said, "Amen," Ruthie dashed for her father, arms outstretched, and the pair embraced. Dinah watched their reunion with envy so deep and stifling she found drawing a breath painful. Had anyone, ever, been as happy to see her as Ruthie was to see her father? How would it feel to run to a father's arms? She couldn't even imagine it.

Ruthie's brothers and sister edged close to Dinah, forming a half circle around her. The tallest boy stood an inch shorter than Dinah, and the top of the little girl's curly head barely reached Dinah's waist. But with all of them staring at her, she felt no larger than an ant. Ruthie and her father joined the circle, and Ruthie went down the line, hugging each of her siblings by turn.

Mr. Mead smiled at Dinah. In his hazel eyes, she saw the same friendliness Ruthie exhibited. "It's so good to have you join us this morning, Miss Hubley. Ruthie has been lonely since her friend Phoebe left the Clifton. I'm sure you're a great comfort to her." When speaking one-on-one, he held his volume to a low rumble, but his tone still sounded strong and certain.

Dinah knew she wasn't a comfort to anyone, but she offered a nod. "Thank you, sir. It's…it's good to meet you." Would God strike her dead for lying in a church?

Ruthie pressed the group of children forward and lightly bounced her hand on each head as she introduced them. "Dinah, this is Seth, Jonah, Noah, Timothy, Joseph, and Dinah June."

The youngest boy, Joseph, jabbed his thumb toward his little sister. "We call her Junebug because she's so little."

Dinah June's round cheeks turned rosier than her strawberry hair. She buried her face in Ruthie's apron. Ruthie laughed and smoothed the child's tumbling locks. "Where's Mama? I wanted her to meet Dinah, too."

"She wasn't feeling well this morning, so she stayed home."

Ruthie's mouth dropped open. "Mama missed church? She must be ailing to stay home from service!"

Mr. Mead patted Ruthie's shoulder. "Now, now, don't get yourself worked up. I'm sure it's just a summer malaise. You know how the heat bothers her."

Ruthie shrugged and turned to Dinah. "Well, you'll just have to come back next week if you want to meet Mama."

"Ruthie, Dinah!" Matilda called from the doorway. "Dean's here with the buggy. We need to go."

Ruthie bade everyone good-bye, bestowing another quick hug on each. Little Dinah June wrapped her arms around Ruthie's waist and wouldn't let go, but Mr. Mead eased her away and lifted the little girl in his arms. The group followed Ruthie and Dinah out to the yard and watched as the wagon rolled away.

Ruthie turned completely backward, bumping Dinah with her elbow as she waved. When the buggy rounded the corner, she flumped into the seat and sighed. "How do you all do it?"

Matilda looked over her shoulder at Ruthie. "How do we do what?"

Ruthie's eyes filled with tears. "How do you survive, being so far from your families? Mine is right here in Florence. I see them every week on Sunday. And I miss them so much sometimes I think my heart will break right in two. Don't you miss your families?"

Lyla shook her head. "Not me. I was only too happy to leave. I'm the 'baby' and my brothers and sisters expected me to stay home and take care of Ma and Pa. Now I just take care of me."

"I miss mine," Amelia said, "but I needed a job. I'll stay as long as Mr. Harvey will keep me."

Minnie shrugged. "I miss mine, too, but my ma really wanted me to work for Mr. Harvey. She said I'd have the chance to meet businessmen with money and find a husband who would provide for me better than Pa's done with his pig raising. What about you, Dean?"

Dean laughed, flashing a grin at the girls. "Miss my folks? Nuh-uh! I'm havin' too much fun to miss anybody." He pulled the reins, and the horses turned the final corner. The wagon rattled over the railroad tracks, bouncing everyone in their seats. Dean hollered over the clatter of the wooden wheels on iron rails. "I'm hoping when I finish my year here, I'll get sent farther up the line. Maybe to Colorado, or even to New Mexico. I hear there's lots of action there."

He drew the team to a stop near the front doors. "Hop on out, girls. Tell Mr. Gindough I'll be in as soon as I get the horses back to the stable."

The girls climbed down from the buggy and headed for the porch. Ruthie and Dinah fell in line at the rear. Ruthie linked arms with Dinah, and even though the familiarity made Dinah stiffen, she didn't pull away. Ruthie seemed to need to hang on to someone, and it felt a little good to be able to provide some comfort, the way Mr. Mead had said.

"I hope you'll go with me again next Sunday because I do want you to meet Mama. She's the dearest woman in the world. I know you'll love her." Ruthie's melancholy tone wove a blanket of sadness around Dinah.

"I'll go." But she wasn't thinking of seeing Ruthie's mama. Instead, thoughts of the egg man filled her head. Remembering his kind smile and gentle nod warmed her. But why had he left before the service ended? Or had she only imagined he was there? She realized Ruthie was talking again, and she pushed her reflections aside to pay attention.

"...you're farther from home than any of the others working here. Well, except for Mr. Phillips. He came from Chicago, too."

Dinah jolted. "Who is from Chicago?"

Ruthie paused beside the hotel double doors. "The hotel manager, Mr. Phillips. People say he's the best paid man in all of Florence. Mr. Harvey hired him away from a fine hotel in Chicago. Didn't you know?"

Her pulse skipped erratically. She shook her head.

A sad smile lifted the corners of Ruthie's mouth. "Isn't that nice for you? Even though you're far from your family, there's someone here who knows about your home. So when you're feeling lonely, you could talk to him. It might help."

Ruthie entered the hotel and Dinah followed. Her entire body trembled. The manager was from Chicago. Did he know about her home? Her head began to swim, and she stopped to lean against the wall until the feeling passed. If Mr. Phillips truly was familiar with her home, she wouldn't be able to become a server. He'd tell Mr. Harvey she wasn't qualified.

Ruthie had continued onward, but when she reached the end of the hallway, she glanced back. Concern pinched her face—as much concern as she'd shown when she discovered her mother wasn't feeling well. She hurried back to Dinah's side. "What's the matter? Are you sick?"

Dinah couldn't honestly say she was ill. She tried to shake her head, but dizziness attacked again.

Ruthie curled her arm around Dinah's waist. "Come with me. This heat must be bothering you the same way it bothers Mama. I'll get you a glass of water. You drink it all down and afterward you'll feel better."

Dinah allowed Ruthie to guide her to their little waiting room, but she didn't answer. A glass of water couldn't possibly make things better.

Amos

Amos dug through the soft straw in the roosting box, but he didn't find an egg. This made the fifth empty box. Yesterday he'd found four empty roosts, and two the day before that. The two hadn't bothered him much. An empty roost now and then wasn't unexpected. But four? And then five? He scowled as he looked down the row of wooden roosts. Were the chickens not laying because they were upset about him bringing home that rooster and separating the flock?

He'd closed eighteen of the hens in the barn to hatch chicks, and the first day the ones outside the barn had carried on as if their tail feathers were on fire. Then the empty roosts followed. Concern churned through his stomach. Either the girls were being cantankerous or he had an egg thief in his midst.

With the basket of eggs cradled in his arms, he made his way out of the chicken house and across the yard. He'd hated leaving church before the closing prayer. Preacher Mead had a way of speaking to the Lord that let everybody know he and his Maker were good friends. Being a witness to the minister's close relationship with God strengthened Amos's resolve to draw ever nearer to his Father. But today, knowing there would be eggs waiting in the straw boxes midmorning, he'd hurried out to count eggs.

He stood for a moment, observing the chickens pecking in the yard. The rooster he'd purchased waved its wings, ducked its head, and charged at Amos. He stood as still as a scarecrow and waited until the bird had nearly reached his boots. Then he shouted, "Hah!" Clucking in angry little bursts of sound, the bird whirled and returned to the pullets.

It paraded around the yard with its head high and wings held at a jaunty angle. He'd chosen the bird from a farmer on the other side of town because of its large size and aggressive attitude. He wanted a bird that would protect the flock. But he didn't like being attacked every time he came near his own chickens. If the obnoxious rooster didn't settle down some, it might end up in a stew pot when the baby chicks hatched and he could replace it.

He carried the basket of eggs into the barn and put it with the ones collected over the past two days. Tomorrow he'd take his eggs to town to sell. Worry descended as he glanced across the smaller number of eggs. Choosing to set some aside for hatching as well as the lower count from the past days meant he'd have none to take the grocer for a credit on his account. And he needed some grocery items.

The morning scripture played through his memory, and he whispered it. "'Thou wilt keep him in perfect peace, whose mind is stayed on thee.'" He sent an apologetic look toward the rafters. "Forgive me, Lord. I'll try to think less about the number of eggs in the chicken house and more about the One who loves me and will always meet my needs. I trust You." The prayer revived him, and he placed the basket he used to collect eggs upside down over the wagon and left the barn.

As he passed the chickens' water pans, he noticed one had been dumped. He shook his head. Probably that strutting rooster again. The bird was almost more trouble than it was worth. He headed for the well to bring up the bucket. The dusty walk to and from town this morning had tired his bad leg, and his foot dragged across the ground. The toe of his boot caught on something, nearly sending him on his nose. He stopped to catch his balance and looked down to see what had created the obstacle. A fist-sized rock lay half-hidden in the grass.

With a grunt, he leaned over and picked it up. He started to toss it into the scrubby brush along the foundation of his house, but sunlight fell on a band of amber circling the stone. He froze. The deep gold matched the shimmering strands in the light-brown hair of the girl who'd turned to look at him in church that morning. He hadn't recognized her at first. With her hair pinned up in a coiled braid and dressed in a hotel uniform, she looked much older than she had when he found her sleeping on the porch. But when he saw her eyes—eyes of larkspur blue—he knew it was her. And something in his chest fluttered.

He bounced the rock in his hand, enjoying the play of sunlight on the jagged band of amber. So the girl worked at the hotel. Good for her. She'd looked so lost and forlorn on the porch, but if she worked at the hotel, she had a roof over her head, meals every day, and a salary to boot. She'd be cared for.

He gave himself a shake. Hadn't he learned woolgathering would lead him to harm? His bum leg proved it—as Pa had often grumbled, if he'd been paying better attention way back then, he might have been able to jump out of the way of the wagon's wheel. So what was he doing, playing with a rock and thinking of a girl when the chickens needed water?

Tucking the rock into the pocket of his overalls, he hurried to the well. He drew up a bucket of cool water, filled the chickens' pan, and shook his finger at the rooster. "Don't dump it this time." The arrogant bird ruffled its feathers and pranced off.

Amos returned the bucket to the well and headed for the house to rest, as the good Lord advised. Inside, instead of settling into his chair, he removed the rock from his pocket and turned it this way and that. Almost without thought, his lips drew upward into a smile. With great care, he placed the rock on his fireplace mantel next to the oil lamp and adjusted it to best display the band of amber. He backed up slowly, admiring it.

A snippet of a hymn rose from his memory—*"He hideth my soul in the cleft of the rock…"*—and he remembered the girl asking what had broken him. He eased into his chair, recalling how he'd wondered what created her skittishness. Concern rolled through him. Why did he worry so much about a girl he didn't know? Didn't he have enough to concern him without adding a stranger's unknown plight to the list? She'd been in church. That should mean she knew to go to the cleft of the Rock when in need of comfort and peace.

He closed his eyes, but behind his closed lids the image of the rock played back and forth with the image of the girl that morning—wispy strands of soft brown hair falling alongside her heart-shaped face and blue eyes lighting with pleasure when they fell on him. And he never did rest.

Chapter 11

Amos

he brooding hens eyed Amos as he crossed the hard-packed barn floor Monday morning. A couple raised their heads and clucked, as if warning him to keep his distance, but he ignored them and limped straight to the wagon, which waited in the deepest shadowy corner of the barn. He frowned when he spotted his egg-gathering basket on the ground instead of upside down over the hay, the way he'd left it.

He sent a frown at the hens. "Which of you has been climbing up here and trying to roost? You stay on your eggs over there. These are for selling, not hatching."

One brassy hen clucked a reply, and he chuckled. He took hold of the handle and set off for town. His chuckle faded as he considered the fewer eggs he transported than he had in previous weeks. Many of his customers would be displeased today.

He cringed, the crunch of the little wagon's wheels on the dirt road seeming to grind out a complaint. But then, maybe it was good he wouldn't be able to provide eggs to everyone who'd come to depend on him. Because when his flock was big enough to meet the needs of the hotel's kitchen, he wouldn't be selling to individuals at all.

The faces of those he'd come to know in the past months paraded through his memory, and it stung to think of disappointing them. But he had to sell to a big company instead of to individuals if he ever intended to build his farm enough to support a family. Unless... He chewed the inside of his cheek, daring to let his dream expand even bigger. If he had sons—or daughters, too, he supposed—they could help on the farm. He'd be able to take care of a much larger flock. He could sell eggs and chickens to the hotel, to individuals, and maybe even to places far away. The railroad could transport his eggs just about anywhere.

His chest went tight, thinking of becoming such a successful business-man. After his accident Amos had listened to his pa bemoan how Amos would be a burden on the family, unable to pull his own weight. When he made his chicken farm a success, he would invite his whole family to visit. Wouldn't it please him to see the surprise on Pa's face?

Eagerness to see his plans through sped his feet, and he pushed his aching hip to cover the distance in record time. When he'd emptied his wagon of all but three lone eggs—in only eight stops—he visited the grocer and gathered staples to carry him through another week.

As Mr. Root tallied up Amos's purchases, he commented, "No eggs to trade today?"

Amos grimaced. "No. Unless you want only three." He must have mis-counted when he put the eggs in the wagon. He thought he should have more than a half dozen left. "Five cents' worth doesn't seem worth the trade."

The man laughed. "You're right there. You must've had good sales today to run out of eggs so soon."

"I sold all but these, true, but I didn't have enough to go around today." Amos shared the changes he was making out at his chicken farm. Mr. Root listened as if deeply interested, pausing with his pencil caught between his thumb and finger above the page. Amos finished, "So it might be a while be-fore I have eggs to bring to you. I hope it doesn't trouble you too much to be without my eggs."

"Doesn't trouble me nearly as much as it might some of my customers." The owner set the pencil to work again, scratching out numbers while he spoke. "You're setting your sights mighty high, especially for someone with—"

Amos sucked in a breath.

"—so few years on him."

Amos's breath eased out, relieved the man hadn't mentioned his gimpy leg.

"I'm not so young." He'd felt older than his age ever since the wagon ran over him.

"No? Well, I reckon when you get as gray headed as me, most everybody under the age of thirty looks like a youngster." Mr. Root wrote the total on the bottom of the pad and turned it around so Amos could check his figures.

Amos trusted the man. He dug in his pocket and counted out the amount needed. He slid the coins across the counter. "I hope to get my farm where I want it before my hair turns gray." He tried to speak lightly, as if he were making a joke, but his voice came out tight and strained instead.

The grocer clanked the coins into his cash register drawer. "Now, don't defeat yourself even before you get started. As I said, you're young. You've got time." He gave the drawer a push, and the massive register echoed with the solid slam. "I'd have to say you're in a better spot than most of the young men here in Florence. Lots of them work at the quarry outside of town. Good work—honorable, with a decent wage. But I can't help but wonder what they'll all do when the rock runs out. It's bound to happen by and by." He shot Amos a smile. "But you aren't likely to run clear out of eggs, and folks will always need what you're peddling. So hang on to your plans, young man. See 'em through."

The man's advice, given in such a fatherly manner, warmed Amos. And encouraged him. He smiled his thanks. "I will, sir. Good-bye now."

Out on the boardwalk beneath the sun, Amos glanced at the three remaining eggs nestled in the straw. He could take them home and eat them—a treat he rarely allowed himself. Or should he give those eggs to the hotel cook as a gift? He could ask him to tell the manager he was working on expanding his flock, as he'd been told to do. *"Hang on to your plans... See 'em through."* Mr. Root's advice propelled him in the direction of the hotel. It wouldn't hurt to let the manager know he'd taken his words to heart and was working to win his business.

Ruthie

Ruthie swung the rug beater like a baseball bat and gave the rug hanging over the clothesline another good whack. Dust swirled from the thickly woven yarns. A gust of hot wind tossed the dust in her face. She turned aside and coughed. From her spot farther down the line, Dinah coughed, too. Of all the tasks assigned to the chambermaids, rug beating was Ruthie's least favorite. Thankfully they only had to do it once every two months.

Raising the beater again, Ruthie took aim. But before she swung, a shadow creeping up alongside her caught her by surprise. She lowered the beater and turned to find one of Papa's parishioners, Amos Ackerman, standing nearby. Immediately, her pulse increased its tempo. She'd never been tongue-tied around anyone, but the first time she'd seen Mr. Ackerman's square, handsome face and broad shoulders nearly a year ago, she'd found herself smitten. Having him so near turned her legs to rubber. Her lips quivered into a shy grin.

He spoke first. "Good morning, Miss Mead."

Up ahead, Dinah was pounding her rug with steady whumps. Between the noise and the dust flying through the air, conversation would be a challenge. But Ruthie could overcome challenges. "Good morning, Mr. Ackerman." Her voice emerged as wobbly as her knees felt. She swallowed a nervous titter.

"You girls are working hard." His gaze drifted to Dinah. Admiration seemed to shine in his eyes.

Ruthie liked his eyes—the color of sapphire with darker blue rims around the irises. He had incredibly thick and long eyelashes for a man, and most of the time he averted his gaze so his eyes hid behind the lashes. She preferred it when he held his head high, the way he was doing now. But she wished he'd look at her instead of at Dinah.

She cleared her throat—partly to rid it of the dusty feeling, but mostly to gain his attention. It worked on the latter. She beamed. "Yes, we are. With all the feet coming and going through the hotel, the rugs needed a good beating.

Dinah and I are only too happy to rid them of the travel dust. Aren't we, Dinah?"

Dinah paused in her pounding and flicked a brief glance over her shoulder. Her gaze bounced from Ruthie to Mr. Ackerman, and color climbed her cheeks. She nodded, then returned to swatting the backside of the rug with even greater gusto than before. If she didn't slow down, her arms would fall off before they finished all the rugs. Ruthie started to issue a warning, but Mr. Ackerman spoke again.

"I came to see the hotel manager, but I wasn't sure if he'd be too busy right now to talk to me. Do you know his morning schedule? I don't want to intrude."

His voice, deep and slow as if every word was too important to rush, reminded her of Papa's when he was reading aloud from the Bible. The warm feeling in Ruthie's chest expanded. "He's likely overseeing the baking. Monday is bread-making day. I think he spends lots of time in the kitchen since he was a head chef at a big-city hotel before he came to Florence. But there are lots of kitchen helpers, so he'd probably have a few minutes to speak with you." She paused, gathering up her nerve. Papa would frown if she behaved flirtatiously—even though she was nearly nineteen and definitely of a marriageable age—while speaking with one of his unmarried male parishioners. "Would you like me to take you in and ask him to speak with you?"

If she wasn't mistaken, Dinah suddenly decreased the strength of her swing. The thuds from her beater seemed less intense. Mr. Ackerman must have noticed, too, because he sent a questioning look in Dinah's direction.

Ruthie said, "I'd be glad to do it."

Mr. Ackerman continued to watch Dinah. She delivered another three, weaker whacks, and then her arms drooped to her sides. The curved wire tip of the beater hid in the grass. In the silence that fell, Ruthie's voice boomed out shrilly.

"Dinah could come, too. She's never beaten rugs before, so I'm sure she's tired." Had she really intended to disparage Dinah? Not deliberately, but she realized her words sounded spiteful. She hurriedly added, "And we both need a drink after swallowing so much dust." She offered Dinah an apologetic look. "So we'll all go, yes?"

But Dinah shook her head. She lifted the beater and returned to work, although her swings showed her weariness.

Ruthie turned to Mr. Ackerman, who gazed at Dinah with sympathy in his expression. Ruthie's heart rolled over. He was such a nice man. She dropped her beater at her feet and took a step toward the open doorway leading directly into the kitchen from the backyard. "Come along, Mr. Ackerman. The kitchen is this way."

He hesitated for a moment. Then he released the handle on the child's wagon he'd been pulling and plucked three eggs from the bed of straw filling the wooden box. Ruthie thought he would follow her, but instead he moved across the yard toward Dinah with the eggs cradled in one of his wide hands. His gait was clumsy, his left leg refusing to travel as far as the right one. But he closed the distance fairly quickly, considering his limp.

Ruthie tipped her head, listening in.

"Are you sure you don't want to take a short break, Di—" Pink stole across his cheeks. He looked at Ruthie.

She read the silent question. "Hubley. Her name is Miss Hubley."

He nodded a thank-you and turned back to Dinah. "Are you sure you don't want to rest a bit, Miss Hubley? Your arms must be aching."

Dinah skittered away from him to the next rug waiting on the line and raised the beater. "I'm fine." She whacked the rug.

He frowned.

Ruthie fidgeted impatiently. As much as she admired Mr. Ackerman's consideration, it was ill placed. Dinah held everyone at arm's length. Why would she treat him any differently? He'd only feel snubbed if he continued trying to persuade her. Ruthie couldn't have that. He was far too kind a person to suffer being rebuffed by a rich girl from Chicago.

"Mr. Ackerman, I'll bring Dinah a cup of water when I return from the kitchen. It's just this way." Ruthie inched toward the building, hoping he would follow.

After another moment of hesitation, he turned and scuffed after her. Relieved, she sent a smile over her shoulder. Even though he marched along in resignation rather than eagerness, victory straightened her spine. She'd saved him from certain humiliation and hurt feelings. She hoped he'd be grateful.

To Ruthie's frustration, the moment she took Mr. Ackerman to Mr. Phillips, she ceased to exist. Or at least it felt that way. The two men began a lightning-fast conversation—Mr. Phillips did everything quickly, and Mr. Ackerman responded in kind, although it seemed out of character for him to rattle off his words—over *eggs,* of all things! Ruthie nearly rolled her eyes. *Eggs* were so important? But apparently they were, because Mr. Phillips turned an egg this way and that with one eye squinted shut. He acted as though he were a jeweler and the egg were a diamond. Even though she'd intended to walk Mr. Ackerman back to his wagon, she realized very quickly the two of them might talk for quite a while.

So she said, "Good-bye, then, Mr. Ackerman."

He didn't even look at her.

Now she felt rebuffed. She took two tin cups from the hooks on the sideboard, filled them with water from the drinking bucket, and carried them out to the yard. Dinah turned as Ruthie approached and reached eagerly for the cup. Ruthie sipped, but Dinah guzzled her water, then wiped her moist lips with the back of her hand—an undignified gesture that took Ruthie by surprise. But if someone from Dinah's background could slurp water without reserve, so could she. Ruthie finished her cup in one long draw.

Dinah twiddled the cup in her hand, her gaze fluttering toward the kitchen doorway. "Was...was Mr. Phillips available to talk with Mr. Ackerman?"

"Yes."

Dinah nibbled her lower lip. Worry creased her brow. "They're talking a long time."

Ruthie stifled a disgruntled huff. Papa didn't approve of snide expulsions of breath. "They are. About *eggs*."

Dinah turned so sharply she nearly dropped the cup. "Did you say *eggs*?"

Ruthie nodded. She held her hands outward, her frustration getting the better of her. "Can you imagine? Mr. Phillips was so intent on examining the eggs Mr. Ackerman had brought, neither of them even noticed when I left the room." She folded her arms across her chest and tapped the tin cup against her shoulder. "I found it rather insulting, to be honest."

A smile grew on Dinah's face. The biggest smile Ruthie had seen since the girl arrived. "Good. That's good."

Ruthie gave a jolt. It was *good* that she'd been insulted?

Dinah thrust the cup at Ruthie and then reached for the beater, which she'd discarded in the grass. Without another word, she set back to work and hummed as she swung the beater.

Ruthie stood staring at Dinah for several seconds. What had made her so happy? Clearly she would never understand Dinah Hubley. She shook her head and started to return the cups to the kitchen. Then she remembered the way the two men had ignored her, and she turned around. After dropping the cups near the clothesline, she yanked up her beater and aimed a mighty blow on the closest rug.

Chapter 12

Dinah

After two hours of swatting at the rugs, Dinah's arms and back ached so badly she wanted to crawl in a hole and wail. She gazed down the line of rugs and gently rotated her neck, willing the stiff muscles to relax. She hadn't been so sore since—

She slammed the door on the thought and turned her attention elsewhere. Despite her physical discomfort, she couldn't deny a great feeling of relief. The chef from Chicago and the egg man—Mr. Ackerman, Ruthie had called him—had talked about eggs. Not about Dinah.

For one brief second, disappointment smote her. He'd been so considerate, asking if she needed a break from the hard labor. Even though his attention made her jittery, it also pleased her. And she'd found herself wanting to hold on to it just a little longer. The feeling surprised her. She'd never wanted a man's gaze to linger on her or to be drawn into conversation, but Mr. Ackerman was different. Maybe she felt safer because she could outrun him, given his limp. But she sensed there was something more. She only wished she knew what it was.

Ruthie walked over, her steps slow and labored, and took Dinah's rug beater from her hand. She heaved a deep sigh. "I'll go tell Mr. Irwin the rugs are ready to go back on the floor. I'm glad the busboys will carry them inside. I can barely lift these things." She swung the pair of beaters and grimaced. "I wish we could take a nap before we start cleaning rooms, but there isn't time. We'll probably both sleep like logs tonight."

Dinah hoped her tiredness would result in deep sleep. Terrifying dreams about the gentleman in Chicago had kept her from fully resting for weeks. At least she'd been able to set aside her concern about being with child. She'd never been so happy to welcome her monthly time. Even so, she needed an uninterrupted night of sleep.

Ruthie started toward the hotel, then paused and turned back. "Oh, Dinah, I almost forgot. Would you take the cups we used to the kitchen? Just put them in the tub for the dishwasher. They're on the ground right over there." She waved one of the beaters in the direction of the clothesline and then headed off across the grass.

Dinah opened her mouth to ask Ruthie to take the cups instead, but she held the request inside. Ruthie would ask why, and Dinah couldn't explain. So she walked stiffly to the discarded pair of tin cups, picked them up, and trudged toward the kitchen. As she crossed the sunny yard, she consoled herself. The washtub would probably be near the back door. At the Yellow Parrot the slop bucket was by the door, and Rueben always said it made sense to have the washtub near the slop bucket. She could probably drop the cups in the tub and slip away without anyone even seeing her.

As she neared the door, which was held open by a brick, the wonderful aromas of fresh bread and roasted meat wafted out to greet her. The smells grew more pungent as she closed the distance, and busy noises—scurrying feet, pans clanking, low-voiced commands to fill the serving bowls and be careful with the gravy—warned her she shouldn't tarry in the kitchen. She'd be in the way.

She peeked inside, cups extended to drop into a tub. But no tub waited near the door. In fact, she couldn't see a washtub at all from this position. She scanned the room, taking note of the workers scurrying around, as industrious as a nest of ants. She'd thought the dining room servers were the only ones who raced to complete their tasks. Serving drinks and a three-course meal to as many as sixty guests during a twenty-minute watering stop left no time to pause between duties. But apparently the kitchen workers were just as taxed. And no one had time to stop and direct her to the washtub.

She considered leaving the cups on the floor inside the door. Someone would come upon them. But how many times had she found items out of place at the Yellow Parrot, which she then had to return to their rightful locations?

She didn't want to create extra work for anyone. With a sigh, she stepped into the kitchen and inched her way along the outer edge, keeping well out of the way of those rushing around to fill plates and slide them through the serving window.

When she'd gone halfway across the room, she spotted a counter with a pump handle sticking up. A wooden tub rested on the floor in front of the counter. The washtub, surely. She hurried in that direction and ran smack into a little girl who was crouched on the floor against the wall. The tin cups went flying as Dinah reached out to catch herself from falling on the child.

The girl began to wail, and a woman carrying a stack of white plates with Mr. Harvey's specially chosen blue swirl design painted on the rims careened from a little room behind the counter. "What's wrong, Laura?" The woman plopped the plates into Dinah's hands. "Take these to the serving window so I can see to my daughter."

Too stunned to argue, Dinah balanced the plates against her ribs and waddled to the counter. Next to Mr. Gindough stood Mr. Phillips, who bobbed his head toward an empty space on the counter. "Put them there and then stand back. We've got to get these filled."

Dinah lowered the plates to the surface, holding her breath. She didn't dare look into his face, fearful he'd recognize her from the Yellow Parrot. The plates clunked together as they met the wooden counter. "Careful," he said, then turned away.

Her head low, Dinah scurried off. She flicked a glance over her shoulder. The man was too busy dishing up food to take notice of her. Relieved, she turned toward the door. But the woman who'd handed her the plates waved her hand and called, "Wait!"

Dinah hesitated. She needed to get to work. She and Ruthie had spent so much time beating the rugs, she was behind on cleaning rooms. She might even need to skip lunch. The woman added, "Please come here," and Dinah couldn't ignore the pleading in her voice. She hurried to the woman's side.

The little girl clung to her mother, hiding her face in the folds of the woman's grimy skirt. The woman offered a quick, apologetic smile. "I'm sorry to trouble you—I know you aren't one of the kitchen workers—but my little girl here needs the outhouse and she's afraid to walk all the way out there alone. I need to bring out more clean plates. Would you take the plates for me? They're in the butler's pantry."

Dinah's stomach churned. The longer she stayed in the kitchen, the more likely it became Mr. Phillips would take a good look at her. She needed to leave. She made a snap decision. "I'll take your little girl to the outhouse." She released a nervous laugh. "I almost dropped those plates, and the cook wasn't too happy with me."

The woman tugged the child loose. "Laura, you go with this nice lady. She'll help you and bring you right back." She pressed the little girl toward Dinah, then disappeared into the pantry.

Dinah looked down at the child. Laura looked back with round, desperate eyes. Dinah said, "Let's hurry."

They took off at a trot. Dinah started to step inside with Laura, but the little girl shook her head, making her silky yellow curls bounce. "I can go by myself."

Arguing would only prolong things. "Go ahead, then."

Dinah waited outside the outhouse while Laura went in and saw to her needs. The child was in there several minutes, and twice Dinah started to go in and check on her, but she could hear her singing, which told her she wasn't distressed, so she paced outside the closed door and waited. Finally Laura emerged. Her skinny little chest rose and fell in a sigh. "All done." The hem of her pink checked skirt was caught in the back of her cotton drawers, and she allowed Dinah to straighten things out. Then she stuck out her hand.

Unexpectedly, tears welled in Dinah's eyes. She was a stranger to the child, yet Laura offered her hand in complete trust. It seemed her entire life she'd ducked away from extended hands, worried about being slapped or pushed aside or pawed in ways that made her shudder. Gratefulness that Laura could offer her hand to a stranger washed Dinah with as much pleasure as a fresh fall of rain, and she found herself hoping nothing would ever steal the child's innocence and trust.

She curled her fingers around Laura's small hand and walked with her back to the kitchen. Her mother was kneeling beside the washtub with her arms submerged in the sudsy water. The rims of various pots and pans created gray circles in the suds. She continued scrubbing a large soup pot as Dinah and Laura approached, but her face pursed into a worried grimace. "Did you make it in time?"

Dinah nodded. Laura still hadn't released her hand. She needed to change her uniform—her apron was gray from dust—and start cleaning rooms, but she didn't want to let go until Laura was ready. So she stood beside the washtub and held the little girl's hand while everyone around her worked.

The woman transferred the clean, sudsy pot to a second tub of clear water. "I don't think we've met. I'm Alice Deaton."

"I'm Dinah Hubley." She held her voice low. With all the noise in the kitchen, she didn't think Mr. Phillips would overhear, but she wouldn't take the chance. Half of the men in Chicago knew of Untamable Tori Hubley. "I'm new here."

"Me, too." The woman plunged her hands into the water and vigorously scrubbed another pot. "My man got hurt working at the quarry a little over a week ago, and Mr. Irwin was kind enough to hire me on until he's well enough to work again." Mrs. Deaton whisked a grateful smile at Dinah. "Thank you for seeing to Laura."

"It was my pleasure." Dinah smiled at Laura, who smiled back.

Mrs. Deaton went on. "She's such a good little thing—helps so much with Francis so I can see to the dishes." She bobbed her head toward a pallet of folded quilts where a small boy slept with his fingers in his mouth. "I don't know what I'd do if I couldn't bring my youngsters with me."

Dinah's stomach tightened into knots. She'd spent her childhood at her mother's workplace. Dismal memories flooded her mind, and sympathy swelled in her chest for these children. Although the Clifton Hotel wasn't anything like the Yellow Parrot, it still wasn't a place for little ones to wile away their days. She hoped Mrs. Deaton's husband recovered quickly so she could give up this job and let Laura and Francis run and play, the way children should.

Mrs. Deaton shifted her attention to her daughter. "Let loose of Miss Hubley now, Laura, and go fetch Mama those tin cups."

Laura slipped her hand from Dinah's and scampered off, the tails from the bow on the back of her dress bouncing against her skirt. Dinah watched her go while loneliness crept over her. She'd enjoyed her few minutes with Laura. She felt good tending to the little girl. Almost motherly. The loneliness changed to longing. Would she ever have the chance to care for a little girl of her own? Probably not. Men didn't want to marry women who'd been used. At least, no decent men would. Any man who'd settle on her wouldn't be any better than the ones who frequented Miss Flo's place. And Dinah had no desire to tie herself to a man like that.

One of the busboys, who everyone called Poke because he moved as slow as a turtle, ambled over with a tray full of dirty dishes. He glanced at Dinah and a curious frown creased his face. "Howdy, Dinah. What're you doing in here? You helpin' in the kitchen now?" He looked over his shoulder at Dean Muller, who followed with a tray of towering stacked cups. "Lookee here, Dean—Dinah's takin' up kitchen work."

"Oh, she is?" Dean smirked and waggled his eyebrows. "Well, I won't complain. Lookin' at her's a big improvement over some of the others, huh?"

Poke laughed.

Dinah wanted to shrink away to nothing. She ducked her head.

Mrs. Deaton scowled at the pair. "You two stop teasing Miss Hubley."

Dean lowered his tray to the counter and began shifting the cups into the dry sink. "Aw, Miz Deaton, don't scold. We don't mean any harm. A fella can't help but tease such a pretty little thing like Dinah."

"Flo told me you were a pretty little thing."

The voice roared through Dinah's head. She broke out in a cold sweat. "I'd better get to work." She turned and darted off before anyone could say another word, choosing to rush through the now-empty dining room rather than going outside and around the hotel to the front doors. She dashed past the lunch counter, not even pausing when Ruthie called for her to stop and grab a sandwich. Around the corner, up the stairs, through the hallway to her room. She fumbled for her key, unlocked the door, then stumbled inside. Her mad dash had taken the wind from her, and she grabbed the cool brass footboard of the bed and held tight until her pulse slowed to a normal rhythm.

When she felt able to move again, she retrieved a clean apron from the wardrobe and exchanged it with the one she'd dirtied while beating the rugs. The apron caught in her hair, pulling a few pins loose, so she crossed to the washstand and reached for her hairbrush. Her gaze lit on the round mirror, and her pale reflection stared back at her.

"A fella can't help but tease such a pretty little thing like Dinah," Dean had said. She examined herself by increments, starting with the straggly, sweat-dampened clay-brown curls plastered to her forehead, then downward to her plain-colored eyes set wide in her face and eyelashes that refused to curl, her long straight nose, and unsmiling lips. Pretty? Dean was teasing, all right.

She hurriedly swept the loose strands of hair into place and pinned them tightly, her hands shaking with her eagerness to step away from the mirror rather than gaze upon her homely appearance one minute longer than neces-sary. The task complete, she turned for the door.

"…a pretty little thing like Dinah."

The comment taunted her, enticing her to turn back for one more hopeful look. But the same reflection greeted her. She must look like her father instead of her mother. Tori had been pretty. Everyone said so. Her prettiness kept the men coming back time and time again. Three or four of them had even pro-posed over the years, but Tori had turned down each one.

Dinah sighed. If she were at least pretty, maybe a man would overlook what she'd done with the businessman and love her anyway. But ugly on the outside *and* the inside? Nobody would ever want her. Not even a kind man like Mr. Ackerman.

She set to work, pushing past her aching muscles to complete the job she'd been hired to do. But she couldn't push past her sadness. It sat on her shoulders and weighed her down as much as those rugs had drooped the wire clothesline. If only someone had a beater that could remove the dirtiness from her life and let her start fresh and new.

Chapter 13

Ruthie

The alarm clock on the bedside table blared its morning wake-up call at five, like always. Ruthie rolled over and, her eyes too blurry from sleep to focus, pawed for the little switch below the clock's round face that would silence the thing. Before she found it, a pair of hands reached in and lifted the clock. Moments later blessed peace fell in the room.

Ruthie flopped back on her pillow, then rubbed her eyes and groaned. "How can something so pretty be such a nuisance?" She'd admired the gold-plated clock with the face of an owl carved onto its front when she moved into this room, declaring Seth Thomas made the prettiest clocks in the whole United States. But the sound it made was far from pretty. Especially when she was still so tired from yesterday's rug beating. The persistent ache in her shoulders had kept her awake last night, and her normally cheerful outlook had departed with the lack of slumber.

"I don't know." Dinah sounded grim. "But you'd better get up. It's Tuesday."

Ruthie groaned again.

"No sense complaining. The ladies will come out in droves, like they always do, to take their turn in the bathing room."

Ruthie forced her eyelids to open, and she scowled at Dinah, who was already dressed and stood at the mirror, coiling her thick braid into its heavy knot. Ruthie thought it a shame to twist such pretty, flowing hair into a plain style. But when she'd said as much to Dinah, intending to pay a compliment, the girl had gotten all stiff lipped and quiet. So Ruthie kept her thoughts to herself about Dinah's lovely, wavy, honey-brown hair.

She crawled out of bed and yanked open the door to the wardrobe. "Some-times I wish Mr. Harvey hadn't made that shower available to ladies twice a week. I never knew so many people in this town had twenty-five cents to squan-der for a bath." She tossed her nightgown onto the floor of the wardrobe and reached for a clean uniform, continuing to grumble as she dressed. "I wouldn't mind if the ladies were more like the men. The fellows just wait their turn and climb in. But the ladies expect a thorough scrubbing between uses. Why don't they save their money and bathe in a washtub at home, the way my mama does?"

"Because at home they have to heat water on the stove, fill a tub, and sit in it. Here, the water is already hot from the tank in the attic, and it trickles over your head in a shower. It's a luxury." Dinah pushed another pin through her hair. "Be glad you don't have to keep the coal heater going. Poke said that isn't a fun job, either, and he has to do it every day."

Ruthie huffed, refusing to see the dark cloud's bright lining. "Well, my arms are still so sore from yesterday it even hurts to button my uniform! I don't know how I'll survive cleaning the tub a dozen times on top of our room clean-ing." She rubbed her aching forearms and glared at Dinah's stoic image in the mirror.

Dinah turned her head left and right, seeming to examine her hair. Strange how she never appeared to look into her own eyes… "You clean the first-floor rooms today, and I'll clean the second-floor ones. Neither of us will have to climb stairs, and I can run to the bathing room and give the shower tub a quick cleaning when it's needed." She stepped away from the mirror.

Ruthie shook her head, wincing when the stiff muscles in her neck and shoulders complained. "That wouldn't be fair. Your arms must be just as sore as mine."

Dinah shrugged and placed her hand on the doorknob. "Not so sore I can't work." An odd expression crossed her face—almost an anguish. She must be hurting more than she wanted to admit. Ruthie started to tell her she'd take turns cleaning the tub, just as they'd done on previous days, but Dinah opened the door and moved toward the hallway. She said over her shoulder, "I'll see you in the breakfast room." And she closed the door behind her.

Ruthie stood for a moment, worrying her lower lip between her teeth. As much as she wanted to let Dinah take responsibility for the bathing room today, she shouldn't do it. They were supposed to divide the cleaning chores. If the hotel manager found out Dinah had done it all by herself, he'd surely reprimand Ruthie, and she'd die of mortification.

She set herself in motion and headed down to the breakfast room. She retrieved a plate of steaming scrambled eggs, crisp bacon, flaky biscuits swimming with butter, and a bowl of creamy grits from the serving window, then scanned the small room in search of Dinah. All the dining room servers and busboys sat around one table, their happy chatter filling the space. And Dinah was at a second table—the one in the farthest corner—by herself.

"Good morning, Ruthie!" Matilda gestured to the open chair beside her. "Join us!"

Ruthie shook her head. "I need to talk to Dinah," she said as she passed the table.

Matilda wrinkled her nose. "Suit yourself." She leaned in and whispered something that set the other servers into wild laughter.

Ruthie tried to ignore them, but it wasn't easy. She'd rather be part of their group, the way she'd been when Phoebe was still here. But Dinah and her standoffish ways had brought changes Ruthie didn't like. She frowned as she slid into the chair next to Dinah. "Why don't you sit with the others? There's room for all of us."

Dinah's plate was nearly empty already. Food went down faster when no conversation accompanied the meal. She nibbled on a strip of bacon and seemed to ignore Ruthie's question.

Ruthie sighed. She said a quick, silent prayer and then looked at Dinah again. "I appreciate your offering to clean the bathing room today, but I'll take turns with you." She waited for Dinah to smile, to say thank you, to acknowledge her in any way. But she just went on munching her bacon, her gaze aimed somewhere on the other side of the room. Ruthie resisted releasing another sigh. She stabbed the tines of her fork into the fluffy mound of eggs and muttered, "You are the most confusing girl..."

Finally Dinah shifted to look at Ruthie. Her brow pinched into a series of furrows that made her look old and tired. "Why?"

Ruthie paused with her fork midway between her plate and her mouth. Should she tell Dinah what she was thinking? It might hurt her feelings. Yet it might do the girl some good to know how others perceived her. Maybe it would help her change her ways.

Ruthie put down her fork and gave Dinah her full attention. "You confuse me because you stay away from everyone else." She spoke quietly so those at the other table wouldn't overhear. "You confuse me because you're a hard worker, even willing to do more work than what's expected, which surprises me since your family was wealthy enough to have its own cook in the house."

Slowly Dinah turned her face away, but she stayed in her chair and seemed to listen, so Ruthie continued.

"You confuse me because you never smile. Well, almost never. You smiled yesterday when I told you Mr. Phillips and Mr. Ackerman ignored me. That seemed to make you happy, which also confused me." Ruthie frowned, wishing Dinah would look at her instead of staring off into nothing. How difficult she found it to converse with this girl. "I don't like thinking this about you, Dinah, because I really would like to be friends, but…you act as though you're better than everyone else. As if talking to us or being with us is beneath you."

Ruthie searched Dinah's profile, waiting for a reaction. Nothing. Irritation stiffened Ruthie's spine and sharpened her tone. "Well? What do you have to say for yourself?"

Dinah finally looked at Ruthie. Her emotionless expression sent a chill through Ruthie's frame. "I have to say…" She spoke in a low, even tone completely devoid of feeling, although a shimmer of unshed tears brightened her eyes. "I'm here to work and to prove to Mr. Irwin that I am dependable so I can become one of Mr. Harvey's servers after I turn eighteen. So you can think whatever you like. It really doesn't matter to me." She picked up her plate and strode to the serving window, staying close to the wall rather than walking through the center of the room and passing the table of servers and busboys.

She handed her dirty plate to the kitchen worker and then headed for the hall-way without a backward glance.

Conversation at the full table in the middle of the room ceased as Dinah made her way across the room and then resumed in a flurry of comments when she'd departed. Amelia turned backward in her chair and pinned Ruthie with a curious look. "What were you two talking about? She looked positively peeved."

Minnie hunched her shoulders and giggled shrilly. "Yes, what did you say to make her storm off that way?"

Ruthie hadn't thought Dinah stormed away. And she hadn't seemed peeved as much as resigned. But to say so would only create a rift between her and the servers. She'd taken the position as chambermaid because Papa hadn't wanted her to become a dining room worker—he didn't like the idea of her serving men. The others already teased her about her overprotective papa. She didn't want to be teased for defending Dinah.

So she forced a cavalier shrug and curled her lips into a weak grin. "Oh, nothing much. It doesn't matter, really."

"Well, now that she's gone, come join us," Lyla said.

If Ruthie went over, she'd probably be coerced into talking about Dinah. She hesitated.

Dean added, "Breakfast's the only time Poke and me get to talk to you gals. C'mon, Ruthie. Start your day with some fun. Once we leave here, it's all work and no play, and we all know that makes Jack a dull boy."

Minnie nudged Dean's shoulder. "Or makes Ruthie a dull girl."

"Like Dinah," Dean said.

They all snickered.

Ruthie did not want them to think of her the way she thought of Dinah—as being snobbish and too good for everyone else. And Dean was right. Once breakfast was over, the chance for fun was gone. She needed a little fun to make up for the dreary start to her day. She snatched up her plate and hurried over to the table.

For the remainder of the week, Ruthie sat with the servers and the busboys at breakfast while Dinah sat by herself. At the end of each day, when the girls gathered for a bit of chitchat in one of their rooms before curfew, Ruthie joined them but never offered her room for the place to gather because Dinah would have to be included. As uncomfortable as it was to share a room and not talk, Ruthie managed to hold her tongue and leave Dinah in peace. If that's what her roommate wanted, and it didn't bother her to be thought of as a snobby recluse, then Ruthie would honor it. By the end of the week, she'd become accustomed to sharing a room and work duties while pretending she was all alone.

On Sunday morning, she dashed out the front doors at a little before nine to climb in the buggy and ride to worship service. Today Poke held the reins, and Lyla and Minnie sat beside him. Matilda was on the closest side of the rear seat and two others, their identities hidden by the shade cast by the leather canopy, filled the other side of the bench. Everyone else was ready to go.

Ruthie grimaced as she trotted to the edge of the buggy. "I'm sorry I kept you waiting. Scoot over a bit, Matilda, and let me come in."

Matilda let out a disgruntled huff, but she shifted to the front edge of the seat and opened a tiny slice for Ruthie to occupy. As Ruthie fell into the seat, she glanced sideways and jolted. On the far side of the seat, Dinah Hubley sat staring straight ahead with her chin held high.

Chapter 14

Dinah

inah watched the buggy roll away from the churchyard and her stomach lurched. Unless she wanted to walk back to the hotel—an unpleasant thought given the already high temperature and dusty streets—she had to stay for the service. And wasn't that why she'd come? To attend the service?

She fell behind the others as they moved as a group toward the church steps. Her uniform marked her as one of them, but she wasn't. Not really. She'd felt so alone all week, but in her solitude Ruthie's comment from her first day in Florence had continually played in the back of her heart. *"God loves you very much,"* Ruthie had said. From the very center of her being, Dinah longed for someone to love her very much. People never had. Not even Rueben, who'd at least been kind to her. But God wasn't people. Maybe...just maybe...God could love her if she took the time to get to know Him. And since church was the place Ruthie had declared the best for meeting God, Dinah had come.

Ruthie darted straight to the front to her family, just as she had last week, but this time she didn't ask Dinah to join her. The servers all filed into a bench on the right in the middle of the worship room. They didn't cast so much as a glance in Dinah's direction, so even though there was room for her, she didn't join them. Instead, she chose a spot on the very back bench on the left side. As far from the others as she could be without sitting outside the doors. She gripped her hands together in her lap and listened to the parishioners quietly chat with one another as they waited for the service to begin.

Dinah's chest felt tight and aching. She might as well be invisible, sitting there all alone. She'd told Ruthie she didn't care what the others thought, but she did care. She cared too much. When Ruthie had accused her of thinking herself too good for everyone, she'd wanted to both laugh and cry. Too good for everyone? Such a ridiculous thought. But it was better to have them think a lie than to know the truth. So she'd allowed the misconception even though it meant being shunned.

Shunned... All she could ever remember was being cast aside. Belittled. Mistreated. Memories of hurtful comments and open snubs from those she'd encountered from childhood on rose from Dinah's mind to haunt her. She cringed, imagining the people now filling the benches—good people, honest people, pure people—discovering just how unworthy she truly was. She had no business sitting among them. No God, not even one humble enough to occupy this simple dwelling, would want anything to do with her. She was only fooling herself, trying to grab on to something that didn't exist.

She shouldn't stay. Not until she'd had a chance to redeem herself. Next year—after she won Mr. Harvey's favor by working hard and earned the position as server—she would come back. Then God might have reason to love her.

Voices faded to silence as the preacher strode through the door and headed up the aisle to the front. In a few seconds, if they did what they'd done last week, everyone would stand to sing. And she'd be able to sneak out, unnoticed. Her heart pounding with the desire to escape, she waited until Mr. Mead called out the title of the opening hymn and invited everyone to rise. She bolted upright and, with her head bowed low, turned to hurry out of the building as the people began belting out, "Shall we gather at the river..."

But she'd only taken one step when someone moved into her pathway. A tall, broad someone in a dark suit and dusty boots who filled the small space between the benches, leaving not even an inch of passageway. She lifted her head, intending to ask the person to excuse her, but when her gaze lit on his face, her tongue seemed to stick to the roof of her mouth.

Mr. Ackerman smiled—a bashful, gentle, almost imperceptible upturning of his lips—and whispered, "May I join you?"

Dinah blinked, gathering her senses. He'd asked to sit beside her. Instead of passing her by or telling her she wasn't welcome on his bench, he'd asked to join her. The tightness in her chest eased as warmth flooded her. She couldn't speak, but she gave a quick nod and turned to face the front, although she couldn't resist peeking sideways at the big man standing beside her.

Mr. Ackerman held his head high and added his voice to the singing. Dinah didn't know the words, so she stood and listened, finding great pleasure in the deep, rich baritone flowing from Mr. Ackerman's throat. "'Yes, we'll gather at the river, the beautiful, the beautiful river; gather with the saints at the river that flows by the throne of God.'" Dinah didn't know where this river would be found, but the expression on Mr. Ackerman's face as he sang— relaxed, happy, even eager—made her pine for the opportunity to go there.

The song ended, and Mr. Mead gestured for everyone to sit. He lifted his Bible and called out, "Turn to Matthew, the first chapter."

All across the room, pages rustled as people opened their Bibles. Mr. Ackerman laid his worn Bible on his knee and opened it gently, as if fearful his large fingers would damage the fragile pages. When he found the page he wanted, he slipped his hand beneath the Book and held it so Dinah could see, too. Her face went hot, but she tipped sideways a bit to peek at the open pages.

She followed along as Mr. Mead read a long list of strange names who begat other strange names. Some of the names, such as Josaphat and Zorobabel, sounded so funny they made Dinah want to giggle. But no one else seemed amused, so she bit the inside of her cheeks and held her humor inside.

When he'd reached the end of the names, Mr. Mead read, "'So all the generations from Abraham to David are fourteen generations; and from David until the carrying away into Babylon are fourteen generations; and from the carrying away into Babylon unto Christ are fourteen generations.'"

He set the Bible aside and smiled at the congregation. "Not very intriguing reading, is it? I saw a couple of you yawn." Self-conscious chuckles rumbled, and Mr. Mead's smile broadened. "And why do all those names matter? It matters because God wants us to know Jesus's lineage. God wants us to know Jesus's forebears. He wants us to know from where Jesus came."

From where Jesus came… Dinah's ears began to ring with such intensity the preacher's next words were lost to her. Lineage mattered to God. And what was her lineage? Her mother was a prostitute and her father someone who'd paid to lie with her mother. Shame, hot and consuming, swept through her. If lineage mattered to God, she was already lost.

She could change her position as chambermaid to server, but nothing would ever change her parentage. Her body trembled. She didn't belong here. Not now. And not ever—not if lineage held enough importance to be printed out in great detail in the Bible, which Ruthie had said was God's Book.

On shaking legs she scrambled to her feet and stumbled past Mr. Ackerman, who looked at her with surprise. He stretched his hand to her as if to hold her back, but she skittered around it and darted out the open doors.

Amos

Amos watched Miss Hubley's dark skirt disappear and then listened to her feet pounding down the front steps. A few frowning faces turned to see who caused the ruckus, but Preacher Mead continued as if there hadn't been any disturbance. So the people faced the front again. Amos kept his gaze aimed forward, but he could no longer focus on the sermon.

Why had Miss Hubley run out? She'd looked frightened. Panicky. The same way she'd looked the day he found her sleeping on the porch. The same way she'd looked when he approached her beneath the clothesline in the hotel's backyard. His heart turned over. Somehow he must have alarmed her again. Had he been too forward, asking to sit beside her and then sharing his Bible with her?

He'd meant nothing by it. He arrived nearly late again, and by sitting in the back, he didn't disturb those who were already settled. He usually sat back here alone. Finding her on the bench had surprised him, but when she said he could sit there, too, he'd been pleased. He liked having some company. But maybe she'd chosen the seat so she could be alone. Of course she wouldn't be impolite enough to refuse his request to sit beside her. He'd intruded. Then when he held his Bible for her to share, he embarrassed her since she apparently didn't have one. So she felt the need to leave.

Remorse soured his stomach. *Lord, I didn't mean to chase her from the church, a place where all should feel welcome.* He needed to apologize. But how? Every time he neared her, she ran away like a scared rabbit. His chest constricted. He supposed by now he should be used to people shying away from him. So often his limping gait made folks uncomfortable. Even his own father kept his distance, as if Amos's bad leg were reason for embarrassment. If he went after her, he'd probably only make things worse. And he had enough troubles right now, what with eggs disappearing daily from the chickens' roosts and some small animal making a feast of two of his birds last week. But somehow he needed to convey his regret for troubling her.

He turned his attention to the front, determined to set aside his worries and listen to the minister's words—how believers, who'd been adopted as brothers and sisters of Christ, could claim the same lineage as Jesus Himself. An uplifting, encouraging message if ever there was one. But his gaze lit on the reddish hair of the preacher's daughter, and his thoughts turned to Miss Hubley again. He could ask Miss Mead to deliver an apology. Then his conscience would be clear.

The service closed with an enthusiastic delivery of "O for a Thousand Tongues to Sing." Amos remained in his spot until Miss Mead made her way down the aisle. Before she could step outside, he called her name and she turned. Her face lit up when she spotted him, and unexpectedly heat filled his face. Maybe he shouldn't beckon to her right there in the church where people might misunderstand. But she was already weaving between others to reach him, so he would give his message and then depart.

"Good morning, Mr. Ackerman. I only have a moment—the buggy will be here soon to transport me back to the hotel." Miss Mead's cheerful voice matched the look of bright expectation on her face.

Amos cleared his throat. "I only need a moment of your time. I wondered if you would tell Miss Hubley something for me."

It seemed Miss Mead's expression clouded, but she nodded.

"Please tell her I'm sorry if I embarrassed her this morning."

Now he couldn't deny the scowl climbing her face. "What did you do?"

His cheeks burned hotter than the late July sun. He swallowed. "She will know. Just, please, tell her I meant no harm and I hope she will come back to church next Sunday." He paused. He wasn't a very good judge of women's feelings, but he sensed Miss Mead was not happy. He added hesitantly, "Do you mind giving her the message?"

A smile formed, but it seemed pasted on rather than genuine. Miss Mead gave a brusque nod. "Of course, Mr. Ackerman, I will give your message to Miss Hubley." She glanced toward the open doorway. "Oh, there's my ride. I need to go." She looked at him again, and something akin to pleading showed in her eyes. "Was there anything else?"

He shook his head, glad to be done. "No. Enjoy the rest of your day, Miss Mead."

"Yes. Thank you. You, too, Mr. Ackerman." She turned and left, but she lacked the usual bounce he'd always seen in her step.

Amos frowned. What had caused Miss Mead's change in demeanor? He hoped it wasn't anything he'd done. Insulting one woman on this Sunday was already one too many. Then he recalled his brothers complaining about women being moody. Since they'd both courted several women before choosing a wife, they had more experience with females than he did. He would trust their judgment. Likely Miss Mead, although generally sunny, was having a moody day. As long as she would deliver his message—and he couldn't imagine a minister's daughter being dishonest with him—she could be moody all she wanted. He was more concerned about Miss Hubley's feelings.

Dinah

Dinah scuttled from the hotel room, her arms overflowing with linens from the bed. Ruthie stepped directly in her pathway, forcing Dinah to halt. The look of displeasure on the other girl's face sent a shiver of apprehension across her frame. After nearly a week of not speaking to Ruthie, Dinah felt strange addressing her roommate, but a nervous question found its way from her throat. "Wh-what's wrong?"

"Why did you leave service early?"

Dinah crunched her lips tight. The pain of realizing she had no place in God's house returned, stinging her anew.

Ruthie waited a few seconds, then drew in a breath that expanded the bibbed front of her apron. She appeared to be gathering courage. "I have a message for you."

From Mr. Phillips, who'd been a chef in Chicago? From Miss Flo? Someone else from the Yellow Parrot who'd discovered where she'd gone? Dinah held her breath, her pulse pounding so hard she wondered if Ruthie could hear it.

"Amos Ackerman—from church—asked me to tell you he's sorry for embarrassing you." For a few seconds Ruthie's lips twitched as if a bumblebee were trapped inside her mouth. Then she blurted, "What did he do to make you leave?"

Dinah hugged the linens to her chest. All he'd done was sit beside her. Share his Bible with her. Acknowledge her presence. He'd been kind. Dinah said, "Nothing."

Ruthie tipped her head and raised one reddish eyebrow. "He must have done something or he wouldn't have asked me to tell you he's sorry. Men don't apologize for no reason."

To her experience, men didn't even apologize when they *had* reason. Dinah stepped past Ruthie. "He didn't do anything. He doesn't owe me an apology." She hurried off before Ruthie could ask anything else.

Dinah dumped her armful of linens into the laundry chute, then stood staring down the dark tunnel. Although she needed to return to work, she allowed herself a few moments to remember the gentle smile Mr. Ackerman offered as he'd asked to sit beside her and the way his deep voice had filled her chest to overflowing when he sang.

He thought he'd embarrassed her somehow, and he felt bad enough to send Ruthie with a message of apology. The warmth that had enveloped her when he'd slipped onto the bench next to her flowed over her again, and she closed her eyes, savoring the essence of acceptance it offered. But then she gave herself a shake. Hadn't she determined she had no place in a church with decent folks? Her lineage didn't belong, and neither did she.

She slammed the door on the chute and marched up the hallway in search of Ruthie. She'd tell her to send a message back to Mr. Ackerman. He didn't owe her an apology, but she owed him one for running off the way she had. Once she'd asked Ruthie to tell him so, she would erase all memory of Mr. Ackerman and his kindness from her mind.

Chapter 15

Amos

mos scraped the rake across the dirty straw, chuckling as the fluffy yellow chicks cheeped and scampered away from the wooden prongs. "Here now," he said gently, "I am not after you. Only the mess you made."

For such little things, they sure managed to muck up his barn. But he would forgive them. They were so small, so innocent, and they stirred his sympathy in their helplessness. Just as the brown-haired chambermaid with eyes of palest blue who worked at the Clifton Hotel stirred his sympathy.

He released a little self-deprecating snort. Now even the chicks were reminding him of Dinah Hubley? He paused and leaned against the rake handle, absently watching the chicks find the courage to return and peck at his boot strings. Why couldn't he erase her from his mind? Each day for the past three days, she had crept into his thoughts at odd times, stealing his focus and making his chest go tight in an unfamiliar way. He'd taken to thinking of her as Dinah rather than Miss Hubley. Dinah... The name suited her. Ma would say it was an unpretentious name—pretty yet humble.

There in the barn with only chicks for witnesses, he dared to speak her name, softly, sampling its sound. "Dinah." Then again, stronger. "Dinah." He smiled. Yes, he liked the way it rolled from his tongue. He laughed a little, glancing around to make sure no one overheard his silliness. Which was also silly since no one else was there. He laughed more and the chicks scattered, leaving him standing alone.

Then he sobered. *Alone...* Just the way Dinah had been on the porch the first time he'd seen her. And on the bench at church this past Sunday. The way he was every day here at his farm. Words from Genesis, spoken by God

Himself, whispered to his memory: *"It is not good that the man should be alone; I will make him an help meet for him."*

He tipped his head, frowning, wondering. In the past when a thought refused to leave his head, he'd eventually accepted the idea was not his own but was planted by God. His chicken farm proved that God-planted ideas bore fruit. So could it be this girl—this girl who was so alone—was meant to alleviate his aloneness?

Of course, after today he wouldn't be alone anymore. The speckled pups he'd located at a farm south of town were finally big enough to leave their mother, and he would bring them home on Thursday when he finished delivering eggs to his customers in town. He'd chosen two pups, both boys, and he intended to name them Shadrach and Meshach. Or Samson and Gideon. Either way, he hoped they'd live up to their names, becoming strong protectors for the chickens. He'd lost a hen only last night to a fox.

The chicks' peeping pulled him to the present. He set the rake to work once more. But another thought sneaked into his mind, bringing his busy hands to a halt. The puppies would give him company, yes, but he could hardly consider a pair of dogs, no matter how helpful, *helpmeets*.

He whispered the name that would not depart from his thoughts. "Dinah…" Did God mean for her to be his?

Ruthie

Ruthie whisked the feather duster over the little scrolled shelves on either side of the dresser's mirror and wished for the dozenth time since Sunday morning that she could sit down with her mother for a long talk. With the half circle–shaped shelves free of even a speck of dust, she draped the delicately embroidered doilies on the shelves, then centered the sweet figurines of cherubs just so on the snowy doilies. Satisfied with their positioning, she moved on to dust the pair of tables standing sentry on either side of the bed.

What advice would Mama give concerning her infatuation with Mr.

Ackerman? Although Papa was the parent most likely to offer advice, even if it was unsolicited, Ruthie preferred to hear Mama's thoughts because she would surely be more understanding than Papa. As a schoolgirl, Ruthie had thought herself besotted on three different occasions, and each time Papa had firmly instructed her to put off such thoughts until she was old enough for marriage. Well, eighteen was certainly old enough. Mama had married Papa when she was three days past her eighteenth birthday, and Ruthie was now nearing her nineteenth year. So Papa shouldn't fuss. And Mama would tell her…what?

Ruthie tapped her chin with the duster's wooden handle, waiting for words of wisdom to fill her head. But none came. With a huff of frustration, she tucked the duster into her apron pocket and began fluffing the bed pillows, finding relief in giving the feather-filled rectangles solid thumps. Did every girl suffer such confusion and longing when a man had captured her heart? If Phoebe were still here, she could share her feelings with her good friend. But she didn't feel close enough to Dinah. Or to the servers, who'd formed pairs the way girls tended to do and left her feeling like an outsider, even though they didn't hold themselves aloof from her the way Dinah did.

She adjusted the pillows so they rested neatly at the headboard, resisting the urge to pound her fist on them instead. Papa would be sadly dismayed to know how jealous she'd become of her roommate. Jealousy was an ugly emotion—Papa had preached fiery sermons on the tenth commandment. She'd managed to set aside resentment concerning Dinah's wealthy background. She'd even overcome coveting Dinah's lovely, flowing hair and eyes of delicate blue that gave her a china doll appearance. But despite her best efforts, she could not quell the envy that filled her when she remembered Mr. Ackerman asking her to deliver a message to Dinah.

To Dinah! Who'd not even been polite enough to give him a simple greeting! Who'd run out of the church last week over some unknown but undoubtedly petty slight. As if Mr. Ackerman would ever be loutish enough to slight anyone.

Ruthie released an unladylike snort and turned from the bed to survey the room, seeking anything else in need of attention. And her gaze fell on the lovely painting hanging above the two graceful chairs forming a sitting area in the corner of the room. Although other rooms required cleaning, she crossed the thickly carpeted floor and stopped before the painting, allowing herself several minutes to absorb the peaceful scene.

Painted in dreamy pastels, the image of a man and woman strolling through a flower-laden garden appealed to her femininity. The garden with its fountains, wrought-iron gate, and many flower beds of rainbow colors was similar to the gardens in front of the hotel. She closed her eyes, imagining placing her hand in the crook of Mr. Ackerman's arm and strolling slowly along the flat rock pathway while the sun beamed down and brought out the deepest colors in every petal.

Lost in her daydream, she began to sway, pretending to match her stride to his. And reality slammed down upon her. Her eyes jolted open. Mr. Ackerman couldn't stroll with her. Not with his limp. His uneven gait would tug her arm with every step. The romance of the inner reflection faded, and sadness momentarily sagged her shoulders. She wished Mr. Ackerman's limp didn't bother her, but it did. Otherwise, he was perfect—tall and handsome, strong yet gentle, a man who wasn't afraid to bow his head in church. All of the qualities she wanted for a husband, Mr. Ackerman possessed. Except...

Ruthie gathered her cleaning supplies and hurried to the next room before Mr. Irwin peeked in and caught her woolgathering. But as she cleaned, thoughts of Mr. Ackerman continued to tiptoe through her mind. What if he'd been born with a bad leg? Some babies came into the world with damaged limbs or other problems. And what if *his* babies were born with bad legs, the way Ruthie had been born with Mama's red hair and Papa's long fingers? It could happen, couldn't it?

Worry followed her as she completed the tasks and moved on to another room. She needed to talk to Mama, to pray with Mama, to search her soul for her true feelings toward Mr. Ackerman. In the meantime, she discovered one consolation that appeased her aching heart. He might be trying to pursue Dinah, but Dinah would never be caught. After all, a girl who'd come from an affluent background would expect more than a lame chicken farmer for a husband. She wouldn't be surprised if Dinah had taken this position to snag herself a wealthy businessman, the way Minnie intended. So even if Mr. Ackerman thought he wanted Dinah, he'd soon be as put off by her as everyone else had been. And that would leave him for Ruthie.

Dinah

Dinah swept away the grit and bits of cut grass the wind had blown onto the long porch fronting the hotel. Although the heat of midday left her sticky with sweat, she didn't mind being given the task. She liked the smell of the flowers, which bloomed in profusion in the well-tended gardens. The fountains sang a sweet melody, and even the distant whistle of the train pleased her ears. She looked forward to the locomotive's approach when the ground beneath her feet trembled, sending vibrations from her soles to her scalp. She felt alive outside.

And out here, away from everyone's eyes, she could relax.

She gave the thick straw bristles a solid push and sent the dust sailing. The *whish* against the porch floor created a satisfying sound, and the clean swath left behind on the painted boards made her smile. How gratifying to see the immediate difference a thrust of the broom made. She moved to the next section and worked the bristles against the lapped siding to free the dust trapped along the edge of the porch.

An odd, offbeat *creak-creak* intruded upon the sound of her sweeping. She'd heard it once before, but she couldn't place it. Lifting her head, she searched for the source of the noise, and she spotted Mr. Ackerman pulling his little wagon along the street. The wooden wheels sent out the creaking. She froze, torn between wanting him to notice her and wanting him to go on without seeing her. Why did this man create such turmoil within her?

She held her breath and watched him pass, his tall form bent slightly at the waist to adjust his height to the handle on the wagon. Then something in the wagon's bed shifted. A little black nose, two bright eyes, and a pair of floppy ears—one black, one white with black spots—appeared over the edge. Dinah let out a little gasp of delight.

The wagon stopped, and Mr. Ackerman turned his head in her direction. She knew the moment he saw her because a smile broke across his face. He lifted his hand in greeting.

She uncurled her fingers from the broom handle and waved back. She returned her gaze to the puppy, which now placed its paws on the edge of the wagon and let its tongue flop from its little mouth. It seemed to be smiling. A giggle grew in her throat and spilled out before she could stop it.

Mr. Ackerman's grin broadened. He pulled the wagon up the walkway between the fountains and stopped at the base of the stairs. "Would you like to pet the puppies?"

Dinah had always liked puppies. And kittens and rabbits and even ducklings. But she'd never been allowed to have a pet. Animals were dirty, Miss Flo said, which Dinah had thought an odd statement, considering the appearance of some of the men she allowed into her parlor. She inched her way to the edge of the porch and peered over the spindled railing into the wagon bed. To her delight, two roly-poly dogs splotched with black on white wriggled on a bed of hay. She couldn't hold back another light laugh.

"Come on down and give them some attention if you like," Mr. Ackerman invited. "I just took them away from their mama, and they'd probably welcome a cuddle or two."

Dinah flicked a glance toward the windows. Would Mr. Irwin look out and scold her for taking time away from work? But it was lunchtime. She was allowed a break at noon. Without another thought, she scurried down the steps and reached into the wagon. Both puppies swiped at her with velvety tongues and batted her with thick little paws. Their entire backsides bounced with the exuberant wagging of their stubby tails.

A genuine smile formed on Dinah's lips and refused to dim. "They're so cute! What are their names?"

Mr. Ackerman chuckled. She caught him scratching his head as he grinned down at the dogs. "Well, I was just thinking on that. I can't decide whether I want to name them Shadrach and Meshach—"

Dinah wrinkled her nose. Those names sounded like the strange ones the preacher had read last Sunday.

"—or Samson and Gideon."

"Samson and Gideon," Dinah said emphatically. Then she cringed. Had she really told him what to call his puppies? She shouldn't be so bold. "That is, if you want something easy for them to learn. I'm sure Shad...Shadrach and Meshach..." Goodness, she could hardly say them. How would a puppy remember them? "...are fine names, but Samson and Gideon could be shortened to Sam and Gid."

Mr. Ackerman squinted one eye and examined the puppies. "But I could shorten Shadrach and Meshach to Shad and Shach. And the pups are black and white with gray smudges, as if they've been scorched. The biblical Shadrach and Meshach spent time in the fiery furnace, as you know. Of course, they escaped unharmed, but even so..."

She didn't know who those people were who'd gone into a furnace, but the thought made her shudder. She curled her hands beneath the puppies' chins and lifted their little faces. The smaller of the pair had one blue eye and one brown one. She was instantly smitten. "They look like Sam and Gid to me."

"All right, then. Samson and Gideon."

Dinah looked at Mr. Ackerman in surprise. He'd agreed with her?

The puppies bounced their wet noises against her palms, and he chuckled. "They seem pleased with the names, too. You made a good choice."

Joy filled her so thoroughly she wanted to laugh. He'd given her a gift, and she wished she knew how to tell him how much he'd pleased her. But all she could do was gaze at him in wide-eyed wonder.

His smile turned tender, as if he read her secret thoughts, and then he took one shuffling step toward her. "Miss Hubley, did...did your roommate deliver a message to you from me?"

Heat filled her face as she recalled racing out of the church last Sunday. She hadn't deserved his apology, and now she had the chance to tell him so. If she could find the courage. With her fingers in the puppies' soft fur, she ducked her head and mumbled, "Yes. But it wasn't necessary. You didn't do anything wrong."

He bent his knees slightly and angled his head to catch her gaze. "Then why did you run out the way you did? Are you sure it wasn't because I frightened you?"

Yes, he'd frightened her. He was frightening her now. She didn't know how to respond to his kindness. She feared his kindness would suddenly change, the way the man in the hotel room had gone from smiling and complimentary to hard and demanding in the space of a heartbeat. She couldn't share all of that with him, but she could assure him he'd been innocent in sending her away from the church.

"You didn't frighten me. I just knew I shouldn't stay. I don't belong in church with—" She sucked in a sharp breath, swallowing the words that had almost escaped, and finished weakly, "I don't belong in church."

His eyebrows descended. Not a scowl of anger, but one of such compassion it caused tears to prick Dinah's eyes. "Why, Miss Hubley, everyone is welcome in church."

Oh, if only it were true. She took a step away from the wagon, away from the man whose tender voice and concerned face raised waves of both panic and longing. "Not me. I...I have to get back to work now."

She raced for the porch, and moments later the *creak-creak* of wagon wheels let her know he'd departed. But her remembrance of their brief time together refused to depart. She carried the image of his stricken face in her memory the remainder of the day.

Chapter 16

Amos

Just as he had last Sunday, Amos waited beside his bench for Miss Mead to move toward the church doors. Dinah hadn't come. He hadn't expected her to after their brief exchange on Thursday, but he still hoped. As he'd shooed the chickens into the chicken house where they'd be safe from predators and then tied Sam and Gid to fence posts with sturdy ropes, he prayed for her to come. The entire dusty walk to town, he repeated the prayer. *Let her be there. Lord, let her come to church.*

But his prayer had gone unheeded, and his need to see her—to explore why she didn't feel welcome in church—kept him waiting for Miss Mead to stop talking and come down the aisle so he could ask her about Dinah.

He fidgeted in place, wishing she'd hurry. She and her mother had their heads together while the youngest member of the family—a cute little girl with curly red hair caught up in a big white ribbon—pulled at her mother's skirt. The boys had darted outside already, and Amos heard their happy shouts from the yard. His heart swelled. He'd like to have a big, boisterous family like the preacher's. Someday. But for now, he just wanted Dinah to feel welcome in the house of the Lord.

A frown pinched his brow even while he nodded greetings to other parishioners and toyed with his hat. As a boy, he'd been taunted in the schoolyard, called Amos Staggerman, instead of Ackerman, because of his clumsiness. When choosing teams for stickball or kick the can, the other kids always picked Amos last and then never put him in to play. Instead, he stood to the side and watched the other children play. When he got older and attended town parties and dances, no girl ever accepted his invitation to dance, put off by his awkward gait.

But at church—ah, at church—he'd found his place of acceptance. There he was at peace, secure in the knowledge that God didn't care if his hips were crooked and he limped when he walked. God didn't care if he raised chickens instead of growing wheat, the way his father and grandfather had before him. God didn't care about what he couldn't do. God cared about *him*—loved him so unconditionally He'd allowed His Son to die for Amos's sins. And it pained him to think of Dinah feeling unwelcome in the one place where everyone should feel openly received.

When all the other worshipers had gone and Amos had nearly given up on being able to talk to Miss Mead, the girl finally hugged her mother and shot down the aisle. Midway, she spotted him and stopped so quickly her feet slid on the wood-planked floor.

"Oh! Mr. Ackerman." Her face flooded with pink, and she repeatedly clasped and unclasped her hands against the white bib of her apron. "You... you're still here."

He nodded and stepped into the aisle. "Yes. I hoped to talk to you."

She glanced out the open doorway and grimaced. "My ride is waiting. I'm on duty in a few minutes. But..." She bit down on her lip for a moment, bringing her fine red-gold brows together. "If I tell the others I'll be there soon, then...perhaps...we could walk to the hotel?" Her gaze dropped briefly to his bad leg, and the color in her face deepened. She looked into his eyes again, her expression apologetic. "That is, if...if you're able."

Amos swallowed a self-conscious chuckle. "Since I don't own a horse, I walk everywhere, Miss Mead. So that suits me fine. As long as you don't mind being seen walking with me." He paused, giving her an opportunity to change her mind. He wouldn't hold a grudge if she did.

A smile curved her lips. "Let me tell the others to go on without me." She dashed out the door, her skirts held above her ankles.

Amos followed in his usual gait, and by the time he reached the bottom of the steps, the hotel's buggy was rolling away. Miss Mead, her face shiny with perspiration and her cheeks glowing pink, hurried to his side.

"It's all arranged. They'll let Mr. Irwin know I'm on my way and will carve this time from my lunch break. So…" She gazed up at him, expectancy glowing in her green eyes. "What did you need?"

Amos held his hand toward the street, and with a little giggle Miss Mead moved in that direction. Amos hitched along beside her, keeping his arm tucked tight to his side to avoid bumping her. "Actually, Miss Mead, I'm worried about something and hoped you might be able to help."

"I'll try." She spoke brightly and seemed to almost bounce as she walked, like a horse being held back by a firm hand on the reins.

"It's about Miss Hubley."

"*Her* again?"

Amos stopped and stared at her. He raised one brow.

She came to a stop, as well, and clapped a hand over her mouth, her eyes rounding in shock. She lowered her hand, once again clasping her fingers and pressing them to her bodice. "Please forgive me, Mr. Ackerman. That was uncharitable of me. It's just that… You see, I was just talking to my mother about my feelings toward…" She waved both hands as if shooing away flies. "Never mind me. Dinah didn't leave service last week because of you. Is that what's troubling you? If so, you can put your mind at ease."

Amos set his feet in motion again, relieved when Miss Mead followed along, although with a more trudging pace. "She already told me so, but—"

"When did you talk to her?"

If he wasn't mistaken, she sounded miffed. He answered cautiously. "I happened upon her this past Thursday when she was sweeping the porch."

The girl set her lips in a firm line.

Puzzled but determined, Amos continued. "But no matter what she says, something must have happened. She told me she feels unwelcome in church. I thought, since you two work together, you might know why. And I thought, since your father is the preacher, you could help her understand she is welcome there."

Miss Mead chewed on her lower lip as they stepped up onto the boardwalk and moved slowly past the town's businesses. Had she slowed her pace to accommodate him, or had her thoughts become so heavy her feet found it difficult to carry her forward?

She finally looked up at him, and the shade falling full on her unsmiling face gave her a grim appearance. "I don't know why she feels unwelcome in church. I've invited her to attend. I even asked her to sit with my family." A hint of defensiveness colored her tone. "But she prefers to be alone."

Amos disagreed with Miss Mead's opinion, but he had no proof to offer as an argument. So he clenched his teeth and remained silent.

"Dinah is nothing like the other girls who work at the hotel. I've never associated with anyone from a big city before." Miss Mead's pace sped as words poured out in a crisp torrent. "Perhaps her behavior is due to being raised in a larger place. I imagine our little town of Florence is quite a change from Chicago. Big-city people are different, Papa says—less likely to know their neighbors. So she might remain aloof because she's always been aloof from those who lived around her. Or perhaps it's the result of being raised in affluence."

"Affluence?" Amos couldn't hold back the startled exclamation. "Miss Hubley is rich?"

Miss Mead nodded rapidly, the ruffle of her little white cap bouncing against her smoothed-back hair. "Oh, yes. Dinah comes from a wealthy family. She even had a cook in her house! Her own cook—can you fancy that?"

Amos shook his head, astounded. "If she's from a wealthy family, why is she working as a chambermaid in the Clifton?"

Miss Mead turned the corner leading to the railroad station, her hands held outward in a gesture of helplessness. "I don't know. But I wonder..."

Amos resorted to a double hop on his good leg as he struggled to keep up with Miss Mead. She seemed to be trying to escape. "You wonder what?"

She flicked a hesitant glance at him and then ducked her head. "I don't know if I should say."

Amos caught her arm and drew her to a stop. His hip ached and his breath huffed out. Sweat trickled down his temples. He removed his hat and swiped the moisture away before giving Miss Mead a firm look. "Please tell me."

Miss Mead released a little sigh. "Very well. I wonder if she came here knowing how many businessmen pass through Florence on the Santa Fe. One of the servers, Minnie, openly proclaimed she hopes to snag a rich husband. I wonder if Dinah has the same intention. After all, she told me she wants to become a server when she turns eighteen. The servers have a better chance of meeting a man than she and I do as chambermaids."

Amos considered everything Miss Mead had said. Some of her statements surprised him. Dinah came from Chicago? Her family had money? He wouldn't have guessed such things about her, given her timid behavior and simple attire. If these things were true, she would certainly want more than anything he could offer. His chest constricted. But he shouldn't think of himself. He still didn't understand Dinah's reason for saying she wasn't welcome in church.

Miss Mead looked toward the hotel, which towered high and proud across the street from the train station. "I need to return to duty, Mr. Ackerman." Regret colored her tone, and her lips turned down in a pout. "I'm sorry if I wasn't as helpful as you'd hoped."

She hadn't been helpful. Not at all. But he'd never be so unkind as to tell her so. He forced a smile. "Please don't concern yourself, Miss Mead. It's apparent you also care about Di—Miss Hubley."

Miss Mead lowered her head and fiddled with the pocket on her apron.

"If you'd be kind enough to tell her that I missed her in service this morning and continue to encourage her to attend, I would be grateful."

"Of course, Mr. Ackerman. I'll…gladly deliver your message." She turned to leave, then spun to face him again. "Oh! Mr. Ackerman?"

Amos paused, waiting.

"It's dinnertime. And the dining room is open to townsfolk. Many of them partake of the scrumptious menus Mr. Gindough prepares." A hopeful smile lit her face. "You've got your own jacket today, so you won't have to borrow one from the cashier. Mr. Irwin strictly enforces Mr. Harvey's 'jackets in the dining room' rule. Why not come in and have a good meal before returning to your home? I would think a bachelor like yourself would appreciate eating someone else's cooking now and then."

Amos rubbed the underside of his chin. The chickens and his pups were safe—he could leave them for a little longer. Good smells wafted across the street from the hotel, making his mouth water. He was hungry, and he'd never treated himself at the hotel, even though he'd heard the townspeople talk about the good cook.

"Roast beef today with whipped potatoes and beef gravy, asparagus in garlic butter, fresh-baked rolls and raspberry preserves, and all the relishes you could want." Miss Mead cocked her head. Her grin turned impish. "And for dessert *Charlotte di Pesche*."

Amos reared back. "What is Charlotte dee peshuh?"

She laughed lightly, but he sensed no rancor. "A delectable concoction of spiced peaches and light cake with a custard-like sauce, all topped with sweet whipped cream."

Amos licked his lips.

Miss Mead giggled behind her fingers. "Have you decided to come in, then?"

He nodded and followed Miss Mead to the hotel. Inside, she bade him farewell and dashed off, hopefully to deliver his message to Dinah. He gave his seventy-five cents—nearly the equivalent of four days' work for a dozen hens—to the cashier, who laid the coins in the cash register drawer so gently they didn't even clink. Then a young man guided him through the crowded dining room to a table where he joined a family with three children of various ages and two couples, one middle-aged and one older. They must have come on the train because he didn't recognize any of them, but they smiled a mild hello as he slid into the one remaining seat. He nodded in reply, and they went back to their conversations as if he wasn't there.

One of the servers—he thought he'd heard Miss Mead call her Amelia— bustled over with a china cup in her hand. "Do you prefer coffee or tea today?"

"Um…" He drank coffee at home. "Tea, please."

She flipped the cup upside down on the table in front of him, then scurried off. Moments later a second server approached and turned the cup rightside up before filling it with steaming, pale-brown liquid. Amos sniffed it. Although not as stout as coffee, it held a pleasant scent. He took a sip. He set it down. He wouldn't waste it, but next time he'd get coffee instead.

The dining room buzzed with the voices of guests, the soft *clump* of plates meeting the cloth tabletops, and the patter of servers' feet. The girls dashed around the room delivering plates of steaming food with such speed, Amos wondered how they managed to avoid running into one another.

And Dinah wanted to be among their ranks…

While he ate his meal—the fanciest food he'd ever had—he watched the servers from the corner of his eye. Especially the short, yellow-haired one named Minnie. Although perspiration dotted her nose, giving evidence of discomfort, she smiled brightly at the men unaccompanied by wives. Miss Mead had said Minnie wanted to snag a husband, and her behavior seemed to prove it. She was friendlier than the other three servers put together, and the others were very pleasant to the guests.

Did Dinah behave this way with the men, too? Maybe she only shied away from him because, as Miss Mead had said, she was wealthy and didn't want to be friendly to someone who wasn't of her class. An unsettled feeling filled his stomach, and he pushed away the last of his peach dessert.

The other men at the table each slipped a nickel or dime under their plates when they finished, so Amos stacked up five pennies beside his—the only coins remaining in his pocket. Then he downed the remainder of his tea, which had grown tepid in the cup, and rose as the train whistle blasted.

Since he had no need to board the train, he stepped out of the way of those who did, allowing them to scurry out ahead of him. Then he waited for the other townspeople to leave, knowing his clumsy gait would slow them, too. When everyone else had made their way to the doorway, Amos followed onto the porch. He paused, his gaze unwittingly turning to the place where he'd seen Dinah three days ago with the broom in her hands.

In his mind's eye he saw her smile. Not aimed at him, but at Samson and Gideon. He tried to recall if she'd ever smiled at *him*. No. Not once. Most of the time she looked at him with a wariness that saddened him. The uncomfortable feeling in his stomach increased. He made his way off the porch slowly, then headed for home. As he walked beneath the blistering sun, he spoke to the One who always walked with him.

"Lord, have I set my sights on something that isn't meant to be? I don't know why Dinah—Miss Hubley—keeps coming to mind if I'm not supposed to think about her *that way*." He knew the Lord would understand. "Maybe my imagination got the best of me, but it sure seemed like she was lonely. Just like me. And maybe she is lonely. But if she's rich and looking for a husband, she sure isn't going to look at me."

He swallowed, his throat so dry the action pained him. He wished he'd asked for a second cup of tea. He squinted skyward at the clear blue expanse. "Maybe it's best. I don't have time to court a girl right now, what with trying to get my farm going good and taking care of puppies. And if she's not yet eighteen, she's awfully young. But I sure wish I could understand why..."

He stopped. His pulse stuttered, and it had nothing to do with tiredness. "She's on my heart, God. She has been since the day I found her sleeping on the porch. I've never met another girl who stayed in my thoughts the way she has. But if she isn't churched, I shouldn't be thinking about her. You warn Your children about being unequally yoked, and I won't go against Your Word."

He pushed himself into motion again. "I'll keep praying for her to come to church. And You keep reminding me to do it. But while You're reminding me of things, remind me not to think of Miss Hubley in ways I shouldn't." He aimed a grimace heavenward and sighed. "It won't be easy. I'm mighty glad with You everything's possible."

Chapter 17

Ruthie

uthie slipped under the covers first, leaving Dinah to extinguish the lamp. She lay quietly while her roommate made her way around the bed, her feet scuffing on the floor and her hand trailing along the edge of the mattress until she reached her side. When she climbed in, the mattress shifted and the springs squeaked, and Ruthie held tight to the sheet to keep it from slipping from her frame as Dinah settled herself against her pillow. A soft sigh carried from the opposite side of the bed, somehow sad sounding in the darkness.

She'd waited all day for the right time to deliver Mr. Ackerman's message, but even though her path had crossed with Dinah's many times, she held the words inside. Now, lying there in the dark with the scented night breeze drifting in from the open window to kiss her cheeks and Dinah silent and still, perhaps even asleep already, she was tempted to forget the message altogether.

Guilt pricked, and she stifled a huff of frustration. Papa had taught her well—her conscience wouldn't allow her to ignore what she'd promised to do, even though it seemed Mr. Ackerman was perfectly capable of seeking Dinah out himself. He'd done it once already. The familiar envy boiled in her middle. Another reason to feel guilty. She couldn't carry two wrongs and get any sleep tonight, and the envy didn't seem to want to leave her. *Oh, all right, then.*

She cleared her throat. "Dinah, I have another message for you. From Mr. Ackerman."

A sharp little gasp, as if she encountered something frightening—or had been given a delightful surprise—escaped Dinah's lips.

Ruthie hurried on before she changed her mind. "He said he missed you in service today. And he hopes you'll come next week." He hadn't come right out and said so, but Ruthie knew he wanted Dinah there. She gave a little jolt, awareness dawning. Shouldn't *she* want Dinah there, too? Papa—and Mama—would be disappointed to know how their daughter had given up on reaching out to Dinah. Granted, Dinah did little to encourage a friendship, but her parents would tell her that wasn't an excuse.

Even more guilt pressed down on Ruthie, and she blinked back tears. But encouraging Dinah to attend service would put her in contact with Mr. Ackerman. Ruthie's whole life, instructed to put others first, she'd let younger siblings and schoolmates crowd her out. She willingly worked to help her family, but if Papa hadn't been so adamantly opposed, she'd be a server rather than a chambermaid cleaning up behind rich people. People like Dinah. Couldn't Ruthie, just once, put herself first? She and Mama had agreed to pray concerning her attraction to the chicken farmer. Couldn't she wait to see how God answered before throwing Dinah at the man's feet?

"I...I want..." Ruthie gulped, a mighty battle waging in her heart. She conceded defeat. Even for herself, she couldn't betray her father's instruction. "I want you to come, too."

Dinah lay in silence so long Ruthie wondered if she'd drifted off to sleep. But then her quiet voice whispered, "No, thank you."

Ruthie collapsed against her pillow, not even aware she'd been holding herself stiffly. Her relief was so immense she let out a little laugh, then bit down on her lip to still the sound. Bits and pieces from a hymn Papa had recently sung sneaked through her thoughts. "'*Rescue the perishing... Tell them of Jesus, the mighty to save...*'" If Dinah died without Jesus, she'd be lost for all eternity. She couldn't simply accept Dinah's refusal. She *had* to *try*. For Papa's sake.

After turning onto her side, Ruthie examined Dinah's profile in the gray shadows. "Are...are you sure?" She held her breath.

Dinah swallowed and blinked rapidly several times. Then she lay unmoving for several seconds before giving an emphatic nod that made the springs beneath their heads twang. "I'm sure."

Ruthie's breath eased out in a long, slow exhale. "Well, you know you can change your mind. Yes? You know the church doors are open to anyone?"

Dinah's lips quirked in an odd wry grin. "Go to sleep, Ruthie." She rolled over with her back to Ruthie.

Ruthie sighed and turned over, too, facing the opposite wall. She closed her eyes, ready for sleep to claim her now that she'd performed her duties for both Mr. Ackerman and Papa. But the slight vibration of the mattress—Dinah crying?—kept her awake far into the night, even well past the time the shuddering movements stopped and all was still.

Amos

Monday morning, even before the rooster crowed, Samson and Gideon burst into a mighty ruckus. Amos sat straight up in bed, his heart pounding. The fox was back! He scrambled out of bed so quickly his bad hip nearly sent him face first on the floor. By hopping on his good leg, he caught his balance, and then he pounded across the floor. Dressed only in his long johns, he snatched his rifle from the pegs above the fireplace and barreled out the door on tender bare feet as quickly as his bum leg would allow.

In the predawn light, he saw both pups leaping at the ends of their ropes. Their shrill barks pierced his ears. He whistled but neither reacted a whit. And all their barking had the chickens in an uproar. An entire chorus of frantic clucks carried from inside the chicken house.

"Sam! Gid!" He tried once more to bring the pups under control, but even though they glanced at him, they still didn't settle down. Whatever they'd spotted, it had them in a mighty dither. He aimed his hop-twice-and-shuffle way of trotting in the direction of the dogs, careful to keep the nose of the rifle barrel aimed skyward. But he changed direction when he noticed his rooster—the brave, cocky bird—in the yard near the spot where the barn wall met the chicken coop.

Wings outstretched and head bobbing, the rooster had cornered some-

thing and prepared to charge. Amos's heart leaped into his throat. How had
the rooster escaped the barn? He always locked it up at night. The obnoxious
bird would be no match for a fox or a bobcat. He jerked the gate to the chicken
yard open and made straight for the rooster, waving his arms and adding a
shout to the cacophony. "Yee-ah! Get outta there! Git! Git!"

The rooster, crowing in indignation, darted between Amos's feet. He
lurched to a stop, expecting a small furry beast to follow, but to his shock
a shadowy figure—too tall to be a fox or bobcat or even a coyote—cowered
against the barn wall. He thought he heard a voice. A *human* voice. But with
the dogs continuing to whine and yip, he couldn't be sure.

Daring to take his squinted gaze away from the intruder, he whirled on the
pups and commanded, "Sam! Gid! Hush!" With a series of whimpers and
weak growls, the pair finally hunkered against the ground, their eyes round
and luminous in the waning moonlight. With the dogs' calming, the ruckus
inside the coop also decreased in volume. "Good dogs. Stay." Then he turned
and faced the barn. "You there. Come on out."

"Please, mister, don't let your rooster eat me. An' don't shoot me, neither."

Now Amos knew the voice belonged to a human. A scared child, based on
the high pitch and quaver. Even so, the kid was a trespasser. Amos kept a stern
tone. "I won't shoot you as long as you come out of there."

"You sure?"

Amos came close to chuckling. "I'm sure. But don't try any shenanigans,
or I'll set the rooster on you."

"I won't try nothin'. Honest." Very slowly the figure shifted, and a boy no
higher than Amos's lowest rib stepped from the deepest shadows. Even in the
dim light, the boy's cheeks looked hollow, his clothes filthy. He dug a bare toe
in the dirt and hunched his shoulders, peering at Amos with round, apprehensive eyes beneath a shock of thick, matted hair. "Y-you gonna whip me? Farmer
up the road whipped me good a couple days ago."

"Is there some reason I ought to give you a whipping?"

"Reckon so. I been stealin' your eggs."

As much as he hated to admit it, Amos admired the boy's honesty. But maybe he didn't think he had any other choice with Amos at the ready with a rifle in his hand. Amos set his feet wide and glared down at the boy. "Stealing's a sin."

"I know."

"Then why'd you do it?"

"'Cause I was hungry."

Amos chewed the inside of his cheek for a few seconds. The kid's confession cleared up the mystery of his disappearing eggs. At least he now knew his chickens hadn't stopped laying. He found the realization assuring. Even though he didn't appreciate this little scalawag helping himself to eggs that weren't his, he experienced a pang of sympathy. The boy would have to be powerfully hungry to eat raw eggs.

Amos snapped out, "You like eggs, do you?"

The boy's skinny shoulders rose in a shrug. "Like 'em best fried over easy with salt pork an' biscuits. But I don't got a stove. Or salt pork. Or flour."

Another chuckle threatened. He'd never heard such a blatant hint.

Pink fingers of light shot upward from the east, and the rooster paused in its scratching to arch its neck and sing out its morning wake-up call. The boy cringed. He pointed at the rooster. "That's a real mean bird, mister. He near pecked my toe off the last time I was here. You might consider fryin' him up for your Sunday dinner."

The boy was almost as bold as the rooster. "I don't know if I should. He does a pretty good job of capturing egg thieves."

His head ducked low, the boy returned to poking his dirty toe against the ground.

Both Samson and Gideon sat up and released twin whines. Amos hitched over to them, hooked the rifle in the crook of his arm, and bent over to give the pups a good-morning scratch behind the ears. He flicked a look at the boy, who stood as still as a statue in the chicken yard, his cautious gaze aimed at the strutting rooster.

Swallowing a chortle, Amos released the pups from their restraining ropes and didn't even call them back when they shot straight for the boy, barking with glee. The boy dropped to his knees and loved on the dogs, his smile so wide it seemed his face might split. Even though he'd lost eggs to this boy— as well as his peace of mind and a half hour of sleep—Amos couldn't help grinning at the happy wrestling match taking place.

But the sun was rising and he had work waiting. So he snapped his fingers. "Samson, Gideon, come."

After a moment's hesitation, Gideon separated himself from the boy and galloped across the yard to Amos. Samson followed closely behind. Both pups plopped down on their bottoms and looked up at Amos with tongues lolling. He gave them each a pat on the head, then looked at the boy, who remained on his knees in the grass.

His heart panged at the child's bereft face. "What's your name, son?"

"Cale."

"Cale what?"

He shrugged. "Just Cale."

"How many eggs do you figure you've snitched from my chicken house or the barn?"

"Dunno." Cale crunched his freckled nose. "Mebbe...nine?"

Amos snorted. "Try again."

The boy ducked his head. "Prob'ly a good dozen an' a half."

"Sounds closer." Amos pretended to think deeply, jutting out his chin and stroking his night's growth of prickly whiskers. "That means you owe me roughly thirty cents."

Cale bolted to his feet. "I don't got any money, mister."

Amos didn't figure the boy did or he wouldn't have been stealing food. "How are you going to pay me back for the eggs you stole?"

In slow, deliberate motions the boy turned his back on Amos and began removing his ragtag shirt. "Guess you can take it out o' my hide, way the farmer up yonder done." He balled the shirt in one hand and bent over slightly to rest his palms on his knees. "Just hurry an' get it over with, huh?"

Amos froze in place, horrified not only by the inches-wide welts striping the boy's narrow back but his resigned expectation of another harsh punishment. His throat tightened, and his words pushed out low and grating. "Put your shirt on. Looks to me like the farmer took his due for both of us."

Cale looked over his shoulder at Amos. "You ain't gonna whale on me?"

Amos turned toward the house. "Nope."

"But what about them eggs I stole?" Panic filled the child's voice. He scampered over to Amos and trailed him across the yard. "You gonna give me over to the sheriff?"

Should he? The boy's hunger, his thieving, his reluctance to share his last name all pointed to him being a runaway. He stopped at the edge of his porch and looked down at the boy, who gazed upward with wide, pleading eyes.

"How old are you, Cale?"

The boy squared his shoulders and stuck out his scrawny chest. "Thirteen an' a half."

Amos raised one eyebrow. "Try again."

Cale grimaced. "I'll be nine come October."

As Amos had suspected, the boy wasn't old enough to be out on his own, and if he kept taking things that didn't belong to him, somebody might do more than take a strap to him—they might aim a rifle at him. He'd better take him in to the sheriff. But first… "How many eggs does a boy your age generally eat for breakfast?"

Cale's eyes grew so round they looked like they might pop from his head. "Two. Sometimes three."

Amos waved his hand toward the barn. "Well, you know where I keep 'em."

"Honest, mister?"

"I don't say anything I don't mean. Bring in three for you and three for me." He'd have fewer to sell, but it was worth the lost ten cents to see the boy's dirty face light with joy.

Cale took off at a run for the barn, and the two pups chased after him. "Cale!"

The boy skidded to a halt and spun to look at Amos. So did the puppies.

"After we eat, you'll help with chores. It'll pay for your breakfast."

"Sure thing, mister. You can use the help. I been watchin', an' you got a powerful bad limp." Cale shot off for the barn with the pups yipping at his heels.

Amos went on inside, shaking his head at the boy's candor. He dressed, and then he stoked the stove and readied a pan for frying the eggs. He didn't have any salt pork, but he could make up some baking-soda biscuits. He might as well let the boy get his stomach filled before he hauled him to the sheriff.

From outside, a pup barked and a child's giggle rose. Amos smiled. It'd be good to have some company this morning.

Chapter 18

Amos

Amos stared in amazement as Cale dug into his breakfast. The boy's nose hovered an inch above his plate. His fork moved so rapidly between the tin plate and his mouth that it reminded Amos of a hummingbird's wings. He must be swallowing the fluffy chunks of egg whole. If he didn't slow down, he might choke.

Amos reached across the table and tapped the top of Cale's head. The boy paused, lifting his head just enough to peek at Amos through the heavy fall of his bangs. Amos pinned a warning frown on his face. "Not so fast there." He added, more gently, "You don't have to worry. I won't take your plate away."

"Sorry, mister," Cale mumbled around a mouthful of eggs. "Just tastes so good I can't hardly stand it."

His appetite gone, Amos pushed his plate aside and watched Cale clean up his own plate and then unashamedly dive into the food remaining on Amos's plate. Apparently his thievery hadn't quelled his hunger. How long had the boy been scrounging on his own? From the looks of his dirty clothes, matted hair, and grime-encrusted fingernails, he hadn't been cared for in a long while. Before Amos took him to town, he'd plunk him in the washtub for a good scrubbing.

When he'd finally finished, Cale swiped his grubby arm across his mouth, leaned back in the chair, and let loose a man-sized belch. "That was real good, mister."

Amos's ma would have had a few words about his manners, but Amos decided to let it go. "You get your fill?"

Cale patted his stomach, which looked round and taut beneath his stained shirt front. "Yup."

"Then let's see to those chores."

Amos headed outside with Cale shadowing him. While they ambled across the yard to the well, Amos said, "Where's home for you, Cale?"

"Don't got one."

He spoke so brightly that Amos drew back in confusion.

Cale dropped the bucket over the edge and lowered the crank. "Used to live in New York. Me an' my brother…we lived there."

Amos stood aside and allowed Cale to bring up the bucket, then carry it across the yard, waddling a bit beneath its weight, to the watering pans. As he worked, the boy chattered on as if he'd known Amos forever.

"Didn't have a bad life, really, just him an' me. But then he took sick with a fever an' died, an' some people—a preacher an' his wife—put me on a train. They said I'd come to ruination if I kept up my stealin' an' such. So they sent me an' a bunch o' other kids who was livin' on the streets, too, to Kansas. Some people north of a town called McPherson took me in, but I run off from there about a couple weeks or so ago. They was too much like that farmer up the road."

Amos cringed, the image of Cale's welted back imprinted in his memory. Little wonder he hadn't stayed with the folks in McPherson.

Cale headed for the barn. Curious to see what he'd do, Amos followed him. While Cale retrieved the egg basket and then sauntered to the chicken house, he continued his story. "So I been travelin' the roads, tryin' to find a place like New York. Easier to sneak off with food an' such in a big city. An' even if you do get caught, nobody whales on ya 'cause there's lotsa places a fella can hide."

He plucked an egg from beneath the belly of a plump hen, then jumped back when the hen fluttered from the roost and clucked in annoyance. He sent a glance at Amos as he sidestepped around the crabby hen. "Where's the closest big city in Kansas?"

Amos took the basket from the boy and limped along the line of roosting boxes, removing eggs as he went. "Kansas doesn't have any cities as big as New York." And he wouldn't direct Cale to one, even if it existed. A boy needed more than the kind of life he'd described.

Cale trailed Amos, lifting chickens from their roosts and shooing them out the door into the yard. "Hmm… Well, it'll take me a while to get all the way back to New York City, but I guess that's where I'll be goin'. Be lonely without my brother, but…" He must have run out of words, because he hung his head and fell silent.

Amos finished gathering the eggs, then curled his hand over Cale's shoulder. Together they left the chicken house and walked between the foraging chickens to the barn, where Amos washed the eggs in the water trough. Cale wiped them dry on his shirt front, then placed them carefully in the wagon, tucking straw between them as protection.

When they'd completed the task, Cale hunkered down and picked at the broken nail on his big toe. "Did I do enough to pay for my breakfast, or do you want me to feed the chicks an' rake the barn, too?"

Amos shook his head in amazement. Cale must have been watching him for days to know the order of his morning chores. "You rake the barn while I feed the chicks. Do a thorough job now—no shirking."

"All right, mister."

Trusting Cale to do as he'd been told, Amos turned his attention to the half-grown chicks. Although the boy had earned his breakfast, he might give him another job when he finished the barn. He had some things to think through, and he needed to keep Cale around until he'd made up his mind.

Dinah

Dinah was in the middle of stripping a bed when a beckon-me bell jangled from the next room. She darted out into the hallway and peeked through the open doorway. A well-dressed woman sat at the dressing table, scowling at her reflection in the oval mirror. On the bed behind her, it appeared a trunk had burst its seams and spewed its contents. Dinah tapped on the doorframe, and the woman gestured her in.

"Thank goodness you've come. I'm in a dreadful spot."

"Are you feeling poorly, ma'am?" Dinah hadn't yet needed to fetch a doctor for a guest, but she knew where to find the local physician.

The woman pursed her lips and shot a frown at Dinah. "Do I look ill to you, young lady? Of course I am quite well. But, oh, my hair…" She touched the dark-brown tresses, which she'd brushed into a loose pouf. "It's all falling down because my combs broke when I took them out last night. My maid ordinarily performs my hairdressing tasks, but I left her home for this journey. Now I regret the decision."

Dinah wasn't sure what to do, so she offered a meek, "I'm sorry, ma'am."

The woman huffed. "I'm not seeking an apology. I must depart shortly after noon, and it is imperative I board the train without my hair straggling around my face." She withdrew two silver coins from the depths of a velvet reticule and pressed them into Dinah's hand. "I need a pair of large hair combs. I prefer those with embellishments, but I surmise *serviceable* is all that will be available in this small town." She released a dramatic sigh. "I shall have to make do."

"But, ma'am…" Dinah held out the money as if it were a snake that might bite her. "I'm cleaning rooms. I can't—"

"When I checked in yesterday evening, the desk clerk told me if I had need of anything, I was to ring this bell and my wishes would be promptly met." The woman lifted her chin and speared Dinah with a glowering look. "Am I to tell the manager that you refused?"

"Of course not, ma'am." Dinah dropped the coins into the pocket of her apron and skittered for the door. "I'll go after those combs right away."

"Be quick about it. My train leaves in less than two hours, and I will need you to pack my trunk when you return."

Dinah paused for a moment, gazing in dismay at the assortment of items covering the bed. It would take an hour to fold and pack everything even if Ruthie helped.

"Miss, why are you dallying?" The woman's strident voice rose. "Go now!"

Dinah went.

As she clattered down the porch stairs and trotted past the gardens, she decided the most likely place to find hair combs was Graham and Tucker Dry Goods. So she headed for the ornate limestone building on Main Street. The coins in her pocket bounced together as she walked, seeming to chide her to hurry, hurry. By the time she reached the store, she was panting from exertion and sweat dribbled down her temples. The wind had tossed handfuls of dust at her, leaving gritty smears on her apron that refused to leave, no matter how many times she swatted them. So she'd need to change uniforms before returning to duty.

Stifling a growl of frustration, Dinah threw the door open and charged into the store. "Excuse me," she called to the clerk, who was waiting on a man and his son. "Where would I find hair combs?"

The man turned, and to Dinah's surprise she found herself being gifted with one of Mr. Ackerman's friendly smiles. Her heart fluttered at the genuine delight shining on his handsome, square face.

The boy poked Mr. Ackerman on the elbow, then pointed at Dinah. "Who's that?" He wore a blue plaid shirt and tan britches bearing crease marks from their time on the shelf. Black-and-brown-striped suspenders held up his pants, which were rolled twice at the cuff, and shiny brown lace-up boots covered his feet. Apparently the two had just completed a successful shopping excursion.

Mr. Ackerman grinned down at the boy. "Are you going to make me introduce you to every person we encounter? You've already met the grocer, the barber, and the store clerk here. Will you remember all the names?"

"Mr. Root, Mr. Cooper, an' Mr. Sellers," the boy recited. "Now, who's she?"

Mr. Ackerman put his large hand on the back of the boy's head and propelled him toward Dinah. "Miss Hubley, please meet Cale. Cale, this is Miss Hubley." He leaned down and whispered in Cale's ear, "Use your manners."

The boy stuck out his hand and lifted his chin. "Nice to meetcha, Miss Hubley."

Dinah gave Cale's hand a quick shake. Her insides trembled, the need to complete her errand and return to the hotel making her fidgety. Or perhaps standing beneath Mr. Ackerman's kind smile caused her discomfiture. Around the men at the Yellow Parrot, she had always been filled with the desperate need to escape. With Mr. Ackerman she also wanted to run, but not as much from him as from herself. Which was even more disconcerting.

"It's nice to meet you, too." She put her hand in her pocket and encountered the coins. Reminded of her purpose for entering the store, she started to move away.

"Miss Hubley, may I ask… Did Miss Mead tell you…"

He didn't need to complete the question. Dinah nodded.

"Good. So will you…"

She'd shed tears last night after refusing Ruthie's request for her to attend services again. She battled tears now, looking into his hopeful face. But she shook her head.

His brow pinched into furrows. "Why? Didn't Miss Mead explain—"

"I came to make a purchase for a guest. I have to get back." Besides, she was in her uniform, acting as a representative of Mr. Harvey's Clifton Hotel. If someone reported her for chatting with Mr. Ackerman while she was on duty, she could be reprimanded, perhaps even let go. Dinah inched in the direction of the counter. "I can't talk." The disappointment crossing Mr. Ackerman's face pierced her, but she had to be firm. With him. With herself.

He offered a slow nod. "We won't keep you, then."

Dinah scurried the final few feet to the counter and gasped out, "Hair combs?" The clerk pointed, and she darted toward the shelf he'd indicated. As she rounded the corner, she heard Mr. Ackerman call, "I hope to see you at service on Sunday, Miss Hubley." She didn't respond.

She quickly located a pair of tortoiseshell combs that looked similar in size to the broken ones lying on the dressing table at the hotel room. Although she needed to hurry back, she stayed hidden behind the tall shelves, listening while Mr. Ackerman paid the clerk. The door to the cash register slammed, and still she waited until she heard Mr. Ackerman's distinctive footsteps cross the floor and the screen door slap into its frame. Assured he'd gone, she hustled from her hiding spot, paid for the combs, then dashed onto the boardwalk.

Without conscious thought, she scanned the street for a glimpse of Mr. Ackerman. She spotted him up the block, ushering the little boy named Cale into the brick building that served as the city offices. Lifting her skirt a little, she took off at a trot, weaving past other morning shoppers. When she passed the city offices, she couldn't resist sending a glance through the plate-glass window. Mr. Ackerman had his hand on Cale's shoulder, and the sheriff seemed to be questioning the boy.

Her feet automatically slowed as questions filled her mind about the child and why he was with Mr. Ackerman. Clearly he was fond of the boy—his tender touch and the kind way he'd addressed Cale in the store indicated such. He'd just bought Cale a set of new clothes, so he must have a relationship with the child. A younger brother? A cousin, perhaps? Or even his son?

The last speculation jolted her feet into motion. She nearly raced the remaining blocks to the hotel, then clattered up to her room and changed into a fresh apron, washed her face, and slicked back the loosened strands of hair from her bun before returning to duty. But while she helped the guest—a Mrs. McClaren from St. Louis, Missouri, who was traveling home from California after visiting her sister—first with her hair and then her luggage, Dinah couldn't clear the images of the little boy from her mind.

What if the child was a stranger, a newcomer to town like her, and the man had simply befriended him? Much the way he'd tried to befriend her. She'd dared to believe Mr. Ackerman's kindness to her meant he saw her as someone special, worthy of attention. But if he reached out to every new person who arrived in town, then she'd have to accept she wasn't really special at all. And the thought hurt more than she would have expected.

Chapter 19

Amos

Amos handed Cale the last clean dish and watched the boy dry every drop with the wadded toweling. With the tip of his tongue poking out of the corner of his mouth and his brow puckered in concentration, he seemed to be performing a more important task than drying a speckled plate. Amos had learned over the past few days Cale did everything with great care, as if fearful of making a mistake.

When the plate was dry, Cale placed it on the stack on the shelf and then grinned at Amos. "All done. I'll go put Sam an' Gid on their ropes now."

Amos held out his hand, stopping the boy from darting for the door. "I already tied them up in the barn."

Cale scowled. "In the barn? How they gonna keep watch over the chicken house if you got 'em closed up in there?"

"I reckon we need to talk about that." Amos didn't relish the conversation. Cale was crazy about the pups, spending every spare minute playing with them, and the news the sheriff delivered earlier in the day would probably worry him. But he'd need the boy's help keeping Samson and Gideon locked up. Pointing to the chairs, Amos silently invited Cale to join him at the clean table. They settled themselves on opposite sides, and Amos said, "Remember how the sheriff rode out this afternoon?"

Cale nodded. His expression turned apprehensive.

"It seems a pack of wild dogs has been roaming the area farms, killing calves and lambs and even a horse at one place. The sheriff's put together a group of men who've been instructed to shoot any dog they see out wandering. So we can't let Samson and Gideon go roaming until the men have destroyed the pack. The sheriff said he knows my two pups haven't been up to any mischief so he didn't shoot them, and he said he'd let me know when it was safe to let them out again."

Cale's tense frown eased. He coughed out a short laugh. "Is that all?"

To Amos the situation was dire. He'd been praying off and on since the sheriff left, and he continued to pray that no other animals or people were put in harm's way by the pack. He spoke firmly, hoping to make clear the seriousness to the boy. "This is nothing to laugh about. Those dogs are a real danger. Not only will we keep Samson and Gideon locked up, but I'll have my rifle ready in case the wild dogs come here. And you stay close to the house, too— no venturing out in the afternoons like you've been doing."

The boy's eyes flew wide, his jaw dropping. "I wasn't laughin' about the dogs, honest! It's just when I seen the sheriff ride in, I thought—" He shrunk down, folding his arms over his chest.

Amos frowned. "You thought what?"

"It don't matter." Cale shot out of his chair. "Gonna get ready for bed."

Amos caught the boy's arm as he charged past. "Hold up, Cale." Cale stood stiffly in Amos's light grasp. And suddenly he understood. "Did you think the sheriff was coming for you?"

Cale's chin quivered. He nodded.

Amos sighed. Although he'd intended to keep quiet about the other reason for the sheriff's visit, he changed his mind. Cale should know. He gave the boy a little nudge toward the chair. "Sit down there. Let me tell you what the sheriff said about you."

Cale slunk back into his chair. Resignation sagged his features, making him seem much older than his not-quite-nine years. "Them Hollisters over in McPherson want me back, do they?"

"He hasn't gotten a response to the telegram he sent." Amos sucked in a breath, praying for strength. He'd grown fond of the boy, and he wanted what was best for Cale. He just wasn't sure yet what "best" might be. "But even if they don't take you back, the sheriff said you'll have to go…somewhere. The church in New York that sent you to Kansas is responsible for you. They'll find a new place for you." Amos angled his head, pinning the boy with a firm look. "Are you sure you don't remember the name of the minister who sent you to Kansas?"

Shaking his head wildly, Cale looked directly into Amos's eyes. "Just know it was a preacher an' a lady. Back in May—maybe June—they hauled a whole bunch of us boys into the church, fed us a good meal, cleaned us up, an' gave us a new set of clothes. Then they put us on a train an' said we'd be goin' to Christian families for a decent upbringin'." He shrugged. "That's all I remember."

Although Amos suspected Cale was wily enough to withhold anything he didn't want to divulge, he hoped the boy wouldn't lie to him. "The sheriff's asked the police in New York for help in finding the preacher. He said there's more than one organization sending city orphans to the West, but he'll find the right one eventually, even without a name."

Cale hung his head and sighed. "Sure don't wanna go back to the Hollisters." He fingered the bone buttons of his new shirt. "They'll probably take the shirt and pants you bought me. They took the new clothes the preacher gave me an' made me wear their boy's worn-out hand-me-downs. I didn't like them Hollisters at all."

Amos didn't like them, either, based on the little bit he'd learned from Cale. *Lord, forgive my un-Christian thoughts, but people like that don't deserve to raise this boy.* "Well, don't fret about it now. You can stay with me until the sheriff works things out with the New York preacher. If you're still here next week when school starts up again, we'll get you enrolled. No sense in a smart boy like you missing out on book learning."

Cale's head bounced upward so fast Amos was surprised the boy didn't jar his neck. "School? Honest?"

Amos anticipated a struggle. He had to wrestle Cale into the washtub for a bath. "You want to go?"

"I sure do!" Cale wriggled in his chair, reminding Amos of the puppies' excitement at breakfast time. "That's the only reason I didn't run off from the preacher. He said we'd get to go to school at our new homes. But the Hollisters said they'd keep me home to work instead. I can really go to school?"

Amos hoped he hadn't mentioned school too soon. What if the sheriff came and took the boy before school started? "If you're still here, yes."

Cale seemed to ignore Amos's cautious warning. He leaped from the chair and punched both fists in the air. "Woo-hoo!"

Amos couldn't stifle a laugh. Had he ever been so enthusiastic about sitting behind a school desk? He didn't think so. He shook his head. "Enough hollering. You'll get the chickens all riled up. It's bedtime. Off with you now."

Grinning, Cale headed for the corner where Amos had laid out a pallet for him. Midway across the floor he stopped and sent a pensive look in Amos's direction. "If the Hollisters don't want me an' the preacher says it's all right, could I just stay here? With you?"

A yearning to agree welled up within Amos's chest. But he wouldn't give the boy false hope. His heart aching, he slowly shook his head.

Cale's shoulders drooped. "Oh. Well."

"It isn't that I don't want you. But—"

"It don't matter." Cale scuffed to the corner and dropped onto the pallet. Rolling onto his side, he faced the wall.

Amos pushed up from his chair and limped across the floor. He bent over and touched Cale's shoulder. He waited until the boy angled his head to peek at him. He cleared his throat, forcing aside a lump of emotion. "If I could, I'd keep you. You're a fine boy. But it isn't up to me. It's up to the preacher, and if the Hollisters don't work out for you, the preacher'll want you to be with a real family. I'm just a bachelor chicken farmer. Do you understand?"

For long moments Cale lay gazing up at Amos with his lips set in a firm line. Then he sighed. "I understand. An' I don't hold it against you."

Amos gave a wobbly smile.

"But," Cale went on, his forehead crunching into furrows of deep thought, "maybe I'll get to stay here after all. Maybe the Hollisters will say they don't want me back—they said I was a peck of trouble. Maybe you'll get married before the sheriff finds the preacher. Maybe—"

Amos lurched upright. Fire flamed his face. "Married?"

Cale flopped onto his back, then propped himself up with his elbows. He blinked innocently at Amos. "Well, sure. You're plenty old. You oughtta get married. What about that lady from the dry goods store? You seemed to like her well enough."

Amos spun on his heel and headed for the stove where the remaining coffee waited in a tall pot. He hoped a splash of strong brew would wash away the feelings the boy's statement had brought to life.

Cale's musing voice carried from the corner. "What was her name? Oh, I remember—Miss Hubley."

Amos filled a cup to its brim. "Go to sleep, Cale."

Dinah

"Oh, there they go…"

The longing in Ruthie's voice pulled Dinah's attention from window washing. She glanced sideways and found her roommate gazing up the road. Curious, she moved to the edge of the porch to see what Ruthie was watching. A few children trudged toward town with lunch pails swinging from their hands. Apparently, with harvest complete, school had started again.

Finding the realization uninteresting, Dinah returned to the bucket of soapy water and plunged her rag into it.

Ruthie heaved a mighty sigh and joined Dinah at the big window that looked into the guests' dining room. "I miss going to school."

Over the past few days, although the servers continued to hold their distance from Dinah, Ruthie had begun talking to her again. Dinah would never admit it aloud, but she appreciated the other girl's willingness to jabber even though Dinah rarely contributed to the conversation. Listening to Ruthie kept other thoughts at bay. If only Ruthie's jabber could make her night terrors flee. She rubbed the soapy cloth over the dusty window and waited for Ruthie to continue. The girl didn't disappoint her.

"Some of my best memories are from my years in the Arnold Grade School."

Some of Dinah's most dismal memories were from her school years.

"And did you know I'm one of the first three twelfth-grade graduates from Florence High School? Mama says I should be very proud of that fact."

Twelve grades… Dinah wondered what the children learned in the upper grades.

"Mama puts a great deal of store in education. She and Papa both, actually." Ruthie finally put her rag to work. "When Seth began talking last year about ending his schooling at grade eight and going to work at the quarry, Papa nearly had apoplexy!" She grinned and bumped Dinah with her elbow.

And Tori had ridiculed Dinah for insisting on earning her eighth-grade certificate. Such differences between Ruthie's family and her own. Dinah moved to the next window.

Ruthie giggled as she drizzled clear water over the sudsy pane. "I'm sure Seth will go all the way through to grade twelve, as will Jonah, Noah, Timothy, Joseph, and little Dinah June. I can't believe she starts school this year already." Ruthie's tone turned musing. "I hope she enjoys it as much as I did." She picked up her bucket and moved beside Dinah again. "Did you attend a private school for your education?"

Dinah thought she detected a hint of envy in Ruthie's voice. If she knew how infrequently Dinah was allowed to leave the Yellow Parrot and attend class at the local school, she'd quickly lose her jealousy. Wouldn't Ruthie be shocked if Dinah came right out and said, "I graduated eighth grade when I was sixteen"? But Ruthie would never know, because Dinah would never tell her.

Dinah said, "No, I did not."

Ruthie wandered to the edge of the porch again and peered up the road. "Hmm. I suppose I assumed you— Oh!"

Dinah jumped, splashing her apron with suds. She drew in a sharp breath and whirled to scold Ruthie for startling her. But the words withered on her tongue when she realized what had caused Ruthie's shrill outburst.

Mr. Ackerman and the little boy named Cale were passing along the street. Ruthie rose on her tiptoes and waved her hand over her head. "Good morning, Mr. Ackerman!"

The man slowed his steps and turned in their direction, his gaze seeking. Dinah quickly ducked her head, her heart hammering and her face flooding with warmth. Would he acknowledge her? She peeked through her fringe of lashes, both hopeful and fearful.

He waved with the hand not pulling his familiar little wooden wagon and smiled. "Good morning, Miss Mead. And Miss Hubley." He chuckled, the sound pleasant. "I think that is Miss Hubley standing there in the shadows."

He'd noticed her! She lifted her face, biting the insides of her cheeks to hold back a smile.

"I see you're shining up the hotel windows this morning." He took a step closer, drawing the boy with him. "A worthwhile pastime. My mother always said clean windows were a sign of a confident soul who didn't mind the world seeing what he was up to because he had nothing to hide."

Ruthie giggled. "Papa says the eyes are the windows to a man's soul. So I suppose looking someone directly in the eyes means the same thing—he has nothing to hide."

"Wise words." Mr. Ackerman's gaze bounced back and forth between Ruthie and Dinah, as if waiting for her to contribute to their conversation.

Dinah had nothing to say, but she had a lot to hide. She faced the window again. Mr. Ackerman's and Cale's reflections peered at her from the clean pane. Their images held her attention as firmly as a miser held a penny.

"I'm taking Cale to school." Mr. Ackerman smiled down at the boy, who beamed upward. "Then I'll deliver eggs to my customers." The school bell's ring intruded, echoing across the distance. Mr. Ackerman gave a little jolt. "We'd better hurry on. It isn't good for him to be late his first day. Good day, Miss Mead. Good day, Miss Hubley."

Ruthie called out cheerfully, "Good day, Mr. Ackerman! Have fun at school, Cale!"

The boy lifted his hand in a wave, and he and Mr. Ackerman set off. But then Cale's voice carried to Dinah's ears. "I changed my mind. I think you should marry Miss Mead instead."

Chapter 20

Ruthie

Ruthie slapped her hands to her cheeks. A giggle of pure delight left her lips. She whirled and clattered to Dinah. "Did you hear what that little boy said?" She waited a moment, but Dinah went on washing the window and didn't reply. So she said, loudly, "That little boy said Mr. Ackerman should *marry* me!"

Dinah's lips pressed into a firm line. She leaned over, picked up her bucket, and moved to the next window. After placing the bucket on the floor—with a hard enough bump to slosh suds over the rim—she shot a quick look at Ruthie. "Better start rinsing before the soap dries and leaves a smear."

Accustomed to Dinah's taciturn behavior, Ruthie snatched up her rag and set to work automatically, her thoughts rolling haphazardly off her tongue. "I wonder who the boy is. I've never seen him before. Maybe a new family moved to town near Mr. Ackerman's place and he offered to show Cale to school. He'd do something like that—be helpful. But then it's odd that Cale told Mr. Ackerman"—her face burned with contained excitement—"he should marry me."

She paused, recalling the exact wording Cale used. "He said Mr. Ackerman should marry me *instead*. Which means Cale and Mr. Ackerman must have discussed possibilities, which means the two of them must know each other fairly well, which means…" She ran out of ideas. Flicking a glance at Dinah's stern profile, she asked a question even though she was certain it would be unanswered. "What do you think it means, Dinah?"

Dinah's hand stilled for a few brief seconds, then began working back and forth with fervor. As Ruthie had suspected, the girl remained silent.

Ruthie sighed and returned to rinsing. "Do you suppose Mr. Ackerman will come to the Calico Ball at the end of the month? He didn't come last year, but then last year he might not have been contemplating matrimony the way he is now." Another giggle formed, tickling her stomach. Could it be her and Mama's prayers were already bearing fruit?

She watched clear water chase the remnants of soap from the pane and kept her musings to herself. If Mr. Ackerman asked her, she'd go. An evening together would help much in determining whether they were, as Mama had said, *compatible.* Mama's concerns hadn't been over Mr. Ackerman's bad leg but more about their age difference and his occupation. Having been raised in town, Ruthie wasn't familiar with the day-to-day operations of a chicken farm. Mama worried the work might be overwhelming but declared if she and Mr. Ackerman were *compatible,* then Ruthie would probably settle into the new duties without resentment.

Her gaze fixed on her own reflection in the glass, she whispered, "Are we compatible?" They both attended church faithfully. They were both hard workers. They both liked children. A flush of pink tinged her reflected face and she smiled at herself. Oh yes, they were compatible. She just needed Mr. Ackerman to realize it.

"Ruthie?"

Dinah's terse voice intruded upon Ruthie's reverie. Slowly, she turned toward her roommate. "Hmm?"

"What is the Calico Ball?"

Although a frown creased Dinah's face and her voice held more irritation than enthusiasm, Ruthie couldn't squelch her own excitement. She dashed to Dinah's side. "It is *the* social event of the year! The entire town is invited. People turn out in droves to partake of the banquet tables' delicious offerings and spend the evening dancing. A band comes all the way from Peabody." She grinned. "Papa thought the songs were a little too fast last year for his taste, but oh, I had such fun!"

Ruthie closed her eyes, imagining the scene. "The men wear jackets, many of them jackets with tails, and they tuck cravats into their collars instead of wearing string ties. Some of them even have handkerchiefs to match. And the women wear fine calico gowns with skirts that flare out when they whirl around the floor, and they put their hair up in beautiful styles." She sighed, pressing her palms to her chest and swaying slightly to the music in her head. "It's an evening of pure magic…"

She popped her eyes open and grabbed Dinah's cold, wet hands. "Best of all, it takes place right here at the Clifton, and since we aren't kitchen staff, we'll be released from duty to attend. Isn't it exciting?"

Dinah pulled her hands free of Ruthie's grasp and picked up her bucket. "I'm sure you'll have fun."

Ruthie grabbed Dinah's arm, staring at her in shock. "You won't go?"

Dinah shook her head.

"But why not? We work all day, every day, and Mr. Irwin will let us off for the Calico Ball. The ball only comes once a year. You have to go, Dinah."

Dinah frowned. She wriggled her elbow until Ruthie released her. But Ruthie couldn't drop the subject and trotted after Dinah as she marched to the remaining window in need of washing. "Why don't you want to go?" She touched Dinah's rolled-up sleeve. "If you don't have a gown, you could borrow mine from last year. Mama is sewing me a new one since my last year's one is too tight. I'm sure it would fit you, though, since you're smaller than me. It's a sweet shade of mint green scattered all over with tiny pink blossoms. And Mama even sewed a peek of lace around the collar."

Dinah froze with her hand in the wash bucket. Most of the suds had dissipated, leaving foamy smears that formed a circle around her wrist. Bent over, her head low, she said, "I don't need a gown."

Embarrassment smote Ruthie. What had she been thinking? Of course, a wealthy girl like Dinah would have scores of gowns. Just because she hadn't brought them with her didn't mean they weren't filling her wardrobe in Chicago. A telegram home and a trunk could be sent. She stepped backward as Dinah abruptly straightened and applied the rag to the window.

"Well, then, if not a gown…" Her voice quivered. She swallowed and started again. "Why don't you want to attend?"

Dinah gave the window one final sweep, dropped her rag into the murky water remaining in her bucket, picked up the bucket, and walked off without a word.

Dinah

Dinah flicked the feather duster across the dressing table's top. The oval mirror captured her from midthigh upward. She found herself pausing, as she had frequently over the past few days, to examine her reflection and imagine herself in a lace-embellished gown, swirling around a dance floor on the arm of a fine gentleman. As a child, she'd engaged in the same daydream countless times. But she wasn't a child anymore.

Her lips set in a firm line, she forced her gaze downward and continued cleaning. Despite her best efforts, her thoughts carried her backward in time to when she was eight, or maybe nine, and Rueben had given her a book filled with wonderful tales written by a pair of German brothers named Grimm. She'd loved it and read the stories again and again, savoring the escape into a world far beyond the confining walls of the Yellow Parrot, but her favorite was "Cinderella."

The girl in the story was so much like Dinah—banished to the attic when guests arrived, forced to labor for a woman who openly disliked her. Cinderella had been rescued thanks to a wishing tree and had found her prince at the castle ball. Castle ball. Calico Ball. Her chest constricted. Fairy tales couldn't come true. It was foolhardy to even consider attending the dance. And yet...

Her gaze returned to the mirror. She took in her simple black dress and bibbed white apron, envisioning a lovely gown in its place. She lifted the feather duster and held it like a bouquet of roses, even daring to sniff the tips of the feathers and smile as the sweet aroma of just-budded blooms filled her imagination. Fluttering her eyelashes, she cast a look at her imaginary dance partner and caught her own reflection again.

She froze, staring into her pale-blue eyes—what Ruthie had called the window to her soul. Within moments her image wavered as tears filled her eyes. How could she even pretend a gentleman would want to sweep her into his arms and dance with her until she was breathless, as the prince had done with Cinderella? The only "gentleman" with whom she'd become acquainted had left a mark on her not even a magic wishing tree could erase.

A beckon-me bell jangled, rescuing her from her dismal contemplation. Dinah swept her hand across her eyes, removing the glimmer of moisture, and darted up the hallway in the direction of the sound. The bell clanged again, more loudly, followed by an angry exclamation. Dinah tapped on the door behind which the noise had escaped, and it opened to reveal a frazzled-looking middle-aged woman and a teenage girl. The girl stood in the middle of the floor wearing a ribboned chemise, ruffled bloomers, and a tear-stained scowl.

Dinah had encountered this pair in the hallway yesterday. They'd been arguing loudly about sharing a room, the woman insisting upon it and the girl demanding her own room. She thought the disagreement petty, considering the size of the rooms, and it appeared their spat hadn't ended. Uncomfortable at having been pulled into their dispute, Dinah aimed her gaze to the side, away from the half-naked girl. "M-may I help you?"

The woman grabbed her arm and pulled her inside the room, then closed the door with a snap. "Yes, you may. Does the hotel have a barrel where rubbish is burned?"

"Yes, ma'am."

"Good." The woman bent over and scooped up a rumpled mass of light-blue fabric with ivory ribbons trailing from the center of the wad. She plopped the mess into Dinah's arms. "Take this."

The girl wailed, "Mother, nooooo!" She raced at Dinah, reaching.

The woman caught the girl and held her tight. "Stop this caterwauling at once, Ernestina! You're not yet fifteen years old and have no business wearing such an elaborate costume."

"But we can save it until my birthday!" Ernestina, tears streaming down her fury-reddened cheeks, strained toward Dinah. "It's too lovely to be burned!"

"You should have thought of that before you commissioned it without my permission." The mother spoke with such harshness that Dinah shrank back, but the girl continued to fight within the circle of her mother's arms. Ernestina's mother looked at Dinah again. "Go ahead—dispose of it. If it remains in our room, this rebellious child will find a way to don it and sneak out again."

With the daughter's howls and the mother's angry reprimands ringing in her ears, Dinah escaped the room with the wadded-up dress in her arms. She went straight downstairs, out the back door, and across the graveled area behind the carriage house where charred barrels stood in a row to receive rubbish. The busboys must have done the burning last night because the smell of smoke still lingered and only one barrel held trash.

She lifted the dress to toss it into the nearest barrel, but curiosity gave her pause. The woman had called it an elaborate costume—too elaborate for a girl not yet fifteen. Flicking a glance left and right, Dinah ascertained no one observed her. Then she shook the gown from its tangled wad and held it up by the shoulders. She gasped. Although rumpled from the woman's rough treatment, the beauty of the frock couldn't be denied. How could Dinah even consider destroying it?

Fashioned in a fabric of weaving vines and sweet morning glories floating on a sea of periwinkle blue, the full skirt ended with a lace-embellished flounce scalloped with ivory ribbon. Its sleeves bore a flutter of delicate lace at the cuffs, and even more lace graced the gently scooped bodice where tiny pearl buttons marched from the neckline to the waist. Ivory ribbons cascaded in streams from both shoulders.

Dinah hugged the dress to her chest, her heart pounding. She'd been instructed to dispose of the gown, but might it be enough to permanently remove it from the original owner? That would be a disposal of sorts, wouldn't it?

Her gaze drifted to the hotel window behind which the mother and daughter probably still fought. The pair were guests, so they'd leave eventually. If she kept the dress, they would never know. Her thoughts teetertottered between keeping the frock and tossing it away, and then another thought screeched into her brain.

She'd envied Cinderella whose wishing tree had tossed down a lovely gown so she could attend the castle ball. Holding the dress at arm's length once more, she pondered whether she should consider the angry mother her "wishing tree."

Chapter 21

Amos

Not until the end of the second full week of school did Amos send Cale up the road alone for the walk to town. The evening before, the sheriff had ridden out to inform Amos that he and his men were confident they'd killed all the dogs in the marauding pack. With the threat of attack gone, Amos felt secure letting Cale walk the road alone without Amos and his ready rifle for protection.

The boy was so proud as he sauntered off, swinging a little tin pail with two buttered biscuits and a chunk of cheese in it. He didn't even stop to wave good-bye before leaving the lane. Amos watched with Samson and Gideon whining at his feet until Cale disappeared around the bend. Then he put his hands on his hips and looked at the pair of growing pups.

"That's it, then. He'll be back later. Come."

The dogs trotted along beside him—Gideon on the left, Samson on the right. Gideon put more distance between himself and Amos's feet than Samson did, however. Amos had stepped on him once due to his hitching gait. Although Gideon didn't avoid Amos afterward, he did take care. Pride filled Amos's chest. The dog was smart.

He enjoyed having his furry companions with him while he did chores. He'd missed them the days they stayed locked up in the barn, and he sent up a prayer of gratitude for the sheriff's diligence in ridding the town of the pesky wild dogs. He'd be able to leave his chickens in their yard during daytime hours again, too, rather than keeping them in the chicken house. Egg production had slowed during their time closed away from the sun, and he looked forward to finding an egg in every roost again.

Amos tossed out handfuls of ground corn for the chickens. He'd put the half-grown chicks into the yard with the laying hens early that morning. He easily spotted the young ones—smaller in body but with long, scrawny necks and feet too big. At first the full-grown hens had clucked in alarm at the new-comers, but they settled down quickly, and now they all pecked in the yard as if they'd always been there together. He released a contented sigh, thinking of the day when the chicks would be old enough to start laying. Not much longer. His plans were going well.

"And as soon as my flock is large enough to bring in twice the money they do now, I will take a wife. Even if I'm not yet selling to the hotel, I will take a wife because I'll have enough to support one." He spoke to Sam and Gid, who whined in reply, his heart thrumming at his bold tone.

Ever since his walk home when he'd admitted his fascination with Dinah Hubley, he imagined her at his farm. Working beside him, cooking at his stove and eating at his table, laughing at Samson's and Gideon's antics... Cale con-tinued to prod Amos to consider marrying Ruthie Mead, but when Amos imagined taking a wife, Dinah Hubley's face always appeared in his mind. He'd come to accept God had chosen her for him. She was young, true, but she'd get older.

Of course, he reminded himself as he emptied the last of the corn on the ground, he'd have to let her know before she signed a contract to be a server. Servers couldn't court for a full year after agreeing to work in the dining room. He didn't want to wait that long. He hoped she'd see marriage to him prefer-able to serving travelers in the dining room.

Shielding his eyes from the sun, he glanced across the feathered flock, nod-ding in satisfaction at how much larger it appeared with the new ones mingling with the full-grown ones. He needed to choose six adult hens to be brooders and close them in the barn with an egg in each hay-filled roost. He'd add an egg each day until there were five beneath every hen. If they all hatched, he'd have another thirty chicks to add to his flock. More than a dozen of the last batch of chicks were showing signs of cocks' combs. He hoped in the next group there'd be much fewer boys. He needed more egg layers than he needed chickens for butchering. But it wasn't up to him whether hens or roosters emerged from the eggs.

Sending a glance skyward, he offered a short plea. "Lots of hens this time, hmm?" Some might laugh at him for praying about chickens, but Amos knew his Lord cared about everything in his life—even the difference between hens and roosters—so he didn't mind sharing every thought with God.

He headed for the barn where his egg-collecting basket waited. "Come, Sam and Gid. Let's see how many eggs the girls left in the roosts since yesterday."

Over the day, Amos spoke to the dogs frequently. He liked the way they looked at him with attentive little faces, their ears alert and stubby tails wagging. Samson even had a habit of lifting his eyebrows, as if amazed at the things Amos said. The dogs made him laugh. He'd been right about them being good company. But he'd also been right about them not taking the place of human company. As much as he talked to them, they didn't answer. Harboring Cale under his roof for the past few weeks had fueled his desire for a family of his own. And even Cale, who never lacked for something to say, wasn't enough. Because Cale wouldn't be with him forever. In fact, Cale would likely be going elsewhere before long.

When the sheriff had told Amos about the wild dogs, he also mentioned he'd found the name of the preacher in New York who'd sent Cale to Kansas. He already sent a telegram to the church and expected a reply within a few days. Amos didn't know whether someone from New York would come get the boy or if the sheriff would be expected to transport him to wherever the preacher chose, but he was already steeling himself for the day when Cale would leave. Because the day would bring a return to his deep loneliness. But only until he took a wife. Then he'd never be lonely again.

Midafternoon, Amos tied Samson and Gideon to a stall post in the barn again. They whined, but he ignored their sad faces. "When I get back, I'll have Cale with me, and he'll romp with you in the yard. So take a nap now."

As if they understood, the pair flopped down, Samson resting his black, moist nose on Gideon's neck. Amos chuckled at the picture they formed. He gave each pup a scratch on the top of the head, then retrieved his wagon. Out-side, he lowered the barn door's crossbar into place and thumped it good into the clamps. The pups were secured to their ropes, but if the door drifted open, the brooding hens might decide to leave their roosts. And he couldn't have that.

He paused beside the chicken yard, observing the flock. Should he chase them into the chicken house before going to town? The day was so nice—calm rather than windy, warm but not hot. A perfect early fall day. It seemed a shame to close them up when they hadn't been able to scratch free for so many days. Hadn't the sheriff said the threat was gone? Of course he had. Amos would leave the chickens to enjoy the sunshine for the hour or so he'd be away.

The decision made, he checked the twisted wire that held the gate closed, then addressed the feisty rooster who lorded over every other bird in the yard. "You're in charge now. Keep everyone safe."

The bird angled its head and blinked at Amos before strutting off.

Smiling, Amos set off for town.

A few mothers, one jostling a baby carriage and two with toddlers balanced on their hips, stood in a little circle in the shade of the elm tree in the schoolyard. Their voices competed with that of the teacher's, whose lesson on grammar drifted from the open window.

Amos parked his little wagon just outside the patch of shade and then sat in it. The wooden wheels groaned beneath his weight, but his tired hip needed the rest. Elbows on his knees, he aimed his gaze at the school doors and counted the minutes until they opened. His eagerness to see Cale emerge sur-prised him. Was this how it felt to be a father? He'd stayed in town a little longer than he originally planned so he could have the boy's company while walking home again. If he'd be bidding Cale farewell soon, he should grab every available minute with him.

Soft laughter rolled from the circle of mothers, and his lips quirked in si-lent response even though he didn't know what had amused them. As a boy, he'd always joined in when he heard someone laughing just in case they were laughing at him. If he laughed instead of cried when someone gibed at him, often the teasing stopped. He never understood why some people took pleasure in another's hurt, and if he was fortunate to have children someday, he'd teach them to defend those being teased rather than being the one to tease others.

The doors opened, and children spilled from the schoolhouse with squeals and laughter. Cale was in the middle of the group, and when he spotted Amos, he grabbed the arm of a red-headed boy and galloped over, tugging the other child along with him.

"Hey, Uncle Amos!" Cale greeted him with such enthusiasm the mothers all turned and sent smiles in their direction.

Amos liked the title the boy had chosen for him. He had nieces and nephews, but in less than a month, he'd gotten better acquainted with this boy than he was with his own family. Sadness tried to wiggle its way through him, but Cale's sunny countenance chased the gray cloud away.

"This is Timothy Mead. He's my best pal."

Amos already knew Timothy, one of Preacher Mead's passel of children. But he stuck out his hand as if they'd never met, and Timothy gave it a solid shake. Amos asked politely, as he'd been teaching Cale to do, "How are you, Timothy?"

"I'm fine, sir. Thank you." Timothy proved he'd been taught manners, too.

Cale went on in his booming voice. "An' guess what? His sister Ruthie works at the hotel—she's the one I think you should marry."

The three mothers broke into titters. Amos pushed himself to his feet, rocking the wagon. He caught the handle. "We'd better head back now, Cale. Good-bye, Timothy."

"'Bye," Timothy said, backtracking in short, quick steps and waving. "See ya Sunday, Cale."

Halfway across town and well away from the others, Amos shot Cale a stern frown. "Listen, Cale, I'll have no more talk about me getting married. Especially in front of other people." The women's laughter echoed in his memory, and such heat filled his face he wondered if smoke rose from his scalp.

Cale scowled in confusion. "But why? You're old enough. Don't ya wanna marry up with some nice girl? Timothy says his sister's real nice. He thinks it'd be fine if you an' her—"

"It isn't up to Timothy." Amos spoke firmly, hoping to quell the boy. "Getting married is a personal decision. I have to choose for myself."

"So why not choose Ruthie?"

Amos tried to think of an answer that would satisfy the persistent boy, but none came. As Cale had said, Ruthie was a nice girl. A pretty one, too. Being a preacher's daughter, she'd have been raised right, and she didn't seem put off by his bum leg. There were several good reasons for him to choose Ruthie, but he had his heart set on someone else. However, he wasn't going to tell Cale and have the boy blab it to everyone in the schoolyard. Amos bit his tongue and stayed silent. Maybe refusing to answer would convince Cale to give up on the topic of him marrying Ruthie.

They stepped off the Main Street boardwalk and headed for the railroad tracks. Cale skipped ahead a few feet and walked sideways so he could look Amos straight in the face. "Didn't ya hear me? What's wrong with Ruthie, Uncle Amos? Huh?"

Amos sighed. He should know by now Cale wasn't easily quelled. He stopped and balled his hand on his hip. "I think you're a little young for this, but since you won't stop asking, I will tell you. I don't love Ruthie. A man shouldn't marry someone just because he's old enough to get married or because the girl is nice. A man should get married because he loves the woman and wants to build a life with her. Not only should a man love a woman before he takes her as his wife, but he should have the means to provide for her. I still have work to do before I can provide for a wife and a family." Longing nearly doubled him over. *Someday soon, Lord, please?* He finished in a quieter voice. "When I'm ready, I'll decide who I should marry."

Cale's face pinched into a scowl. "How will you know?"

"How will I know what?"

"How will you know when you're ready?"

Amos knew how to answer this question. "When the good Lord says so." A picture of Dinah Hubley as she'd knelt beside the wagon, laughing at the puppies, flooded his memory. How sweet she looked, how gently she stroked their little heads. Wouldn't she gaze down just as tenderly at a baby? He closed his eyes, imagining her cradling an infant in her arms.

Cale tugged at his sleeve. "Uncle Amos? Uncle Amos?"

With effort, Amos forced himself to focus on Cale. "What?"

Worry furrows formed across the boy's forehead. "When will the good Lord tell you? Will it be soon?"

Amos swallowed as the image of Dinah faded. "I don't know."

Cale stomped his foot. "Well, He's gotta hurry. 'Cause if you don't get married soon, I'm not gonna be able to stay with you. An' I don't wanna go someplace else."

Amos put his hand on Cale's shoulder, the sheriff's visit fresh in his memory, and spoke gently. "As I told you before, that isn't up to us. We have to let the New York preacher decide where you're to live."

Cale knocked Amos's hand aside and took a giant step away from him. "You don't care if I go away."

This surprise was greater than the first one. Hadn't he already proved to Cale how much he cared about him? He'd been feeding him, sheltering him, helping him with his homework, and even bought a second pair of clothes for him to wear. "Of course I do."

"No, you don't, or you'd do what you have to so I can stay. Well...well..." Cale raised his fists and glared at Amos. "Then I don't care, neither!" He took off running.

"Cale!" Amos grabbed the wagon handle and bolted after the boy in his hop-skip jog, but with two sturdy legs and no encumbrances, Cale outdistanced Amos within a few minutes. Grunting with irritation, he allowed himself to slow his pace. He'd reach home eventually and Cale would be waiting. Maybe by then the boy would have settled down enough for them to talk reasonably. Amos didn't know being a father could be so difficult. As he walked, he prayed for wisdom to know how to best handle Cale's anger, which he suspected was based on fear and disappointment. He'd do his best to be patient with the boy.

When he was less than a half mile from his house and his aching hip was shortening his stride, he heard Cale's frantic voice calling his name. Alarm sent chills across his frame. He released the wagon and broke into his clumsy trot. Cale came running, his face wet with tears and his eyes wide with horror. He fell into Amos's arms, pulling him to his knees. The boy sobbed against Amos's chest.

He tugged the boy loose and held him by the shoulders. "What is it, Cale? What's wrong?"

Shaking with sobs, Cale choked out, "There was a big dog in the pen! I chased him off, but the chickens—they're...they're dead!"

Chapter 22

Amos

The sun was setting, igniting streaks of bold pink and yellow in the pale sky by the time Amos buried the last of the dead birds near the row of hedge apple trees at the far edge of his property. Cale, his anger forgotten in the face of tragedy, sat off to the side with Samson and Gideon tucked beneath his arms, watching Amos pat the soil smooth. Although his sobs had faded, silent tears continued to roll down his cheeks.

Amos's heart ached. For the boy, who was so distraught. For the poor chickens, who'd been helpless against the attack of the dog. And even for himself. Such a loss… Thirteen dead birds, including the feisty rooster. It could have been worse. A pack of dogs might have wiped out his entire flock. The dog could have turned on Cale instead of running away. But Amos found it difficult to be grateful in light of what had been taken from him. Why hadn't he put the birds in the chicken house before leaving?

Propping the shovel on his shoulder, he turned to Cale. "That's the last of them. Let's go back to the house."

With a heavy sigh, Cale rose and scuffed along beside Amos, his shoulders slumping. Samson and Gideon seemed to reflect the humans' sadness, plodding rather than frisking, their ears drooping and their heads held low.

Cale followed Amos into the barn and watched him return the shovel to its hook on the wall. He trailed Amos to the roosts, his chin bumping Amos's elbow as he checked to be sure the eggs were still beneath the softly clucking hens. Then, so close the toes of his boots nearly touched Amos's heels, Cale followed him to the house. Inside, the boy got in the way while Amos prepared a simple supper, but he didn't scold. Cale needed comfort, and Amos needed it, too. So they took solace from each other's company. Not until they'd finished eating and were washing their plates did Cale finally speak.

"Uncle Amos, Sam an' Gid are dogs, an' they don't kill chickens. Why'd that dog do it?"

Amos's chest grew tight. "I don't know, Cale." He wished he had a better answer. A fox or other wild animal would have taken one and would have eaten it, leaving only feathers behind. But not one of the birds had been eaten. Just killed. Out of sport? Or meanness? He didn't understand why the animal had attacked his flock, but right after he deposited Cale at school tomorrow, he intended to hunt it down and keep it from attacking anyone else's barnyard creatures. He said, more bitterly than he intended, "Why do animals or people choose to do hurtful things? I suppose only God knows the answer to questions like this."

Cale hung his head. "I didn't even like that big ol' rooster. But it still makes me sad he's dead."

For the second time that day, Cale moved into Amos's arms. He didn't cry but just clung, his face pressed against Amos's chest. He held him for as long as he wanted, and then when the boy finally pulled back, Amos gave his skinny shoulders a gentle pat. "Go to bed now. Things will look brighter in the morning."

Cale tipped his head and gave Amos a pleading look. "Can Sam an' Gid sleep in here with me tonight?"

Every night Cale had asked the same question, and every night Amos had refused. He didn't want the pups thinking the house was their domain. But tonight he said, "Go get them." And Cale dashed off.

While Cale slept, Amos sat at the table, sipped strong coffee, and contemplated the setback the wild dog had created with its rampage. Nine of the dead birds were hens of laying age. It would take months before the eggs in the brooding roosts hatched and the chickens grew large enough to produce eggs. If at least nine of the hatchlings were girls, he'd be able to replace the lost hens, but he wouldn't gain more layers to meet the needs of the hotel kitchen.

And, his thoughts continued as a bitter ache settled in his chest, it meant postponing providing for a family.

"Why, God?" He whispered the question in the quiet room. He listened for a long time, but no answer came.

Dinah

No, no, please… Not again… Dinah awakened with a soft moan, her body drenched in sweat. She blinked into the dark room, confused and frightened, her heart thumping at twice its normal rhythm. She was in Florence in her room at the Clifton Hotel, not in the room at the fancy hotel in Chicago. She was *safe*. Safe…

She worked so hard each day—deliberately worked herself to exhaustion. Worked hard to prove herself worthy, and worked hard so she wouldn't have to *think*. During the daytime hours she mostly managed to keep the images at bay, but at night—oh, at night—they crept back to haunt her and rob her of the rest she needed.

Beside her, Ruthie slept soundly, unaware of Dinah's turmoil. If only she possessed the ability to remain peacefully asleep all through the night. She'd sometimes been troubled by nightmares as a child, and she learned to roll into a tight ball and whisper comforting words in the darkness until she calmed herself. But here she didn't dare tuck up her knees the way she had in her younger years—the bed was so narrow she'd surely bump Ruthie and waken her. She couldn't whisper to herself, either, without Ruthie hearing. So Dinah forced herself to take slow, deep breaths. Eventually the wild thump in her chest calmed and her body ceased to tremble.

Tired but afraid she'd return to the same place she'd just left behind, she lay with her eyes wide open. Bits and snatches of the dream continued to play in her mind's eye—disjointed images of a leering face, accompanied by feelings of helplessness, terror, and pain. Her heart begged for freedom from the ugly memories. When, *when* would they finally leave her for good?

Ruthie mumbled, a soft mutter ending with a sigh. Dinah blinked back tears. Obviously Ruthie's dreams were pleasant ones. But why shouldn't they be? Ruthie had grown up as part of a loving family in a small town where no brothels tempted men to squander their time and money. Everything Dinah had ever wanted—two parents, siblings, a happy home—Ruthie had always had. In that moment Dinah envied Ruthie with such ferocity she nearly forgot to breathe. Why did good come to some people and not to others? Why did she have to be one of the "others"?

"God loves you very much." Ah, those words again… Just as the nightmares haunted her, the statement Ruthie made on Dinah's first day in Florence repeatedly played through her mind. No matter how many times she tried to ignore it or argue against it or scoff in disbelief, the comment returned to tease her heart with the desire to accept it as truth.

In the dark room, with distressing images of her frightening dream still lingering in her memory, she chose to let the words soak in and chase away the vestiges of unpleasantness. Just as sunshine sent golden light over shadows, dispelling the murky gray, the simple statement—*"God loves you very much"*— flowed gentle peace through Dinah's frame. Slowly, hesitantly, she let her eyes slip closed. No leering face appeared behind her closed lids.

And then another voice spoke from past days. *"I hope to see you at service on Sunday…"* An image of Mr. Ackerman, his face wearing a gentle smile and his eyes shining with sincerity, filled her mind. Remembrances of his kindness to her, his sweet apologies, even his tenderness to the floppy-eared dogs and the little boy named Cale paraded through her memory. With each sweet remembrance, the ugly one retreated further and further into the recesses of her mind, and her body relaxed until a grateful sigh whisked from her throat.

She could sleep now. And come morning, when the others climbed in the buggy for the ride to the clapboard chapel where Ruthie's father preached, Dinah would go, too. She still wasn't sure that God loved her very much, but contemplating the possibility had given her peace. So she would go to His house and tell Him thank you.

And she'd also give Mr. Ackerman a smile. It was the least she could do after all his kindness to her.

Amos

Amos jolted and stared in disbelief when he entered the chapel. She was there, on the back bench, and the moment she saw him, she smiled. The shock of finding Dinah Hubley in church, of seeing her face light with the most beautiful smile he'd ever seen, stole the bones from his legs. He dropped into his familiar seat, and his backside collided with the wooden surface hard enough to hurt, but what did he care? She was there. And she was smiling.

Smiling. At him.

Cale hadn't even had a chance to sit down before Preacher Mead invited the congregation to rise for the opening hymn. Amos wasn't sure his legs would support him—he quivered from head to toe in suppressed happiness—but he pushed himself upright and tried to sing. However, the furious pounding in his chest kept him from drawing enough breath to support the words.

So instead, he stood gazing at Dinah, who peeked at him out of the corner of her eye, a shy smile toying at the corner of her lips and cheeks blushing a rosy red. He'd asked God to open Dinah's heart to him if he was meant to pursue her. And here she was, in his church, at his bench, with a smile on her face that could melt the hardest soul.

And she chose to offer it when he couldn't possibly respond to it.

He bowed his head and battled a wave of regret. *God, I can't court a girl unless I have the means to provide for her. Why would You give me hope that she might find me acceptable when You know the loss I just suffered at my farm?*

Caught up in his thoughts, he didn't realize the hymn had ended and everyone had sat until a rumble of stifled chortles rolled through the room. He glanced first at Cale, noting the boy's impish grin, and then at Dinah, who gazed to the side. Her face was a bolder pink than before. He sat so quickly the bench legs squeaked against the floor. A few more titters escaped, but then Preacher Mead began his sermon and people turned their attention elsewhere.

As hard as he tried, Amos could not focus on the preacher's message. His awareness of Dinah went too deep for anything else to penetrate. He wanted to question her reason for attending. Had she come because of him? Why had she chosen his bench for her place in the chapel? Why had she smiled at him after so many weeks of carefully looking away? But he didn't know if he'd have the courage to ask the many questions, or if she would have the time to stay long enough to answer.

When the service ended, Cale dashed off with Timothy Mead, leaving Amos and Dinah standing side by side in the little space between benches. He should step aside and let her pass, but she made no effort to leave, so he stayed in place, gathering his courage to ask the questions plaguing him.

With the other people visiting and laughing as they filed from the chapel into the yard, Amos believed no one would overhear him. His heart pounding in both eagerness and apprehension, he leaned forward a little. "Miss Hubley? I wondered—"

"Hello, Mr. Ackerman!" The cheerful voice interrupted from behind Amos.

Amos made a slight turn. Miss Mead stood in the aisle, beaming at him. Cale's comments about marrying her rose in his memory and a worry struck. Had her younger brother repeated Cale's words to her? He battled the urge to duck beneath the bench and hide. But courtesy demanded he remain upright and acknowledge her. "Hello, Miss Mead. How are you today?"

"I'm very happy."

"That's good." He started to turn to Dinah again.

"Because Mama told me she finished my new gown for the Calico Ball." Miss Mead was still talking, and Amos felt obliged to look at her again. She raised her shoulders and clasped her hands beneath her chin as she smiled at Amos. "I'm so excited to attend. I went last year, too, and had such an enjoyable night." She paused and bit her lower lip. "Are…are you going to the ball, Mr. Ackerman?"

Amos attend a dance? He nearly laughed. He couldn't even walk gracefully. He'd only humiliate himself by stumbling around on a dance floor. But if Miss Mead was going, then she—and Dinah, too—must have the evening free. If Dinah was at the dance and he went to the dance, then he would have the time he needed to talk to her, to get to know her better, to find out if her smile meant what he hoped it meant. He couldn't court her—not yet. But he could find out if she would be open to it when he'd built his flock again.

He jerked to face Dinah so quickly he almost lost his balance. When he regained his footing, his voice escaped in a breathless rush. "Will you be at the Calico Ball?"

An odd little squawk, as if someone had swallowed a gnat, sounded from behind him. Then Miss Mead's disbelieving voice filled his ears. "Are you inviting Dinah to the ball?"

Dinah's eyes widened and her lips parted in an expression of wonder. He'd seen the same look—a look of pleased astonishment—on her face when he agreed to name the puppies Samson and Gideon. Did it really take so little to delight her? What would she say if he asked her to attend? He had to know.

"Yes. That's what I'm doing." He pinned his gaze to her larkspur-blue eyes, noting a sheen of moisture had brightened the pale irises. "Miss Hubley, would you go to the Calico Ball? With me?"

Chapter 23

Dinah

inah's heart fluttered like a moth caught in a jelly jar. Maybe she'd been wrong. Maybe, sometimes, fairy tales could come true. Mr. Ackerman—the kindest man she'd ever met—wanted to take her to the Calico Ball. She held her breath, savoring the sweet moment. When her chest felt ready to explode, she expelled her lungful of air and uttered, "Oh, yes," in a breathy rush.

The smile that broke across his face brought tears to her eyes. After a lifetime of being shoved aside, Dinah finally had someone who wanted to be with her. She had never experienced such deep happiness. Her feet itched to dance right there in the church. Then his smile wavered as a hint of apprehension pinched his features. She flicked a glance at Ruthie, who stood in the aisle as if the soles of her shoes had sent down roots, and a worrisome thought trailed through her mind. Had he made a mistake? Did he want to take Ruthie instead? She braced herself for rejection as he parted his lips to speak.

"Miss Hubley, I need to apologize…again."

Dinah hung her head, battling tears of fierce disappointment.

"My feet… They're too clumsy to move to music. So if we go together, I won't be able to escort you onto the dance floor."

She jerked her gaze to meet his, blinking to clear her vision to better examine his contrite face. Realization bloomed through her heart, bringing a fresh rush of joy. He didn't regret asking her. He regretted not being able to dance with her. She couldn't stop a smile from growing on her face. "I don't know how to dance, either."

His eyebrows rose. "A pretty girl like you has never been to a dance?"

"Flo told me you were a pretty little thing." The voice swooped in, bringing a chill that shuddered her frame. Dinah hugged herself and shook her head, unable to push words past her tight throat.

"Well, then, you should have the chance to fully enjoy this one. If you want to allow other men to sign your dance card, I won't mind."

"Oh! No, I..." She was speaking too shrilly. She unfolded her arms, forcing herself to relax her stiff stance. "I don't mind just watching." But she'd not been completely truthful. Hadn't she always been on the outside, watching others seek and find happiness? She wanted to be part of the circles of people who talked, laughed, and danced. But being invited was so much more than she'd ever expected. She could be happy watching the other attendees dance. She added, with complete honesty, "Thank you for asking me, Mr. Ackerman."

He leaned forward, bringing his mouth close to her ear. He whispered, so sweetly her heart ached, "Thank you for accepting."

Ruthie reached past Mr. Ackerman, caught Dinah's arm, and gave a jerk. "The buggy is here. We have to go."

Dinah didn't even have time to bid Mr. Ackerman farewell as Ruthie dragged her out the door and across the yard to the waiting buggy. The moment after they climbed in, Dean brought down the reins and the horses jolted into motion, sending Dinah smartly against the back of the seat and Minnie's shoulder. Minnie grunted and wriggled sideways a tiny bit. Dinah shot the girl an apologetic look, but Minnie didn't seem to notice.

As the buggy rolled from the churchyard, Ruthie announced, "Dinah has been asked to attend the Calico Ball."

Minnie's head turned so sharply Dinah marveled that her neck didn't crack. "You have?"

Amelia and Lyla shifted to peek over their shoulders at Dinah, their eyes alight with interest. Amelia squealed, "Oh, myyyy! You're so lucky. We servers have to take care of the food tables, so we can't attend with a gentleman."

Lyla pinched Amelia's arm. "We couldn't attend with a gentleman even if we didn't have to take care of the food tables. Our contract prohibits courting." The jealousy in her voice startled Dinah. Had anyone ever been jealous of her?

Matilda leaned across Minnie and aimed an interested look at Dinah. "Who asked you?"

Dinah held on to the scrolled-iron armrest. They were all looking at her—well, all but Ruthie, who stared straight ahead with her arms folded tightly over her chest. They envied her. All of them. Delightful shivers raced up and down Dinah's spine. She allowed herself a moment to bask in their attention before offering a reply. "Mr. Ackerman."

Matilda's eyes bugged. "Mr. Ackerman? You mean the man who limps all over town selling eggs?" She burst into gales of laughter.

Lyla and Minnie joined her, their hoots of merriment like knives in Dinah's heart. Amelia nudged Lyla, frowning, then hunched her shoulders and giggled. Even Dean barked out a guffaw.

Minnie announced, "Of all the eligible men in town, he's the last one with whom I'd attend a dance."

Matilda snickered. "I bet he's good at waltzing, though. With his limp, he'd go round and round and round…"

Dean roared and the servers' giggles grew louder as they competed with one another in adding teasing comments about Mr. Ackerman's limp, the bits of feathers decorating his clothes, and the little wooden wagon he used as his delivery conveyance.

Dinah's frame went hot to cold. Fury built in her chest. Their words were hurtful. Belittling. She wanted to defend Mr. Ackerman, but just as she'd stood mute before the taunts of her former classmates, her tongue remained incapable of forming words now.

"Stop it!"

Dinah nearly leaped out of her skin at Ruthie's curt command. The others' remarks and laughter abruptly stopped.

With her hands balled into fists, Ruthie glared at the other girls. "You should all be ashamed of yourselves, disparaging Mr. Ackerman for something over which he has no control. Would you want to be teased for your freckles, Minnie? Or for the gap between your front teeth, Amelia?"

Bright red flooded Minnie's face, masking the tiny dots of pale brown that marched from her forehead to her chin. Amelia sucked in her lips and ducked her head. Both Lyla and Matilda shrank back as if fearful of what Ruthie might say about them.

Ruthie went on, speaking so harshly Dinah cringed. "You are criticizing him for being a hard worker, for making an honest living! And you're poking fun at his misfortune, which I find particularly disturbing. Mr. Ackerman is exactly the kind of man every girl should desire for a beau. He is respectful, industrious, and possesses strong faith in God. Mr. Ackerman has done nothing to earn your disdain. Every one of you should ask God to forgive you for your unkindness. And then you should tell Dinah you're sorry for being so rude to her."

Minnie, Amelia, and Matilda continued to stare at Ruthie in silence, but Lyla released a light, self-conscious giggle. "My, my, Ruthie. If I didn't know better, I'd say you were smitten with the chicken farmer."

Pink splashed Ruthie's cheeks. "So what if I am? As I said, there is much to admire about Mr. Ackerman. And if he had asked me to the Calico Ball, I...I would have proudly accepted his invitation, just as Dinah has done." She shifted slightly to cast a regret-filled look on Dinah. "If I'd known how they were going to react, I wouldn't have mentioned the invitation you received. Everything they said was out of jealous spite." Ruthie paused, nibbling her lower lip. "And I suppose I told them because I was jealous, too. I hope you will forgive me, Dinah."

The others all muttered apologies, although with less sincerity than Ruthie. Then Matilda sent a sheepish look across the other girls. "You know, Mr. Ackerman is handsome."

"He has very broad shoulders," Minnie said, fluttering her lashes, "and strong hands. I like a man who has strong hands."

Lyla and Amelia added their praises as Dean brought the buggy to a stop outside the hotel's doors. The girls continued jabbering while they departed the buggy and darted for the porch.

Dinah and Ruthie climbed out last, and Ruthie looped arms with Dinah as they ambled up the walkway. "Please don't let what the others said bother you, Dinah." Ruthie released a deep sigh. "They want to go to the ball, too, and since they know they can't, they feel the need to ridicule the event and those who are attending."

Dinah gently removed her arm from Ruthie's grasp. "Why should I care what the others think?" She forced a glib tone, although her lips quivered with her smile. "I'm going to the ball." Just like Cinderella in the storybook. She didn't care a whit if her prince limped.

"Good for you." Ruthie flashed a quick yet somehow sad-looking smile. "We'd better get busy." She darted off.

Dinah headed up the hallway to begin her duties, but she didn't hurry as Ruthie did. Troubling thoughts plagued her despite her effort to set them aside. The girls' praises for Mr. Ackerman had only come after Ruthie proclaimed her interest in him. In the others' eyes, he hadn't been worthy of affection until Ruthie had deemed him so.

The realization stung. Her opinion didn't matter. Nor did her feelings. Not to the servers. Just as she'd never really mattered to her mother or to her schoolmates or her teacher or Miss Flo… She took the feather duster from her basket of cleaning supplies and gave a vicious swipe across the surface of the room's dressing table. Tiny particles sailed through the yellow beam from the wall's gaslight and rained downward in a silvery explosion.

She met her gaze in the mirror, assumed a firm expression, and pointed at her reflection with the splayed feathers on the duster. "But you matter to Mr. Ackerman." Warmth flowed from her head to her toes, and tears pricked her eyes. "You must matter because he invited you to the Calico Ball. So think of him instead of everyone else."

As she set to work again, she inwardly listed the reasons why Mr. Ackerman was a worthwhile prospect. Handsome. Strong. Hardworking. Honest. And, as Ruthie had said, he was a godly man. Dinah knew very little about God, but if God loved her the way Ruthie claimed and if Mr. Ackerman was a godly man, then she trusted him not to hurt her. She didn't understand why she knew this, but from the very center of her being, she believed she could trust Mr. Ackerman.

"He will be my prince…" One warm tear rolled down her cheek, tickling her as it trailed to her chin. With the belief came a lightness in her chest that tempted her feet to give vent to the happiness inside. Extending her hands, still with the feather duster in her grip, she twirled on one toe in the middle of the room. She ended her spontaneous pirouette with a giggle that doubled her over. Was this how it felt to be smitten? Oh, if it were, it was a glorious thing. She positioned herself for another swirl.

"Miss Hubley, I would like a word with you." The manager's stern voice carried from the open doorway.

Dinah froze for the beat of three seconds with her hands outstretched and the toe of her shoe planted against the plush carpet. Then she quickly dropped the carefree pose and turned to face the unsmiling man. "Y-yes, Mr. Irwin." She scurried toward the door, her stomach quaking.

Amos

"Yes, Sheriff." Amos heard himself speak calmly and wondered how he managed, considering how his insides were flopping like a trout on a creek bank. When the sheriff had ridden up the lane, Amos had expected a casual greeting. Who'd have thought the long-awaited telegram would arrive on the Lord's day? "Tomorrow morning, I'll bring Cale to your office. Thank you for letting him spend this last night with me so we can…" A lump filled his throat, and he couldn't finish his sentence.

The sheriff nodded, his face creasing into a sympathetic grimace. "I know you've grown fond of the boy, but I have to agree with the preacher in New York. Boys, especially ones as young as Cale, need raising by both a ma and a pa."

Amos knew the sheriff was right, but it didn't make saying good-bye any easier. "Do you know where he'll be living?"

"The city preacher—name of Reverend Silas Joiner—gave me responsibility for finding a home for the boy." The sheriff scratched his head. "That's a little outside my usual duties, so I asked Preacher Mead to locate a family. Soon as I know, I'll be sure and tell you. Maybe you can visit him from time to time if he ends up close enough to Florence."

The thought cheered Amos somewhat. He bade the sheriff farewell, then waited until the man swung himself onto his saddle and aimed his horse for the road. Then Amos scuffed out to the patch of ground behind the barn where Cale had taken the pups to play. He leaned against the sturdy barn wall and watched the three of them for a few minutes, smiling.

Cale had taken it upon himself to teach the pair of puppies to perform tricks like a street vendor's dog in New York. Amos didn't see much sense in dogs rolling over, shaking hands, or sitting up on their back legs, but Cale seemed to think it a fine thing, and it wouldn't do Sam and Gid any harm. Maybe he'd keep working with the dogs after Cale left, just so they might remember the boy. He'd never forget Cale—that was certain.

His heart heavy, Amos took a forward step. "Cale?"

The boy paused with one hand stretched over Gideon's nose and the other holding Samson by the ruff. His face lit up. "Hey, Uncle Amos, watch this!" He turned a serious look on Gideon. "Stand. Stand, Gid." He bounced his hand, and Gideon rose up on his haunches and nosed Cale's palm. He scratched Gid's ears, grinning broadly. "Good dog!" He aimed his grin at Amos. "Did'ja see it? He stood up, just like I wanted him to!"

Amos thought the pup had just lunged upward to see if Cale had anything of worth in his hand, but he chose not to discourage the boy. "Yes, I saw. Now bring Sam and Gid to the house. I need to talk to you."

Cale's expression went from happy to stubborn in the space of one pulse beat. "Why?"

Amos could be stubborn, too. "Because I asked you to. That's reason enough." He turned toward the house and took two plodding steps.

"If you're plannin' to send me away, I ain't goin'."

Amos paused but refused to turn around. Partly so the boy wouldn't know he'd gotten Amos's dander up, but mostly because saying good-bye was hard enough without having to look into Cale's angry face. "Sam, Gid—come!"

Amos snapped his fingers. The pups raced to him. He set himself in motion again. "Come on to the house, Cale."

Trusting the boy to follow, Amos crossed the yard and entered the house. He left the door open, but Samson and Gideon plopped down on an old rug he'd put on the porch and didn't enter. They were smart dogs. And Cale was a smart boy. Eventually he'd come to understand Amos wasn't sending him away out of meanness but because it was the best thing to do.

He'd barely settled himself at the table when Cale stepped over the threshold. He stood just inside the door, hands deep in his pockets and feet set wide apart, scowling. Amos pointed to the chair across from him. "Come on."

Cale held out for a few seconds, working his jaw back and forth and squinting. But finally he let out a huff and stomped to the table. He flopped into the seat and threw one arm over the chair's ladder back, as insolent as Amos had ever seen him. "All right. Whaddid you want?"

Amos frowned. "First of all, sit up and behave yourself. You're too fine a boy to act so uncivil."

In slow motion Cale brought his arm down from its floppy position and rested his linked hands on the edge of the table. Although he still held his lips in a sulky line, Amos decided to ignore it. This wasn't easy for Cale, either.

"It's time, Cale. The sheriff wants me to bring you to his office tomorrow. He and Preacher Mead will take you to your new home."

Cale sat up ramrod straight. "Where?"

"He didn't tell me. I'm not sure he knows yet. But Preacher Mead won't give you over to someone who won't take good care of you." Amos found comfort in his words. He hoped Cale would be comforted, too. "You don't need to worry."

"But I don't wanna go. I like it here. Like it better'n anyplace else I ever been." A thread of panic wove its way through the boy's tone. "An' you need me! I help with the chickens. I help with Sam an' Gid. You need me, Uncle Amos."

Amos placed his big hand over Cale's joined hands. His palm easily covered them. Cale was so young. So small. A wave of protectiveness swept over him. *God, put him with a family who will love him and teach him Your ways.* "Somewhere, Cale, there's a family who needs a boy like you. And you need them—a family with a father and a mother. That's what every boy needs."

Cale yanked his hands away. "So get me a mother. It ain't gotta be that hard. People get married all the time. Timothy told me so—says his pa's always speakin' the words for folks. If you'd get married, then I could stay. You could be my pa."

Pressure built in Amos's chest. An intense, deep ache. If only his flock were bigger. Then he could afford to take a wife. Then he could keep Cale. Assuming, of course, his wife would want the boy, too. Somehow he sensed Dinah wouldn't send Cale away. But the timing was all wrong.

He spoke gently. "The decision's been made. It's out of my hands. We have to do what the minister in New York says. So tomorrow you're going to Preacher Mead and then on to your new home."

Cale's gaze narrowed, his eyes shooting darts of fury.

"We don't have to like it." Amos pulled in a big breath and let it go in a mighty whoosh. "But we still have to do it. Do you understand?"

Cale angled his face away from Amos. His jaw quivered. He muttered, the words emerging on a growl, "Sure, mister. I understand."

Chapter 24

Dinah

inah left Mr. Irwin's office with his warnings ringing in her head. Someone must surely be very jealous to have run to him with the news of her invitation to the Calico Ball. But she would do everything Mr. Irwin said was necessary. She would finish her work before changing into her ball gown. At the ball she would conduct herself with the decorum expected of an employee of the hotel. And until the day of the ball, she would keep her attention on the tasks required of her rather than escaping into flights of whimsy.

Her face flamed with humiliation as she hurried back upstairs. How silly she must have looked, waving the feather duster and twirling like a child! If Ruthie had caught her instead of Mr. Irwin, she wouldn't have been quite so embarrassed. Ruthie seemed to understand Dinah's excitement. At least partially. No one understood the deepest reasons why the invitation meant so much. And no one ever would, because she wouldn't tell.

Would she have ever imagined a man like Amos Ackerman asking her to attend a ball? No. Never. Yet he had. A niggle of guilt pricked. Would he have asked her if he knew who she was...and what she'd done? She shook her head hard. She wasn't that girl anymore. What mattered was now. No longer Untamable Tori's unfortunate mistake, she was one of Mr. Fred Harvey's employees. Perhaps only a chambermaid in the Clifton Hotel now, but in nine more months when she turned eighteen, she would become—

She came to a stop right outside the door of the room she'd vacated at Mr. Irwin's interruption. She hadn't come to Kansas to be courted. When had she lost sight of her reason for accepting the position as chambermaid? She hovered in the doorway, as if it were a portal between two choices. Stay with her original intention to secure a position that would grant her the respect she'd never previously received, or move forward into the new opportunity that seemed to be presenting itself?

Ruthie had scolded the servers with the statement that any girl should be pleased to be courted by Mr. Ackerman. He'd asked her to the ball. Which meant—oh, how her heart pounded—he could very well be interested in courting her. A man didn't invite a girl to something as important as the Calico Ball unless he truly liked her. But if she went, if she allowed herself to be courted, she wouldn't be able to become a server after all. Servers weren't allowed to court or marry during the year of their contract.

Which did she want more—to become a well-respected server or to have a beau?

As the golden days of September slipped away and October arrived with chilly nights and naked tree branches tapping their tips together in the wind, Dinah struggled with the question. During the weekdays when she performed her cleaning duties and observed the servers in their crisp telltale uniforms signifying them as Mr. Harvey's specially chosen workers, she convinced herself she must set aside thoughts of all else except donning one of those uniforms for herself. But on Sundays when she sat on the back bench with a respectable space between herself and Mr. Ackerman and peeked at the Bible he held in his broad hand for her to share, she longed for something entirely different.

The confusion wore at her, stealing what little sleep she caught between the persistent nightmares. Ruthie expressed concern about the dark circles beneath Dinah's eyes and questioned whether she needed a tonic, but Dinah knew of no tonic that would cure uncertainty. So as the days moved steadily toward October 19—the night of the Calico Ball—Dinah accepted she wouldn't find her answer until she'd experienced her evening of enchantment with Mr. Ackerman.

Amos

Amos moved as fast as his bad leg would allow up the road toward town. Cooler, damp weather had descended, giving the landscape a gloomy appearance. The cool always made his hip ache worse, and he grimaced against the discomfort. He missed having Cale walk with him. But if the boy was still with the Meads, as he'd been for the past two weeks, he'd see him in church. He looked forward to a little time with Cale, as well as with his fellow believers. Sundays were his favorite days, because for the hour of the service, he wasn't alone.

And today he would stay after church and enjoy a meal with the Mead family. They'd invited him last week, but he had declined since a new batch of chicks was breaking free of the shells, and he liked to be close by during the process. Sadly, two of the new ones had drowned in their watering dish, and another had apparently suffocated beneath the straw. The losses, added to the dismal gray weather, had combined to create a difficult week for him. But surely time at the Meads' table with the preacher's lively family would give his heart a lift.

And then on Friday, there was the ball…

He'd never anticipated anything as much as he looked forward to the night of music, eating, and visiting. So what if he'd only eat and visit rather than dance? He didn't mind because Dinah had said she didn't mind. And he would have three hours to visit with her. Three hours! His pulse stuttered in happiness. The few minutes he'd grabbed after church services these past Sundays had only heightened his desire to get to know her better.

Such a delicate, pretty girl she was, with a gentle and humble spirit. Ma would like her—Amos felt sure. And once they'd spent their evening together—when they'd finally become well acquainted—he would write to Ma and tell her all about Dinah. In Ma's last letter she'd asked, "Aren't there any girls of marriageable age in that church of yours? It's high time you settled in with a family." He agreed, and he hoped to do just that. But first, he needed those hours of the ball with Dinah. To be sure the little seed of affection planted in his heart was meant to bloom.

Dinah was already at the back bench, as he'd come to expect, when he limped into the church. The singing had already commenced, too, so he stepped into his familiar spot, swept off his hat, and joined his voice to the others joyfully singing of the holy God. Dinah was singing today, too, and he gave her a smile of approval. In her shyness, she rarely participated in hymn singing. Her doing so now told him she was feeling more at home here, just as he'd prayed she would. Some of the gloominess of the past days melted away as he listened to her soft, reedy voice blend with his.

He shared his Bible with her, finding it difficult to concentrate with the sweet scent of her floral soap filling his nostrils. But the sermon was a good one about the shepherd seeking the lost lamb of his large flock and expressing the determination of Jesus, the Good Shepherd, to bring every soul into His flock—none were so lost that the loving Savior would abandon His search for them. Hearing of Jesus's love for him always brought joy to his heart, and the minister's words seemed to impact Dinah, as well, for she listened more intently than he'd seen before.

When the service ended, he enjoyed a few short words with Dinah, telling her he would meet her in the hotel's lobby at eight thirty on Friday night. She blushed prettily when he gave the reminder. He found the sight so appealing he gripped the brim of his hat to keep from cupping her cheeks and lifting her face to him. Wouldn't she make a beautiful bride? Impatience smote him. He wished he had the means to provide for her now. When she scurried out to meet the buggy and return to the hotel, he gazed after her, battling loneliness. But then Cale bounded over and caught Amos's hand, and he turned his attention to the boy.

Amos walked with Cale and Timothy to the Meads' house. Mrs. Mead seated Amos next to Cale at the long table in the warm kitchen that held the wonderful aromas of the food she prepared to feed the family's growing brood. As everyone settled into chairs and Mrs. Mead carried full bowls and platters to the table, Amos noted the difference between the smell of the Meads' kitchen and his own. His smelled of beans and salt pork—not unpleasant but of a bachelor's dwelling. This one, though… He inhaled deeply, savoring the unique fragrance. It smelled like home. He hoped his kitchen would smell just this way someday.

Preacher Mead offered a prayer of gratitude for the food and the hands that had prepared it. Amos echoed the prayer in his heart. How had the woman managed to prepare such a feast and have it all ready, hot and aromatic, the moment they returned from the church? His mother had possessed the same ability. Women were sometimes magical creatures.

Amos enjoyed every bite of the crusty bread, roasted meat swimming in rich gravy, oven-browned potatoes, and buttery green peas. He also enjoyed the conversation flowing around the table as they ate. But as much as he enjoyed himself, he also fought against melancholy. Sitting here surrounded by happy chatter and pleasant scents, his little house seemed to grow more empty, his solitary existence more dismal by the moment. The upcoming Friday, when he could talk with Dinah, express his deep desire for family, and discover whether she desired the same, seemed so far away.

Mrs. Mead brought out apple pies for dessert. As she placed a large slice before Amos, he said, "This is the best meal I've had since I left my ma's cooking, Mrs. Mead. Thank you for sharing it with me."

Mrs. Mead released a light laugh and moved on to serve Cale. "Now, Mr. Ackerman, you know you shouldn't fib. Especially on Sunday in a preacher's house."

Amos blinked at her in surprise. "I'm not fibbing, ma'am."

She smiled as she rounded the table, dishing up juicy slices of pie to her waiting children. "Now, now, I'm only teasing. Our Ruthie told us you'd had a meal at the Clifton's dining room. Everyone says Mr. Harvey stole the hotel's manager away from Chicago because he is the best chef in America. I'm sure the meal he set the cook to making there was better than this simple dinner."

Amos lifted the first bite of pie. The cinnamon-laced apples melted on his tongue. He shook his head. "Ma'am, if Mr. Harvey had tasted your cooking, he would have asked you to cook for the hotel instead."

Both the preacher and Mrs. Mead laughed, but Amos could tell he'd pleased her with his comments. When his wife cooked for him, he would remember to praise her often for the meals she put on their table.

After the children finished their pie, they dashed off to play, leaving the three adults at the table. Amos started to rise and head home, but Mrs. Mead put her hand on his wrist. "Stay, Mr. Ackerman. Have a cup of coffee with Jacob and me and visit a bit. That is, if you have time."

Return to his lonely house or stay here and talk for a while? The choice was easy to make. Amos settled back into his chair. "Thank you, ma'am."

While Mrs. Mead cleared the dishes, Preacher Mead rested his elbows on the table edge and fixed his attention on Amos. "Many of my parishioners speak well of your egg business and appreciate having eggs delivered to their houses. Will you be able to continue the deliveries when winter sets in?"

Amos took a sip of the coffee—strong and black, just the way he liked it— before answering. "I'd hoped to have enough money set aside for a horse and wagon before the snows fell, but I think I will probably have to wait for another year at least." He considered sharing the troubles that had befallen him lately, but a preacher probably had to listen to everyone's calamities. He would let the man enjoy his Sunday in peace. "Until then, I will deliver eggs on the days when the wind isn't too strong or the snow too deep for me to come into town."

"You have a good work ethic."

Mrs. Mead's compliment made Amos blush in pleased embarrassment. "Well, the chickens do most of the work."

Both the minister and his wife laughed. Then Mrs. Mead's face pinched in sympathy. "It must be difficult for you, though, with your leg. Or is it your foot that gives you pain?"

Amos didn't mind talking about his injury when people asked kindly. "My hip. I broke it when I was a boy, and it didn't heal correctly." Lest he sound like a complainer, he added, "But I manage. The Lord has given me the strength to endure."

Mrs. Mead gave him another warm, approving look before continuing her cleanup.

Preacher Mead said, "Cale tells us often how he helped you at the chicken farm. Are you managing well without him?"

The chores weren't too much. It took longer on his own, but he could get them done. He mostly missed the company. He wasn't sure how to reply, so he chose a question instead. "Have you found a family to take in the boy yet?"

Preacher Mead and his wife exchanged a look, as if seeking permission. The woman gave a slight nod, and the minister cleared his throat. "Yes, I think we have."

Amos's heart fell. As much as he knew Cale needed to get settled with a family quickly, he'd still clung to hope he might be able to take the boy himself. He took another sip of his coffee to drown the sadness rising in his chest. "Who will be his new family?"

"Us."

Startled, Amos looked from Mrs. Mead to Preacher Mead. Had he heard correctly? "You are keeping him?"

Mrs. Mead placed the last of the dirty dishes on the dry sink and returned to the table. "Yes." Preacher Mead took her hand and squeezed it. The two smiled at each other, leaving Amos feeling like an interloper.

Amos's thought spilled from his lips. "But you already have so many children."

The pair laughed, and Preacher Mead looked at Amos. "I suppose with five boys already in the house, it would seem we have no need for another one. But our oldest and youngest have always been very close, with Joseph looking at Seth almost like another father. Noah and Jonah, being so close in age, are best buddies. So Timothy was left out until Cale came along. It's as if our family was waiting for another boy so Timothy would feel as if he belongs."

Mrs. Mead added, "Cale and Timothy have become such good friends. To separate them now would be cruel. So Jacob and I decided, what's one more boy? An even eight children gives us a full quiver."

Amos recalled his father speaking of his full quiver of sons, quoting the verse from Psalm 127, but Pa had considered three enough. Amos wouldn't mind having as many as eight children in his quiver if the Lord chose to bless him. But discovering Cale wouldn't be one of them pierced him. "Well... well..." He didn't know what to say.

Mrs. Mead slid into the chair next to her husband. "Cale speaks so highly of you, Mr. Ackerman. I can tell you'd be a good father."

Amos lowered his head. Her words pleased him. "Thank you, ma'am."

She went on in the same pert tone. "There are several young women in our congregation who would make fine wives. Have you considered courting?"

Preacher Mead cleared his throat. "Leah..."

Mrs. Mead crinkled her nose at her husband. She looked very girlish despite the threads of white in her red hair and the fine lines around her eyes. "Oh, now, Jacob, I'm not pressuring him." She looked at Amos again. "Forgive me if I seem nosy. But a young man as yourself, with his own prospering business, is probably eager to begin his family. Am I right?"

Amos shrugged, chuckled softly, then nodded.

Her smile grew. "And have you found a young woman who interests you?"

Again, a soft chuckle escaped before he managed a quick nod. "Yes. She attends your church. Her name is Dinah Hubley."

Mrs. Mead jerked slightly, and a look of disappointment flittered across her face before she formed a smile again. "Dinah...a very sweet girl. She works at the Clifton with our daughter Ruthie."

Amos nodded. "I am taking Miss Hubley to the Calico Ball on Friday. I don't know for sure that I will court her, but..." Why was he telling the preacher's wife all this? Apparently he spent too much time with only chickens and two speckled dogs for company. Embarrassed, he fell silent.

Preacher Mead lifted his coffee cup, a silent invitation for his wife to refill it. She rose, and he turned to Amos. "Ruthie asked her mother and me to pray for Miss Hubley. Ruthie is concerned for Miss Hubley's lack of faith."

Amos frowned. "But she attends the church. Your daughter invited her." He was grateful Dinah had set aside whatever misgivings she'd held about the simple church and accepted the invitation. He couldn't court an unchurched woman, but her attendance had reassured him. Preacher Mead's odd statement raised prickles of unease across his scalp.

"Yes, she's attending, which is a good first step," the minister said, "and we're praying she discovers her need for a Savior."

"You're sure she's...faithless?" Amos nearly held his breath, waiting for the answer.

Preacher Mead sighed. "I wouldn't presume to judge someone else's heart. But she hasn't made a profession of faith, so we will pray until she does."

Mrs. Mead held the coffeepot near Amos's cup, but he put his hand over the opening. He wouldn't be able to swallow anything else. He'd prayed for Dinah, too, but only for her to form a relationship with him. He shouldn't even entertain such thoughts until he knew if she had faith in the one true, living God.

He pushed clumsily to his feet, his hip stiff from his time of sitting in the hard chair. "I should get back to my place. I've left the chickens unattended long enough."

Preacher Mead also stood. "I'll drive you. The children and I often go for a drive on Sunday afternoons. They enjoy the outings. It will only take me a few minutes to hitch the team."

Amos needed time alone. "Thank you for the kind offer, but I'll walk." He patted his bad hip, forcing a smile. "Walking loosens the joint."

"Very well."

Amos thanked the minister's wife for the good dinner. Then Preacher Mead walked him to the door. So eager to get off by himself and consider the revelations the preacher had shared, he even forgot to say good-bye to Cale. On the walk home, he prayed. As he performed his afternoon and evening chores, he prayed. Before dropping into his bed that night, he knelt awkwardly and asked God to give him peace concerning his upcoming evening with Dinah. But the heaviness in his chest was still there the next morning. And the morning after that.

Rather than anticipating the evening at the Calico Ball, he now dreaded it. What would he do if he asked Dinah "Are you a believer?" and she said "No"?

Chapter 25

Ruthie

uthie gritted her teeth and reached for another cluster of flowers. She should be the one preparing to meet Mr. Ackerman in the fancy parlor in the turret. Instead, she was inserting tiny sprigs of dried field pennycress into the thick braid circling Dinah's head. Some people called the wildflower stinkweed because it grew in the most unlikely places, and its white fingernail-sized blossoms had never been one of Ruthie's favorites. But when nestled in Dinah's dark honey–colored tresses, the unremarkable bloom took on a beauty.

With her coronet of flower-bedecked braids, Dinah appeared to wear a crown. And her dress! Oh, such a lovely gown… In a sweet shade of periwinkle with delightfully pink morning glories climbing on weaving vines of palest green, it couldn't be more suited to the girl. The light blue brought out the pale color of her eyes, and the flowers matched the splashes of rose on her blushing cheeks. Obviously Dinah's seamstress knew her well to choose such a complimentary fabric.

Jealousy nearly turned Ruthie's stomach inside out. Peering at their reflections in the oval mirror, she felt downright homely even though she wore her new gown and had swept up her hair in a loose, poufed style she'd always felt accented her slender neck. She stepped away from the mirror to check the curling tongs, which she'd placed over the lamp to heat. She fingered the iron barrel and deemed it hot enough to form spiraling coils of the loose strands falling from Dinah's temples and nape.

As she wrapped a strand of hair around the barrel, she contemplated why she was helping the girl who was going to the ball with the man she'd hoped would be her escort. Two biblical admonitions simultaneously ran through her mind—*"Love your enemies, do good to them which hate you"* and *"If thine enemy hunger, feed him; if he thirst, give him drink: for in so doing thou shalt heap coals of fire on his head."*

She gave the tongs a gentle downward pull, and a perfectly shaped coil trailed over Dinah's shoulder. She lifted another strand, reminding herself Dinah was hardly an enemy. And certainly the girl didn't hate her even though she couldn't honestly say they were friends. But performing these kind deeds for Dinah, considering the envy Ruthie held, was as difficult as if she did them for a hateful enemy. Even so, the teaching she'd received from her earliest memories would not allow her to be cruel. Not even to the girl who'd stolen her would-be beau.

But then, by the end of the evening, maybe Dinah's aloof behavior would prove off-putting to Mr. Ackerman. By the end of the evening, maybe he would decide he'd rather have a girl who gaily talked and laughed and—

"Ruthie!"

Dinah's shrill squeal started Ruthie so badly she dropped the tongs. A thin line of smoke rose, followed by the foul scent of singed hair. Dinah stared in horror at her reflection. Ruthie matched Dinah's expression, remorse striking with more ferocity than the jealousy ever had.

"Oh, Dinah, I'm so sorry. I allowed myself to become lost in thought, and I left the tongs on too long. Oh!" She scrambled for the barrel, which had landed on the carpet beside her slippered feet. A scorched mark showed on one large cabbage rose. Ruthie groaned. "Oh, what a dolt I am…"

Dinah turned in the chair. "You aren't a dolt. Anyone can have an accident." She fingered the heat-stiffened lock. A small grimace creased her face, but she seemed to deliberately replace it with a weak smile. "Hair grows back, and if we reposition the rug, the bed will cover the mark. Please don't feel bad."

Tears pricked behind Ruthie's eyes as guilt struck like a gale wind. *Lord, forgive my unfavorable thoughts. Dinah is behaving more Christlike right now than I am.* She sniffed hard and returned the tongs to the lamp. "I have some extra hairpins. I'll weave the scorched strand into your braid, and no one will ever know it happened."

An odd look flitted across Dinah's face—both hope and agony. She ducked her head, and when she raised it again, the look was gone. She offered a quavering smile. "Thank you, Ruthie."

"You're welcome." Ruthie carefully lifted the damaged curl and wound it gently into her roommate's hair. "To be honest with you, Dinah, we could burn off all your hair and you'd still be the prettiest girl at the ball." Her chest went tight as envy tried once more to take control. "You look beautiful."

Dinah's eyes widened and met Ruthie's gaze in the mirror. "I do?"

Ruthie nodded emphatically. "You do."

A genuine smile lit Dinah's face. "Thank you." Then she added shyly, "So do you."

"I do?"

It was Dinah's turn to nod.

Ruthie smiled. Then she laughed, remembering. "Last year Phoebe and I helped each other dress for the ball. We primped and posed before the mirror and even practiced waltzing before going up to the ballroom! That was the night Phoebe met Harold, and now she's married and has her own house in Newton…" Her thoughts drifted away again, imagining the blessing Phoebe had received. Ruthie wanted it, too—a husband, a house, a family of her own.

"Ruthie?"

Dinah's timid voice pulled Ruthie from her reverie. She looked into her roommate's pale eyes, which glistened with unshed tears.

"Maybe…maybe tonight you'll meet a 'Harold' who'll be smitten with your red-gold hair and fine figure."

Ruthie turned away. The only man who'd piqued her interest hadn't chosen to escort her. And after Dinah's sweetness to her, how could she even consider hoping he'd reject Dinah? A lump filled her throat, bringing with it the strong desire to cry. She lifted her lightweight shawl from the end of the bed and draped it over her shoulders. "Come, Dinah. It's eight thirty already. We'd better go."

Amos

Amos wished he could pace. His walk to town through the chill evening air had tired his hip, and pacing would make things worse. But standing still when his insides quivered in impatience was agony. He checked the face of the stately grandfather clock standing guard against the parlor wall. Eight thirty-two. He'd only been waiting seven minutes, but it felt like seven years.

He fidgeted, shifting from foot to foot and absently rubbing his hip. The same prayer that had lingered in the back of his heart all week winged heavenward again. *Lord, if I'm not meant to pursue her, let her be displeasing in my sight.* An image of Dinah's smile the Sunday he'd found her sitting on his bench in church flooded his mind. Something in his chest fluttered in response to the remembrance.

He couldn't call her beautiful—not in the classic sense. But there was a sweetness about her, an innocence that touched him. And her features were soft and pleasant, fitting well with her quiet demeanor. He especially liked her unusually pale eyes, as gently blue as a cloudless summer sky. She was young—not yet eighteen—but he sensed she possessed a soul wise beyond her years. She intrigued him. He closed his eyes and shook his head. *And now I'm only finding her pleasing again, Lord. What are You trying to tell me?*

The delicate sound of a clearing throat brought his eyes open. His gaze fell on two young women who stood before him, each with shy smiles gracing their faces, each wearing fancy gowns, each with elaborate hairstyles…but only one with eyes of larkspur blue. He settled his attention on Dinah, and his heart fired into his throat, making it difficult to draw a breath.

Had he really thought her only pretty and not beautiful? He blinked twice, amazed by the transformation from chambermaid to belle of the ball. He gulped and wheezed out, "Miss Hubley, you… You look…" He searched for an adequate word. Nothing seemed fine enough. He finished, "Very nice."

His simple statement apparently found favor because she blushed and ducked her chin in a demure pose. "Thank you, Mr. Ackerman."

Amos, striving to be polite, turned briefly to Miss Mead. "As do you, Miss Mead." He spoke truthfully. Miss Mead's bright-yellow dress decorated all over with red rosebuds suited the preacher's daughter well. He glanced around the small room, noting the others who had entered the parlor were in pairs. "Are you waiting for your escort?"

Miss Mead's rosy lips formed a tight smile. "I am without escort, Mr. Ackerman, but I discovered at last year's ball there is fun to be found by even those who come alone."

He'd never attended a ball, either alone or with a companion, so he couldn't attest to her statement. But he nodded politely. "Good. Well…" He held out his elbow to Miss Hubley, his pulse scampering into double beats of nervous excitement.

Her hand extended slowly, as if traveling against a tide, and her fingers trembled as she placed them lightly on the crook of his arm. The sight of her slender hand ignited a wave of protectiveness. Ungloved and so very small compared to his thick forearm, with chipped nails and chapped fingers telling a silent story of toil.

Dinah was humble. Attractive. Willing to work hard. *She's too pleasing, Lord, far too pleasing…* He swallowed hard. "Are you ready?" He waited for her timid nod. Then with Dinah at his side and Miss Mead trailing behind, he headed toward the ballroom.

Dinah

With a slight shake of her head, Dinah refused the offer of a dance card from the formal-looking man outside the ballroom's wide double doors. Mr. Ackerman's hitching gait led her over the threshold, and the moment she entered the room, she released a gasp of delight.

Gas lamps set shoulder high all around the wood-paneled room cast soft-yellow light over the scene, giving it a fairy-tale quality. Swags of sheer fabric formed festoons from the chain of the glistening chandelier in the center of the high stamped bronze ceiling to each corner. Caught within the folds of cloth, dried rose petals in deepest pink and buttery yellow took on the appearance of jewels. More petals formed dotted trails of color around and between the silver platters and crystal bowls that filled the buffet tables. Snow-white satin tablecloths draped all the way to the floor, the folds shimmering in the glow of the lamps.

Her lips parting in wonder, she allowed her gaze to drift beyond the tables to the narrow windows stretching from no higher than her knees to well above her head. Bare of any covering, the glass rectangles offered views of the night sky in all directions. Stars twinkled against the gray expanse, seeming to add to the festivity inside. Dinah could think of no better adornment than the exposed patches of stars and endless sky.

She caught a reflection of the dancers in one pane, and she turned to smile at the pairs of men and women who filled the marble-tiled floor. Their attire was surely fine enough to grace any big-city social event. Above them, the dangling crystals of the chandelier caught light and sent out tiny shards of rainbows. With precise rhythm, the dancers swayed to the tune played by a six-piece orchestra positioned on a platform at the far end of the ballroom.

A desire to join the dancers swelled, and without conscious thought she took a step toward the center of the room. But Mr. Ackerman didn't move with her. His firm stance reminded her she'd told him she didn't intend to dance. Swallowing the lump of longing, she turned her face up to him and found him gazing at her with deep regret in his dark eyes. Abashed at having inflicted discomfort on him within moments of arrival, Dinah bit down on her lower lip. How could she have been so thoughtless?

The song ended, and the dancers and those standing in groups along the periphery of the dance floor patted their palms together in polite applause. As the orchestra members retrieved their next piece of music, people milled in pairs or small groups. Voices rose in conversation, interspersed with soft bursts of laughter. Dinah stood as still as a fence post, holding on to Mr. Ackerman's steady arm, wishing he'd say something to break the awkward silence between them.

Ruthie leaned close to Dinah's ear. "I'm going to get a plate of food—I'm famished!—and then join the other unescorted girls." Ruthie's forehead puckered as she added, "The chairs fill quickly, so unless you want to lean on the wall, you should probably claim a pair of them before you visit the buffet tables."

Dinah smiled her thanks for the advice, and Ruthie hurried off in the direction of the tables. Her departure left Dinah tingling with unease. Even though dozens of people filled the room, she felt as though she and Mr. Ackerman stood on a tiny island with a moat keeping them separate from the others. What should she do now? She sent a sidelong glance at her escort.

Apparently Mr. Ackerman had overheard Ruthie's whisper because he was scanning the room. He tucked his elbow against his ribs, pinning her fingertips against his scratchy wool suit coat, and pointed with his other hand. "I see a place to sit there between two windows. We'll have a good view of the dancers, but we'll be far enough from the band to...talk." His clean-shaven cheeks streaked with red. "Is that...all right with you?"

Dinah nodded and allowed him to guide her to an armless settee. A few people standing nearby shifted aside as they approached. The musicians struck up a new tune, livelier than the last, and partners dashed onto the dance floor, giving Dinah and Mr. Ackerman plenty of berth. He released her hand, and she seated herself at one end of the brocade settee, smoothing her skirt over her knees as she did so. He lowered his backside toward the other half. Midway down, it seemed his bad leg gave way, and he landed with a plop that bounced her slightly. She pretended not to notice. Crossing her ankles and resting her hands in her lap, she tried to relax.

As much as she'd anticipated this evening, now that it was upon her, she felt completely out of place. Beside her, Mr. Ackerman tugged at his collar—a stiff white band of celluloid. His fingers mussed the black ribbon tie, destroying the perfectly shaped bow. Then he lifted his hand to his head and scratched behind his ear, ruffling his thick, dark-brown hair. Sympathy twined through her. He was uncomfortable, too. Suddenly she realized he wore his Sunday suit.

Black wool pants and jacket over a white starched shirt and familiar string tie—not a cravat, like most of the other men were wearing—and no top hat.

Perhaps if she pretended they sat side by side on the church bench, she might be able to enjoy the evening after all. As the song went on, she observed Mr. Ackerman's stiff form slowly easing to lean fully against the back cushion. His tightly clamped hands on his knees also lost their tense grip, the white dots on his knuckles fading. He shifted his head a bit and caught her peeking at him from the corner of her eye. A grin twitched at his cheeks.

"The music is nice," he said, as if testing his voice.

Dinah offered a wobbly smile. "It is. The band is very good." She assumed it was very good. She'd never heard a band before tonight, but the combination of stringed instruments pleased her ears.

"And the ballroom..." He glanced around, his forehead pinched in a thoughtful expression. "It's a fancy one."

"Yes. It...it is." She wished she had the courage to tell him the room was better than the one from her childhood imaginings.

The music increased in volume, the dancers' soles clopping and clicking against the marble in beat with the merry tune. He sighed and angled his body toward her. His knee bumped hers, and he abruptly jerked it back as she jerked away from it. Heat rose in her face, and color climbed from his neck to his hairline. Her discomfort grew. To hide the rush, she made a pretense of plucking a bit of lint from her skirt, then smoothed the fabric again.

She raised her face in time to see him lick his lips—one nervous swipe of the tip of his tongue. He cleared his throat and blurted, "Miss Hubley, may I ask you an important question?"

Dinah's heart thrummed and moisture dampened her palms. This was it! He would ask if he could court her! What would she say in response? She clamped her hands firmly together and forced her chin to bob in silent approval.

His chest expanded in a mighty intake of air. He opened his mouth, and his breath whooshed out, carrying with it the oddest question. "Do you know God?"

Chapter 26

Dinah

*H*aving expected something completely different, Dinah took a moment or two to comprehend the question. Then she needed another full minute to decide how to answer. Did she know God? The inner reminder of His love for her had become as familiar as a friend. She had attended church service faithfully and listened when the preacher spoke of God. Although there was much she didn't know, she believed she could honestly say she knew of God.

"Yes." Dinah nodded. "Yes, I do."

Mr. Ackerman's face lit. "That's good. That's very good."

She'd pleased him. Happiness exploded within her breast. She couldn't help but smile back at him.

The musicians moved directly into another song, one with slow, long-held notes that seemed to invite a lingering conversation. Mr. Ackerman propped his elbow on the seat back and leaned in a bit. "What is your favorite scripture?"

Dinah raised her brows. "Scripture?"

"Yes. Your favorite Bible verse."

"Oh…" She grimaced. "I don't really have one yet, but I like the part about the man who went looking for his lost lamb." Thinking of the story again, and recalling how the preacher likened the man's search to God's desire to save every lost soul, created a sweet ache in the center of her breast. But the story wasn't a scripture, which was what Mr. Ackerman had requested. She hoped her reply wouldn't disappoint him. To her relief no frown marred his face.

"You are new to believing in God, then." A statement rather than a question.

Her knowledge was only as long as her time in Florence—a scant four months. "That's right."

He smiled, his expression tender. "In time you will find those scriptures that speak to you more deeply than others, but all of God's words are beneficial."

She smiled, finding confirmation that her interest in the Bible story met with his approval.

"May I share one of my favorites with you?"

Curious to hear what he'd say, Dinah nodded.

"From Philippians, the fourth chapter, 'I can do all things through Christ which strengtheneth me.'"

When he quoted from the Bible, his voice took on a different tone—peaceful, sure, intimate. A tiny chill of pleasure quivered through her frame. "The words are lovely." They were, even though she wasn't certain what they meant.

"I have drawn on this scripture many times since my accident." His expression became serious. "It reminds me to be grateful even when I hurt, for God gives me the strength I need to finish my work."

Grateful even when he hurt? Dinah's admiration for him rose. She didn't think she'd ever be able to experience gratitude for the things that had hurt her in her past. She tipped her head and braved a question. "Your leg...does it pain you a lot?"

An odd smile curled one side of his mouth. "Not too much. Not...too much."

Relief flooded her. "I'm glad."

His bright smile returned. "While so many are dancing, maybe we should visit the buffet. It isn't crowded right now. Are you hungry?"

Although when she'd arrived, the thought of eating made her queasy, she now recognized a hunger. She relaxed enough to lose the stone of dread that had filled her stomach. "Yes. And everything smells so good."

"Then let's go." He pushed himself upright, then held his hand to her.

In place of his extended hand, another one suddenly appeared. One raised to strike her. Instinctively, she winced, anticipating a vicious blow. She heard his soft intake of breath, and she peeked at him. Confusion clouded his features. What was she doing? Mr. Ackerman wouldn't hurt her. She shouldn't even hesitate. *Take his hand, you foolish ninny!*

Despite her stern self-talk, she couldn't keep her hand from shaking as she placed her palm in his. She stood, and he transferred her hand to the crook of his arm. He gave her hand a pat, his smile tender in spite of the uncertainty in his eyes, before turning her toward the tables.

His limp made him brush his upper arm against her shoulder with each step, but she discovered it wasn't difficult to walk beside him. His stride matched hers, although the top of her head barely reached his shoulder. In the few moments it took for them to cross the floor to the food-laden tables, Dinah was able to set aside the apprehension that had gripped her. She liked walking with Mr. Ackerman. She felt safe with him. Secure. A wonderful feeling.

They filled their plates with quail pie, roasted lamb with finely chopped cucumber and dill relish, crab-stuffed shrimp, candied carrot coins, garlic- and rosemary-infused asparagus, and duck-liver pâté on thin wedges of toasted rye. The offerings, with the exception of the quail pie, were familiar to Dinah thanks to Rueben's elaborate menus, and she nearly licked her lips in anticipation. At first Mr. Ackerman turned up his nose at the pâté, but when Dinah laughed at him and promised to finish it if he didn't care for it, he took two pieces.

Back at the settee, they balanced their plates on their laps and ate, continuing to chat between bites and applications of their linen napkins. By the time they'd finished, Dinah was so at ease with Mr. Ackerman she felt as if she'd known him forever. And indeed she had. In her heart, her life—her real life, the one that mattered—began with her arrival at the Clifton Hotel.

Minnie approached with a large silver tray and asked for their empty plates. Mr. Ackerman placed his on the tray and then reached for Dinah's, pleasing her with his consideration. They continued their easy conversation as if no interruption had occurred. Dinah giggled when he shared the ways Samson and Gideon entertained him, and he shook his head in wonder at her tales about some of the guests' unusual demands.

As the evening progressed, their talk shifted from casual topics to more serious ones. When Mr. Ackerman asked about her family, she gave a vague yet honest answer. "I never knew my father. He was gone before I was born. My mother died shortly before I came to Kansas. I had no brothers or sisters, so I am without a family."

"I'm sorry." His tone held such sympathy Dinah blinked back tears. He went on. "I am fortunate to have a big family. A mother and father, and two brothers, Titus and John. They're both older and are married with children. So my family numbers ten in all. My father and brothers grow wheat on land near El Dorado that Grandfather Ackerman claimed in 1854 when the government opened the region to settlers."

Dinah wondered why he alone had left the family land holding, but she decided not to pry. He might reciprocate by delving more deeply into her background. It was better, sometimes, to leave the past in the past. "Do you miss them?"

The same strange look he'd assumed when she asked about his leg bothering him returned. "Yes. Especially at night when my house is so quiet. But I hope to have my own family someday, and then my house won't be quiet anymore." He paused, looking into her eyes so intently. Could he see beneath the surface to her soul? She squirmed beneath the sharp scrutiny. Then he said, "Miss Hubley, do—"

"Last song, folks!" The violinist waved his bow over his head. "Last chance to dance, so grab your partner and find a spot on the floor. We're winding up the evening with a fairly new tune called 'Roses from the South' by a German composer named Johann Strauss. We hope you'll find it a fitting finale for our evening together." He settled the glossy violin beneath his chin, placed the bow on the strings, and began a haunting yet heart-stirring melody. The others took up their instruments and, one by one, joined him.

The music was so lovely Dinah's chest ached. She pinched her hands between her knees and gazed at the dancers moving gracefully in a gentle waltz. So many crowded in the space that the women's skirts couldn't flare with their turns, but it didn't matter. She tried to memorize the image so she could dwell upon it when the night terrors attacked.

"Miss Hubley?"

Mr. Ackerman's quiet voice intruded. She sent him a quick sideways glance. "Hmm?"

"Would..." He swallowed. "Would you like to dance?"

She gawked at him, uncertain she'd heard correctly. "You want to dance?"

A nervous smile trembled on his lips. "I'm willing to try if you aren't afraid to have your toes trampled."

"I'm not afraid." She bounced upright, her heart pounding with eagerness, and waited while he pushed to his feet. His look of uncertainty was almost comical, but she stifled the giggle pressing for release and placed her hand in his.

They couldn't enter the dance floor—there wasn't an extra inch of space—so they moved to the tiny patch of floor between the settee and a wing-backed chair. He held open his arms. The suppressed giggle escaped on an airy note as she moved into position. His hand descended lightly on her waist—a hand so big, so strong. Unbidden, memories of another man taking hold of her waist rose from the recesses of her mind. Apprehension ran like spiders up and down her spine, and she shivered.

He frowned slightly. "Are you cold, Miss Hubley?"

The concern on his face, in his tone, calmed her. This was Mr. Ackerman. Gentle, kind Mr. Ackerman. She'd seen his big hand stroke a puppy's head and curl around a small boy's shoulder in tenderness. She drew a breath and released it, the busy spiders changing to fingertips running lightly over a keyboard and bringing forth a sweet melody.

"I'm fine." And in that moment she truly was.

A smile tipped up his lips, and then in unison they began to move to the music. *One-two-three, one-two-three,* she counted in her head as they turned in small circles. The first count jolted Mr. Ackerman the most, so their movements were far from graceful, but Dinah didn't mind. Not a bit. She gazed into his square, honest face, admiring the dark blue of his eyes and the sweet curve of his shy smile. She would rather dance with him in his clumsy gait than with any man on two good legs.

The song ended far too soon, and Dinah experienced a sense of loss when he dropped his hands and moved backward a step, distancing himself from her. They joined in the applause for the musicians, and then people began to amble toward the open doors. Mr. Ackerman offered his arm, and they fell into place at the rear of the group.

Laughter, chatter—the sound of happiness—filled the room, and Dinah found herself wanting to laugh and cry at the same time. The evening had been all she'd hoped it would be and more—her own fairy-tale story. She didn't want it to end. When they reached the lobby, Mr. Ackerman turned to face her. She sensed he held the same wish for more time, and she found it easy to say, "Thank you, Mr. Ackerman. The evening..." She released a contented sigh. "I enjoyed it very much."

"I did, too." His voice came out gruffly, as if he constrained himself. "Thank you for accepting my invitation."

She allowed her smile to respond.

"Miss Hubley, I wondered..."

Still feeling dreamy from their time moving to the sweet melody of song, she murmured, "Hmm?"

"Would you allow me to court you?"

All wistful remembrances dissolved. For the past two weeks, she'd contemplated how she would respond to this question if it was asked, but she never found an adequate answer. She'd enjoyed her evening. She admired him even more now than she had before. But courtship led to marriage, which would lead to intimacy. Her stomach rolled. Additionally, courtship would prevent her from becoming a server, the means of earning the respect and admiration she'd lacked her entire life.

But oh, how she'd enjoyed her time with him. If she were to consider marriage with anyone, she would choose gentle Mr. Ackerman. Yet the thought of

marriage—of him discovering her loss of innocence and of giving up the opportunity to be held in high esteem—held her speechless.

He sighed, lowering his head. "I understand if you refuse. After all, I am a
stranger to you, and I can't— I'm unable to—" He shook his head, then looked
her in the face again. "If I were to court you, it would be a long courtship. I have
much to do yet on my farm before I can support a wife and...a family."

Red filled his face, and Dinah felt certain her cheeks glowed, too. Fortunately the other townsfolk had all left. She wouldn't want anyone overhearing
and then gossiping about her.

"But I thought, if you were willing, we could get to know each other.
Slowly. And then, in time..."

Dinah liked the idea of advancing slowly. If she had time with him, she
might find it easier to make a decision concerning her future. But how would
they find time to be together? It was impossible given her schedule. She blinked
back tears of disappointment. She should tuck this evening away in her memory, be thankful she'd had the fairy-tale hours, and send Mr. Ackerman on to
court someone else. Someone worthy of his attention. Like Ruthie.

She bit back a groan of regret. "I work seven days a week. My only free
hour is the one on Sunday when we attend service. I have no time for us to
become better acquainted."

His brows beetled and he tapped his pursed lips with his thick fingertip.
Then he brightened. "We could write letters!"

Dinah frowned. "Letters?"

"Yes." Enthusiasm made his voice thready. "I keep in touch with my family by writing letters. Because of the words going back and forth, they know
about me and I know about them. We could do the same—we could write to
each other."

His zeal stirred her excitement. She'd never received a letter. Rueben had
sent two postcards in response to her correspondence, but that wasn't the same.
A letter would be a treasure. "How would we exchange them? On Sundays at
church?"

"At church, yes, we could do that. And on the days I come in to deliver eggs, we could exchange letters, too."

Dinah cringed. "Mr. Irwin wouldn't approve of me leaving my post to meet with you and exchange letters."

He shrugged. "Then we'll choose a spot where we can leave them. Someplace here at the hotel that you can reach and I would have access to. Where would be a good place?"

Immediately an idea popped into her head. "The porch, under the cushion on the wicker chair." She didn't explain which chair, but the way he smiled she knew he needed no further instruction.

"No one would bother them there?"

"No one fluffs the cushions except Ruthie and me. It's part of our job to keep the porch dust-free. Ruthie wouldn't keep a letter if she found it—she'd give it to me." Odd how she'd come to trust these two people, both Ruthie and Mr. Ackerman.

"Then we have a plan." His eyes twinkled, giving him a boyish look. "Letters on Sundays and on egg-delivery days, Mondays and Thursdays, yes?"

She shouldn't agree. She would only be misleading him. A man as kind and giving as Mr. Ackerman deserved someone free of ugly blemishes and dark secrets. Yet when she opened her mouth, she said, "Yes."

"Good."

The pendulum clock on the lobby wall began bonging its tolls for midnight. Both of them jumped at the first bong, glanced at the clock, then at each other again. They both smiled, then released soft laughs, then fell silent in unison. The last bong rang and the chimes vibrated for several seconds, slowly fading. Not until the sound had completely died did Mr. Ackerman speak again.

"I should go."

Dinah whisked a look at the night sky. The moon showed round and full. He would be able to find his way beneath the moon's bright glow. Even so, she said, "Be careful," surprising herself with the deep concern in her voice.

Tenderness drifted over his face. "I will. I will see you on Sunday, Miss Hubley." He took her hand, raised it to his mouth, and brushed his lips over her chapped knuckles. Then, before she could respond, he turned and hitched his way out the door.

Dinah moved slowly to the doors and watched through the oval window as he made his way across the garden stepping stones and onto the road. Long shadows tried to shield him from view, but she followed his tall form until he reached the corner. Her nose pressed to the glass, she observed him pause and turn back. Even though she couldn't make out his face from this distance and she knew he couldn't see her, she raised her hand and waved.

He set his shoulders square. Moonlight glinted on his dark hair. His hand lifted to touch his lips and then swept outward as if freeing a dove. Holding her breath, she counted the seconds before gently clapping her hands together to catch the imaginary kiss. She put it in her pocket. Then, with a smile in her heart, she headed to her room.

Chapter 27

Amos

lthough it was nearly one o'clock in the morning when Amos reached his home, he was too awake to sleep. The evening with Dinah—discovering she did know God, witnessing smiles bloom on the young woman's normally reserved face, and then holding her in his arms as they moved to beautiful music—had ignited something inside of him he hadn't even realized lay dormant. How could he sleep when he felt more alive than he ever had before?

He tugged open the top drawer of his bureau and removed the writing tablet and pencil he used to communicate with his mother. As he headed for the table, he caught a glimpse of the rock he'd placed on the mantel. Smiling, he snatched it from its spot and then settled it on the table next to the lamp. His eyes on the rock, he plopped into a chair and laid out his paper and pen. But his smile faded when the lamp's glow flowed across the writing tablet. He needed something pretty on which to put the words intended for Dinah. The dingy-looking paper with pale lines marching from side to side didn't suit her at all. But he supposed the message was more important than the message holder.

Placing the tip of the pencil on the page, he willed his trembling hand to calm so the letters would be legible. Very carefully he wrote, "Dear Miss Hubley." He stared at the salutation. He'd thought of her as "Dinah" for so long, the heading seemed too formal. Anything less would be inappropriate. Still, the title longed for something friendlier. With a smile he added the word "My" in front of "Dear." Satisfied, he set to work on the body of the letter. An hour later he tipped it to the light and read the missive in its entirety.

My Dear Miss Hubley,

Thank you again for accepting my invitation to the Calico Ball. I have never attended a dance before, and now I know what I was missing. But I think the reason it was so special is because I was there with you.

It was good for us to talk and get to know each other better, but there is still so much I don't know. I find myself wanting to know everything. So I am going to ask you some questions that you can answer in your letter to me. Please ask me anything you want to know, too. I will do my best to answer.

Here are my questions:

Miss Mead told me you were raised in wealth. Was your money lost when your mother died and that is why you work as a chambermaid?

I could see how much you liked talking about Samson and Gideon. Did you have dogs at your house?

When I was a boy, my favorite day of the year was my birthday because Ma baked a chocolate cake and I got presents. I still have the carved wooden dog my grandfather made for me when I turned six. I will be twenty-five on January 11. When is your birthday, and what was your favorite birthday present when you were a girl?

I suppose that is enough prying for now. I look forward to your reply.

I remain faithfully yours,
Amos Ackerman

He still wished he'd had prettier paper, and his penmanship could be neater, but for a first letter he was satisfied. He folded it and placed it inside the cover of his Bible so he wouldn't forget it on Sunday. Then he yawned, tiredness striking. He should be able to sleep now. He extinguished the lamp's flame, then felt his way to his sleeping room. In the dark, he skimmed down to his long johns and flopped onto his bed. The straw-filled mattress felt good after his long walk from town. He yawned again, ready to succumb to sleep. But before he allowed himself to drift away into slumber, he sent up a brief prayer.

Lord, thank You for giving me this evening with Dinah. Please give her good dreams to carry her through the night. Amen.

Dinah

Dinah couldn't sleep. Or perhaps, more accurately, she refused to sleep. She wanted nothing to cloud the sweetness of her blissfully wonderful evening with Mr. Ackerman. If she closed her eyes, the nightmares would surely come just as they came every night. She'd already laid out a sheet of plain paper and the stub of a pencil when she returned to the room, but Ruthie had fussed about wanting to sleep, so Dinah had set the items aside. But they beckoned to her from the dresser top.

She slipped from the bed and tiptoed to the dressing table. By pawing around, she located the paper and pencil. She tucked the items underneath her arm. Then she lifted the globed lamp in one hand and cradled the little tin of matches in the other. Holding her breath, she crept out to the hallway where the light wouldn't disturb Ruthie.

After quietly closing the door behind her, she removed a match and flicked it on the doorframe. It flared to life, making her squint. She touched the tiny flame to the lamp's wick, and then she blew out the match and waved away the pungent smoke. For several seconds she stood as still as a mouse beneath a cat's scrutiny, listening for any signs her nighttime activities had awakened any of the other girls. But only silence greeted her ears.

Relieved, she set the lamp on the floor and sat beside it, taking care not to bump it. Using her bent knee as a desk, she flattened the paper and gripped the pencil between her fingers. Although she'd struggled to write school assignments and had only written letters to Rueben—hardly the same as writing to a potential beau!—she found words flowing easily onto the page.

Dear Mr. Ackerman,

Thank you so much for inviting me to the Calico Ball. I have never had as much fun as I did this evening. You were a perfect gentleman—

Her heart caught as the meaning behind the simple statement rose up to torment her.

—and I couldn't imagine a better escort. I especially enjoyed our dance at the end of the night. From now on "Roses from the South" will always be my favorite song.

She paused. Was the statement too personal? The admission came from the center of her heart, a place she tried to shield. But in the end, she chose to leave it. It was the truth, and there were so many things she had to keep secret. She would be transparent whenever she could.

Your idea to write letters is a good one, and I look forward to getting to know you better as time goes by. Thank you for your kindness to me, Mr. Ackerman.

Sincerely yours,
Miss Dinah Hubley

She held the page at arm's length. The content was short but heartfelt. Would he expect more for a first correspondence? She wanted this letter to be perfect in every way. She found nothing to fault in her penmanship, at least. Over time, as she grew more comfortable in her relationship with Mr. Ackerman, the length of her letters would increase. She could be satisfied with a short one for now.

Her eyes felt scratchy, and she set the letter aside and rubbed her eyes with her fists. Her mouth stretched in a yawn, and she rested her head against the wall, allowing her eyes to drift shut for a moment. Behind her closed lids she envisioned the ballroom with its swags of fabric and scattered rose petals. She saw Mr. Ackerman hold his arms open to her, tenderness shining in his eyes. The sweet melody of "Roses from the South" sang through her memory.

A smile formed on her lips without conscious thought. With the pleasant sights and sounds filling her head, she eased into sleep.

Ruthie

The alarm clock's clang roused Ruthie. She clumsily swatted at the clock until she managed to silence the discordant sound. Balling her hands into fists, she enjoyed a leisurely stretch and then reached over to tap Dinah awake. To her surprise, her arm descended on an empty slice of mattress.

Sitting up, she searched the room. Her confusion mounted when she realized the lamp from their bureau was missing. Where could Dinah have gone during the night that required a lamp's guiding glow? If Dinah had sneaked off to meet Mr. Ackerman somewhere and Mr. Irwin found out, she'd be in terrible trouble. Torn between aggravation and worry, Ruthie flung herself out of bed and scrambled into her robe. Then she charged for the hallway.

As she tugged the door open, she heard a muffled giggle. She looked across the hall to Lyla, who stood in her open doorway. One door down, Matilda hissed to capture Ruthie's attention and then pointed. Ruthie peered out and then reared back in shock. There sat Dinah, sleeping on the floor with her head lolling to the side and her nightgown bunched up around her knees. The lamp, still flickering, stood sentinel over a rumpled piece of paper and a stubby pencil.

While Lyla and Matilda continued to giggle behind their hands, Ruthie exclaimed, "Dinah! What on earth are you doing out here?"

Dinah came awake with a start that lifted both of her bare feet off the floor and brought her head up with snap. She released a little yelp, and then her face contorted into a horrible grimace. Clutching her neck, she glared at Ruthie. "Did you have to scare me that way? I think my bones cracked."

Ruthie snorted. "Your bones are fine." She yanked up the lamp, scowling at the small amount of oil left in the bottom. "But our oil supply isn't. You nearly used it all up!"

Lyla and Matilda exchanged smirks. Matilda said, "Does Ruthie snore, Dinah? Is that why you slept in the hallway?"

Lyla teased, "Or did you get locked out of the room last night?"

Dinah jolted to her feet, pressing her palms on the wall to help herself rise. She said nothing to either of the servers as she bent over and snatched up the paper and pencil still lying next to her bare toes. She pushed past Ruthie into their room, and Ruthie slammed the door on Matilda's and Lyla's laughter.

Ruthie set the lamp on the bureau and turned to Dinah, placing her fists on her hips. "What were you doing out there? I thought you'd given up sleeping in odd places." She'd not forgotten finding Dinah asleep behind the wardrobe on her first day in Florence.

Dinah, red faced, crushed the paper to her chest. "I wanted to write a note, but I couldn't see in the dark, and I didn't want to wake you by lighting the lamp, so I went into the hallway. And I must have fallen asleep out there."

Ruthie couldn't stifle a laugh. Dinah was prattling worse than Ruthie usually did. Maybe she was rubbing off on the girl. "It must have been an important note."

A soft expression crossed Dinah's face. "Yes. It was."

They needed to dress and go down to breakfast, but curiosity held Ruthie in place. "To whom did you write?"

Dinah ducked her head, her cheeks filling with such color she looked as though a fever raged. Her hands convulsed on the paper, which was becoming irreparably wrinkled. Then she whispered, "Mr. Ackerman. A...a thank-you note."

"So you enjoyed your evening?" Ruthie would never admit how much time she'd spent gazing at the pair of them snug on the settee, lost in conversation while the ball went on around them.

"It was a lovely evening." Dinah's tone turned wistful. "But..."

Ruthie's pulse tripped into hopeful double beats. Might the note be a means of letting Mr. Ackerman know Dinah was no longer interested in spending time with him? She braved a quavering question. "But you needed a gentle way to tell him…farewell?"

Dinah's wide-eyed gaze collided with Ruthie's. "What do you mean?"

"Well…" Ruthie floundered. She wished Dinah were easier to read. She never knew what was going on behind the girl's pale eyes. "It's nice that you went with him, since he's merely a chicken farmer and you hail from a wealthy background. Generally, those of such different social classes don't mix well. So the two of you wouldn't be"—she drew on Mama's word—"compatible."

Dinah gazed at her for long minutes, her brow all puckered. Finally she sighed. "Ruthie, I am not from a wealthy family."

Ruthie raised one brow. "But you had a cook."

Shaking her head, Dinah offered a sad smile. "The owner of the house where my mother and I lived had a cook. So we didn't do any cooking on our own. We were…employed…there, as well."

Realization dawned. All this time she'd envisioned Dinah with servants and a lifestyle of leisure, but instead she'd worked as a servant for someone else. The jealous thoughts she'd harbored now made her feel petty and mean. Embarrassment washed over her. Ruthie marched to the wardrobe and reached for her uniform. "Why didn't you tell me this before?"

Dinah followed, still pressing the note to her heart as if she needed the message to keep her blood pumping. "I should have." She touched Ruthie's arm. "I'm sorry. It was wrong of me to stay silent."

"It surely was." Ruthie didn't mean to speak so sharply. She stepped aside, uniform in hand, so Dinah could get to the wardrobe. "So you've decided to…" Her tight throat didn't want to release words. She pushed her question past a lump of resignation. "To be courted?"

Dinah paused with her hand on the uniform apron. "I don't know."

A flicker of hope rose to life within Ruthie's breast. "You don't know?"

Dinah took down the apron and turned toward Ruthie. "Not yet. Mr. Ackerman and I are going to"—another blush rose in her cheeks, so girlish and happy a new wave of jealousy captured Ruthie—"get to know each other a little better first. By writing letters." She waved the paper she clutched between her fingers. "We'll leave them beneath the cushion on one of the wicker chairs. So if you find a letter out there, it's meant for me."

But he was meant for me. Ruthie managed to hold the dismayed comment inside. She forced a trembling smile. "I won't read them. I promise."

A genuine smile grew on Dinah's face, transforming her. "I know you won't. I told Mr. Ackerman we could trust you."

Dinah couldn't have hurt her more if she'd poked her with the point of a freshly sharpened pencil. Ruthie turned her back on Dinah and tossed her nightgown over her head. "We're late for breakfast. Hurry now."

The scrambling noises behind her let her know Dinah was taking her advice. As Ruthie brushed her hair and twisted it into a bun, she gave herself a stern talking-to. Mr. Ackerman and Dinah trusted her. So no matter how temptation clawed at her, she would not peek at their love notes. She wouldn't!

Chapter 28

Dinah

*S*aturday passed so slowly Dinah wondered if it would ever draw to a close. She yearned for her bed—between the ball and staying up to write her letter to Mr. Ackerman, she'd gotten very little sleep the night before. She also yearned for Sunday, when she would see Mr. Ackerman again, would sit beside him in church service, and would exchange a missive with him.

As she worked, forcing her tired limbs to perform her given tasks efficiently, she pondered what he would say in his letter. Would it be very short, like hers, or longer? Would he speak of the ball or of chickens or of other things—more personal things? Or would it hold apologies for his impulsive idea and a request to forget the whole thing? The wondering and worry had tangled her insides into knots, and she wanted to crawl in a hole and hide.

The clock chimed twelve, alerting her to lunchtime. She set aside her cleaning supplies and made her way toward the lunch counter for her noon meal, but halfway down the hall the intrusive clang of a beckon-me bell brought her steps to a halt. Dinah sighed and changed direction. She located a gentleman guest peeking out his door with a look of consternation on his face. She hurried the last few steps.

"Yes, sir? What can I do for you?"

He scowled and flapped a newspaper at her. "This is missing the center pages. Which means part of an article—one which I found particularly interesting—is absent. Kindly retrieve a complete paper for me." He thrust the crumpled sheets of newsprint at her, then closed the door in her face.

Dinah hurried to the front desk where a supply of daily papers usually sat on the counter. But the spot was empty. She summoned the desk clerk. "Are there more newspapers somewhere?"

"They've all been claimed, Dinah. Lots of people are interested in that story about the Supreme Court calling the Civil Rights Act of 1875 unconstitutional. Some are downright riled over it."

She sighed. "The guest in room 112 requested a newspaper. I suppose I'll have to tell him none are available." Considering his brusque demand, she didn't look forward to disappointing him.

"Wait." The clerk rummaged beneath the counter and then pressed a fifty-cent piece into her hand. "Take this and purchase a handful more at the newspaper office. I'll go up to the room and let the guest know you'll have a fresh paper for him soon."

Although she'd lose her lunch break running the errand, Dinah didn't dare fail to meet a guest's specific request. "All right. Thank you."

As she headed for the porch, an idea struck. If she had to go to town anyway and she was using her own lunch break, why not perform an errand or two for herself while she was out? The morning's doldrums faded momentarily as she dashed upstairs to retrieve her little money pouch. The cloth bag with its drawstring closure was weighty, filled with all her earnings for the past months as well as the small amount of money left over from Chicago. Uncertain how much her purchases would cost, she looped the pouch's string over her wrist and took off for town at an eager pace.

Amos

Amos arrived at church early. The earliest he'd ever arrived. Even before any other parishioners arrived. He settled onto his bench in the quiet sanctuary and released a sigh of relief to be off of his feet. His hip ached from the rapid pace he'd forced upon himself, but he didn't regret hurrying. By arriving early, he might be able to steal a moment or two of time with Dinah before the service started. What was a little pain compared to the pleasure of gazing into her pretty face and hearing her soft, timid voice greet him?

Inside the cover of his Bible, he carried the letter he'd written after the ball. He still regretted the plain paper on which it was written, but her next letter would be more appealing. Saturday morning he'd gone into town and bought a packet of fine stationery decorated with a cluster of violets tied with yellow ribbon. Although the clerk raised his eyebrows in silent surprise at Amos's choice, causing him to fidget in embarrassment, he bought the pretty paper anyway, not because it suited him, but because it suited her. And it pleased him to think of pleasing her.

Now he wriggled on the bench, waiting for her to arrive. His hands trembled, and he clutched them tightly around the leather cover of his Bible. Without conscious thought he closed his eyes and lapsed into prayer. *Dear Lord, I'm as nervous as a chicken in a den of foxes. Calm my spirit. I believe You gave me this idea to get to know Dinah better, and I trust You to guide our friendship. You know my heart's desire concerning Dinah, my Father, but most of all my heart's desire is to follow Your will. So let me only go where You would have me go.*

Even as he prayed, he recognized how much he wanted God to bless him with a wife. How much he wanted to be blessed with Dinah as his wife. Surely God wouldn't allow this deep affection for her to sprout if Amos wasn't meant to act upon it. He bent forward over his Bible, finishing his prayer. *Your will, Father. Let me seek Your will above all…*

Footsteps on the stairs alerted him to others arriving. He sat upright and aimed his gaze at the double doors, which opened and closed dozens of times, each time bringing in a cool breeze along with clusters of worshipers. But not until it was nearly time for the service to begin did the young women wearing uniforms from the Clifton Hotel finally enter. When he spotted the familiar black-and-white uniforms, his heart leaped. And when Dinah stepped into the room with her sweet face aimed in the direction of their bench, his heart seemed to lodge in his throat. He read in her eyes the same eagerness thrumming through his veins.

He scooted over, allowing her to sit on the end rather than having to climb over his knees. Not until she'd seated herself in a graceful motion that made his pulse trip did he notice she cradled a book in her arms. Its black leather binding and gold-tipped pages identified it even before he saw the scrolling, stamped words *Holy Bible* on its cover. If he'd thought her lovely before, her beauty increased tenfold in that moment. Her possession of God's Word seemed to grant approval of him pursuing her as a life's mate.

Thank You, Lord.

She placed her Bible on the bench between them as the congregation rose to sing. He laid his Bible next to hers. Although his cover looked even more battered and worn next to the crisp newness of hers, it pleased him to see the two Bibles side by side. He lifted his attention to the front of the church as Preacher Mead announced their opening hymn. As one, the worshipers burst forth in song. "'How firm a foundation, ye saints of the Lord, is laid for your faith in His excellent Word!'"

Amos shook his head, marveling at how the hymn's first line seemed to point toward the Bibles butted against each other on the bench. In his mind, they presented a picture of oneness, and his chest went so tight he could hardly draw enough breath to sing along with his favorite hymn.

As usual, Preacher Mead delivered a biblically based sermon that spoke truth. But Amos had trouble staying focused, aware of Dinah painstakingly turning the crisp pages of her Bible in search of the references on which the minister drew. Having been raised in church and participating in Bible reading at home with his parents from the time he was old enough to read the words for himself, he was as familiar with the contents of his Bible as he was with his own reflection. He battled a strong urge to help her locate the books and verses mentioned, but knowing she'd learn faster if she sought them out herself, he kept his hands to himself.

After the closing prayer, in unison he and Dinah sat back on the bench. As parishioners filed down the aisle and out the door, they opened the covers of their Bibles and withdrew folded sheets of paper. His hand trembled as he held his letter to her, and the pages pinched between her fingers fluttered, too.

Lifting his gaze from the letters to her face, he caught her biting on the corner of her lower lip.

He formed a quavery smile and bobbed his letter. "This is for you. Is that for me?"

She nodded and pushed the letter toward him.

He took hers, and she reached for his. Not until her fingers closed on it did she finally look at him. Her cheeks bore rosy circles and apprehension widened her eyes. She swallowed, her shoulders lifting into a pose of protectiveness. "I-I'm not much of a writer. I hope you won't be disappointed."

He shook his head, touched by her concern. "I can't imagine being disappointed by you, Miss Hubley." He slid her letter into his Bible, continuing to offer a smile he hoped would set her at ease. "I hope you won't be disappointed with mine. My penmanship..." He rubbed the underside of his nose and chuckled. "I didn't get very high marks on that in school."

To his delight her lips tipped into a shy smile. She placed his letter in her Bible, then lay her open palm on the cover, as if shielding it. "I'm sure it's fine. I've..." She met his gaze, and although her face still held its embarrassed flush, a hint of boldness entered her expression. "I've never received a letter before. I'm eager to read yours, but I'll have to wait until I'm finished with my work today."

He took her final comment as a hint she needed to return to the hotel. Although reluctant to part company already, he pushed to his feet, his stiff hip making him clumsy and slow. Dinah rose as well and stepped into the aisle. Together, they followed the last few straggling worshipers into the yard. The cool breeze nipped at them, and she hugged herself, locking her Bible between her folded arms and the white bib of her apron.

She angled a timid grin at him. "I'll put another letter—a longer one, I promise—under the cushion for you tomorrow morning."

He liked the way the sunshine brought out the amber highlights in her hair, the way she crinkled her nose as she squinted against the sun's bright beams, even the way she hugged her Bible, as if she held something precious. If they hadn't been standing in a churchyard in full sunlight with more than a dozen townspeople nearby as witnesses, he might be tempted to steal a kiss from her. Ma would be mortified to know he was thinking such things on Sunday morning.

He took a backward step. "I'll be sure to look for it. And I'll leave one for you, too." The other Clifton Hotel workers were already in their buggy, and they all seemed to be watching him and Dinah. Another hitching step put a few more inches between them. He pointed at the buggy with his chin. "You'd best skedaddle—your carriage is waiting."

She flicked a look in the direction of the conveyance, and a scowl marred her sweet face. The scowl pleased him even more than a smile would have. She wasn't eager to leave his company, either.

Dinah

Dinah stifled a sigh. How pleasant to stand here in the scant shade of a nearly leafless elm with Mr. Ackerman. Next to his tall, broad form, she felt safe. She'd feared the wonderful feelings of her time with him at the Calico Ball had been figments of her imagination—that when she saw him again, her illusions of his princeliness would shatter. But no, if anything her feelings had magnified. His kind nature and gentle manner of speaking soothed her and made her long to remain near him, like a chick tucked beneath its mother's protective wing. But of course she had to go. Work awaited.

But when work was over, she would read his letter. The letter he'd written just for her. She inched backward, holding her Bible and its letter between the pages as if it were her lifeline. "Good-bye, Mr. Ackerman." The farewell escaped on an airy sigh.

"Good-bye, Miss Hubley. Have a good day."

He sounded formal, no special inflection in his tone to indicate he found their parting painful, but she noted the lack of sparkle in his eyes. Illogical, perhaps, but her heart lifted to know he was sad to see her go. With the image of his serious countenance seared in her memory, she whirled and scampered the remaining few feet to the buggy.

"Finally." Minnie sent a sour look over her shoulder as Dinah climbed in and squeezed into the tiny spot left. "I thought you were going to stand there and talk forever."

Dean flicked the reins and set the horses in motion. "Aw, let her be. We'd have had to wait a whole lot longer if it'd been you grabbin' words with a fellow. Especially if it'd been that dandy who stayed at the Clifton three nights ago."

Minnie nudged Dean's arm.

He gave her a light bump with his elbow in return. "How long past curfew did you dally behind the carriage house, Minnie?"

"Dean…"

"Bet you thought nobody saw you, huh?"

Dinah and Ruthie exchanged a look. Ruthie's brow crunched in worry. Dinah swallowed against her dry throat. If Minnie was caught flirting with a man, she'd be released from her position as a server. Why would she take such a risk?

Minnie nudged Dean again, hard enough to rock him in his seat. "And just how late were you out, Dean Muller? You're a fine one to berate me when you were breaking the silly curfew rule, too."

Dean laughed. "Don't worry, Mins. I won't tell. And none of the girls will, either." He sent a look across the buggy full of women. "Her secret's safe with us, right?"

"Oh, of course," Lyla said quickly. "I won't tell a soul." Matilda and Amelia murmured their assents.

Ruthie leaned forward. "Minnie, you know better than to be out after curfew. Especially with a man."

Minnie shifted sideways in the seat and glared at Ruthie. "We were only talking. There's nothing wrong with talking. And just because your father is a preacher doesn't mean you can preach to me."

Dinah cringed at the girl's harsh tone, but Ruthie didn't even flinch. She said quietly, "I'm not preaching to you. But we can all get in trouble if you don't follow the rules. If you're caught and Mr. Irwin finds out we all knew you were sneaking out with a man, we could be released from duty, too. Maybe you should think about that before you decide to stay out past curfew."

Minnie sniffed and turned her back on Ruthie. Dean stopped the carriage near the hotel's front doors, and Minnie gave Lyla a push that nearly sent the girl over the edge of the seat. She clambered out behind Lyla and stormed into the hotel. Lyla waited beside the carriage for Amelia and Matilda to climb down. Then the three of them hurried in with their heads together, whispering excitedly.

Ruthie and Dinah climbed out and followed. Ruthie's steps lagged, and Dinah stayed close to her. Ruthie was clearly burdened, and Dinah wished she knew how to help. Before she could think of anything to say, Ruthie spoke again.

"I wish Dean had kept quiet about Minnie's late-night dalliance. I won't tattle to Mr. Irwin, but our contract requires us to be honest, so if I'm asked…" Ruthie sighed. She turned a sad look on Dinah. "I fear Minnie is heading for trouble. A girl's reputation can be permanently marred by sneaking off with a man, even if they're only talking."

A wave of guilt struck Dinah with such force she stiffened her knees to keep herself upright. The secret she carried burned like a fire in her middle. She hugged her Bible so tightly the edge of the cover dug into her ribs.

Ruthie went on in a somber tone, seemingly unaware of Dinah's turmoil. "I hope she doesn't lose her job, but mostly I hope she doesn't lose her reputation. A reputation isn't easily restored."

She headed into the hotel, but Dinah remained rooted on the porch, her stiff legs refusing to carry her forward. *"A reputation isn't easily restored…"* Ruthie's parting comment rang in her mind, stinging her with its truth. Her reputation in Chicago had been deplorable given her connection to the Yellow Parrot. She'd traveled a far distance from that place, but she carried bits of it with her still.

Her breath gasped out in little puffs as her pulse sped more rapidly than the wheels on the train at full throttle. How could she escape every vestige of her past? A throbbing pressure in her ribs reminded her she'd been holding the

Bible too tightly. She relaxed her grip but still cradled the Book. Inside the pages was Mr. Ackerman's letter—a missive from a man unlike any she'd known before. She'd so anticipated getting to know him better. Perhaps allowing his attentions. But if he got to know her—and all her secrets—what would he do?

"I can't imagine being disappointed by you, Miss Hubley." His sweet words, which had offered such assurance earlier in the day, returned. Were they true? Had she finally met someone who could overlook her past and only see who she was today—a hardworking girl who attended church and conducted herself with dignity? Her chest ached with the desire to be loved. Unconditionally loved.

"I can't imagine being disappointed by you, Miss Hubley." Clinging to the promise of those words, Dinah returned to work.

Chapter 29

Amos

*U*nable to wait, Amos read Dinah's letter as he walked home. As she'd told him, it was very short, but he didn't mind. He read it again and again, memorizing the words. Then he held it in front of him and admired the precise slant of the letters, the straight cross on the *t*'s, and the perfectly formed loops falling below the line. The letter was a work of art. But he wouldn't frame it.

As soon as he reached the house, he checked on the chickens and the dogs. Finding nothing amiss, he hop-skipped inside and got out the pretty paper he'd purchased and laid it on the table. Then, with the rock next to his ink pot, he set to work penning his second letter. He opened by thanking her for her letter and assuring her he found it pleasing. In the second paragraph he expressed his approval of her possessing her own Bible and encouraged her to read it regularly—her familiarity would increase with each use. And then he wrote about himself.

> *My flock now numbers seven dozen hens, although eight of those are too young to lay yet. But they will start laying soon enough. While I wait, I've set aside another six hens to brood, with three eggs in each roost. So there will be more chickens coming.*

Amos paused, the pen gripped in his fingers. Would Dinah find this information about his chicken farm interesting? His father and brothers didn't seem interested, although Ma asked questions and offered encouragement in her weekly letters. It would pain him if Dinah seemed uncaring, but he needed to tell her about his farm. About his plans. If she was to consider marrying him, she should know how he intended to support her.

He dipped his pen and continued.

I want to build my flock until it is large enough to meet the needs of the chef at the Clifton Hotel. It will take time, as long as two years—

His heart lurched. Would she be willing to wait? He nibbled the end of the pen, contemplating whether to share this with her already. But he needed to be honest. With a sigh he placed the nib on the page and continued.

But in the meantime I sell to people in Florence and manage to make a comfortable living.

He hoped "comfortable" would be enough to satisfy Dinah. He filled the page describing the responsibilities of running a chicken farm, all the while imagining her working by his side. On the second page he told her about his farm—his house, the outbuildings, the spot of ground where he grew corn and barley for the chickens. His future dreams spilled onto the sheet as he added,

My vegetable garden is small now, since I only grow enough to feed myself, but I have space to expand it when more is needed.

He hoped she would understand the hidden meaning behind his simple statement.

His hand was starting to ache from gripping the pen so tightly, and his writing was getting sloppier with every line. He should close. Dipping the pen one last time, he formed his final thoughts.

Did you know that my name, Amos, and your name, Dinah, both come from the Bible? There is a book called Amos, written by the

prophet Amos. Dinah's story is found in the thirty-fourth chapter of
Genesis. She was a woman from a family of strong faith but had much
heartache.

He closed the letter with the same salutation he'd used on the first letter, then set the pages aside for the ink to dry. He glanced at the clock and gave a start when he realized he'd spent two hours writing. Two hours? He couldn't spend two hours each day on letters! But after this one, he would have three days to write the next one. So he could spend a little time each evening adding to his letter. Almost like a journal. He smiled, thinking of the chance to "talk" to Dinah every day.

He stood to put away the ink pot, pen, and paper but decided to leave it out instead. If he'd be writing every day, it would save him time. But he returned the rock to its place on the mantel. With his fingers resting lightly on the rock's rough surface, he focused on the band of amber. In the pale sunlight flowing into the room, the band shimmered like gold. A verse from Proverbs 31 trailed through his memory. *"Who can find a virtuous woman? for her price is far above rubies."*

He ran his finger across the gold-like stripe. Did gold cost more than rubies? He didn't know the answer. He'd never purchased either. But he did know gold was costly. Precious even. He smiled. Precious… Just like Dinah.

Dinah

Dinah grimaced as Ruthie pulled the covers over her head. The light must be keeping her roommate from sleeping. She should extinguish the lamp. But she hadn't finished her letter yet. She'd promised to write a longer one, and she intended to keep her promise. But she should hurry.

Sitting as still as possible on the edge of the mattress to keep from jouncing Ruthie, she glanced over what she'd written so far on the fine stationery she'd purchased from the mercantile. The rows of words in black lead stood out proudly on the background of tan. Three stripes—two of brown with a narrow band of dark blue in the middle—formed a border on the left side of the page. The brown stripes reminded Dinah of Mr. Ackerman's dark hair, the blue of his eyes. She hoped he wouldn't suspect her reason for choosing this stationery over some of the prettier ones, but in her mind it matched him perfectly.

She'd answered his three questions, finding it fairly easy to post a response. He might be surprised to learn she came from a humble background, but she sensed he wouldn't be put off by it. Her reply concerning pets took only a few words: "I've never had a pet." But thanks to Rueben she had some happy memories to share about birthdays. She gnawed a dry piece of skin on her lower lip as she reflected on the difference between hers and Mr. Ackerman's ages. Would he think her too young when he learned she wasn't yet eighteen? Even so, she wouldn't lie. Not about that.

Now that his questions had been addressed, she needed to write something more. What could she say? Since he'd asked her questions, maybe it was all right for her to reciprocate. Bending over the page once more, she wrote,

I would like to know more about your family. Will you tell me all about them? What is your favorite food? I know you like dogs and chickens. What other animals do you like?

She'd filled an entire page. Twice the length of her first letter. Satisfied, she folded the sheet into thirds and placed it on the bureau. A twist of the lamp's key shrunk the wick, and the flame flickered and went out. Tiptoeing, Dinah made her way back to the bed and crawled in, taking care not to bounce the springs or rustle the blankets too much. She held her breath, waiting to see if Ruthie roused. But not even a mumble came from the opposite side of the bed.

Relieved, Dinah relaxed against her pillow and closed her eyes. She deliberately conjured images of Mr. Ackerman—of him sitting straight and attentive beside her on the church bench, of his finger underlining the words in his

Bible as the minister read, of his hand offering his missive to her. She played the pleasant remembrances over and over, hoping they would keep the nightmare at bay when she finally drifted off to sleep.

But they didn't.

Ruthie

October eased into November. Although winds blew colder as Thanksgiving neared, no snow arrived in Florence. The servers wistfully spoke of the first snow of the season, but Ruthie was grateful for its delay. Last winter she'd spent much time on her hands and knees scrubbing up the muddy footprints left by guests on the hotel's carpets. She'd rather beat out dust than scrub up mud. Besides, snow made it harder to get to church, her one and only outing each week. She looked forward to that hour of service and the chance to grab a few minutes with her family.

Ruthie had heard about winter doldrums—experiencing melancholy as skies turned gray and the temperatures dipped—but she'd never suffered them until this year. Perhaps, because the holidays were nearing, she missed her family even more and longed for hours of uninterrupted time with Mama, Papa, the boys, and little Dinah who was growing up so fast. Last year she'd at least had Phoebe, and the two of them managed to find reasons to be merry even though they worked on Christmas Day. Certainly some of her sadness came from being separated from the ones she loved. But some of it, she knew, was a continuing battle against envy.

Each time Dinah retrieved a letter from beneath the cushion on the porch chair, Ruthie felt as though someone pierced her soul. When Dinah kept the lamp burning past curfew to write to Mr. Ackerman, Ruthie pulled the covers over her head and plugged her ears against the *scritch-scritch* of pencil on paper while gritting her teeth so tightly her jaw ached. When she observed Dinah reading—or rereading—one of Mr. Ackerman's messages, the urge to peek over the girl's shoulder nearly overwhelmed her. She was older than Dinah.

She'd been waiting longer for a beau. Why couldn't she be the one receiving the attention, the affection, the promise of a family to come?

Then with the arrival of December came a new routine—one which Ruthie found even harder to bear than the exchange of letters between her roommate and the man who continued to pique her interest. Mr. Ackerman began visiting the hotel on Mondays and Thursdays at noon—taking his lunch at the counter. And Dinah always sat with him, as bold as brass, right in front of everyone!

Ruthie knew she shouldn't grumble. Their innocent lunch meetings didn't break any rules. Dinah was a chambermaid, not a server, and the chambermaid contract didn't forbid courtship. But the servers simmered at the blatant display, and Ruthie had to guard against siding with Minnie, Matilda, Lyla, and Amelia. Knowing the servers weren't allowed the same freedom, shouldn't Dinah be more considerate? Yet she also knew if Mr. Ackerman were taking the time to lunch with her, she'd seat herself on a stool next to him and engage in conversation as openly and unabashedly as Dinah did.

The Friday before Christmas the first snowflakes of winter fluttered from the sky. Ruthie paused in her cleaning to peer out the window and watch the fluffy bits drift downward to create a lacelike pattern on the brown landscape. So beautiful… A lump filled her throat. The entire hotel was decorated for the season with evergreen boughs and fat red candles and strings of gold and white beads. Everywhere she looked, her eyes met beauty. Yet inside, she was more empty and sad than she'd ever been. What was wrong with her?

"Ruthie?"

Dinah's voice pulled her attention from the scene outside. She turned to find Dinah framed in the doorway, peeking in. A soft smile curved her lips and brightened her eyes. Ruthie sighed. "What do you want?"

"Would you like to walk into town with me during our lunch break? I need to do some shopping."

Ruthie stifled a groan. Why hadn't she stopped to remember Christmas was only days away? She hadn't purchased any gifts for her family yet. She and Phoebe had exchanged gifts last year, so she should probably buy a little something for Dinah, too. If she could manage it without Dinah seeing. And maybe letting a few of those fluffy flakes fall on her hair might cheer her a bit. "Yes, I'll go."

Joy lit Dinah's face. "Good. And may I ask a favor of you?"

Ruthie shrugged.

"You have brothers. And a father. So you'd know better than I what a man might like." The girl's cheeks flushed as scarlet as if she stood in a frigid wind. She toyed with the shoulder strap of her apron and angled her head downward in a timid pose. "Will you help me choose something appropriate…for Mr. Ackerman?"

Her request bruised Ruthie's heart. The groan she had held inside escaped. "Oh, Dinah…"

Dinah blinked several times, confusion pinching her brow into furrows. "What?"

Closing her eyes for a moment, Ruthie prayed for guidance. With a sigh she looked at her roommate. "Choosing a gift is a very personal thing. If I were to pick something, it wouldn't really be from you, would it?"

Her frown remained intact. "But I'd be the one buying the gift. So of course it would be from me."

Ruthie snatched up her feather duster and set to work, whisking the feathers over the dresser's surface with a vengeance. "But it wouldn't be your idea. It should be your idea, Dinah."

She blew out a heavy breath. "That's the problem. I don't have any ideas. Not a single one!"

Ruthie rolled her eyes and aimed the duster at the bed's ornate headboard. "With all the letters he's sent, he's never hinted at what he likes?" Only a fool would miss the sarcasm in her tone.

"No." Dinah trailed Ruthie, wringing her hands. "Oh, please, Ruthie? I'm sure you've bought presents over the years for your father. I'm sure he's been happy with what you chose. So can't you help me find something? I don't want to make a mistake."

Ruthie paused, her conscience pricking her. Dinah sounded desperate and near tears. She hung her head. Was she resisting helping because she was jealous that Dinah had reason to purchase a gift for Mr. Ackerman? She searched herself, but she couldn't discover an honest answer.

Facing Dinah once more, she forced herself to speak kindly. "You're right that my father has always been pleased with whatever I gave him." She placed her palm against her bodice. "But he was pleased because he knew I gave from my heart. So the item didn't matter to him as much as the thought behind it." She cupped her hand over Dinah's shoulder. "Are you sure you don't want to choose something without my help? So you'll know, without doubt, the gift really did come from you?"

Dinah sucked in her lips and stared at Ruthie for several long seconds. Beneath Ruthie's hand, the girl's muscles were tense. For a moment, sympathy twined through Ruthie's chest. She'd never witnessed such turmoil. Maybe she should just tell Dinah what to buy to put her at ease. She started to offer a few suggestions, but Dinah spoke first.

"All right. I'll pick something. But will you give me your opinion on it? Just in case I…I make a foolish choice?"

She must be the biggest kind of ninny for agreeing to help another girl buy a gift for the man she'd hoped to snag for herself. "Yes, Dinah, I will."

Chapter 30

Dinah

hristmas Eve morning Dinah awakened before dawn, images of the nightmare still floating in the back of her mind like mist over a pond. Eager for sunshine to erase the haunting fog, she slipped from the bed, donned her robe and slippers, then made her way to the outhouse. The cold, crisp air stole her breath momentarily, but the first taste of morning was pleasant on her tongue. She sucked lungfuls of the frigid air, allowing its clean freshness to chase away the ugliness of her dreams.

When she stepped from the outhouse, she caught sight of a flash of red. It took a full second for her brain to recognize what her eyes had seen. But then she smiled at the cardinal darting between the scraggly boughs of a bare lilac bush. Shifting from foot to foot on the frosty ground, she basked in the beauty of the bird's bright feathers against the plain background. In her Bible reading, she'd encountered the story of God providing quail to feed the children of Israel in the desert. Might God have sent this bird to her this morning to feed her soul? It was a ridiculous thought—why would the mighty God of the universe send something just for her?—but she clung to the idea anyway.

The patter of feet on the hard ground met Dinah's ears, and the bird shot out of the bush and disappeared around the corner of the hotel. Disappointed, Dinah turned to see who had startled the beautiful red bird into flight. Minnie bustled up the path leading to the outhouse, holding her robe closed at the throat. Minnie was always the last girl to rise and had been late to breakfast more than a dozen times due to her unwillingness to roll out of bed in the morning. Of all the people to encounter in this predawn hour, Minnie was the last one Dinah expected.

Apparently Minnie hadn't expected to find anyone else up, either, because when she spotted Dinah, a sour look crossed her face. "You're up early." She spoke softly, yet her tone held a hard edge.

"So are you."

Minnie flicked a glance right and left. "Are you going to stand out here all morning or go inside?"

Stung by the girl's impatience, Dinah scuttled around her and went inside. Ruthie still slept, so rather than lighting the lamp and dressing, Dinah eased open the door to the wardrobe and took out the gift she'd purchased for Mr. Ackerman. After sinking down on the floor, she laid the slim, leather-covered box in her lap and lifted the lid. Although heavy shadows shrouded the room, the mother-of-pearl inlay on the pocketknife's handle glowed like a full moon in a black sky.

Dinah ran her finger up and down the smooth mother-of-pearl. The knife came all the way from Sheffield, England, designed and crafted by a man named George Wostenholm. The clerk at Graham and Tucker claimed Wostenholm knives were of the finest quality and would last a lifetime. When Dinah had seen the pearl inlay, as creamy as the shell of an egg, she deemed it the perfect knife for Mr. Ackerman to carry in his pocket.

Ruthie had agreed it was a fine gift, something Mr. Ackerman would certainly enjoy, but she raised her eyebrows at the price. However, Dinah willingly handed over four dollars and twenty-five cents. How could one put a price on the kindness she'd been given from her very first time of meeting him? She owed him a much bigger debt than a four-dollar pocketknife. Now, smiling down at the knife nestled in its protective box, she tried to imagine his face as he opened it. Oh, she hoped he would be pleased with it.

The bedsprings creaked, and then the covers rustled. Moments later Ruthie peered over the edge of the bed, her face scrunched as she squinted through the murky light. "Why are you on the floor again?"

Dinah swallowed a giggle at Ruthie's sleep-roughened voice. "I couldn't sleep, and I didn't want to disturb you."

Ruthie's gaze dropped to the box in Dinah's lap, and she flopped onto her belly with her head half on, half off the mattress as she continued to stare at the knife. "You should have asked to have that wrapped."

Dinah replaced the lid and laid both of her palms over the box. She'd allowed the clerk to wrap her other purchases. She accumulated quite a pile by the time she chose something for the servers, Ruthie, each of the members of Ruthie's family, and the kitchen dishwasher and her two children. But she deliberately left Mr. Ackerman's gift unadorned by paper and ribbon. He was a no-nonsense man. Frippery seemed out of place for him. Besides, the stamped leather box was too fancy to hide beneath a layer of paper. "It's fine as it is."

Ruthie yawned. "Suit yourself." She rolled onto her back, stretched, then rubbed her eyes and yawned again. "Ohhh, I'm Minnie this morning. I don't want to get up."

Dinah pushed to her feet, still holding the knife box in her fist. "Minnie is you, then. She's already awake."

Ruthie's eyes widened. "She is? So early?"

"I saw her on the way to the outhouse awhile ago." Dinah lit the lamp, hiding her smile when Ruthie scrunched her eyes shut against the yellow glow. Then she frowned. Had Minnie returned? Although the hotel was well built, she usually heard the click of doors closing. She didn't recall hearing feet in the hallway or a door closing. But maybe Minnie had crept in quietly, the way Dinah had tried to do, to keep from disturbing those still sleeping.

She rounded the bed and removed her uniform from the wardrobe. Not until she was fully dressed and had tucked Mr. Ackerman's gift into her pocket did Ruthie finally crawl out of bed. Dinah considered laughing at her room-mate. She moved as slowly as a ninety-year-old woman. But considering the lack of sparkle she'd witnessed in Ruthie's countenance of late, she decided laughing would be cruel. She should find a way to cheer her instead.

She clapped her palms together as an idea struck. "Would you like your present now?"

Ruthie stopped halfway across the floor. "But it isn't Christmas yet."

Dinah's lips twitched as she battled a smile. "No, but I'm giving Mr. Ackerman his when he comes for lunch. So I could give you yours today." Ruthie's stoic expression didn't soften. Dinah added, "That is, if…if you'd like."

Ruthie's brow furrowed. Several seconds ticked by while Dinah waited for Ruthie to make up her mind. Eagerness to bestow the present she'd sneaked to the cashier when Ruthie was busy shopping for her siblings made her want to wriggle out of her skin. She'd never realized how much fun could be found in giving gifts.

At last Ruthie heaved a mighty sigh. "All right. Yes. We can exchange gifts now."

Dinah blinked in surprise. "Exchange?"

Ruthie drew back. "Yes. I got you something."

A gift! Ruthie had gotten her a gift! Mr. Ackerman had indicated in his last letter he would be bringing her a "little something," but he was trying to court her. She hadn't expected a present from Ruthie, who had to buy presents for so many people in her family. The thought that Ruthie would buy something for her made her feel joyous, befuddled, and undeserving all at once. Tears stung Dinah's eyes. "Y-you did?"

"Of course I did." She inched around Dinah, moving toward the bureau. "I'll get it."

Dinah shook her head so hard her hair, which she hadn't released from her nighttime braid, flipped up and whacked her on the side of the face. She tossed the thick plait over her shoulder with an impatient flick of her wrist. "No, please! I don't want anything from you today. You'll be getting presents tomorrow when you go see your family at dinnertime. So I want you to have mine today. But I—" For a moment sadness attacked. She swallowed and finished, "But I don't have a family to visit tomorrow. And since Mr. Ackerman is coming today, I…I won't have any other Christmas except with you. So may I wait until tomorrow?"

At first it seemed Ruthie would argue, but then she offered a slow nod. "All right, Dinah." She sat on the bed, and an odd smile lifted one side of her lips. "I'm ready."

With a little giggle Dinah dashed to the wardrobe and reached into the far corner. She pawed through the jumbled pile of presents and located the box intended for Ruthie. Another happy chortle left her throat as she plopped it into Ruthie's hands. "There you are! Merry Christmas!"

Dinah perched next to Ruthie, holding her breath as Ruthie released the red ribbon and peeled away the green-sprigged paper to reveal a hinged velvet box. Ruthie sent a quick, puzzled glance at Dinah before snapping open the lid. Then she gasped and clapped her hand to her cheek. "Oh, it's beautiful!" Ruthie gawked at Dinah, her eyes so wide Dinah could see her own happy reflection in Ruthie's pupils.

Dinah hugged herself to hold on to the wonderful feeling coursing through her. "You like it?"

"Yes…" Ruthie's fingers trembled as she lifted from its box the oval locket Dinah had selected.

So happy she couldn't contain herself, Dinah began to babble. "It's not solid gold. Only plated. And it's rolled rather than etched. But the clerk said that's a real diamond chip in the center of the flower. And inside there's a place for a picture. Just one. I…" She took a deep breath, feeling as though she'd just run a race. "I thought, when you have a beau, you could put his photograph inside."

Ruthie held the locket between her fingers and stared at it. The serpentine chain flowed across her wrist and swayed gently above her lap. "That's a grand idea, Dinah."

She frowned when she realized tears rolled down her roommate's cheeks. "Ruthie? Why are you crying?"

Ruthie's shoulders heaved with one sob. Then she took in a shuddering breath. "They are happy tears."

"You don't look happy."

Ruthie licked her lips, wrapping her fist around the locket. "I am, though."

She turned to look directly into Dinah's eyes. No joy lit her expression. "It's a wonderful gift. Thank you."

Confused by Ruthie's reaction, Dinah stood and looked uncertainly at the chain dangling from Ruthie's tight grasp. "You're…you're welcome." She glanced at the clock and gave a start. "Oh, it's almost six. We'd better finish getting ready before we miss breakfast."

Ruthie nodded and rose. Dinah moved to the mirror and began brushing out her hair. In the mirror's reflection, she observed Ruthie uncurl her fist and stare down at the locket resting in her palm. She expected her roommate to slip the chain over her head, but after several seconds of seeming intense concentration, Ruthie returned the necklace to its box and put it in her pocket.

A disappointment more intense than she'd ever experienced—and her life had been filled with disappointments—smote Dinah. She'd been so sure Ruthie would love the locket. But apparently she didn't like it at all. Why else would she hide it away? Blinking back tears, Dinah finished fashioning her hair in its familiar coil, then moved to the door. "I'll see you downstairs." Without waiting for a reply, she hurried into the hallway.

On the other side of the closed door, she allowed one tear to slide down her cheek. Ruthie hadn't liked her gift. Dinah's hand went to her pocket where Mr. Ackerman's box waited. She hoped he would like the knife. If he didn't, she'd never buy a present for anyone ever again.

Amos

Had he made a mistake? Amos waited beside the lunch counter for Dinah to join him. His hip ached fiercely and he wanted to sit, but uncertainty kept him from relaxing. The gift he'd chosen burned in his coat pocket like a hot coal, and he was tempted to toss it out onto the snow-dusted yard and pretend he'd forgotten her gift at home.

When he'd picked it, he was so sure it was the right thing to do. Although their acquaintance was short, although they'd had very little time to spend together, he felt as though he'd been waiting for a girl like her for years. A girl who would look past his limp and see the man. A girl who was gentle, kind, humble, of like-minded faith. Who wanted a family as badly as he did.

And now he'd found her. The eagerness to make her his stole his sleep at night and his focus during the day. He couldn't marry her. Not yet. She was too young. He still had much work on his farm to accomplish. But he wanted to know she would one day be his. He wanted the promise. His gift was meant to be a promise from him to her—a promise of his intentions. If she accepted it, she would pledge to save herself for him. But was she ready to make such a promise?

His heart might pound out of his chest if he didn't settle down. He paced back and forth, willing his racing pulse to calm. Others entered the hotel, shuddering as they left the chill behind, and filed to the lunch counter. The stools quickly filled, and Dinah hadn't come down yet. Amos moved to the wall and leaned against it, his gaze aimed at the hallway leading to the guest rooms. Nervousness made his stomach churn. Had Dinah forgotten they were supposed to meet? Maybe he wouldn't have to give her his gift after all. Maybe he would have time to find something else. He could save the gift he now carried for another time. Later. Next year.

"Mr. Ackerman?"

Amos jolted. Dinah stood before him in her uniform, her head tipped in puzzlement. How had he missed her coming up the hall? Now that he gazed down at her—at her sweet, innocent face—how could he possibly wait to offer his promise and receive hers?

"I'm sorry I'm late. I had to finish a room before I could come for lunch." She glanced at the counter, her face pursing in regret. "Oh, all the seats are taken."

His tongue seemed stuck to the roof of his mouth. He cleared his throat. "We can wait for seats to open."

"But that might not be until my break is over." Dinah brightened. "I know! We'll take plates to the chambermaids' little parlor. It will be quiet there."

The thought of finding a private spot to exchange their gifts appealed to him. If she refused it, at least there wouldn't be witnesses.

She went on, lifting her shoulders in an apologetic gesture. "That is, if you don't mind holding your plate in your lap. There's not a table suitable for dining."

He smiled, recalling another time he sat with a plate in his lap and ate with Dinah. "I don't mind." He trailed her to the counter and waited while she asked one of the luncheon workers for two lunch specials. Amos didn't ask what the special was today—he would happily eat boot leather and sawdust if it meant dining with Miss Dinah Hubley.

She turned with two plates containing thick slabs of meat loaf, roasted potatoes, buttery carrots, and a perfectly browned biscuit. He licked his lips. That looked a lot better than boot leather and sawdust.

She grinned at him, her eyes sparkling, and for a moment he wondered if she'd read his secret thoughts. "This way," she said, and he followed her up the hallway, behind the check-in counter, to a small room tucked off the lobby. A pair of wicker chairs similar to the ones on the porch sat side by side along one wall, the seats angled slightly toward each other. Dinah moved to the chair farthest from the door and nodded at the second chair. "Go ahead and sit down, and I'll give you your plate."

Both embarrassed and pleased by her serving him, Amos aimed his back-side at the cushion on the second chair and let himself plop down. Two guests wandered through the lobby, sending a curious glance into the little room. Wouldn't it be nice if they could close the door and enjoy complete privacy? But propriety demanded they leave it ajar. The moment the seat of his pants met the chair, Dinah handed him his plate. As she did so, she flashed a winsome smile that warmed him from the inside out.

Once she'd sat and settled her plate on her lap, he held out his hand to her. Without pause, she placed her small hand in his. Linked with her, Amos closed his eyes and offered a brief prayer of thanks for the food. Inwardly, he added, *Lord, grant me the favor of acceptance from Dinah.* "Amen."

"Amen," she echoed. She picked up the fork balanced on the edge of her plate, then paused. "Mr. Ackerman, would…would you like to exchange gifts before we eat?"

A hint of trepidation crept through her tone, matching the feelings he'd been battling. A lump seemed to sit in his stomach. He might not be able to swallow until he knew how his gift would be received. He nodded. "I think that's a fine idea."

With a nervous giggle, she ducked her head. She slipped her hand inside her pocket, withdrew a narrow, embossed leather box, and thrust it at him without ceremony. "I didn't wrap it because I thought the box too nice to cover. I hope you'll like it."

"I'm sure I will." Amos took the box. The leather was warm from its hiding spot. He placed the box on his knee, then reached into his pocket for the package he'd brought for her. The sharp edges of the box poked his flesh just as uncertainty stabbed his heart. His hand froze. Once again he wondered if he'd made a mistake. Then he looked into her face, and his apprehensions melted like snow in a hot skillet. This was no mistake. She was meant to be his.

He reached across the little table and took her hand. Turning it palm side up, he battled an urge to lift it to his lips and plant a kiss on the soft pad at the base of her thumb. Instead, he laid the box across the row of calluses that offered silent evidence of her labor. "Miss Hubley, this is a Christmas gift, but it's also…more." Her expression turned curious. He squeezed her fingers closed over the box. Her hand was so small the tips barely curved over the top edge. His heart set up a wild thrum. Settling back into his chair, he nodded at her. "Open it."

Chapter 31

Dinah

lthough Mr. Ackerman sat watching, unmoving, clearly eager for her to open his gift, Dinah took her time. Gifts were few, and she wanted to savor this one. So she slowly slipped the ribbon from the box, leaving the bow intact, and laid it on the arm of the chair. With the ribbon's release, the paper came loose. Careful not to tear it, she removed it, folded it, and tucked it in the space between her hip and the chair's side. Now she held a plain brown box with a fitted lid similar to a hatbox but much smaller.

She allowed herself a few moments to speculate on the contents. Christmas and something more, he'd said. Chocolates? Hair adornments? Perhaps a pretty lace shawl? No, it was too heavy to be a shawl. Maybe the box held a bottle of sweet-smelling perfume... The curiosity built until she couldn't bear it any longer. She popped the top from the box and peeked inside. A highly varnished wooden box with a painted image on its top greeted her eyes, and she released a little laugh of pure pleasure.

"Oh, Mr. Ackerman..." Where had he found such a perfect box? She touched her finger to the painting of a little girl perched on a fallen log with two bright-eyed puppies leaning their paws against the child's leg. On a drooping branch above the girl's head, a cardinal sat with its head tipped to the side as if carrying on a conversation with the child. She couldn't stop smiling.

"T-take it out." Mr. Ackerman's voice quavered, as if his excitement matched hers. "It's a music box."

"It is? Oh my!" Forgetting her determination to extend the moment, she pulled the box from its container and located the brass key. She gave the key several twists, then held her breath. Within seconds, a tinkling melody spilled forth. Dinah beamed.

Mr. Ackerman offered a remorseful grimace. "It isn't 'Roses from the South,' but I thought it sounded nice."

"It sounds beautiful." Dinah gazed in wonder at the music box. She'd never expected to receive anything so lovely. She waited until the music slowed and finally stopped with one echoing note. She sighed and pressed the box to her heart. "It's wonderful. Thank you."

"Miss Hubley…" The hesitation in his tone pulled her attention away from the box. "The music box is only part of the gift. The other part is…inside."

Dinah lowered her brows, puzzled. "Inside?"

"The box is also a trinket box. There's a…trinket…inside."

Looking again at the box, Dinah noticed a tiny drawer tucked on the opposite side of the turn key. She pinched the little rosebud-shaped brass knob serving as a drawer pull and slid the drawer open. She nearly dropped the box on the floor when she saw what rested in the velvet-lined bottom of the drawer.

Rueben had always given her a little something for Christmas, things he called trinkets, but they'd been childish whatnots—a tiny tin dog, a string of glass beads, a coin purse. But now she gazed at a gold ring bearing an amber-colored stone between four silver prongs. After examining the lockets with the clerk at Graham and Tucker, she recognized at once this ring was no cheap trinket. Her mouth went dry. Her hands seemed to forget how to function. She sat staring into the drawer but couldn't find the ability to take out the ring.

Mr. Ackerman reached over and plucked it out, his big fingers barely fitting into the tiny space. He held the ring aloft, the circle of gold and the deep yellow stone reflecting light. "This is what is called a promise ring. It is meant to signify a commitment."

Dinah shifted her gaze from the ring held between his thick, work-roughened fingertips to his face. His voice had emerged low and tight, as if something blocked his throat, but his face bore a deep tenderness. Dinah found herself mesmerized by the emotion in his eyes of darkest blue—the windows to his soul—as he went on quietly.

"I offer it to you as commitment to build my business to support you. I offer it as a promise to someday—when we are both ready—be a faithful husband to you." He rotated the ring slightly back and forth, causing tiny sparkles to blink in offbeats. "I want you to keep it. It's yours. But I..." The last two words growled out.

He ducked his head for a moment, his eyes slipping closed, and when he looked at her again, a soft, gentle, heart-melting smile curved his lips. "But I ask you to only wear it if you are willing to make a commitment to me. I know you're very young. You might want something more in life than to be the wife of a chicken farmer. If so, you don't need to wear the ring. But keep it as a token of my affection for you. Take it out from time to time and think kindly of me."

He dropped the ring in the little drawer and pushed it closed with one finger. His smile wavered as the ring disappeared from sight, but then it grew broader when he looked at her again. "And now, may I open my gift from you?"

Dinah hadn't realized she'd been holding her breath. All at once it whooshed out, and a nervous laugh followed it. The mother-of-pearl knife seemed so paltry when compared with what he'd given her. But she had nothing else for him. Cradling the music box against her chest again, she nodded. "Yes. Please open yours." She bit her lower lip, waiting for his reaction.

He lifted the box from his knee and popped the lid in one smooth motion. His eyes lit up. He pulled the knife free and snapped open the blade. The knife looked ridiculously small in his big hand, but the polished silver glinted almost as brightly as the gold ring had. "Well, would you look at that..." He turned the knife this way and that, examining it from every angle. He ran the tip of his thumb along the blade's edge, whistled through his teeth, then did it again.

Dinah, beyond pleased by his eager examination, pointed to the stamp at the base of the blade. "The clerk at Graham and Tucker said an English company makes these knives. He said they're pur—" She sought the fancy word the clerk had used. "Purported to be among the finest in the world."

Mr. Ackerman continued admiring the knife. "I believe him. It's grand, Dinah—the nicest pocketknife I've ever seen."

Heat raced from Dinah's chest to her face. He'd called her Dinah. Not Miss Hubley, but Dinah, with such ease and familiarity she was certain he hadn't even realized his blunder. The utterance surprised her, thrilled her, and frightened her all at the same time. Unsure how to respond, she blurted, "Should we eat now? My break will be over soon."

With seeming reluctance, he returned the knife to its box. Then he pulled it out again and slipped it into his right-hand coat pocket. He shoved the box in the left-hand pocket. He looked at Dinah. His gaze dropped to the music box, which she still clutched to her bodice, and a crooked smile creased his cheek. "It'll be pretty hard to use your fork when you've got both hands busy."

A self-conscious titter escaped her throat. She shifted her knees to make space on the chair seat for the music box. She placed it very gently on the cushion, then lifted her fork. Although the ring was well hidden in its little drawer, she could see it plainly in her mind's eye. As she took her first bite of now-cold meat loaf and congealed gravy, she tried to imagine how it would look on her hand.

"Only wear it if you are willing to make a commitment to me." Mr. Ackerman's sweetly uttered words echoed through her memory. He was a good man. A better man than she'd known could even exist in the world. And he'd given her the ring as his commitment to her. Should she put it on? Doing so would secure her future. She'd never known security, and its pull was strong. Yet her dream of becoming a server—of being recognized as one of Mr. Harvey's specially chosen girls—also tugged at her.

The respect and admiration she'd been denied all her life waited on one hand. Security and the affection of a good man waited on the other. Which should she choose? She risked a glance at Mr. Ackerman, who sat erect and ate his lunch with proper manners yet also with obvious enjoyment. A smile grew on her face without effort. He was a handsome man pleased by simple things. She found him attractive.

Her eyes drifted to his lips. When he'd touched them to her knuckles the night of the ball, she hadn't shrunk away. The touch had been so tender, so kind. But she also remembered another man's lips, and the recollection brought a roll of nausea. What would she do if Mr. Ackerman pressed his lips to her mouth rather than to her hand?

She set her plate aside, her appetite gone. She lowered her gaze to the music box where the painted girl lifted her face to the cardinal. How unburdened and innocent the artist's rendition appeared. A lump filled Dinah's throat. Had Mr. Ackerman chosen this box because the picture reminded him of Sam and Gid, or of her? The puppies' pose and inquisitiveness certainly reflected his pair of pups, but the image held nothing of her. She wasn't unsullied. She wasn't carefree. Her dreams reminded her of that truth each night.

But... Her pulse stuttered as an idea crept through her melancholy thoughts. If Mr. Ackerman saw her as innocent, as someone to be desired, then perhaps the admiration she'd been seeking could be found by accepting his ring. Wouldn't others look upon her differently if they knew Mr. Ackerman had chosen her as his own? Her mother's poor reputation had impacted others' views of Dinah. Didn't it then stand to reason the community's respect for Mr. Ackerman would trickle over on her? And if others viewed her as such, perhaps her view of herself could be altered, as well.

Excitement trembled through her belly. Respect—and healing from the scars inflicted by the man in Chicago—could be hers...now...by simply placing his ring on her finger. Her hand inched toward the little drawer on the music box, some inner voice prodding her. *Put it on, put it on...*

"There you are."

Dinah jumped at the intrusion of Mr. Irwin's stern voice. The man stood in the doorway with a dark scowl marring his brow. Dinah scrambled to grab her plate and rise without knocking the music box onto the floor.

"I've been looking everywhere for you. We've had a calamity, and Miss Mead informs me you might be willing to help bring a speedy resolution."

Dinah shook her head in confusion. "I'll do what I can, Mr. Irwin. What is the calamity?"

He folded his arms over his chest. Bold streaks of red colored his cheeks. "I've just had to dismiss one of our dining room servers for consorting with a traveling salesman, a clear violation of the rules of conduct. Consequently I need a dining staff server at once. I realize you are not yet eighteen, but given the circumstances and given your thus-far exemplary employment with the Clifton, I believe Mr. Harvey would be willing to make an exception and allow you to assume the position as server immediately."

He took a deep breath, and the bold red faded to a rosy pink. "Of course, you would be required to sign to a year's service and abide by the rules outlined in the contract." The manager's gaze flitted to Mr. Ackerman and then returned to Dinah. "Are you interested, Miss Hubley, or do I wire Mrs. Walters to request a new server?"

Chapter 32

Amos

$\mathcal{A}$ mos listened with interest but carefully kept his head angled low so Dinah wouldn't read any silent messages from his face. A year's service was a big commitment, and he'd heard about the stringent rules for servers. If she accepted the position, she wouldn't be able to write to him or spend time with him. Bringing their budding relationship to a halt would pain him. He'd come to treasure her letters and their twice-weekly luncheons. But the job was a good opportunity for Dinah. Better pay and less strenuous work. And Miss Mead had told him long ago it was what Dinah wanted. He wouldn't blame her if she told the manager yes.

Out of the corner of his eye, he watched Dinah place her plate on the chair's seat. Her hands, without hesitation, reached for the music box he'd given her. She opened the little trinket drawer, took out the ring, and slipped it on her finger.

Amos sucked in a sharp breath as his head came up. Had he seen correctly? Yes, the ring sparkled on her finger. He'd chosen one too large—she had to curl her fist to keep it on—but it was there, circling her finger as a symbol of his commitment to her. And hers to him.

He set his plate on the floor and rose. He forced himself to be unselfish. "Are you sure? We have to wait until you're eighteen anyway. We have to wait until I've built my flock. You could work as a server for a year and then…"

Her pale-blue eyes glowed with certainty. She nodded. "I'm sure." She stepped away from him to address Mr. Irwin. "I appreciate your confidence in me, sir, but I want to keep working as a chambermaid." Shifting her head, she met Amos's gaze. A smile of promise appeared on her face. "I don't want to give up being courted by Mr. Ackerman."

Amos swallowed. If Mr. Irwin hadn't been in the room, he'd have swept Dinah into his arms. But he had to satisfy himself by offering her a brief nod of approval. Her answering smile told him she understood.

Mr. Irwin released a disgruntled huff and threw out his hands in a gesture of frustration. "Very well, Miss Hubley, very well. The three remaining servers will simply have to cope with the extra work until a new server is hired." He whirled and stormed from the room.

Amos touched Dinah's shoulder, and she turned to fully face him. He sought words to tell her what her decision meant to him. But nothing seemed enough. So he said simply, "You've made me very happy, Miss Hubley." He smiled, warmth flooding his chest. "Dinah."

Tears swam in her eyes, brightening her irises. "Merry Christmas, Amos."

Ruthie

"Merry Christmas, Mama. Merry Christmas, Papa." Ruthie embraced her parents by turn, then held her arms to her younger brothers and sister. Little Dinah June dove against Ruthie, and Joseph, Timothy, and Cale pushed in for a hug. But she had to pursue Noah, Jonah, and Seth. They complained at her insistence on greeting them with a hug, making her laugh, but inwardly she ached. They were getting so grown up. Seth was already taller than her, and Jonah wasn't far behind. As much as she relished helping her parents with her salary, she wished she could spend more time with her family. She would savor every minute of this lunch break on Christmas Day.

"We waited for you to open presents!" Dinah June bounced in place, her red ringlets dancing around her rosy cheeks. "Come on!"

Ruthie grabbed up the bag of presents she'd brought and allowed Dinah June to tug her toward the bedraggled tree in the corner of their small parlor.

The boys followed in a jostling cluster, and everyone sat on the floor. Ruthie emptied her bag, and Joseph reared back in surprise.

"Lookit 'em all!" Her seven-year-old brother grabbed the closest two packages and showed them to Seth, who sat next to him. "Ruthie must be rich to buy so many presents!"

Mama leaned in, frowning a bit as she surveyed the pile. "My, Ruthie, this is extravagant. I hope you didn't overextend yourself."

Ruthie knew Mama was asking if she'd charged items at the store. "Don't worry, Mama. I only bought one present for each. I had enough money."

Her mother held one hand toward the impressive stash. "But—"

"My roommate, Miss Hubley, purchased something for all of you, too."

Now Papa scowled. "Well, why didn't she come with you, then, so we could thank her?"

"Yes, Ruthie," Mama added. "Did you invite her?"

Guilt pricked. She should have asked Dinah to join them. But wasn't it enough that the man she'd set her sights on was pursuing Dinah? Did her family have to claim Dinah, too? Instead of answering her mother, Ruthie began calling the names printed on the paper tags attached to the packages' bows. To her relief, her parents' attention shifted to distributing the gifts under the tree. In only a few minutes, each Mead family member held a small cluster of presents.

Dinah June crowed, "I'm youngest, so I get to open first!"

Papa put his hand on Dinah June's head. "This year, Junebug, let's all open our presents at once."

Seth frowned. "But we always take turns so we can see what everybody got."

"Your sister has to hurry back to work. If we take turns, she'll have to leave before we're finished."

The younger children all dove into their presents with glee, but Seth grumbled under his breath. Another wave of guilt struck Ruthie. Was it fair for her family to sacrifice their long-held and favored traditions for her? Paper and ribbons flew, and happy chatter filled the room, but Ruthie found little plea-sure in watching her younger siblings tear through their packages. What should have been a leisurely celebration of gifting one another turned into a three-minute-long melee, robbing her of seeing her family's delight in what she chose for them.

As soon as the children had unwrapped everything, Mama shooed them to the dining room table. She called over her shoulder, "Come along now, Ruthie and Jacob. We'll have to eat quickly if Ruthie is to partake of any of our Christmas dinner."

Ruthie set her lips in a disgruntled pout. Hurry through presents. Hurry through dinner. Where was the joy of which the angels sang? Papa didn't even have time to read the Christmas story while she was here—something she'd cherished since she was a small girl. She thumped her fist on the braided rag rug filling the middle of the floor. "I'm not hungry."

Papa stood over her with his hands on his hips. He sent her a disapproving look. "Ruthie, such behavior. And on Christmas."

Looking up from her spot on the floor, she felt like a little girl again. She wished she could be a little girl, as little as Dinah June, so she could climb into her father's lap and find comfort the way she used to. She ducked her head as tears filled her eyes. "Oh, Papa…"

He crouched on his haunches and cupped her chin, forcing her to look at him. "Tell me what's wrong." Only kindness colored his tone and expression.

Ruthie sighed. "I wish I knew. I've been sad for…for weeks." A tear trailed down her cheek in a warm rivulet. "I feel as though nothing is right in my world."

"Ah, Ruthie…" He shifted to sit beside her, resting his elbows on his bent knees. "I think you're experiencing growing pains. Your mother told me you have interest in Amos Ackerman."

Ruthie gawked at him. "She told you?"

A soft chuckle rolled from her father's chest. "Your mother and I discuss everything involving our children's well-being. So yes, she told me. And we haven't missed the fact that he is taken by your roommate." He raised one eye-brow. "Is that why you didn't invite her to join us today?"

Remembering her shock and dismay at the ring on Dinah's finger, Ruthie closed her eyes against another rush of tears. "He gave her a ring, Papa." She braced for a lecture about putting others before herself instead of behaving selfishly.

But Papa's arm slipped around Ruthie's shoulder and pulled her close. She snuggled in, grateful for her father's understanding. His chin tipped against her temple. "I'm sure it hurts, having to give up on thinking of a future with him. I wouldn't have opposed it. Mr. Ackerman seems to be a good Christian man. But apparently God has something else in mind for you."

Ruthie angled her head to peer at her father. "Do you think so?"

Papa feigned surprise. "Why wouldn't I think so? Doesn't the Bible we believe say God's thoughts of us outnumber the grains of sand? And doesn't it tell us God makes good plans for His children?"

Ruthie sniffed and laid her head on Papa's shoulder again. "Then why did He let Mr. Ackerman choose Dinah instead of me? God knows how much I…I like Mr. Ackerman."

"Ruthie, you're looking at Mr. Ackerman's choosing to court Dinah instead of you as an end to a journey."

She jerked upright. "Because it is! Maybe it's childish, Papa, but I imagined a life with him. The imaginings felt good and right. But now—"

"But now you're being sent down a different path." Papa took her hand and squeezed it, his touch assuring. "Instead of the end, Ruthie, this is the beginning. You stand ready to take the first step on the road God wants you to follow. Now that your plans have been set aside, your heart is open to explore the plans God has for you."

Ruthie wasn't sure her aching heart was open for anything. But she wouldn't argue with Papa. Especially not on Christmas Day. She sagged against him again, letting his strength bolster her. He curved his arms around her and held her close for several seconds. Then he planted a kiss on the top of her head and gave her a little shake.

"All right now. No more moping. New beginnings are happy things. Maybe a little uncertain, even a little scary, but mostly happy and exciting."

Papa stood and pulled Ruthie up with him. "Your mama peeked in a bit ago and didn't interrupt us, but I'm sure she'd like a few minutes with you before you have to go back to work. So let's join her and the children, hmm?"

They started toward the dining room, but after only two steps Ruthie stopped and caught Papa's hand. "Will you pray for me, Papa, so I will know what I'm meant to do? I'm so confused."

He delivered a tender kiss on her forehead. "I pray for you every day, my darling daughter. Your mama and I both pray for you." He cupped her face in his hands. "Remember God wants good things for His children—the best things—but we have to be willing to listen for His guidance and then go where He leads. Will you listen, Ruthie, and respond with obedience?"

When Papa spoke to her so seriously, with tears glittering in his eyes, Ruthie couldn't refuse what he asked. "I will. I promise."

"That's my girl."

Ruthie joined her family at the table for a few bites of the wonderful meal Mama had prepared. She talked and laughed and teased as if she hadn't a care in the world. But underneath, a question tormented her. What if God's plan was for her to work as a chambermaid at the Clifton Hotel for the rest of her life? Would she be able to be obedient to such a call?

Chapter 33

Dinah

inah finished her work by noon on Christmas Day. Only a few guests resided beneath the hotel's roof on this holiday, giving her a rare day of leisure. But she had to be available if someone needed something, so instead of going to her room, she took her lunch, her Bible, and her writing paper and pencil to the chambermaids' parlor. While she listened for a beckon-me bell to jangle, she could read or write a letter to Mr. Ackerman.

To Amos…her beau.

Just the thought of her beau made her heart flutter, but she couldn't deny experiencing a stab of loneliness as she entered the beautifully decorated yet empty room. As a child, she'd been lonely both at school and in her home even though people were always around. But none of those people had included her in their circles, making her feel isolated. Remembering past days of sitting in her attic room or on the playground or in the schoolroom all alone raised an ache in the center of her breast. How she hated being all by herself…

She gave herself a little shake. Shouldn't she be accustomed to loneliness? Of course she should. Being alone wasn't anything new. She placed her Bible and paper in one chair and sank into the second one with her plate, determined to set aside the melancholy feeling. But she couldn't. Christmas Day—a time when families gathered—was the worst day to be by herself. She lowered her head and caught sight of the ring Amos had given her. For a moment she paused and pointed toward the ceiling to admire the slim gold band circling her first finger.

Amos had expressed disappointment that the ring didn't fit her ring finger, but it fit perfectly on her first finger. And she liked it there. In only one day, she'd developed the habit of rubbing her thumb along the smooth band or tapping the yellow-orange gem to her lower lip when she was thinking. The ring offered a constant reminder that someone—someone kind and good and loving—wanted to build a life with her. She pressed the stone to her lip again. Like a kiss. Hope flickered in her heart. Would the knowledge of Amos's care for her chase away all the ugly feelings of unworthiness that had plagued her for as long as she could remember?

Thinking of Amos drew her attention to her Bible. He'd mentioned a biblical woman named Dinah in one of his letters. While she ate, she could find the story and then let him know she'd read about the Bible-Dinah. Her smoked-ham sandwich in one hand, she opened the Bible with the other and leafed through page by page until she found the thirty-fourth chapter of Genesis. Leaning toward the chair seat, where the Bible lay open, she began to read, whispering the words.

"'And Dinah the daughter of Leah, which she bare unto Jacob, went out to see the daughters of the land. And when Shechem the son of Hamor the Hivite, prince of the country, saw her, he took her, and lay with her, and defiled her.'" Dinah gasped. She dropped the sandwich onto the plate and slapped the Book closed. But even though the printed words were hidden, they continued to blaze in her memory.

"He took her, and lay with her, and defiled her."

"He...defiled her."

"He...defiled her."

She pressed the ring to her lip until her teeth cut the tender skin inside her mouth, willing the pain to rid the ugly reference from her mind. But the images remained, bringing with them agonizing memories of being taken, being forced upon a bed, being defiled. Stifling a little cry, she rose and paced the room. Such heartrending pictures the few verses painted in her mind. Such empathy she felt toward the woman of long ago. Chills broke out over her body followed by waves of heat as she battled an intense emotion she couldn't even define.

She whirled toward the Bible, which lay at an angle on the chair's cushion, so innocent looking. So inviting. She quivered from head to toe. Bits and pieces of the stories in her fairy-tale book tiptoed through her mind. Many of the stories included difficulties, but always evil was conquered and the hero and heroine lived happily ever after. Hugging herself, she struggled to bring her tremors under control. She should read the rest of the story about Dinah. It could have a happy ending.

Feeling as though she walked through waist-deep water, Dinah moved slowly, painstakingly, toward the chair and picked up the Bible. No longer hungry, she set the sandwich aside, curled in the seat, and opened the Book again. She read the chapter in its entirety. And when she finished, the words swam on the page as tears filled her eyes. Perhaps some would say the story ended well, with the defiler and his entire clan punished by death, but the ending gave Dinah no satisfaction.

Where was the happily ever after? All that remained at the close of the tale was a woman defiled, her reputation permanently ruined. Brothers with blood on their hands. A father now fearing revenge against his entire family. Knowing what had happened to the Bible-Dinah, even though her brothers defended her, made her heart ache. Why had Amos mentioned the woman in the Bible named Dinah?

When she saw him Thursday, she would ask him if he thought the brothers had been right to kill an entire clan because of one man's vile act. She would ask if he thought Dinah, who had been defiled, ever recovered from the harm inflicted upon her. She would ask—

She sat upright, shaking her head. No, she wouldn't ask about the Bible-Dinah. Because if she talked about the woman in the Bible who'd been defiled, she would surely cry, and Amos would wonder why she'd been moved so deeply. He might guess she really asked about herself. He might react the way Bible-Dinah's brothers had—seeking revenge. And she couldn't bear to see her gentle, loving beau stirred to such anger and hatred.

So she wouldn't ask. She would bury the knowledge of the Bible-Dinah the way she tried to bury the memories of her time in the hotel in Chicago. She hugged the Bible and closed her eyes against a fierce sting of tears. She would remember Dinah's defilement—she would remember her own defilement—no more.

In the nights following Christmas, Dinah's dreams changed. No longer only reliving terrifying moments from her own experience, she became a helpless witness to Bible-Dinah's attack. She would awaken crying, riddled with guilt at her inability to save the poor woman from pain and suffering.

Ruthie had begged Dinah to share her dreams—"Mama always told me, once you say out loud what's frightening you, it will lose its power over you."

Dinah was tempted. She longed to be free of the horrible nightmares. But she didn't want to put the pictures into Ruthie's head. So she suffered in silence.

On Thursday heavy snows fell, carried on a strong wind that kept everyone holed up inside. Amos didn't come for their lunch meeting, and although Dinah hadn't expected him to make his way into town in such frigid conditions, she missed her hour with him. By Sunday the snow had cleared, but a guest rented the buggy the girls used for transportation to church and the ground was too mucky for them to walk. Ruthie moped all day over missing the service and the minutes of time with her family, adding to Dinah's doldrums.

Monday, New Year's Eve, Dinah hurried to the lunch counter at noon, almost desperate to see Amos, only to receive a message from one of the luncheon-counter workers that he couldn't meet with her. He'd had to hurry back to the farm with a little coal-oil stove he hoped would keep the newest batch of chicks from freezing. When she found a letter anchored beneath one leg of the chair on the porch—they'd stored the cushions during the winter months—she was cheered. Until she unfolded it and realized the damp porch boards had caused the ink to run. She couldn't read most of the message, and she spent the remainder of the day mourning not only her lost hour with Amos, but also the lost words from him.

The hotel hosted a New Year's Eve dance for the townspeople of Florence to welcome the year 1884, and both Ruthie and Dinah were released to attend. Dinah had no desire to go to a party—she wasn't in a festive mood—but Ruthie's parents would be there, so Ruthie eagerly donned the dress she'd worn to the Calico Ball and asked Dinah to fashion her hair.

As Dinah pinned Ruthie's wavy red-gold locks into a mass of curls on top of her head, Ruthie said, "Why don't you come, too, Dinah? It would do you good, I think, to have a little fun."

Dinah shook her head.

Ruthie's green-eyed gaze begged Dinah from the mirror's reflection. "Not even for an hour or so? You wouldn't have to dance. Except maybe with my papa."

She'd promised herself to Amos, and she wouldn't dance with anyone else, not even Ruthie's father. "No, thank you."

Ruthie caught Dinah's hand. "But if you dance with Papa, you can talk to him. About your night terrors."

Dinah tried to withdraw her hand, but Ruthie held tight.

"Papa is a minister. He's a very good listener. And he gives wonderful advice. He could help you stop having the bad dreams."

"Ruthie..." Dinah nearly groaned her roommate's name. How could she convince Ruthie to let her be? Ruthie thought her father could solve any problem, but the only person who could help Dinah was Amos. He was her beau— her rescuer. Surely the severity of her dreams these past few days were because she hadn't seen him for a week. She needed to stockpile good memories with him so the ugly memories would be forced out of her mind. Talking to Preacher Mead would be a useless frittering of time. She needed only Amos.

Ruthie tugged on Dinah's hand. "I really think you should—"

Dinah slipped free of Ruthie's grasp and picked up another hairpin. "You go. Enjoy your time with your folks. I'll be fine. Don't worry about me."

Ruthie set her lips in a grim line and sat quiet and still while Dinah finished her hair. When Dinah secured the last pin and turned away from the dressing table, Ruthie said, "What will you do this evening if you don't go to the party?"

Dinah shrugged. "I'll probably spend the evening in our parlor in case someone rings the beckon-me bell. We do have guests in the hotel, you know."

Ruthie heaved a mighty sigh. "Well, I don't mind telling you I feel guilty going to a party when you plan to work." An impish smile crept up her cheek. "But I don't feel guilty enough to skip the celebration." She opened a little drawer on the dressing table and took out the locket Dinah had given her for Christmas. She slipped the chain over her head, then gave the mirror a peek. "Perfect."

She fingered the oval locket, her expression turning pensive. "Who knows? Maybe tonight I'll meet the man whose photograph will go inside this locket someday." She spun and captured Dinah in an impulsive embrace. Taken by surprise, Dinah didn't have time to stiffen before Ruthie released her and crossed to the door. She flashed a quick smile over her shoulder. "By the time I get in, you'll probably be asleep, so I'll say happy New Year now."

Dinah echoed, "Happy New Year." But her voice held little gaiety.

Ruthie clicked the door closed behind her, and her pattering footsteps receded. Dinah waited until she was certain Ruthie had made it down the stairs before collecting her writing paper and pencil and scuffing to the door. For a moment, she considered putting on her Calico Ball dress and going to the party after all. Just to watch. Then she shook her head. If Amos couldn't be there, she didn't want to be there. She'd only be lonely without him. She'd do as she'd told Ruthie.

As she headed downstairs and through the hallway to the chambermaids' parlor, she reasoned she'd likely have a quiet evening. The desk clerk indicated only two people had checked into the hotel that day. With the holidays upon them, most people were staying home rather than traveling. She'd write a bit to Amos and maybe turn in early. Her body gave an involuntary jerk as she remembered that going to sleep meant the possibility of another nightmare. She shuddered. No, she'd keep herself awake as long as possible. Maybe even until the chimes announced midnight. Then, if she were very lucky, she'd be too tired to dream.

She sat in the chair in the corner, laid the paper across her knee, and began to write.

My dear Amos,

It is New Year's Eve, and the town is celebrating with a party. If you were in attendance, I would be at the party, too, like Ruthie and many of the townspeople. But you aren't here, and I don't want to go without you. So instead I will write you a letter. Writing to you is almost as good as talking to you. It makes me less lonely.

With a start she realized she didn't feel quite as alone with thoughts of him filling her mind. Smiling, she bent over the page again.

I hope the stove you bought is keeping the chicks warm. It must not be a very large stove if you carted it home in your wagon. But chicks are so tiny they probably don't need a large stove for warmth. Have you trained Samson and Gideon to cuddle with the chicks and help keep them warm? I think smart dogs like Sam and Gid could learn just about anything. Even being kind to baby chickens.

Since you haven't been able to get into town easily, are the eggs—

A light "ahem" intruded. Startled, Dinah jerked, and the pencil lead left a thick mark on the page. Sucking in a breath of aggravation, she set the paper and pencil aside and turned to see who had disturbed her. But the person framed in the doorway wasn't Mr. Irwin, one of the hotel employees, or even a guest. Her heart gave a happy leap, and she dashed toward the door.

"Amos!"

Chapter 34

Amos

inah stopped just short of reaching him. Amos would have welcomed her leaping into his arms, but the expression of delight on her face was reward enough for making the long, chilly trek to town. How could he end this year without one more glimpse of her sweet face? The ache in his hip, the pain in his ears, toes, and fingers from the biting wind were a small price to pay to have pleased her so much.

He smiled and stretched out one hand, which she gripped between both of her palms. The warmth of her flesh felt good against his wind-chilled fingers. "Happy New Year, Dinah."

"Oh, happy New Year to you, Amos." Her voice trickled out, carried on a soft sigh. "I didn't know you were coming. This is a wonderful surprise."

The way she clung to his hand was a wonderful surprise for him. Although he often reached for her, to cup her hand or graze her arm with his fingertips, she usually scurried away from his touch. He admired her restraint, while at the same time he longed for signs of affection. But she held to him now, and his ring sparkled on her finger. Both promised him that one day, when they had become man and wife—and such a day it would be!—she would respond differently to his affectionate advances.

"I came to take you to the New Year's Eve party." He glanced across her uniform, and his spirits sank. "But you must be working."

She released him and took a dainty backward step. "Mr. Irwin told both Ruthie and me we could go to the party, but I didn't want to go without you."

Her statement made his heart sing.

"So I decided to stay in my uniform. If you're willing to wait, I'll run up-stairs and change into my ball dress."

"I'll wait."

She inched toward the door. "I'll only be a few minutes."

Amos would wait hours if need be. "Take whatever time you need. I'll be here when you come down."

She flashed a grateful smile and grabbed the doorframe as if to propel herself into the hallway. "Good! I'll—" The clatter of a bell sounded from somewhere up the hall. Dinah gave a little stomp and pursed her lips into a scowl. "Oh, pooh, there's a beckon-me bell. I need to see to a guest."

Her reaction tickled him, and he stifled a chuckle. "Well, go ahead and take care of it." Consternation marred her brow. He added, "We'll have the whole evening together." He intended to stay until midnight so he could start the new year with Dinah at his side.

With a sigh she rounded the corner. Curious to see her at work and unwill-ing to let her out of his sight after their long week apart, Amos followed, keep-ing a few yards' distance between them. The bell jangled again, more loudly, and Dinah sped into a little trot. When she halted outside a door, he stopped, shifting to lean against the opposite wall where he had a good view, and watched her flick her apron smooth, tuck a wayward curl behind her ear, and finally give a few taps with the brass door knock.

Moments later the door swung wide. A gray-haired man with a thick mus-tache stood in the doorway. His shirt was untucked and unbuttoned at the throat, giving him a slovenly appearance. Amos scowled. Was Dinah subjected to such sights daily? Protectiveness tightened his chest. *Lord, let me complete my plans quickly so I can take Dinah away from this job. Witnessing men in states of half dress isn't suitable for a young, innocent woman.*

The man seemed to examine the thick towel draped over his arm. "I was preparing to make use of this towel, but I discovered a stain." He pointed at a spot. "Has this been washed?"

Dinah leaned in slightly, peering at the fabric. "I'm sure it's been laundered, sir, but I'll gladly retrieve a fresh one for you." Her courteous voice contrasted with the man's brusque tone.

He thrust the towel at Dinah, lifting his head as he did so, and his brow furrowed as if he puzzled over something. Then recognition burst across his face, and he barked out a brief laugh of surprise. He gave the towel a toss toward her waiting hands and then leaned his shoulder on the doorjamb. Folding his arms over his chest, he sent his leering gaze up and down Dinah's length.

Dinah's face drained of color. Her frame began to tremble, and the towel fell to the floor at her feet. She stared at the man in mute horror.

Amos's blood ran cold as fury writhed through him. How dare the guest eye Dinah as if she were a common strumpet. He balled his hands into fists and started toward the insolent man. If only he could charge like a bull instead of limping over the carpet in his awkward gait.

"Well, well, well…" The guest laughed again—this time the sound low, knowing, mocking. "If it isn't little Dinah from Chicago. Working as a chambermaid, are you? I don't imagine it pays as well as your former occupation."

Amos froze in place, confusion and revulsion replacing the ball of fury.

The man went on, his voice wheedling. "But if you'd like to earn a few extra dollars while I'm in town, maybe we could…"

Nausea flooded Amos's gut as the guest's meaning became clear. He forced one word past his aching throat. "Dinah?"

Dinah

Standing there beneath the lewd grin of the man who had haunted her dreams while Amos—her beau, her prince—looked on with an expression of pain and disillusionment, Dinah wanted to die. She tried to go to Amos, but her foot caught on the discarded towel. The tremors shuddering through her made her clumsy, and she couldn't free herself to move. So she remained in place, aware of the businessman from Chicago witnessing her appeal to Amos with her eyes.

Amos shifted his gaze from her to the man in the doorway. He snapped, "You know Miss Hubley?"

A chuckle rumbled from the man's chest. "I certainly do. I know her well."

Shame burned in Dinah's middle. She folded her arms across her waist in a feeble effort to tamp it down. She sent Amos a pleading look. "It...it isn't what you think."

Amos hitched toward her, his face set in such a grimace of agony she thought her chest might explode from pain. "What I'm thinking, Dinah, I cannot bring myself to say aloud." Although he spoke softly, even kindly, his words flayed her. "This man... In Chicago..." His dear eyes slipped closed, as if he couldn't bear to look upon her. He whispered in a grating voice, "Did you take money from him?"

"I... He..."

Amos opened his eyes and pinned a steely look on her. "Answer me. Did you lie with this man in exchange for money?"

Regret and disgrace and so much sorrow—she marveled that she could hold it all—rolled through her, making her body go hot, then cold, then hot again. For a moment, she felt incapable of drawing air into her lungs, as if her very breath had been snatched away. Could someone drown from shame? Icy waves seemed to break against her frame, growing stronger and more stifling with each ebb. The cloying feeling of being sucked beneath a whirlpool stole her ability to speak. Her lips flopped helplessly open and closed. But she didn't need to answer him. Amos saw the truth. Her body sagged in defeat as the raging seas consumed her. Her humiliation was complete.

He took a step backward, angling his head away from her but shifting his eyes so his gaze continued to bore into her with accusation and disbelief. "You...are a harlot?"

Dinah threw her fists outward, rejecting the name he'd thrown at her. "No!"

"What else except a harlot takes money for something that should only be given in love?" His tone was flat, his expression dead, but his blue eyes had never seemed so dark and foreboding. "How many men did you favor in Chicago?"

Men? Did he really think so little of her? Too hurt to speak, she stood in silence, rubbing her thumb over the gold band of the ring he'd given her as a promise of good things to come. Now, with the opening of a door, all the bright promises had crumbled. If only she hadn't responded to the beckon-me bell. If only Amos had stayed away this evening. If only she could turn back time and choose a different path. If only those crashing waves would swallow her up.

Bible-Dinah's brothers felled an entire village in retaliation for their sister's defilement. Dinah had no brothers. She only had Amos. And instead of attacking the defiler, he'd turned on the defiled. She'd never felt such torment. The pain she'd experienced during the hours in the hotel room in Chicago were only a scratch compared to the deep wounds Amos's reaction inflicted on her soul. Had she really believed he wouldn't hurt her? How wrong she'd been. With only one question—"How many men did you favor?"—he destroyed every bit of trust she placed in him. How could her heart keep beating? How did her lungs keep drawing in air? Her body went on living, but inside... Inside she surely died.

The guest—the gentleman who was no gentleman—pushed off the doorframe and scooped up the towel from the floor. "I suppose I can tolerate a little stain on my towel. Never mind bringing me a fresh one." He closed the door, leaving Dinah and Amos standing several feet apart in the hallway.

Gas lamps flickered. Music and laughter and chatting voices floated from the ballroom. The pendulum clock in the lobby ticktocked its familiar cadence. Minutes slipped by as if nothing were amiss. Yet her world had crumbled. She stood so still and stiff her muscles ached while she waited for Amos to say something, do something. But he remained as motionless and stone faced as a statue. She couldn't let him go on believing she had sold her body to men. She must at least tell him that much truth.

Dinah forced her tight chest to fill with air, gathering courage. "Not men."

He visibly jerked, as if jolted from a stupor. His head swiveled and his emotionless gaze fell on her. "What?"

She dared to inch forward two tiny steps. Linking her hands together, she beseeched him with her eyes. "It wasn't men. A man. Only one, Amos."

His brows rose and his mouth fell open. He shook his head as if removing stones from his ears. "Only one. Did you say, 'Only one'? The number doesn't matter. You took money from a man for——" His face contorted. He clutched his temples and groaned. A horrible, pain-filled groan that seared Dinah's heart. "I...I have to go." With a stumbling step, he aimed himself for the front doors.

Dinah darted after him, reaching out with both hands but not touching him. "Amos, wait. Please." He pumped his arms, his feet falling heavily on the floor as he broke into a clumsy trot. Even though he wouldn't look at her, she scuttled alongside him, gazing into his stern face and hoping for some hint of softening, some small glimmer of understanding. But they reached the double doors leading to the porch and his expression remained forbidding.

He reached for the doorknob, and she caught his sleeve. Through gritted teeth he said, "Let go of me."

She shook her head. "No, I won't." When had she grown so bold? She never exhibited such fortitude, but she never faced losing something so precious before. She tightened her grip, feeling the strong cords of his muscles even through the sleeve of his wool coat. "Not until we've talked."

"There's nothing left to say."

Where had her gentle, tender beau gone? This mask of cold indifference had no place on Amos Ackerman's face. And she—what she had done—had brought the change. She'd destroyed herself. She'd destroyed him. Her burden of shame heightened, nearly collapsing her. She swallowed tears. "Please, Amos, let me—"

He whirled on her. "Explain?" His icy tone lashed her like a whip. "There is no explanation, Dinah. Nothing you can say will excuse what you did. You are a trollop. You sold yourself. And the man who purchased you might be willing to use something that bears stains from another's use, but I—" His body jolted as if someone had plunged a knife into his heart. Tears spurted in his eyes, and he crunched his face into a horrible grimace. He jerked free of her grasp and lunged for the doorknob. "I cannot."

He threw the door open with force and then left it standing wide when he lurched onto the porch. Cold wind blasted through the opening, carrying fluttering snowflakes that fell on Dinah's skirt and glistened like stars in a blackened sky. She shivered, but she made no effort to close the door. Instead she stood in the doorway while wild winds tossed her hair and penetrated her dress to chill her limbs.

Eyes dry and unblinking, she stared into the darkness where Amos had disappeared and waited for the frigid gusts of winds to freeze her heart. Maybe then it would stop beating. Maybe then she would feel nothing. Maybe then the pain would end.

Chapter 35

Amos

mos held on to his fury the entire long walk home. With every step he took, the drawling comment of the guest in the Clifton—*"I know her well"*—repeated itself in his mind. With every blast of cold wind, an image of Dinah's pleading face appeared in his memory. With every wink of a star in the sky, he recalled the sparkle of the ring she wore on her finger. And with each remembrance, his anger grew—an anger more intense and encompassing than any he'd faced before.

He thought he'd been angry when as a young boy, he'd awakened to hear a doctor tell him he'd never walk normally again. But the anger he felt then paled in comparison to this. Then, he'd been angry at the circumstance. This anger was personal. Which made it much more difficult to bear.

Despite the cold, sweat trickled between his shoulder blades. She'd duped him. He'd pledged himself to a girl whose innocence was a farce. A girl who'd sold herself would be looking for a man too green to see the truth. And along came Amos… So stupid he'd been—so naive. He was angry at Dinah, yes, but even more he was angry at himself. How could he have been so blind?

By the time he reached his farm, the anger had begun to cool, and a deep, throbbing ache sneaked in to replace it. As he layered wood on the glowing embers in his fireplace, he tried to rekindle the fury. But it faltered, much like the little tongues trying to take hold of the larger chunks of dry hedge apple. On one knee he remained in front of the fireplace and fed log after log to the inner hearth, hoping as the fire grew his anger could return to burn out the pain.

But even when the fire blazed, searing him with its heat, he couldn't renew his anger.

He hurt. Worse than he'd ever hurt. Worse than when he'd faced his father's disappointment. Worse than when he'd been rebuffed on the school playground. Worse than when he'd heard disparaging comments whispered behind his back about his gimpy way of passing. Even worse than when the wagon wheel snapped his bones and he'd screamed in agony. He'd opened his heart to her. And she ripped it from his chest.

In his mind's eye he saw Dinah kneeling beside his cart, her fingers twining through Gideon's ruff, her face alight with pleasure. His arms tingled as he remembered her tiny hand resting in his palm the night of the Calico Ball. Without conscious thought, he swayed slightly as if moving to the melody of "Roses from the South." An image of her delighted dash across the carpet when he'd surprised her earlier this evening—of her hands reaching toward him, her smile igniting the pale blue of her eyes—filled his memory, and a bolt of pain stabbed through him.

He lowered himself to sit on the braided rug in front of the hearth and rested his weight on his good hip, burying his face in his hands. "Why, God?" Tears formed in his eyes, but the fire's heat dried them before they could fall. "Why did You let me love her when You knew…You knew what she was?"

Too weary to rise, he remained there until the flames consumed the logs and turned them to chunks of glowing, red-eyed char. He remained there until the embers had died, and a chill fell around him. When the clock on the mantel announced the arrival of the new year, he was still sitting there, waiting for an answer. But it never came.

Ruthie

Ruthie crept into the sleeping room on her tiptoes, cringing when a floorboard creaked. Dinah snuffled and a bedspring twanged, letting Ruthie know her roommate had roused. She froze in place until no sound carried from the bed.

Then, without lighting the lamp, she made her way through the heavy shadows to the wardrobe and changed into her nightclothes.

What a wonderful party it had been! She'd danced with Papa three times, Dean Muller twice, and once each with more than a dozen townsmen. She'd sipped glasses of fruity punch, feasted on boiled shrimp and miniature artichoke and mushroom quiches, and sang "Auld Lang Syne" at midnight with her arms around Mama's and Papa's waists. The weight of worry she'd assumed on Christmas Day had slowly melted as the evening progressed, and she found herself wanting to hum for the first time in a week. But humming would have to wait until morning.

Her nightgown did little to protect her from the chill in the room, and she shivered as she turned from the wardrobe. Eagerness to climb beneath the heavy layer of quilts tempted her to scamper around the end of the bed and dive in. But she shouldn't disturb Dinah. So, staying on her toes to make as little noise as possible, she placed her feet cautiously on the floor and prayed the boards wouldn't announce her progress.

Hugging herself for warmth, she lengthened her stride as much as her nightgown would allow. And her foot descended on something sharp. Stifling a yelp, she jerked away from whatever had pierced her tender sole. The quick movement toppled her balance, and she plopped onto the edge of the mattress.

With a cry of alarm, Dinah bolted into a sitting position. Her pale face searched the dark room. "Who...who's there?"

Holding her throbbing foot in her hands, Ruthie aimed an apologetic look in Dinah's direction. She whispered, "It's just me, Dinah. I'm sorry I woke you. But something..." She slipped to her knees and felt around on the carpet with her open palm. After only a few seconds of searching, she located the offending object. Pinching it between her fingers, she held it toward the faint band of moonlight filtering through the lace curtains. Dinah's ring. It must have fallen off her finger while she slept. Ruthie frowned as a puzzling question entered her mind. How had the ring fallen clear on Ruthie's side of the bed?

She straightened and held the ring to Dinah. "You must have dropped this."

Dinah clutched the quilts to her chin and made no effort to retrieve the ring.

Ruthie bounced it, shivering. "Take it so I can get into bed. My toes are freezing!"

Dinah flopped onto her side, facing away from Ruthie. "I don't want it."

Ruthie drew back, so startled she forgot to shiver. "You don't want it? But it's your promise ring!" She grabbed Dinah's shoulder and forced her onto her back. She stared into Dinah's face. Although the room was shrouded in the darkest gray, she noted thin lines trailing down Dinah's cheeks. Alarm bells rang in the back of her mind. "Why have you been crying?"

Dinah grunted and strained against Ruthie's hand. "It doesn't matter. I threw the ring across the room. I don't w-want it anymore." But the longing in her voice belied her words.

Ruthie eased onto the mattress and knelt beside Dinah. "But why not? You were so happy when Mr. Ackerman gave it to you." Recalling how jealous she'd been, Ruthie experienced a sharp pang of remorse. Had her envious reaction influenced Dinah not to wear the ring?

"I said it doesn't matter."

At Dinah's harsh tone, Ruthie withdrew her hand from her shoulder, but she had to know if she had inadvertently created a rift between Dinah and Mr. Ackerman. Holding her voice to a whisper, she said, "Dinah, did—"

Dinah came up from the mattress, her face drawing so close she nearly bumped noses with Ruthie. "Can't you ever stop talking? Go to bed and leave me alone!"

Ruthie scrambled under the covers, too stunned to do otherwise. She curled in a ball and tugged the quilt to her ear, holding herself as still as possible while her heart pounded. What might Dinah do next? Her behavior was so irrational, so unexpected. Maybe she should sleep in Minnie's vacated room.

For long seconds Dinah stayed sitting up, and Ruthie sensed her angry glare fixed on the back of her head. Finally the mattress bounced, the springs whanged, and the quilts jerked into place. Silence fell. An uncomfortable, tense silence that kept Ruthie from relaxing. Several minutes passed before she realized she still held the topaz ring in her fist. The prongs poked the flesh of her palm, but she lay very still and didn't release her grip.

Dinah

Strong fingers held her wrists in an iron grip. A heavy body pinned her to the mattress. Hot breath whisked over her face as lips—hard, insistent, punishing—pursued her mouth. Frantic, Dinah writhed against her pillow, shifting her head this way and that way while emitting little animalistic grunts of terror. *Help me, help me,* her thoughts begged. *Oh, please, someone save me!*

The doorknob turned. Hinges squeaked. She fought to turn her gaze to the door where her rescuer was now entering. A tall, broad-shouldered man stepped into the room. Shadows hid his face from view, but she recognized him. Joy and relief exploded through her breast. *Amos! Amos, help me!* Dinah panted, her chest heaving, her body bucking in terror-filled jolts while she waited for him to storm to the bed and fling the defiler away.

But he came slowly. The heavy line of shadows eased downward as he advanced, revealing his face, inch by agonizing inch. Brow etched with lines of fury. Eyes glittering with indignation. Lips set in a grim line of condemnation. After what seemed an eternity, he finally reached the edge of the bed.

Dinah held one hand toward him, everything within her yearning for him to take hold, to pull her to safety. He leaned down, his fists rising. And he hissed through clenched teeth, "Dinah…what have you done?"

Sobs racked her body as Amos, his face set in a stony glare of disgust, turned and stalked away. "I'm sorry! I'm sorry! Oh, please forgive me. I'm so sorry!"

Someone shook her shoulder, and a voice filled with concern and worry carried over her cries. "Dinah, wake up! You're dreaming, Dinah. You're only dreaming."

A dream? A tiny spark of hope flickered in her heart. Maybe…maybe it wasn't real. But then words swooped through the fog to attack her memory.

"Only one, Amos."

"The number doesn't matter."

"Let me—"

"You are a harlot?"

"Only one, Amos."

"The man who purchased you might be willing to use something that bears stains from another's use, but I cannot."

Ruthie, her voice kind, strong, and comforting, repeatedly murmured, "You're all right, Dinah. It was only a dream."

She shook her head, resisting Ruthie's assurance. It wasn't a dream. It was real. Amos knew her dark secret. He knew. He knew. Coiling on the sweat-damp sheet, she convulsed with throat-drying, gut-wrenching sobs of anguish. But not for herself. For Amos. For the pain she'd caused him.

That day on the porch, when he'd frightened her and then asked her forgiveness, she saw his tenderness. Over the months she'd witnessed his acts of kindness, benefited from his patient understanding, reveled in his sweet attention. He offered her all things good, and she repaid him by exposing the ugliest, dirtiest, most shameful piece of herself. She deserved his disdain and anger, but knowing she deserved it didn't make it any easier to receive.

Behind her, Ruthie continued to rub her shoulder and offer soothing words. Dinah wanted to thank her, but if she spoke, Ruthie might ask questions. In her quivering, weakened state, she might accidentally answer. And then Ruthie would know, too. Having disappointed Amos was already too much. She couldn't look into Ruthie's face and see shock and revulsion.

With several shuddering breaths, she fought to bring her crying under control. "I…" Her raw throat resisted speech. Dinah swallowed and tried again. "I'm fine now. Go back to sleep."

Ruthie's hand closed over Dinah's shoulder and squeezed. Gently. Encouragingly. "Are you sure you don't want to tell me about your nightmare? It might help." Ruthie's voice quavered, as if she, too, battled against tears.

Dinah crunched her sore eyes tight. Ruthie's kindness, especially considering how Dinah had treated her earlier, was like salt in a wound. "Please, Ruthie, just…" She couldn't finish.

Ruthie's hand slipped away. A heavy sigh whisked past Dinah's ear. The bed bounced slightly. And then Ruthie began to speak. To pray.

"Dear God, please take away Dinah's nightmares and let her sleep. Give her good dreams instead. Thank You. Amen."

A few minutes later, Ruthie's deep, even breathing spoke of peaceful rest. Although Dinah lay very still with her eyes closed, she didn't allow herself to slip into sleep. She wouldn't trust Ruthie's prayer. She'd trusted Amos, and he turned from her. If God knew what caused her nightmares—and according to Ruthie's father, God knew everything—He wouldn't help her, either.

Chapter 36

Dinah

W hen Dinah glanced in the mirror on the first morning of 1884, she gasped in horror. Purple smudges—dark as bruises—underlined her red-rimmed eyes. In contrast, her face was stark white. Colorless. Lifeless. She touched her pale cheek with her trembling fingertips just to ascertain it really was her reflection peering back from the looking glass. The touch confirmed the haunted image was no apparition. Such a change a night of tears and sorrow had wrought.

She turned from the dismal sight and hurriedly dressed in her uniform. Apparently she'd finally fallen asleep because Ruthie was gone, and she hadn't even heard the girl leave. Part of Dinah wanted to crawl back under the covers and hide—was the businessman from Chicago still in the hotel?—but with Amos's departure from her life, she needed to hold on to her job. She didn't dare miss a day of work.

As she plodded downstairs on wooden legs, she wondered if Mr. Irwin had already hired a server to replace Minnie. Another girl hadn't taken over Minnie's room yet, but one might be en route. As soon as the manager arrived, she would ask if the server position was still available. And if so, she would ask to fill it. No anticipation stirred within her at the thought of becoming one of Mr. Harvey's servers. After the blissful contemplation of a life with Amos Ackerman, Dinah realized nothing else appealed.

But if she won the position as server, as she'd originally intended, she would be financially secure. And she'd finally have the respect denied her for her entire life. That is, if the Chicago businessman hadn't told anyone else about what she'd done before coming to Kansas.

Her pulse sped, and she hurried as quickly as her stiff limbs would allow to the check-in counter. Feigning a nonchalance she didn't feel, she pasted a quavery smile on her face and addressed the morning clerk. "Is…is the guest in room fourteen planning a lengthy stay?"

"Fourteen, fourteen…" The clerk turned the registry book on its revolving stand and peered at the open page half-filled with signatures. He tapped one name with his finger. "Ah, yes, Mr. Sanger."

Sanger… She finally knew his name. Chills broke out across her frame. She chafed her arms with open palms as the clerk continued.

"He leaves on this morning's train for Denver, but he's already arranged to stay with us again on his return trip at the end of the month." His brows rose, and he sent Dinah an apologetic look. "I wish I'd thought to tell you about his arrival sooner, Dinah—I forgot you were originally from Chicago. You and he might have enjoyed a chat yesterday evening. Were your families acquainted?"

Dinah shook her head and backed away from the counter, needing to distance herself from the man's bold signature in the registry. "No. Our families weren't acquainted."

He shrugged and then whirled the registry so it faced the entry doors again. "Well, since you hail from the same community, you might enjoy talking about the sights of the city with him. Shall I tell him you're employed here so he can make arrangements to visit with you when he returns?"

"No!" Dinah didn't realize she'd yelled the word until the man's eyebrows rose and he drew back. She forced a light laugh, which sounded more like a strangled sob, and spoke calmly. "There's no need to bother him by mentioning me. I'm sure a busy man like M-Mr. Sanger prefers his solitude when he travels. I'd better go have my breakfast so I can get to work." She turned and fled before he could ask any other questions.

Amos

On Thursday, Amos prepared the eggs for transport to town. With winter's shorter days and sometimes cloudy skies, the chickens had slowed their laying.

The Leghorns could be a bit finicky, only gifting him with eggs when the sun shone. A lesser number of eggs meant receiving less money for his chilly walk to town, but could he let the eggs sit and spoil in the barn? Of course not. So, grumbling under his breath, he nestled the creamy orbs between thick layers of straw to keep them from freezing.

He knew why he was so reluctant to deliver the eggs today. In the previous weeks there had been fewer eggs, too, but he'd headed to town with an eager bounce in his step. Because going to town meant seeing Dinah. Today, however, there was no promise of time with Dinah, no anticipation of a letter, no joy waiting at the end of the trek. He sighed and hung his head.

Samson and Gideon sat at his feet and whined up at him, as if sensing his melancholy. He took the time to give them each a scratch under the chin, but he didn't speak to them as he usually did. A lump of sadness filled the back of his throat, and talking took too much energy. With another heavy sigh, he caught the handle of his wagon and set out at a trudging gait.

He'd waited until early afternoon, when the sun was high and had burned away the dark chill of morning. Even so, the air was cold, and he shivered. Automatically his hand lifted to pat his pocket, and he gave a start when he found the pocket empty. He shook his head. He would not be taking envelopes of folded pages all covered in words intended for Dinah to town anymore. Yesterday he'd thrown away the pretty stationery paper. The temptation to sit and write had tugged at him one too many times, so tossing the paper into his fireplace eliminated the means to pen words to her.

But the urge remained in his chest. How long before the habit died and he would chuckle at Samson and Gideon romping together or see a hawk circling in the sky or watch the moon slip above the empty tree branches without murmuring, "I should write to Dinah about that"? He sent an accusing glance skyward. "You put her in my thoughts and heart, God, and it's caused nothing but heartache. So take her out now, do You hear me?"

His belligerent tone when addressing the Almighty would shock his mother and rile his father, but Amos chose not to hide his disdain. He'd repeatedly asked God not to let his affections for Dinah grow if they weren't meant to be together, and God had callously sent him down a pathway to destruction. So God would just have to get used to Amos's antagonism. He would foster it until all thoughts of Dinah had been stripped from his head.

He stopped at the houses of each of his usual customers, but he didn't take the time to exchange cheerful chatter as had become his custom. When one woman expressed concern about his stoic countenance, he gave the excuse that it was too cold to visit. His conscience stung because he'd lied. Cold had never frozen his tongue before. Losing Dinah had crushed the joy out of him. No joy within made for a sorry existence.

When he'd finished delivering the eggs, he headed to the grocer to purchase a few food items. Instead of passing the Clifton, which was the shorter route, he rattled the wagon two blocks out of the way to avoid the hotel. But when he left the store, by habit his feet carried him in the direction of the hotel. Not until he spotted the gardens, now brown and shriveled in the height of winter, did he realize what he'd done.

Immediately the desire to see her, talk to her, regain the friendship they'd created struck like a gale force. He stood with aching chest and galloping pulse, staring at the chair where they had left notes for each other. Caught up in the past, he began moving toward the porch. At the base of the stairs, his hand released the handle of his wagon, and he hitched his way up one, two, three steps, then crossed the boards to the painted wicker chair. It seemed as barren as the unadorned landscape with its floral cushion gone.

How many letters had he left beneath the cushion? A dozen? More? He'd lost count. He only knew he'd poured himself out on the pages, sharing pieces of himself with the girl he hoped would become his bride. All that time he spent writing and dreaming and praying now mocked him with its uselessness. Releasing a low moan of frustration, he turned to go, but his gaze caught sight of a small, square, folded paper pinned to the porch beneath one of the chair's legs. His heart lurched.

Glancing right and left, he searched for prying eyes. Then, in an awkward movement, he bent over and yanked the paper free. His hands shaking, he worked to unfold the weather-dampened sheet. The layers wanted to stick together, and he tore one corner, but eventually he peeled it apart and found a simple message: "Dear Mr. Ackerman, I beg your forgiveness. I truly hope we can be friends again someday. Sincerely, Dinah."

Forgive her? He crumpled the note into a wad and groaned. He should. Jesus Himself instructed His followers to forgive seventy times seven. He'd forgiven his father for rejecting him, his brothers for disdaining him, his schoolmates for taunting him. Would he be able to forgive Dinah someday when the pain wasn't so raw? when time had erased the affection he held for her? Maybe he'd eventually find the ability to forgive her. But he'd never forget. And with the knowledge of her indecency always in the back of his mind, they could never be friends. Not again.

"Mr. Ackerman?"

The soft female voice came from behind Amos. His heart gave a leap— Dinah? He immediately squelched the hopeful reaction. She would have called him Amos. He looked over his shoulder and found Miss Mead standing a few feet away, her head tipped to the side as she gazed unsmilingly at him. Her green eyes held compassion, and Amos found himself wanting to lose himself in the kindness she silently offered.

She held the handle of a stiff-bristled broom in both gloved hands, and she twisted her wrists as if trying to ignite a spark in the length of unpainted wood. A nervous gesture. "Did you come to see Dinah?"

"No." Amos jammed the wadded note into his pocket and took two clumsy steps toward the stairs.

She moved into his pathway, as stealthy as a panther. "She would welcome you."

The memory of Dinah dashing across the floor toward him, her face bright with happiness, stabbed him with fresh pain. Amos set his jaw.

"She never smiles. She hardly eats. And every night she cries."

Amos closed his eyes. He wanted to close his ears, too, his heart aching at the image Miss Mead's words painted. But was Dinah's anguish over losing his affections, or was it only because she'd been found out?

Miss Mead went on in a quiet voice. "She's so...broken, Mr. Ackerman. I don't know what happened between you, but I know she's sorry. Every night I listen to her proclaim apologies in her dreams. And her dreams... She's had night terrors before, but now they must be especially awful, the way she moans and thrashes about." She released the broom with one hand and reached toward Amos. Her fingers descended on his sleeve, the touch gentle. "At the end of the month, Mr. Irwin is sending her to train as a server. If she goes, you won't see her again. Are you sure you—"

He sidestepped past her, ignoring the sorrowful look in her eyes that reminded him too much of the pleading look Dinah had turned on him New Year's Eve. "It's better this way. It's what she'd wanted all along. Tell her I... wish her well."

Miss Mead sighed, her breath forming a little cloud of condensation that billowed, then dissolved. A bitter thought entered his mind—*If only feelings could dissipate so easily.* She trailed him to the stairs, dragging the broom behind her like a deflated balloon on the end of a string. As he grabbed the handle on his wagon, she spoke again.

"If you need to talk to someone, you can call on me." A hint of a smile tipped up the corners of her full lips. "Even though I'm often berated for talking too much, I'm also a good listener. So if you need a friend..."

Amos nodded a thank-you. "I'll think about it, Miss Mead. Good-bye now." He took off in his hitching hop-skip, eager to escape. His breath came in puffs, his ears stinging from pushing himself into the wind. A half mile up the road, he finally slowed his pace. He paused and looked back at the cluster of rooftops and the recognizable turret of the Clifton Hotel standing tall and proud. The farther he got from town, the deeper his loneliness grew. All he had waiting at home were two dogs and a henhouse full of clucking chickens.

"If you need a friend," Miss Mead had said. He needed a friend. Even more than a friend, he needed a helpmeet and a family. Cale had come and then gone. He'd sent Dinah away. In their stead they'd left gaping holes that begged to be filled. He chewed the inside of his lip and pondered whether someone else—perhaps Miss Mead—could fill the emptiness inside.

Chapter 37

Amos

*B*roken… As Amos went about his work during the weeks of January, the word Miss Mead had used to describe Dinah continually rolled through the back of his mind. His limp was more pronounced with the descent of cold, damp weather. Perhaps his lurching gait contributed to him not being able to set aside the ugly word. Whatever the reason, just as the ache in his hip was always with him, the reference clung to him and refused to let go.

He knew too well how it felt to be broken—unfixable. Compassion tried to stir to life in his heart for Dinah's brokenness, but he stubbornly refused to let it flare. His brokenness and hers were different. He had done nothing to deserve his broken state—he'd only been a young boy, daydreaming a bit as he'd followed his father's instruction to walk alongside the hay wagon and fork straw into its bed. Brokenness had been thrust upon him, but she had chosen to sell her body and then pretend to be chaste. Whatever sorrow she now experienced was a consequence of her choices. If she were broken, it was the result of her own doing, not his. So why did he feel sorry for her? The constant pondering left him unsettled and edgy.

He entered the barn early the Sunday after his birthday to grind dried corn to feed the chickens before leaving for service. Samson and Gideon roused from their sleeping spot beneath the egg wagon and dashed at him, releasing yips of happiness. Gideon danced around Amos's feet, his stubby tail wagging so quickly it became a blur. Samson, the more reckless of the pair, leaped against Amos's legs.

Amos grabbed the top rail of a stall to keep from falling, then aimed a swat at the dog's speckled hindquarters. "Samson, bad dog! Down!"

With a whine Samson crept away, head low and little tail tucked downward. Gideon backed away, too, looking at his master in confusion. Amos watched the pair huddle together at a safe distance, both keeping watchful eyes pinned on him. Unbidden, two pictures formed in his mind—one of Dinah's delighted expression when he'd entered the chambermaids' parlor on New Year's Eve followed by her stricken face when he'd confronted her about her indecency.

He shook his head, and the images of Dinah fled as he focused again on Sam and Gid. He groaned. What was he doing, getting angry with the dogs when they were only happy to see him? Propping one hand on his knee, he bent down and offered his palm to the cowering dogs.

"C'mere, boys. I'm sorry. I'm glad to see you, too."

After a moment Gideon's tail gave a hesitant wag, and then the dog rushed to Amos. He swiped Amos's hand with his tongue, his multicolored eyes losing their apprehension. Samson required a little more coaxing, but finally he, too, offered forgiveness by licking Amos's hand and placing his paw on Amos's knee.

Although he needed to see to the chickens' feed, Amos spent several minutes scratching the dogs' ears, rubbing their bellies, and speaking kindly to them until he felt sure he'd made up for his shortness. Finally he pushed to his feet, stumbling a bit as he rose, and limped to the corn grinder. While he fed ears of dried corn into the spout of the grinder and turned the crank, his thoughts moved ahead to the church service.

He'd skipped last week, unwilling to risk seeing Dinah, but he couldn't stay away forever. In the tenth chapter of Hebrews, believers were cautioned not to avoid gathering together for worship. He should go. But would Dinah be in attendance? If so, would she sit on their bench? His chest tightened, slowing his hand on the crank, as he contemplated what he would do if he found her waiting there.

The dogs' growls caught his attention, and he shifted his gaze from the stream of ground meal filling the bucket to their playful wrestling match. He wanted to smile at their antics, but only sadness filled him. They'd forgiven him and forgotten his harsh treatment already and returned to joyful romping.

As he watched the dogs, a memory rose from long ago. He'd come home, upset at being deliberately left behind when other youngsters trotted off to the swimming hole. Ma let him spout his anger, and then she put her arms around him and advised, *"Forgive them. They were thoughtless, but harboring anger won't hurt them. It will only hurt you. So forgive them and free yourself from the chains of resentment."* At the time, Amos hadn't wanted to do anything more than feed his anger, but at his mother's kind counsel, he agreed to forgive.

He put his hand to work again. As he finished grinding the corn, he pondered what Ma would say about Dinah. Would she advise him to forgive, or would she think he was justified in holding a grudge? He knew Ma well enough to know she'd quote Scripture, just as she'd always done when admonishing her children. In this situation she'd probably recite Luke 17:3 or Ephesians 4:32. He knew the verses by heart, and thinking of them now raised a prickle of guilt.

No, he wouldn't tell Ma. But could he talk to Preacher Mead? This burden of sorrow and hurt weighed him down. He wanted freedom. And the preacher would probably tell him the only way to be free was to choose to forgive. But he couldn't. He couldn't! How could anyone forgive such a grievous slight as had been perpetrated on him?

With a grunt of aggravation, he grabbed up the bucket of meal and hurried to the chicken house as fast as his bad leg would allow. He scattered the meal for the chickens, then headed for the house. Inside, he dressed for service. His Bible waited on the fireplace mantel, and as he reached for it, his fingers brushed the brown-and-amber rock. He froze for a moment, his unblinking gaze refusing to move from the reminder of Dinah's thick, wavy hair.

Gritting his teeth, he curled his fist around the rock, tromped clumsily across the floor, and flung the door wide. He drew back his arm and prepared to throw the rock as far as his strength would allow. But as his muscles tensed, another scripture winged through his mind. *"He that is without sin among you, let him first cast a stone at her"*—Jesus's words to the men preparing to stone the woman caught in adultery. One by one, in recognition of their own trespasses, the men had dropped their rocks and walked away.

Amos's hand clenched and unclenched on the rock. Should he let it fly… or let it fall? One action denoted condemnation, the other compassion. Which was an appropriate response? For long seconds he stood poised on the threshold, his arm in position. Every muscle in his body ached with tension. Cold air lifted strands of his hair and sent chills through his frame. Behind him, the logs in the fire popped and crackled. Beneath the buttons of his shirt, his heart pounded with ferocity.

Condemnation…or compassion?

His fingers tightened on the rock until it cut his palm. A trickle of warm blood dripped from his clenched fist and formed two dark blotches on the floorboards. Amos stared at the blots. Jesus had possessed the grace to forgive even those who pierced His hands with nails and mocked Him as He hung on the cross.

An anguished growl built in Amos's chest. He clutched the rock to his pounding heart and stepped onto the porch. Looking skyward, he railed, "I loved her! You let me love her. You let me imagine bringing her here. You let me dream of working together, forming a family, becoming as one. She betrayed me, but…" A sob wrenched from his throat, and he shook the fist holding the rock at the heavens. "But You betrayed me, too."

His face set in a snarl, he brought back his arm and threw the rock with such force he lost his balance and fell to his hands and knees on the rough porch boards. Splinters needled into his palms. He hissed at the throbbing pain, but at the same time he welcomed it. Because for a few minutes he could focus on physical discomfort rather than the deep bruises on his heart. For a few minutes he could forget his resentment toward the One he'd always trusted and the one he'd grown to love. For a while—albeit a short while—he might experience a breath of peace.

Ruthie

At the end of her father's closing prayer, Ruthie separated herself from her siblings and darted onto the raised dais where Papa was gathering his Bible and sermon notes. She caught hold of his hand. "Would you hitch the team and give me a ride back to the hotel today?"

Papa offered a mild scowl—his thoughtful look. "Will your employer mind if you don't ride back with the others? The Clifton's manager has been very kind allowing you to take off time each Sunday for service. I don't want to take advantage of his kindness by delaying your return."

"If I send a message with the others so Mr. Irwin knows and I get my work done on time, he won't mind. I've done it before."

Papa's scowl deepened, indicating disapproval. "You have?"

Ruthie held up both hands in a gesture of innocence. "Only one time, Papa." Recalling her walk through town with Mr. Ackerman, she felt her lips twitch into a smile despite the worries she carried. "But I need to talk to you. Please?"

His expression softened. He cupped her cheek and gave a nod. "I'll tell your mother to go ahead and serve the children their dinner. Let the others know I'm taking you back, and then wait for me out front. I'll be there shortly."

Ruthie watched the hotel carriage roll away, then paced in front of the church while waiting for her father. How would Papa respond to the question that had plagued her since last week when Mr. Ackerman had rejected reconciling with Dinah? So often she'd heard Papa and Mama say "God works in mysterious ways" when situations seemed dismal from one viewpoint yet proved to be a blessing from another. Would Dinah's heartache be Ruthie's opportunity for happiness? She needed to know, and she trusted Papa would have an agreeable answer.

The rattle of a wagon's wheels alerted her to her father's approach, and she darted to the edge of the street to meet him. As she settled herself on the high seat, she said, "I hope Mama doesn't feel slighted that I didn't ask to talk to her. But I don't need a parent right now. I need my minister."

Papa shifted the lap robe to cover her, as well, and then he flicked the reins.

As the wagon rolled forward, he made a little *harrumph* sound in his throat, then spoke in a stiff, formal tone. "Well, then, Miss Mead, with what may I assist you today?"

Ruthie sighed. "Please don't tease. This is serious."

Papa squeezed her knee through the thick layers of the lap robe. "I'm sorry. I suppose I feel a little awkward treating you as one of my parishioners rather than one of my children. But I'll do my best. Now, what is on your mind?"

Hunkering into her coat, Ruthie turned slightly to face her father. "Do you recall what you told me at Christmastime when I was upset because Mr. Ackerman gave Dinah a ring?"

"I told you to consider their pledge God's way of sending you in a different direction."

Grateful she didn't need to waste precious time reminding him of their conversation, she gave an eager nod. "That's right. But something happened at New Year's—Dinah and Mr. Ackerman broke their pledge. She isn't wearing his ring anymore, and he isn't interested in trying to reconcile with her. So I began to wonder…" She bit her lip. She'd been taught from her earliest memories it was more blessed to give than to receive. Being selfish was not acceptable in her family. Her question might very well be perceived as selfish, but she had to know. She looked into her father's face. "Did they break their pledge because God wants Mr. Ackerman to pursue me instead?"

Ruthie held her breath in anticipation of his response, but Papa didn't reply. The wagon rolled on toward the hotel, the horses' hoofbeats and the wheels' crunch against the hard dirt road filling Ruthie's ears. In moments they'd be at the Clifton and she'd get down and go to work. If Papa didn't answer quickly, she'd face another week of worry and wondering. She wriggled, nervousness and eagerness combining to make her want to climb out of her skin as she waited.

Papa guided the horses in front of the hotel, then pulled back on the reins. He set the brake, wrapped the reins around the handle, and finally turned to face Ruthie. Her heart pattered in hopeful double beats. Papa said, "I don't know."

Ruthie's breath whooshed out. Disappointment sagged her shoulders. "But, Papa, you're a preacher. You should know!"

"Now, Ruthie…" Mild reproach flickered in Papa's eyes. "I'm only a man, not God. I teach His Word, yes, but I can't presume to know His inner workings and reasons."

Ruthie fought tears. She'd been so certain Papa would offer direction. She was as aimless now as she'd been for the past two weeks. Her thoughts poured out in a bitter torrent. "I'm happy to help you and Mama, but I don't want to be a chambermaid forever. I want a family, like you and Mama have. I want to be a wife and a mother. I want a godly man to love me. If you, as a preacher, don't know if Mr. Ackerman is the man God has chosen for me, then how can I know what I'm supposed to do?"

Papa slipped his arm around Ruthie. "I can't tell you whether this conflict between Mr. Ackerman and Miss Hubley is meant to bring you and Mr. Ackerman together, but Matthew 6:33 tells us, 'Seek ye first the kingdom of God, and his righteousness; and all these things shall be added unto you.'" Papa's fingers closed over Ruthie's shoulder, his touch comforting and encouraging. "You want a husband and a family. Those are normal desires for a young woman. But could it be you are so intent on gaining what you want that you've lost sight of what your soul needs most?"

She blinked rapidly, determined not to break down and cry like a little girl. "What does my soul need, Papa?"

"What every soul needs. Right relationship with God." Papa smiled gently, and the tears Ruthie had tried so hard to squelch rolled down her cheeks. He wiped them away with his thumb as he went on. "Seek Him and His righteousness, my darling daughter, instead of pursuing your own wants. He will fulfill you in ways no human relationship could. When you put Him first in your life, before beaus and jobs and motherhood, then all else can fall into place. And only then will you be at peace with yourself and with others. Do you understand?"

"I think so." She affected a frustrated pout. "But it's so hard, Papa…"

He chuckled. "Those things that are most beneficial to us generally are. But they are also worth the effort."

She sniffled and rubbed her gloved finger under her nose. "I have to go to work."

"Then you'd better climb down."

Ruthie propped her hands on the edge of the seat in readiness to descend, but then she whirled and impulsively threw herself into her father's arms.

He squeezed her hard before setting her aside. "Go on now. Your mother and I will continue to pray for your pathway. God will lead you when the time is right, Ruthie. Turn your heart to Him and have faith."

"Yes, Papa." She hesitated, uncertain whether she should share her other concern with her father. She might be breaking a confidence. But if she thought of him as Preacher Mead instead of Papa, then it should be all right. "Papa, Dinah has horrible nightmares—nearly every night. I've asked her to talk to you, but she won't do it. I think she's afraid of saying it all out loud. Lately they've been even worse." Ruthie gave a little start as she realized Dinah's night terrors had become more severe at the same time she'd stopped wearing Mr. Ackerman's ring. Confusion smote Ruthie. She finished lamely, "Will you pray for her, too?"

Papa's brow formed lines of concern. "Night terrors are usually a result of a deeper problem. Holding it all inside won't do her any good. I will certainly pray for Dinah."

"Thank you."

"And, Ruthie, don't give up on her. You're likely her only friend. Especially now that she and Mr. Ackerman have parted ways. Take every opportunity to remind her God can heal whatever is causing her night terrors."

"I will." She gave Papa one more quick hug, then climbed down. She waved as the wagon carried him away. Then she hurried into the hotel, eager to be out of the cold. Inside, she deposited her wool coat in her room, straightened her hair that had been loosened by the relentless Kansas wind, then went down to eat her dinner.

When she entered the luncheon room, she spotted Dinah sitting at the far end of the counter. She paused and observed the other chambermaid for several seconds, noting her downcast face, the way she poked at her food with the fork rather than carrying any bites to her mouth, the cloak of sadness that drooped her frame. Clearly, Dinah was in agony. And Mr. Ackerman had missed church two Sundays in a row, so he must be suffering, too.

Sympathy welled within her. What should she do? Papa's admonishment rang through Ruthie's head. "Seek ye first…" Closing her eyes for a moment, Ruthie consulted her heavenly Father. Then, with a determined bounce in her step, she made her way across the floor to the empty stool beside Dinah.

Chapter 38

Dinah

"Mmm, is that roast pheasant with mushroom stuffing? It smells wonderful."

Dinah glanced at Ruthie, who slipped onto the stool next to her and looked with interest at the uneaten food on Dinah's plate. The aromas rising from the meat and mound of moist, seasoned breadcrumbs were making her stomach churn. She should have requested the cream of asparagus soup instead. Not that she would have been able to swallow that, either.

She pushed the plate toward Ruthie. "You can have it if you want. I haven't touched it."

"Are you sure?" Ruthie pursed her face into a worried frown. "You've hardly eaten enough to keep a sparrow alive lately. You'll make yourself sick if you aren't careful."

Dinah shrugged, and after a moment's pause Ruthie bowed her head to pray. As Dinah observed her roommate's humble pose and her lips moving in silent communication, she experienced a deep pang of longing. How must it feel to lift one's heart to God and believe He cared enough to listen?

Ruthie raised her head and reached for a fork from the little basket on the counter. She stabbed up a small bite of stuffing, then closed her eyes and murmured in pleasure. "Oh, Dinah, you really should have tried this. Mr. Gindough must have used rosemary and sage as flavorings. Even cold, it is delicious. Are you sure you don't want it?"

Dinah shook her head. "No. I…can't eat."

Ruthie had lifted another bite, but at Dinah's comment she set the fork on the plate and shifted to look full into Dinah's face. "My papa always says when someone can't eat, it's because his stomach is full of something else." She placed her hand over Dinah's. "I know you're sad, and I understand why. But not eating won't fix anything. You need to eat, Dinah."

"I know you're sad, and I understand why." Ruthie's gentle statement echoed through Dinah's mind. Well-meaning as she might be, Ruthie didn't understand. How could she? She hadn't lived Dinah's life. She hadn't suffered scorn and rejection and mistreatment. Resentment and anger welled, creating a maelstrom in her heart. If she didn't escape, she would explode.

Dinah yanked her hand free of Ruthie's light grasp and hopped off the stool. "I'm going to go to work."

Ruthie abandoned the plate and scampered after Dinah. "Dinah, wait!"

People awaiting their turn in the dining room or at the luncheon counter loitered in the lobby. Dinah wove between them, wishing she could lose Ruthie in the process. But the relentless girl stayed with her pace for pace.

When they reached the storage closet where cleaning supplies were kept, Dinah whirled on Ruthie. "Would you please leave me alone? You don't know why I'm sad, and you're only frustrating me by trying to pretend you know. So leave me be!" She turned to enter the closet.

Ruthie grabbed her arm and gave a fierce yank. "You aren't getting rid of me that easily. You are going to talk to me, Dinah Hubley. You owe me that much."

Dinah's mouth dropped open. She'd seen Ruthie's stubborn side before, but she'd never witnessed such forcefulness. She squirmed against Ruthie's firm grip, remembrances of another time someone held her so tightly raising a wave of panic. "I owe you nothing!"

"Oh, you don't?" Ruthie's eyes glittered, and she held her head at a contrary angle. "For months now you've interrupted my sleep with your nighttime screams and moans. I know you're sad about losing Mr. Ackerman as your beau, but there's something else bothering you. Something that came with you from Chicago."

Flashes of memories played through Dinah's mind, dizzying in their dance of torment. The leering faces of the men at the Yellow Parrot, her mother's bawdy costumes, her teacher's contempt, Miss Flo's harsh treatment, the businessman's uncaring ravage of her body… Her chest ached. Her throat grew tight. Her breath began to puff in little bursts as if at that very moment she was being ogled, humiliated, rejected, defiled.

Ruthie shook Dinah's arm again and leaned close. "I will not leave you alone until you tell me what plagues your nights and makes you hold yourself aloof from anyone who would be your friend. Say it! Let the secret out!"

Dinah gritted her teeth and gave a vicious twist of her arm. Ruthie's hand finally fell away, and Dinah backed up out of the girl's reach. She rubbed the spot where Ruthie's fingers had bit into her flesh. The secret, as Ruthie had called it, burned in the center of her being. She wanted to release it, to send it far, far away. But its exposure on New Year's Eve hadn't bought her freedom from its grip. Instead, it had cost her Amos. There was no escape. She would carry the ugly stain of what she'd done to her grave.

Ruthie advanced, backing Dinah into the closet. She smacked the door closed behind her, sealing the two of them in the murky space infused with the scent of mildew from the damp strings on the mops. Her voice cut through the gray—firm yet somehow also kind. "I'm waiting. You won't feel better until you let it all out. So tell me. Tell me. Tell me."

Dinah clutched her temples and squeezed her eyes tight. "It won't help. Nothing can change it. Nothing can take it away."

"Take what away?" Warm hands closed over Dinah's shoulders. "What are you trying to lose, Dinah?"

Her body trembled so badly she wondered how her legs held her upright. If Ruthie let go, she might crumple onto the floor. Drawing in a shuddering breath, she willed her quivering limbs to still. She rasped in an anguished whisper, "M-my past." With the simple utterance she collapsed into Ruthie's arms.

Ruthie

Ruthie blinked, straining against the deep shadows as she held Dinah. She should have chosen a different place to talk, but it was too late now. She glanced left and right, seeking something on which to sit. Two buckets waited on a low shelf. Holding on to Dinah with one arm, she bent forward slightly and slipped the buckets free. She turned one upside down and guided Dinah onto its bottom. Then she upended the second one for herself. She'd never perched on such an uncomfortable stool, but the seats weren't nearly as important as Dinah's reedy admission.

Clutching her hands together in her lap, Ruthie prodded, "What about your past?"

Dinah's face appeared pale and haunted in the dim light. "I've already lost Amos. And if Mr. Irwin discovers wh-what happened, I won't be able to be a server. Servers are required to be—"

Ruthie internally finished Dinah's sentence. *Young, attractive, intelligent, of good moral character.* But why should Dinah worry? She was all of that. Or was she not? Ruthie gulped as an uncomfortable thought crept through her mind.

Dinah began to sob. "I'm—I'm dirty. Amos knows it. That's why he left me." Suddenly she reached for Ruthie, catching her hands and clinging with a frightening ferocity. "But you can't tell anyone! Please? I have to become a server. It's my only hope."

A hymn swept through Ruthie's memory, and without thought she began to sing. "'My hope is built on nothing less than Jesus' blood and righteousness.'"

Dinah drew back. "Wh-what?"

Ruthie ignored Dinah's puzzled query and continued singing. When she reached the third verse, she sang louder while tears pricked in her eyes as the reality of the words ignited joy in her heart. "'When all around my soul gives way, He then is all my hope and stay.'" Her voice caught, and she couldn't sing any longer.

She closed her eyes and lapsed into silent prayer. *Papa was right, dear Lord. You are what we need most of all. Please help me show Dinah the truth that You— not a beau, not a server position, not anything in this world except You—are her Hope. And thank You for reminding me of the truth, as well.*

"Ruthie?" Dinah's voice cut through Ruthie's reflections.

She opened her eyes and blinked until her vision adjusted enough to make out Dinah's uncertain face. She smiled. "Dinah, do you want to lose your past?"

"Yes, but—"

"Then listen to me. There's a verse in the Bible—John 3:16. It says, 'For God so loved the world, that he gave his only begotten Son, that whosoever believeth in him should not perish, but have everlasting life.'

"God knew we would make mistakes and do things we shouldn't. Those wrong things are called sins, and when we carry them, we feel, as you said, dirty." Ruthie's words poured out faster and brisker as she inwardly prayed for Dinah to accept the touch God wanted to offer. "But God loves us, and He doesn't want us walking around with the burden of sins weighing us down. So He sent Jesus, His Son. Even though Jesus was blameless, He died on the cross so His blood could wash away our sins and remove our dirtiness. There's another verse—in Hebrews, I think. The seventh…no, eighth chapter."

Why hadn't she brought her Bible with her? She pressed her memory, trying to recall the exact words. Eyes closed, she envisioned the text on the page of her well-worn Bible, and she began to recite, "'For I will be merciful to their unrighteousness, and their sins and their iniquities…'" She opened her eyes, and tears spilled down her cheeks. She finished in a breathless rush, "'…will I remember no more.' Oh, Dinah, you want to lose your past? This is how. You ask Jesus to save you from your sins. You believe He will do it. And in God's eyes it will be as if you never sinned at all. Your faith in Him will make you whole."

Dinah stared at Ruthie. Agony and desire warred in her eyes. "But Amos said I was stained. He said he…he couldn't touch something that carried a stain."

Ruthie shook her head slowly, remembering her foolishness in wanting Papa to know as much as God. A bubble of laughter built in her throat. She and Dinah were more alike than she'd ever realized. She knew just what to say to Dinah now. "You can't depend on Amos Ackerman. He's just a man. But

God is God. He loves bigger and forgives better and gives more abundantly than any man ever could."

Ruthie eased off the bucket—by now its hard edge had surely left a bruise where she sat—and knelt before Dinah. She placed her hands on her friend's knees. "Earlier today my papa told me I needed to seek God and His righteousness instead of thinking that getting married and starting a family would make me happy. So now I'm telling you the same thing. Don't think being courted by Mr. Ackerman or becoming a server will fulfill you. Those things aren't bad, but they aren't eternal. Only a relationship with God will last forever. God loves you. He sent His Son to die…for you. He wants to take your sins away. He wants to be your Father."

Dinah's eyes flew wide. "I…I never had a father."

Ruthie swallowed hard. Little wonder Dinah had made such a mistake without a father's tender guidance. She gave Dinah's knees a brisk pat. "Well, you can have one now. Do you want Him, Dinah?" She stared at Dinah's unsmiling face, waiting, hoping, praying.

Several seconds ticked by while Dinah seemed to gaze into nothing and her hands repeatedly clenched and unclenched. Then she sagged forward, her forehead nearly meeting Ruthie's. "I want Him. What do I do?"

Ruthie smiled through her tears. "All you have to do is ask. Believe on the Lord Jesus Christ…and you will be saved."

With hesitance, in a voice so small Ruthie might have imagined it, Dinah said, "I believe." She straightened her shoulders and spoke with more boldness. "I believe." Wonder broke across her countenance. Tears flooded her eyes. She raised her face to the ceiling. "I believe, God. I believe." Although the words emerged on a sob, no one could deny the joy ringing in her tone. "I believe, I believe…"

Ruthie situated herself on the bucket again and sat in silent witness to Dinah's awakening. She'd never seen anything more beautiful. A lump of gratitude filled her throat. Such an honor, to play a part in guiding Dinah to the everlasting love of her heavenly Father. Tears rolled unendingly down Dinah's cheeks, and warm rivulets flowed down Ruthie's face, as well. She felt God's presence in the closet with them, penetrating both of their beings.

She folded her arms across her middle, envisioning God's arms holding her close. She and Dinah had each received a healing today. *Whatever You want for me, wherever You want me to go, God, I'll follow.*

Dinah had found her peace. And so had Ruthie.

Chapter 39

Dinah

fter dressing for bed Dinah turned from the wardrobe to find Ruthie closing the Bible she'd purchased. The tips of several strips of paper stuck out from the Bible's top edge, splaying in various directions. Their haphazard arrangement reminded Dinah of wildflowers along the side of a road. Her lips twitched into an amused grin. "What did you do to my Bible?"

Ruthie skittered forward, her face alight. "I marked several of my favorite passages. See? At the top of each marker is the reference I want you to read. And so it's easy for you to find them, I inserted a paper at the right page. Now that you've decided to be a follower of God, you will want to grow in your faith. Reading your Bible is the way to grow. So"—she thrust the Book at Dinah with a little giggle—"here you are! Grow!"

Dinah took the Bible and gazed in wonder at the number of slips protruding. Ruthie had an envious grasp of God's Word to be familiar with so many different passages. "Where do I start?"

Ruthie pressed her finger to her chin, seeming to examine the markers. Then she tapped her fingertip on one. "This one. It's a story, a very short story, about a woman who reminds me of you. This woman had—" She waved her palms as if erasing something in the air. "Oh, me and my talk-talk-talk! Don't let me tell it to you. Read it yourself." She hurried to her side of the bed and knelt on the floor, folding her hands in her familiar prayer pose.

Dinah peeked at the reference written on the paper's tip in Ruthie's flamboyant handwriting—Luke 8:43–48. A part of her desired to open the Bible and absorb herself in the story, but another part of her resisted. Amos had told her about a story in the Bible, and the images of Bible-Dinah's assault still hovered in the back of her mind. Did she want to risk filling her mind with yet another heartbreaking tale?

"Did you forget which one I showed you?" Eagerness quavered through Ruthie's voice.

Dinah sent her roommate a sheepish look. "I know which one you said. But…it isn't a sad story, is it? I read about a woman named Dinah, and I…" Unpleasant remembrances dried her throat. "I can't forget how sad it was."

Sympathy showed in Ruthie's eyes. "What happened to Dinah in the Bible was sad. Even though she went to the neighboring village when she'd been instructed not to, Shechem should not have…er, taken her. And Dinah's brothers… Oh my." She shook her head sorrowfully. "That story has troubled me, too. There is so much wrong in it." Then her expression brightened, and she nodded toward Dinah's Bible. "But I think you'll find the one I marked full of right. Read it, Dinah. Go ahead." Ruthie closed her eyes and bowed her head.

While Ruthie prayed, Dinah sat on the edge of the bed and placed the Bible in her lap. Swallowing a knot of worry, she slipped her finger between the pages and flopped the Book open. She scanned the little numbers beneath chapter eight until she located forty-three. Drawing in a breath, she leaned forward and began to read about a woman who had suffered a blood disorder no physician could cure. But then she touched the hem of Jesus's robe, and her illness was healed.

Her heart caught as she read the final verse. "And he said unto her, Daughter, be of good comfort: thy faith hath made thee whole; go in peace." Dinah placed her palm over the wonderful words as warmth flooded her. Setting the Bible aside, she dropped to her knees beside the bed and bowed her head. Although she'd listened to Ruthie's prayers countless times in the past months, she wasn't sure what to say. Her relationship with God—her Father—was so new. So she prayed what was on her heart.

Dear God, thank You for healing me. Thank You for loving me. Thank You… *Amen.* She rose as Ruthie rose. Ruthie extinguished the lamp, and both girls slipped into bed.

Ruthie's content voice carried across the darkness. "Good night, Dinah."

"Good night, Ruthie." But she lay with eyes open, staring at the gray ceiling. Closing her eyes meant dreaming. The images—familiar and frightening and unwelcome—began to take shape in the back of her mind. Then, as sweet as a lilac's bouquet wafting on a fresh spring breeze, Jesus's statement to the woman who touched His robe whispered through her heart. *"Thy faith hath made thee whole; go in peace."*

Dinah closed her eyes.

"Go in peace."

Her body relaxed, every muscle becoming loose and liquid.

"Go in peace."

Dinah slipped off to blissful, dreamless sleep.

Amos

Amos tossed and turned on his straw-filled mattress. Why couldn't he sleep? His hip ached, but he was used to the pain. He'd learned to sleep through it long ago. Wind blew, whistling through a crack in the window frame. But that, too, was familiar. He rubbed his hip and listened to the night sounds—an occasional *pop* as the blaze in the fireplace died, the distant howl of a coyote, the wind… None were intrusive enough to hold him awake. Yet sleep refused to come.

When had he last enjoyed easing quickly off to sleep and resting well all night? Staring at the thick ceiling beams running from side to side above his bed, he counted backward in time. It took very little effort for him to settle on a date. December 30. Three weeks ago.

He shifted, seeking a more comfortable position. But all the wriggling in the world didn't relieve the throbbing ache in his hip. Or the lonely ache in his heart. Other than making egg deliveries and engaging in the short conversation with Miss Mead on the hotel porch, he had isolated himself at his farm. He'd had one visitor—Preacher Mead, who expressed concern about Amos's lack of church attendance since the new year began.

Remembering the excuse he gave the minister—*"It's a long, cold walk into town, and keeping this new batch of chicks warm and flourishing takes a lot of attention"*—his conscience pricked him. He hadn't fibbed, but the cold and the chickens hadn't kept him home from church before. The bigger truth was he didn't want to encounter Dinah. So he stayed away. And in so doing, he removed his remaining means of fellowship from his life.

Another thought tormented him. Was his haunting loneliness related to the anger he chose to hold toward God? Since the day he'd thrown the rock, he hadn't prayed. Hadn't read his Bible. Hadn't acknowledged God's presence in any way. And each day, his despondence grew ever deeper and harder to carry. He could almost hear his mother's voice chiding, *"Well, now, what do you expect? You're His child. Of course you're going to be lonely when you hold yourself from Him."*

With a disgruntled huff, Amos heaved himself out of bed and tromped to the table in front of the fireplace. Although only coals remained, a small flow of warmth crept across the floor and touched his feet. He sank into a chair in the dark room and rested his head in his hands. Dinah's indiscretion had stolen so much from him. He still worked hard, but it all seemed pointless with the promise of a wife now gone. Because no matter how he tried to set his sights on someone else—Miss Mead, or one of the servers from the hotel who attended church, or any of the other young women in town of a marriageable age—he couldn't push Dinah from his thoughts.

He slapped the table, irritated with himself. Why did she hold such prominence in his heart? Of course he couldn't marry her now. Not knowing what she'd done. But thinking of pursuing anyone else left him cold and empty.

"So just stay alone, then!" The command burst from his lips without him planning to speak out loud. The sound of his own voice startled him, but once he'd started talking, it was as if his tongue had taken on a power of its own. He rose and paced the floor, charging through the shadows in a stumbling gait.

"Didn't you spend most of your boyhood alone, left behind by the ones who ran on two good legs? Didn't you stay at home alone when your brothers trooped off to the fields with Pa? Didn't you come to Florence and start your chicken farm alone? And you've managed just fine by yourself. So stop your moping." He puffed to a halt behind one of the chairs and caught hold of its top rung. Curling his fists around the sturdy strip of wood, he growled, "Stop being a blamed fool, Amos. You don't need anybody else."

His final comment hung in the room like a veil of smoke from Pa's pipe. Except Pa's pipe smoke held a sweet essence. No pleasant aroma clung to his bitter utterance. He let his head sag and finished in a ragged whisper, "I might not need anybody, but I sure did want someone." The desire to pray—to pour out his hurt to the God he'd trusted from the time he was very young—nearly sent him to his knees. But he stiffened his legs and set his jaw tight to hold the entreaty inside.

Even though he returned to his bed, so tired his heels dragged as he moved across the floor, and even though he closed his eyes and willed himself to lapse into sleep, the weight of resentment pressing his chest held sleep at bay for many more hours.

A pounding noise awakened Amos from disjointed dreams. He bolted from the bed, aghast at the sunlight pouring through the window. He yanked up his britches from the foot of the bed and fumbled into them as he headed out of the bedroom. How had he stayed in bed so long? The angle of the sunbeams across the floor indicated it was midmorning already. He was late in feeding and watering the chickens. And poor Sam and Gid probably thought they'd been forgotten.

Bang! bang! bang! A fist pounded on his front door again. Amos limped past his shoes and opened the door. Cold air whisked in, chilling his bare toes. But when he drew back, it wasn't because of the cold. Preacher Mead stood on his porch holding a set of reins. At the end of the reins stood a gray-nosed, swaybacked mule. Was he still dreaming? Amos rubbed his eyes with his fists, then looked again. The smiling minister and the mule were still there.

"Good morning," Preacher Mead said brightly. Then his brows furrowed as his gaze bounced up and down along Amos's strange attire of britches over long johns. "Did I wake you? I waited until nine o'clock to come out, figuring you'd be done with your morning chores. I'm sorry if I disturbed you."

Amos flapped his hand in dismissal. "It's all right. I—I needed to get up." He winced as the sunlight hit his sore eyes. He took another backward step. "Come on in. I haven't got my fire stoked yet, so I can't offer you a cup of coffee, but if you don't mind waiting, I can get a fire going and then…" Why was he blathering? He never blathered. Apparently his long stretch of aloneness had stored up words that needed release.

Preacher Mead tangled the reins around the rail running the length of Amos's porch. Then he stepped over the threshold. "I won't stay long, and I've already had my morning coffee, so don't worry about fixing anything on my account. But get your fire going if you need to. I'll talk while you work."

With a shrug Amos hitched around the table to the wood box, loaded his arms, and then crouched in front of the hearth to begin the chore of fire building. He flicked a look over his shoulder, noting Preacher Mead standing halfway across the floor. He'd said he would talk while Amos worked, but he remained silent with a serious, almost uneasy expression on his face that set Amos's teeth on edge.

As he arranged the logs over yesterday's coals, Amos prodded, "What brought you out this morning?" He'd never had visits from anybody two days in a row.

Preacher Mead took in an unsteady breath and moved two steps closer to the fireplace. "Actually, Mr. Ackerman, I'm here because of Cale."

Amos planted his palms on the floor and pushed to his feet more quickly than he knew he could move. "Did something happen to Cale?"

The man swept his hat from his head. "No, no, Cale is fine. It's only—" He gestured to the table. "Could we sit?"

Nervous, Amos sidestepped to the table and eased into a chair. Preacher Mead sat opposite him and placed his hat on the table. "Mr. Ackerman, I hope you'll receive this gift in the manner it's intended."

Amos scowled. "Gift? What are you talking about?"

"That mule hitched outside your door? Cale wants you to have it."

Amos might've been mule kicked the way the statement affected him. He lurched back in the chair, banging his spine against the hard rails. Then he bounced forward and rose from the chair in one jarring motion. As he crossed to the door, Preacher Mead's explanation followed him.

"Shortly after Christmas one of my parishioners gave the boys the mule and a pull cart. They've had great fun with it."

Amos cracked the door and peeked at the mule. By the gray on the animal's muzzle, clearly it had lived awhile. Although its back was swayed, its chest was fully muscled, and its legs were long and straight. The boys had received quite a gift. Amos closed the door and faced the preacher again.

The man continued. "When I came back from visiting you yesterday, I told my wife about your difficulty walking into town when it's so cold and the length of time you had to be away from the farm because of the long walk. Apparently Cale was listening, and he gathered up his brothers and convinced them you needed the mule more than they did. Then he came to me and asked me to bring it to you."

Amos's throat tightened. Cale had been very open about Amos's limp, often expressing concern about how long it took Amos to get from one place to another. Ordinarily he didn't like having people make a fuss about his gimpy leg, but he couldn't help but be warmed by the boy's consideration. He returned to the table and sat heavily. "That's kind of him."

"I hesitated about bringing the mule to you. I know you're a proud man—a competent man—and I don't want you to feel as though the boys gave you the mule because they think you are less than able. Cale wanted you to have it so you could come to town even when it's cold outside. He's missed seeing you at church."

Amos rubbed his palms up and down the thighs of his trousers. Head low, he muttered, "I…I've missed seeing him, too."

"Then you aren't offended?"

Amos managed to lift his gaze and offer a weak smile. "No. I appreciate the boy thinking of me."

Preacher Mead slipped his hat over his hair and stood. "He's a good boy.

We're blessed to have him in our family. If you discover having the mule—by the way, its name is Jehoshaphat Isaac—"

Amos burst out laughing. Genuine laughter. He enjoyed letting it roll.

The preacher chuckled, too. "We didn't name him. He came with that moniker, but since he responds to it, we didn't change it." He ambled toward the door. "Cale didn't think about feeding and stabling the animal when he decided you should have him. If he's too much trouble to keep, let me know. I'll take him back and explain to Cale. I'm sure he'll understand."

Amos wouldn't send the mule back. Ol' Jehoshaphat Isaac was a marvelous gift. "Tell Cale and your sons thank you for me. Jehoshaphat Isaac will be of good use to me, I'm sure."

Preacher Mead gave Amos's shoulder a solid clap. "Cale is very fond of you, Mr. Ackerman. Every night when he says his bedtime prayers, he asks God to bless 'Uncle Amos.' He hasn't forgotten you."

"He hasn't forgotten you." The sentence echoed through Amos's mind, making his eyes sting. Unable to talk, he nodded.

The minister headed outside, pausing to give Jehoshaphat Isaac's nose a rub as he stepped from the porch. He climbed into his wagon, waved good-bye, then aimed the horses for the road. Amos, on bare feet, moved to the edge of the porch and cupped the underside of Jehoshaphat Isaac's jaw. The mule snorted but allowed Amos's examination.

Amos sent a hesitant glance toward the sunny sky and spoke to God for the first time in weeks. "I don't begrudge the gift. I'm glad Cale hasn't forgotten me. But don't think an old mule is enough to replace what I lost. I'm still mad." He chuckled. A self-deprecating chuckle. Ma would probably say Ol' Jehoshaphat Isaac wasn't the only stubborn mule on his property. And Ma would be right.

Chapter 40

Amos

ehoshaphat Isaac, or "Ike" as Amos preferred to call him, proved to be a greater blessing than he'd even imagined. Amos rigged a makeshift harness so Ike could pull the egg wagon. Although it pained his hip to straddle the mule's broad back for the trek into town, he found it much less tiring to climb up and down than it had to walk the distance himself.

He learned to pace Ike to avoid bouncing the eggs too much. One customer teased, "I'd rather my eggs didn't get scrambled in the shell, so keep that noble beast from breaking into a run." Even holding Ike to a gentle saunter let him deliver in half the time it had taken him to walk the route. Which gave him time to meander past the schoolhouse and let Cale and the other Mead boys leave the recess grounds to give their former pet a few nose rubs and sneak him a carrot or apple from one of their lunch pails.

He'd worried how Sam and Gid would react to having the mule take up residence in the barn, and he also worried how Ike would react to the dogs. Although full grown, the pair still scampered and played like puppies, and their rambunctiousness might startle the mule into kicking. A mule's kick could do a lot of damage. But the worry was for naught.

Dogs and mule formed a fast friendship, and each morning Amos entered the barn to find the two speckled dogs curled next to Ike's snoring form in the stall. Ike might have been the grandfather to the pups, the patient way he tolerated their antics. Sam and Gid showed their affection by washing Ike's ears and giving his bristly back a scratching with their paws. Observing them, Amos often experienced a touch of jealousy over how well the three animals got along.

As January moved steadily toward its end, Amos looked ahead to spring and made careful plans. As soon as the snows were gone for good, he'd tear down the last of the small outbuildings and give the chicken house one more expansion to accommodate his ever-growing flock. He'd plant corn, oats, and barley to feed his animals and put in a sizable garden of vegetables for his own table. Thanks to Ike's service, he would extend his delivery route. Each month over spring and summer, he'd set aside brooders to hatch chicks to increase his egg production.

He intended to ask Preacher Mead about hiring out a couple of his boys—Cale and the oldest one, Seth—for the summer months in exchange for eggs and butchered chickens. To get it all accomplished, Amos would need the extra hands. Cale already knew how to care for the chickens, and he trusted the preacher's son to be a good worker. If all went well—if more hens than roosters emerged from the shells, if Sam and Gid kept wild animals away from his flock, if no illness or weather calamity affected his birds—by the end of the year, he would be close to having enough eggs to meet the needs at the Clifton Hotel. As he planned for the future, he added one more goal to the list: forget Dinah.

He needed to visit the hotel's manager and assure him he was still working to provide the chef with eggs. But he couldn't go there until Dinah had left. So he put off making the trip to the Clifton. He also continued to avoid Sunday services so he wouldn't risk seeing her. No matter how hard his conscience poked him, he stayed away from the places where his path would most likely cross hers, determined to forget how she once filled every corner of his dreams for the future. And despite his efforts, Dinah persistently lingered in the back of his heart.

But, he consoled himself, once she was gone from Florence, he would be able to forget her. Only a few more days and she would be gone—off to train for a server position. He would be happy for her. And he would be fine here by himself. Of course he would.

Dinah

"Dinah, may I confess something to you?"

She paused in removing her ball dress from its hook in the wardrobe to send a surprised look in Ruthie's direction. Over the past week of studying the Bible and praying together, Dinah had grown closer to Ruthie than she'd ever been to anyone. Except Amos. She gave herself a little shake. Hadn't she decided not to think about him anymore? Yes, she had, but deciding it was one thing—actually doing it had proven to be quite another.

She focused her attention on Ruthie. "You can tell me anything."

Ruthie sighed and sank down on the edge of the bed. She fingered the lip of Dinah's travel valise and gazed into its open pouch with longing. "I envy you. I wish I was going off to train to be a server."

Dinah recalled how smug she'd felt when the other servers and Ruthie all seemed to envy her invitation to the Calico Ball. This time Ruthie's statement raised no hint of smugness. Instead she experienced a stab of remorse. She hated to see Ruthie sad, and she hated to tell her only friend good-bye.

She touched Ruthie's hand. "Maybe your father will change his mind and let you train after all. Mr. Irwin said there are openings all up the Santa Fe line. I might go to one of the Harvey restaurants farther west once I turn eighteen."

Ruthie tipped her head and frowned. "Why wait? If there are openings now, couldn't you take one of them when you finish your training?"

Dinah shook her head. "No. I'm too young. Mr. Harvey made an exception because no other girls were interested in working in Florence. So he told Mr. Irwin I would have to come back here after my training. But once I'm eighteen, I could go to Colorado or Wyoming or even New Mexico."

"Oh, how exciting it would be to travel…" Ruthie's expression turned dreamy.

At one time the thought of traveling to such amazing places would have filled Dinah with delightful eagerness. But now, knowing what she would leave behind, she was plagued by a sense of loss. But it was best that she leave

Florence. Best for her, and best for Amos. She began folding the Calico Ball dress into a neat square. "You can ask your father again at service tomorrow morning. Since I'm going, he might think it's all right for the two of us to go together."

Ruthie crossed her arms over her chest and scowled. "He'll never let me go. No matter how many times I've told him Mr. Harvey's servers are well respected, he still considers waitressing a less-than-acceptable occupation for his daughter. Papa doesn't seem to understand that Mr. Harvey's standards are so high that becoming one of his restaurant servers is an honor." With another melodramatic sigh Ruthie flopped flat on her back on the quilt with her arms up over her head.

Dinah sucked in her lower lip. Ruthie's downcast rumination flamed to life the spark of doubt that had been flickering in Dinah's heart ever since Mr. Irwin told her he'd received special permission for her to attend the training sessions in Kansas City so she could fill the position Minnie's departure had caused. She fully accepted that God had forgiven her for going to Mr. Sanger's hotel room in Chicago, and in His eyes the stain the man's treatment had left on her soul was gone. But what would Mr. Harvey think if he knew she'd been raised in a brothel and had received money for the forfeiture of her chastity? Would he still approve her becoming a server?

Uncomfortable with the direction her thoughts had taken, Dinah turned her attention to packing. She lay the dress she'd worn to the Calico Ball in the bottom of the valise to serve as a cushion for her little painted music box. She doubted she'd ever wear the lovely frock again, but she would take it along on her adventure as a keepsake from the third happiest event of her life. The music box, with the topaz ring snug inside the little trinket drawer, would serve as the second happiest. But she needn't pack a reminder of the most happy event. She carried it within her heart. Now that she'd accepted God's Son as her own Savior, wherever she went, she would never be alone.

After nestling the music box in the folds of the dress, she slipped the valise under the bed. She wouldn't leave Florence until the last day of the month—still five days away. And sometime during those five days, Mr. Sanger would return from his business dealings in Colorado. Her stomach gave a flip, and she folded her arms across her middle as nausea attacked. She hoped she could keep her distance from the man while he was here.

God had forgiven and forgotten—she believed it from the bottom of her heart. Now if only she could forget, too.

Sunday morning Dinah joined Ruthie's family for service. How strange to sit in the front instead of the back. Although nine other people crowded onto the bench with her, she was more lonely than she'd been on the back bench with only Amos for company. She sent a quick look over her shoulder, hoping he might be in his familiar spot. According to Ruthie, her brothers had given him a mule that he could ride into town. But the glance confirmed the bench was empty.

Sadness attacked. He was staying away because of her. Such harm she had caused him. Would he return to services when she left Florence? After today, many weeks would pass before she listened to Preacher Mead's teaching again. Six at least. A very long time. But during her time away, maybe she'd finally be able to erase her affections for Amos Ackerman. And maybe he would find the ability to forgive her and return to fellowship with his congregation.

She blinked back tears as a prayer filled her heart. *God, let him come back, please. Don't let him leave church because of me.* Her prayer came to an end when Preacher Mead stepped onto the dais and invited the worshipers to rise for an opening hymn.

He led them in "My Hope Is Built on Nothing Less." Dinah couldn't help exchanging a smile with Ruthie as she joined the others in singing out loud and clear, "'My hope is built on nothing less than Jesus' blood and righteousness…'" By the time they'd finished the hymn, her doldrums slipped away, and she settled onto the bench, eager to hear what Preacher Mead would share today.

He opened his Bible and, without preface, began. "From the book of Numbers, the thirty-second chapter." Dinah followed in her Bible as he read an account of Moses chiding the families of Reuben and Gad for choosing to see to their own needs rather than protecting the children of Israel. The leader Moses used strong words of rebuke toward the men, reminding them of God's anger in past times when His children had chosen to disobey His commands. The men eventually agreed to defend the Israelites if they could build their homes and fences first. Moses offered approval of their plan, then followed it with a warning.

Dinah almost thought she could hear Moses's thundering voice as Preacher Mead read, "'But if ye will not do so, behold, ye have sinned against the LORD: and be sure your sin will find you out.'"

The preacher set his Bible aside and lifted his gaze to the congregation. "For generations, people have sinned. They have chosen their own pathways rather than following God's. They have sought their own desires rather than asking God what He wanted for them. And each time people sin—each time they go astray—God knows. They might be able to hide their sins from their families and friends and townsfolk, but God knows. And Moses reminds us right here, 'Be sure your sin will find you out.'"

Dinah squirmed. Of all the people in Florence, only Ruthie and Amos knew about Chicago, and she didn't want anyone else to know. She'd suffered so many disapproving looks, so many rebuffs, so much ridicule. Would it all start again if people in her new town knew where she'd lived? Yet by keeping it all a secret, was she sinning? She leaned forward slightly, eager to hear what Preacher Mead might say next.

"I've always told my children it's better for them to be found out when they've done wrong rather than succeed in hiding it." A grin twitched on his cheeks as he glanced at his row of offspring, who hunched their shoulders and sent sheepish looks to one another. "You see, finding success in wrongdoing only leads us to think we can get by with more wrong. And before we know it, we're up to our elbows in sins…and living with a mighty regret. Or, even worse, we've hardened our conscience to the place where we don't even care if we do wrong anymore. Both situations are not good for a person's soul."

Preacher Mead rested his elbow on the corner of the simple wooden podium and sent a fatherly smile across the congregation. "If you read God's Word, as Christians are called to do, you know what God requires of His children. He gave us all the instruction we need. He also gave us the Holy Spirit, who whispers to us when we need to change our ways. If you knowingly do wrong, you stir God's anger." He tapped his Bible. "It says so in this passage."

He moved to the opposite side of the podium, and Dinah followed him with her gaze, gripped by his message. "Of course we don't want God's wrath against us, but I hope more than wanting to avoid His anger, we want to please Him. Just as a child seeks the approval of his father, we should live in a way intended to bring the approval of our Father in heaven."

Preacher Mead bent his head over the Bible again and continued reading the story. Dinah stared at the passage in her Bible, but the words melted together. Her thoughts turned inward as realization bloomed. The niggle she'd been experiencing over the past days was the Holy Spirit trying to get her attention. She'd been wrong to withhold the truth from Mr. Irwin and Mr. Harvey. Now that she'd recognized her wrongdoing, she couldn't, in clear conscience, get on the train Thursday without divulging the secrets of her past to her employer.

She hung her head. Telling would be hard, but not telling wouldn't please the God who had saved her. *I want to stand faultless before You, Lord, just as we sang at the beginning of the service. Give me the courage to tell my secret.* Worry struck. If she told, she might not be able to become a server. She might even be released from her position as chambermaid. As she contemplated the possible consequences, worry gnawed through her gut. What would she do if she lost her job? Then, in a warm, welcome wave, peace flooded her.

She finished her prayer. *You are my Hope and Stay. If I lose the chance to become a server, I will accept it as Your will for me. I'll trust You to take care of me. Amen.*

Chapter 41

Ruthie

uthie grabbed Mama's hand and pulled her toward Papa. At the same time, she shooed her young siblings away. "You all go on. I need to talk to Mama and Papa without you underfoot. Go pester Dinah for a few minutes." She laughed at her friend's shocked face, then hurried Mama across the floor.

All night she'd contemplated what becoming a server might mean. Girls who honored their contracts were allowed to ride free on the Santa Fe trains. She could visit Phoebe in Newton, or travel all the way to Wichita to see Mama's parents and brothers. Maybe she could even go to the nation's first national park—the one President Grant named Yellowstone—and watch the geysers shoot into the air. She'd take Seth along for propriety's sake but also because she knew he would love to see those geysers.

The plans rolled through her mind and sped her tongue when she had Mama's and Papa's attention. "Papa, I know you've said you aren't in favor of me becoming a server for Mr. Harvey, but I would like to ask you to consider it one more time."

Papa made a sour face. "Now, Ruthie…"

She talked over the top of his mild protest. "Dinah is leaving on Thursday for training in Kansas City. So I could travel with her rather than going alone. If I became a server, I would earn more money, which I could share with you, and I would also have several months free from work to spend more time with the family. So—"

"I will not have any daughter of mine becoming a waitress." Papa spoke firmly. "Waitresses have a very poor reputation, Ruthie."

Although she knew better than to argue with her parents, Ruthie couldn't stop herself. "But you are talking about waitressing in a raucous roadhouse. Papa, Mr. Harvey's restaurants aren't anything like the establishments that concern you. He has very high standards for his restaurants, and his servers are clean, modest, well-respected women."

Papa's stern expression didn't change, but Ruthie glimpsed a hint of softening in Mama's face. She plunged on. "Come to the Clifton today for dinner. Watch Lyla, Amelia, and Matilda. If after seeing how they serve and how the people treat them you are still vehemently opposed to the idea, I won't mention it again." She bit her lip to prevent herself from further pleading.

Papa and Mama looked at each other. Mama said, "I put a stew on the stove before we left. I could set it aside and save it for our supper."

Papa said, "It would cost more than I have in my pocket for all of us to eat at the hotel."

Ruthie snagged Seth's sleeve and yanked him onto the dais. "Then have Seth take the youngsters home and feed them the stew while you and Mama eat at the hotel. He's capable of ladling stew into bowls."

"Hey!" Seth wriggled loose. "How come I'm gettin' stuck with all the work?"

Ruthie wrinkled her nose at her brother. "It's only one dinner, Seth. And Jonah and Noah can help you." She turned from her brother's disgusted scowl and aimed a hopeful look at Papa and Mama. "Please? At least come see?"

Papa looked at Mama. She raised one shoulder in a slight shrug and quirked her lips. Papa sighed and nodded. He gave Seth a little nudge toward the younger ones waiting at their bench. "Take your brothers and little Dinah June home and give them their dinner. Your mother and I will be there after we've eaten at the hotel."

Dinah

Instead of eating, Dinah tapped on the door to Mr. Irwin's office. His blunt voice invited her to enter. Although a man of small stature, Mr. Irwin possessed an intimidating bearing. The hotel manager, Mr. Phillips, had certainly taken that into account when he'd placed responsibility for hiring and firing into Mr. Irwin's hands. From her first encounter with him, she'd been cowed by his brusque, no-nonsense demeanor. Uncertainty about how he'd respond to her planned admission left her quivering inside, but she slipped into the chair facing his desk and met his unsmiling gaze.

"Mr. Irwin, may I talk with you about my training?"

Apparently she'd caught him in the midst of an important task because he drummed his fingers on the stack of papers on his desk in an impatient gesture. "What about it?"

Lord, help me... "I want to make sure I'm...qualified."

The manager frowned. "We've already discussed the qualifications. Mr. Harvey requires his servers be at least eighteen but not older than thirty years of age, attractive, intelligent, and of good moral character. We're aware of your young age, but we waived the requirement given our unique circumstances here."

Dinah's pulse pounded with ferocity, making her breath come in short spurts. Her voice emerged in a mouselike squeak. "It isn't the age qualification that troubles me. You see, I...I was born to a Chicago prostitute and raised in a brothel."

The man's eyebrows came together sharply. He drew back. "Oh?"

"Yes, sir. When my mother became very ill and I needed to pay for her care, I...I arranged to meet a businessman for an evening's companionship." As she spoke, she felt as though the dark cloud that had hovered over her head since her arrival in Florence broke apart into small, less threatening puffs.

She sat up straighter in the chair, and her voice lost its quaver. "I changed my mind and told him I didn't want to do it, but he took his pleasure from me. And then I took his money. I used it to care for my mother in her last days, give her a proper burial, and buy train tickets to get out of Chicago."

"You..." Mr. Irwin stared at her with horror-filled eyes.

Bravely, Dinah nodded. "I don't ever intend to do something like that again. It was..." She swallowed, briefly reliving the pain and degradation of

that night in Chicago. She forced out in a rasping whisper, "It was awful."
Then she squared her shoulders and faced the manager again. "God has for-
given me. The Bible says He has thrown away my sin as far as east is from west.
But what I did carries consequences. I didn't want to mislead you, Mr. Irwin.
I didn't want to lie to you."

The man sat as still as a fence post, seeming to stare straight through
Dinah. She waited, but he didn't speak.

While he sat in silence, she told him the rest. "I've recently accepted
God's Son as my Savior and God as my Father. From now on, I want to be an
honorable child of God. Please forgive me for keeping my past a secret. If you
decide this disqualifies me from being a server, I'll accept it without a fuss."
Rising, she held her hand to him. "Thank you for the opportunity to work at
the Clifton."

Mr. Irwin made a strange little gurgling sound, as if someone had tied his
tonsils in a knot, but he took Dinah's hand and gave it a very brief shake. "I
appreciate your...candor, Miss Hubley. I will share this information with Mr.
Phillips, and certainly he'll wire Mr. Harvey to seek his counsel. You'll be ap-
prised of our decision concerning your training for a server position before
Thursday."

Dinah expected a cloak of dread to drop over her. After all, her security
was being threatened. But instead she only experienced a great sense of relief.
She'd told. She said it all out loud. And admitting it had somehow diminished
its power. Her lips tugged into a smile while tears of gratitude stung her eyes.
"Thank you, Mr. Irwin. Coming here has changed me, and I will always be
grateful."

She stepped out of his office and walked directly into Ruthie, who stood
just outside the door with her hands clamped over her mouth and her eyes wide
and stricken looking. A bolt of fear sliced through Dinah. She grabbed Ruthie's shoulders. "What is it? What's wrong?"

"Oh, Dinah..." With her hands over her mouth, her words became a
strangled mutter. "Oh, Dinah..."

She wove her arm around Ruthie's waist and guided her into the chambermaids' parlor. She closed the door behind them, then pulled Ruthie's hands down and held them tight. "What has happened?" It must be something terrible for Ruthie to be so distraught. Dinah held her breath, preparing herself for whatever tragedy Ruthie would share.

Ruthie shook her head, tears pooling in her eyes. "I didn't mean to listen. I only came to deliver a message to Mr. Irwin from Mr. Gindough, but you were talking, and I heard and…and…" Bursting into tears, she flung her arms around Dinah. She stammered through sobs. "I'm so sorry for what happened to you. You really are like Jacob and Leah's Dinah, who suffered harm because of Shechem's selfish want. Oh, Dinah, I'm so sorry the man hurt you that way."

As Ruthie continued to weep against her shoulder, Dinah's tears spilled, too. She cried for Ruthie's broken heart. For her own lost innocence. Even for the Bible-Dinah. The shared sorrow was healing, and a few of the black puffs remaining from the heavy cloud faded, washed away by the cleansing tears.

After several minutes the girls pulled apart. Dinah looked into Ruthie's red, puffy face. "You're a mess." She pulled her handkerchief from her pocket and gave it to the other girl.

Ruthie huffed out a short laugh as she mopped her face. "No more than you." She withdrew a lace hanky from her pocket and handed it to Dinah. "Here. Blow your nose."

Dinah did so, and then they stood, holding each other's rumpled handkerchief and staring sympathetically into each other's eyes. Ruthie spoke first.

"I wish I'd known." Regret pursed her face. "I was jealous of you, Dinah. First I was jealous because I thought you came from affluence. Then I was jealous because Mr. Ackerman gave you his attention. I was even jealous because you could make decisions for yourself without having to ask permission from anyone. I was so foolish and childish and wrong." More tears quivered on her lower lashes. "Will you please forgive me?"

Dinah gave Ruthie an impetuous hug, amazed at the ease with which she embraced the girl. "I forgive you. And will you forgive me? All of those misunderstandings could have been avoided if I'd just told you the truth."

"Of course!" The girls embraced again, then drew back, both smiling.

The emotional release left Dinah weak. She eased into one of the chairs and sagged against its sturdy back. "I feel so…free."

Ruthie sniffled hard as she perched in the other chair. She gazed at Dinah with sympathy. "What an awful thing to carry. Little wonder you had such nightmares." Then she jolted. "But they've stopped, haven't they? I haven't heard you cry out in days."

Dinah released a contented sigh. "God took them away when I asked Him to take my sins away."

A frown marred Ruthie's face. "I need to tell you something. About your sin…" She nibbled her lip for a moment as if gathering her thoughts. She cupped her hand over Dinah's before speaking more quietly and slowly than Dinah could remember. "You made a mistake by going to meet that man. Even though you needed the money to take care of your mother, which was an honorable thing to do, selling yourself wasn't the right way to earn it. So you made a mistake."

Dinah nodded, accepting Ruthie's words without a sting of resentment.

"But the man who…who bought you—he is also at fault. You changed your mind. You said no and he didn't listen. You tried to do right, and he forced himself on you." Ruthie squeezed Dinah's hand, the pressure pinching yet comforting at the same time. "You shouldn't feel shameful over what he did. Do you understand?"

Dinah considered Ruthie's statement. Was her guilt the result of her choice or the choice Mr. Sanger made? The feelings were all tangled together, making it difficult to sort them out. "I think I understand. And I'll pray about it. God has already taken away my nightmares. He's forgiven me for going to the hotel room. He can remove the shame from me, too, can't He?"

Ruthie beamed. "He can do anything, Dinah. Remember what we read in Ephesians last night? He is able to do 'exceeding abundantly above all' we ask or think."

Desire writhed through Dinah's middle. "Can we ask Him now?"

Without a word Ruthie moved to her knees. Dinah knelt beside her and they held hands. Ruthie prayed aloud. "Dear God, Dinah was hurt by someone, the same way Dinah in the Bible was hurt by Shechem. Shechem's mistreatment of Dinah left a mark on her soul, and the man in Chicago did the same thing to my friend Dinah. But You don't want us to cower beneath burdens of shame. So, God, erase the mark. It isn't hers to carry. Give her complete freedom so she can be whole in body, spirit, and soul. Thank You for bringing us healing when we ask. In Your Son's name, amen."

They rose, and Ruthie gave her face one more swipe with the handkerchief. "We'd better go to work before Mr. Irwin bellows at us."

As they left the parlor and went their separate ways, something whispered a reminder to Dinah. There was someone else who deserved to know the truth of her past. It would be harder to tell him than it had been to tell Mr. Irwin because she wanted his approval so badly. But she sensed once she'd told him, not one wisp of black cloud would haunt her.

Somehow, before she left town, she had to talk to Amos.

Chapter 42

Amos

mos reached the edge of town as the morning train was pulling in. He brought Ike to a stop a few feet from the tracks and watched the locomotive roll past. The engine whistle blasted, and Ike laid his ears flat to his skull and snorted, dancing in place. Amos gave the mule's solid neck a pat. "There now, boy, I know it's noisy but don't bolt on me." His cart still held ten dozen eggs—if Ike took a notion to escape the noise, the cart would likely tip.

Ike snorted again, but to Amos's relief he only pawed the ground. He continued to give the animal comforting pats and talked softly into his flattened ears until the caboose had passed. Then he gave Ike's sides a little nudge with his heels, and they headed up Main Street. He couldn't resist sending a glance toward the Clifton Hotel as they crossed the tracks. His heart lurched when he spotted two women on the station's boarding platform, one with a red-gold bun and the other with upswept waves the color of honey. Miss Mead and Dinah. A brocade bag rested on the platform next to their feet.

Instinctively he tugged the reins and intoned, "Whoa." Ike stopped, and Amos watched the two women embrace, then catch hands. He frowned, wishing he could hear what they were saying. He fidgeted on Ike's back, battling the urge to go to the station, to give Dinah a farewell the way Miss Mead was now doing. Seeing her again, even from a distance, raised the familiar mingle of love, anger, regret, and disillusionment.

She was leaving now. He would be able to bury the dream of building a life with her. He should be happy. But the heaviness in his chest wasn't from joy. He sighed and tapped Ike's sides again. "Come on, boy. Let's get these eggs delivered."

Over the next three hours, he went door to door and sold all but one dozen of the eggs to people in town. With noon approaching he decided he'd been in town long enough. "Let's go to the grocer, Ike—buy a few provisions." Ike snorted a reply. As Amos looped Ike's reins on the hitching post, the store-keeper stepped out on the porch and flicked a glance across the sky.

"Look at that. Clear as clear can be." Mr. Root sounded disgusted.

Amos chuckled. "I'm enjoying the clear sky. Even though it's still cold, that bright sun makes it seem warmer. And there's no wind today for a change. I'd say it's a good day."

Mr. Root shook his head. "Sure it's a good day. But I don't understand it." He pointed at his right knee. "This thing's telling me a storm is brewing. For seven years now, I've been able to predict every storm whether summer, spring, winter, or fall by the ache in my knee. But I don't see one single sign of a storm. So that means my knee's now giving me aches over my age." He flung one more venomous look toward the sky, then marched back into the store, mumbling under his breath.

Hiding his smile, Amos followed the owner inside and collected the items he wanted to purchase. As he laid them on the counter, he started to ask if he could get credit for the last dozen eggs in his cart. But another idea struck. Why not take them to the Clifton? He wanted to remind the manager how he was building his flock. Now that Dinah had left—his heart panged, but he gritted his teeth and pushed the ache aside—he could go there without worry. After talking to the manager, he could give the eggs to the chef as a promise of more to come. So even though the credit would be a boon, he paid for his purchases out of his pocket and then aimed Ike for the Clifton.

Not until he slid down from Ike's back and limped to the cart did he remember he hadn't brought a basket to carry the eggs into the hotel. Grimacing, he scratched his head and finally decided to fill his jacket pockets. The large squares of cloth stitched on three sides to the flaps of his coat were big enough to each hold a half-dozen eggs. He carefully placed the eggs in his pockets, then made his way into the foyer.

Up the hall the luncheon counter was crowded with diners. Good smells wafted from the area, and happy chatter filled the air. But the pleasant scents and cheerful noises reminded Amos of the many lunches he'd shared with Dinah. He hadn't realized how hard it would be to enter this place of memories. He came to a halt midway between the door and the check-in counter.

The clerk looked up and sent Amos a puzzled look. "Good day, Mr. Ackerman. I haven't seen you in a while."

Amos forced his feet into motion. "I've stayed busy. Is Mr. Irwin available? I'd like to talk to him."

"I believe he's in his office. Let me fetch him for you." He bustled off.

Amos turned and leaned against the counter while he waited. The first time he'd brought eggs to the hotel, he arrived at breakfast time when everyone was busy. Maybe he should have considered the poor timing of this stop, too. But if Mr. Irwin was busy, as he'd been that first time, Amos could wait, just as he had then.

Without warning, a memory surfaced—Dinah, peering over the back of the chair with wide, compassionate eyes. Her voice whispered from the past: *"What...broke you?"* He hung his head and closed his eyes, willing away the remembered images. If he'd known how broken he'd become by allowing her into his heart, he would have made a different choice. But how to change it now? She was gone from town, but she was still with him.

Lost in thought, he muttered, "Why can't you leave me alone?"

"Amos?"

He jerked upright, his eyes seeking. There, not six feet away, stood Dinah. Was he imagining things? He blinked twice and looked again. No, she was there, her crisp maid's uniform and upswept hair with its few escaping tendrils both familiar and somehow new at the same time. He shook his head, confused by his thoughts. "What are you doing here?"

A slight smile curved her lips. "I work here."

"But you left." He bounced his palm toward the railroad station across the street. "I saw you on the boarding platform with a bag. You left."

Her smile remained, but it seemed sad. "I wasn't leaving. I was seeing

Ruthie off. She's going to train and then come back and work as a server here at the Clifton."

"Then you aren't leaving…"

She lowered her head. He stared at the neat part in her thick, wavy hair. She said softly, "No. I'm not leaving." She lifted her face and met his gaze, her expression bold. "And I'm glad to see you. There's something I've needed to tell you. Since it's my dinner break, can we…talk?"

Before he could form an answer—before he could determine whether he wanted to agree or refuse—intrusions came from two directions. Mr. Irwin approached from the right, and the guest whose proclamation had destroyed Amos's world on New Year's Eve wheeled around the corner from the left.

Mr. Irwin said, "Mr. Ackerman, what can I do for you?"

At the same time, the guest spoke to Dinah in the same deprecating tone that had set Amos's teeth on edge. "Well, hello there, honey."

Dinah shrank away from the man, bringing her closer to Amos.

Mr. Irwin turned from Amos and toward the guest, his brows set in a sharp V. "Sir, in this hotel, as in all Harvey-owned establishments, we address ladies with courtesy."

The man shrugged. "I always address ladies courteously. But this little gal is not a lady."

Amos balled his hands into fists. No matter what she'd done, this man shouldn't publicly disgrace her. After all, he'd been in the wrong, too, to hire Dinah. He took one step toward the guest to warn him to silence, but Mr. Irwin darted in front of him, forcing him to move aside or be toppled.

"From where do you know Miss Hubley?" Mr. Irwin bit out the question. His stance reminded Amos of the cocky rooster he'd once owned.

The guest slipped his hands in his pockets and peered down his nose at the hotel manager. "She and I go way back." He aimed his smirk at Dinah. "Don't we, honey?"

Mr. Irwin looked at Dinah, and Amos held his breath. The protectiveness welling within him took him by surprise. Without thought, he moved half in front of Dinah, blocking her from the other men's view. But Dinah stepped out of his shadow as Mr. Irwin said, "Miss Hubley, is this the man from Chicago?"

Dinah nodded, neither with hesitance nor in a frightened manner. She looked composed, strong, confident. Amos stared at her in wonder. What had brought this change?

Quick as a lightning strike, Mr. Irwin's hand shot out and grabbed the man by his jacket front. "Mr. Sanger, get your things and leave this hotel."

The man slapped the manager's hand aside. "I'm paid up for two days. I'm not going anywhere."

"You will or I'll call the sheriff on you."

Sanger's jaw dropped. "You'll evict me for calling her 'honey'?"

Mr. Irwin rose up on his tiptoes and glared into the guest's face. "I'll evict you for being a lowdown, grimy, snake-in-the-grass who preys on young girls. I might not be able to do anything about what you did to Miss Hubley in Chicago, but I can make sure every female under the Clifton roof is safe from the likes of you now." He jabbed both palms against Sanger's chest. "Get out."

Sanger swung an incredulous look from Mr. Irwin to Dinah and back. "What about the money I paid for my room?"

"If you want a refund, take it up with the sheriff," Mr. Irwin replied in a glib tone. "I'll be glad to explain to him why I sent you from my hotel. I think he'd find it very interesting how you forced yourself on a young girl who tried to refuse your advances."

Amos stared at Dinah, who stood gazing at the diminutive hotel manager with her spine straight and her head high. Mr. Irwin's statement reverberated in his head like a clapper against a bell's bowl. This guest, this man named Sanger, had...had... Amos couldn't complete the thought.

Fury roared through his chest. With a growl, he raised his fists and advanced on the man. Sanger darted up the hallway like the coward he was. The slam of his door carried clear to the lobby.

Mr. Irwin touched Dinah's elbow. "I don't trust that man. He might cause trouble. I'm fetching Mr. Phillip's pistol and then sending one of the busboys for the sheriff. He'll make sure Sanger gets on the next train. It's probably best if you go to your parlor and stay there until Sanger leaves." His grim expression took on a hint of compassion. "Don't worry. He won't bother you again."

"Thank you, Mr. Irwin."

The manager snorted. "Such riffraff in the Clifton! Mr. Harvey would be appalled." He strode off, arms swinging.

Dinah started for the little parlor tucked behind the counter. Midway there, she stopped and looked back. "Are you coming?"

Amos gave a start. "Do you want me to?"

The same smile—half-sad, half-hopeful—appeared on her face. "I haven't had a chance to talk to you yet."

He saw no need for her to say anything else. So much had become clear in the past few minutes. On their first meeting, he'd wondered why she seemed so nervous and distrustful. He thought about the times he'd reached to touch her and she flinched away, how she stood so stiffly within his arms at the beginning of their one dance the night of the Calico Ball, the wary way she watched people, even her reasoning that she wasn't welcome in church.

She'd been broken by a man who disregarded her feelings. And he'd broken her again, by refusing to listen when she tried to explain. Recalling how he'd thrown that rock from his front door—thrown it in condemnation—Amos wanted to hide. He'd wronged her.

What should he do? While he now realized she hadn't callously sold herself to a man, he also knew something precious was gone that couldn't be recovered. When he was a boy, he'd overheard his mother and one of her friends discussing the sad fate of a girl whose purity was stolen. Ma said, with such sorrow, "How will she ever be able to allow a man to touch her?" It had taken years for him to understand the meaning behind their conversation, but he understood it now.

That girl's circumstance applied to Dinah. Since she had been robbed of her maidenhood, would her trust also be permanently scarred? Would he only be causing her more discomfort and fear by reestablishing a relationship with her? And—he had to acknowledge the question teasing the deepest part of his heart—could he touch her now without wondering if his hands reminded her of the man who'd desecrated her? Was it best for him to leave…or stay?

"Amos?" She still waited.

When he looked into her pale-blue eyes glimmering with hesitant hope, refusing her request became an insurmountable challenge. He started to slip his hands into his pockets, but his fingertips encountered the eggs. He needed to deliver them to the kitchen before he broke them. Regretfully, he said, "I can't." He wanted to ask if he could meet with her later, but before he could say the words, she gave a little nod and darted around the corner.

Chapter 43

Dinah

inah closed the parlor door behind her, then immediately knelt before one of the wicker chairs. Her encounters with first Amos and then Mr. Sanger had left her reeling, and she needed to sort her thoughts. But mostly she needed to find relief from the sting of rejection Amos's hasty departure had caused. Closing her eyes, she addressed her heavenly Father in prayer.

"God, did You see? He walked away from me. I prayed for the chance to talk to him, and then there he was, as if waiting to see me. I wanted to tell him what I'd done so he'd know why I asked for his forgiveness. But then he walked away again." Her chest tightened with a fresh ache, and she swallowed a lump of hurt before continuing. "Thank You for promising to never leave me or forsake me. As much as I want Amos to be my friend again, I know I will be all right if he chooses not to be because I have You. I will always have You."

Tears threatened—tears of both gratitude and disappointment. She went on in a raspy whisper. "When Mr. Irwin told me I wouldn't be able to be a server after all, it was hard but I accepted it. When Ruthie was sent to train in my place, I found the means to be happy for her instead of jealous. So I know You are helping me. Thank You for being my Father, my Comforter, my Strength, my Protector, my Everything. Even if I'm a chambermaid for the rest of my life—even if I never find someone on this earth to love me—I will have You. Please help me remember, dear God, that with You I am whole. Help me remember You are my Enough."

A sweet trickle of peace flowed through her being. Her lips quivered into a grateful smile, recognizing God's Spirit in the room. "Mr. Irwin told me to stay here until Mr. Sanger left, but I have a job to do and I will go do it now. You are with me, God, and You will keep me safe as I go about my duties. Amen."

She rose, wiped the moisture from her cheeks, and then with a light step set to work.

Amos

By the time Amos finished speaking with Mr. Irwin and delivered the eggs to the chef, the clock in the foyer showed a quarter of two. He shook his head. How had he managed to spend so much time waiting? He started toward the chambermaids' parlor, but halfway there changed his direction and aimed himself for the front doors instead. Dinah wouldn't be there any longer. And he didn't know what to say to her anyway. It was best to just go on home.

When he stepped outside, a chill blast of wind took him by surprise. He fastened the top button of his coat and folded the collar around his ears before moving to the edge of the porch. The sky, which had been a clear blue at noon, now held the color of a galvanized washtub—an ominous gray. Far in the north, dark clouds rolled in a billowing mass. He whistled through his teeth. Apparently Mr. Root's achy knee wasn't related to age after all.

Amos hop-skipped to Ike and swung himself onto the mule's back. The way the wind blew, that storm would be upon them soon. He didn't worry about a tornado—tornadoes were spring storms—but he didn't want to be caught out in the open by a blizzard. He clicked his tongue on his teeth, prompting the animal to get moving.

Twice on the ride toward home, the wind turned the wagon over. Amos's hip ached with ferocity from having to climb down, right the wagon, and clamber onto Ike's back again. When the little wagon tipped a third time less than a quarter mile from home, Amos released the rigging and left it in the road. Everyone in town knew it belonged to him so they wouldn't bother it. He'd come back for it when the storm had passed.

Particles of dust, tossed by the stout wind, stung his cheeks and neck, and he heaved a sigh of relief when Ike trotted the final yards to the farm. Amos slid down and limped his way to the barn, pulling Ike along with him. Samson and Gideon dashed over, greeting Amos with low whines and moist nose-bumps against his hands. He gave the dogs a halfhearted greeting as he led Ike to his stall. A shiver rattled his frame. He longed to go to the house and sit in front of the fire, but he needed to tend to the mule first.

He tossed a blanket over Ike's back, then filled the hay trough. With the dogs trotting alongside him, he lifted down a bucket from its hook to bring in water. He held the rope handle firmly in one hand and gave the barn door a push with the other. He gasped as a mighty gust of wind yanked the bucket from his grasp and forced him to stumble backward. The door slammed into its frame, sending the brooding hens into wild squawking. Amos stood, dumbfounded. Kansas was a windy state—he knew that full well—but that was the most forceful blast he'd ever experienced.

One small window looked out on the east side of Amos's property. He crossed to it and stood for a moment, watching the trees bow low among clouds of dust stirred to life by the wind. The thought of venturing out lost its appeal regardless of the animals' need for fresh water and his desire to warm himself before a toasty fire. As quickly as the storm was blowing in, wouldn't it blow itself out just as fast? Maybe he should just hunker down in here and wait rather than try to go to the house.

He blew out a breath of irritation. Why hadn't he followed the advice given by longtime residents when he moved onto the farm? All of the local farmers strung ropes from the house to outbuildings in case a winter storm caught them by surprise. Then they could follow the ropes from one place to another without fear of getting lost. But Amos had put it off, too busy with the other tasks required to get his chicken farm up and operating. If he tried to get to his house without hanging on to something, the wind might send him head over heels into Indian territory.

"I reckon I'll be staying here with you for a while," he told the dogs. They looked up at him with bright, trusting eyes. For some reason the confidence in their warm gazes made him want to cringe. He limped across the barn to Ike, ignoring Sam's and Gid's furry company. The blanket he'd tossed over Ike was mouse chewed and smelled like mold, but it would offer him warmth. "Sorry, Ike, but I need this worse than you do." He tugged the battered square of brown wool free, then moved to the corner of the stall.

He sank down in the hay and spread the blanket across his lap. At once, the dogs plopped beside him. Gid rested his chin on Amos's knee. Sam pressed himself against Amos's thigh and busied himself licking his paws. Idly Amos stroked Gid's silky, black-splotched ears and listened to the wind howl. A mournful sound. The door bounced in its frame and the windows rattled. Amos shuddered. He hoped the wind didn't damage any of his buildings before it moved on across the plains.

The afternoon hours crept by slowly, painfully. Despite the blanket, his body convulsed from cold. The wind beat the building, raising thuds and creaks and rattles. The dogs slept, their snores competing with the wind's howl, but Amos sat stiffly upright, occasionally checking his watch and willing the storm to pass.

By four o'clock full darkness had descended, and the storm still raged. Impatient and tired of sitting, he gritted his teeth against the stiffness in his hip and pushed himself upright. Sam and Gid whined and rose with him, their curious gazes aimed at his face. He gave the dogs an absent pat on their heads and shuffled to the window. His breath steamed the pane, so he cleared it with his hand and squinted through the shadows. Strange clumps of white, some of which were shedding smaller bits of fluff, rolled across the yard, tossed by the gusting wind. He leaned closer to the window, trying to make sense of the sight, and realization broke through like a grain sack bursting its seams.

"Stay, Sam and Gid!" Breaking into a clumsy hop-skip, he trotted across the dirt floor and threw open the barn door. Wind blasted him, but he fought his way against it to the chicken yard. The chicken-house door flapped on broken hinges. More than a dozen chickens, probably frightened, had vacated the safety of the house and found themselves treated callously by nature's fury. Weak clucks reached Amos's ears, piercing him with their helplessness.

One by one, Amos gathered them. Three were already dead, their glazed eyes staring sightlessly, but those still breathing he cradled against his jacket and placed gently in a nesting box inside the chicken house. It took fourteen trips to collect them all, but when he'd laid the last one on the straw, he wedged the door closed against the wind, then went down the row of boxes, giving each a thorough examination.

Of those he'd brought in, four seemed in shock and near death, but he believed the others would survive if kept warm and safe. He ached. His muscles felt stiff and his hip throbbed. A headache pounded at the base of his skull. But mostly his heart hurt for the poor chickens that had been at the mercy of the wind.

Releasing a growl of frustration, Amos shook his fist toward the low ceiling. "We're all at the mercy of wind, aren't we?" His heart thumped against his rib cage. He dropped to his knees, his hand falling into one of the nesting boxes where a weak hen lay panting in the straw. He stroked the hen's straggly feathers as he continued to speak to God—not in prayer, but in protest.

"We're helpless. We can't prevent hardships. As much as we make our plans and strive for success, everything can be wiped out in the blink of an eye. So why do we bother? Why did You open us to falling in love when our hearts can be so easily broken? Why do You allow us to build our houses and farms when winds can come roaring into our lives and steal it all away? Do You find pleasure in seeing us struggle like those poor chickens being thrown across the ground by the driving wind?"

A dry sob wrenched from his throat, anger and frustration and powerlessness pressing at him as relentlessly as the wind slapping against the wooden structure. "We're helpless against driving winds and wagon wheels and unscrupulous men who take whatever pleases them!" He came to a stop as his own words penetrated his ears. Had he just equated Dinah's state to the haplessness of the chickens and his own encounter with the hay wagon?

An image of Dinah filled his mind—her calm, steady stance as Mr. Irwin berated the man at the hotel for taking advantage of her. He'd never seen her so sure, so strong, so poised. Something had changed her. Even though she was still working as a chambermaid instead of going to train to be a server, even though he'd broken his promise to her, even though a man who'd apparently harmed her in the most vile of ways stood only a few feet away from her, she'd exhibited a stalwart strength. A strength he now lacked. And in that moment, he envied her.

The wind's howl nearly covered his voice as he lowered his tone to a whisper as weak as his trembling limbs. "How is it possible she remains standing after losing so much?" The answer whisked from the depths of his soul, from that secret place where his mother had taught him to hide away words of wisdom. Words penned by the apostle Paul while imprisoned and with chains hanging from his hands and feet—*"I know both how to be abased, and I know how to abound: every where and in all things I am instructed both to be full and to be hungry, both to abound and to suffer need. I can do all things through Christ which strengtheneth me."*

Kneeling on the floor of the chicken house with a storm raging outside and hens softly clucking in nervousness around him, Amos realized how far he'd slipped from the faith he'd received as his own when only a boy of nine. He allowed the perceived betrayal by Dinah to steal his peace and his source of strength. How could he have given her such power? He relied too much on her—had put too much attention on developing an earthly relationship instead of keeping Christ where He needed to be.

He hung his head and spoke to God again, but this time in reverence and humility. "How foolish I've been, chasing Dinah and eggs and my own plans. When I bought this farm, I asked Your blessing on it, and I worked hard as if I were working for You. But somewhere—when I met Dinah—it became for me. I forgot that You made it possible for me to buy this farm. I forgot that You put Dinah in my pathway and brought her to my heart again and again. You gave me good gifts, and I squandered them, thinking only of myself and what I could achieve."

Gulping back knots of sorrow, he continued laying bare the thoughts and feelings God already knew but which he needed to divulge for his own purging. "I'll make things right with Dinah. I'll be happy with a small operation instead of trying to build a bigger one, if that's what You want for me. Please forgive my stubborn selfishness and let me walk with You again. I'm so…lonely without You."

The God of his childhood held out His hand, and Amos took hold. The helplessness over which he'd railed only minutes ago remained, yet joy, peace, and contentment descended. The storm raged outside, but within Amos, all was still.

Chapter 44

Amos

On the tail of the storm came snow—dry, crystal-like flakes that arrived sideways on the wind and blew between the cracks of the barn and chicken house walls, falling like confetti on the shivering creatures housed beneath the roofs. Amos, reluctant to leave the chicken house with its damaged door, stayed with his flock until the storm blew itself out early Friday morning. By then two of the most traumatized hens had died, so—with a heavy heart—he butchered and stewed them. But even though he hadn't eaten since breakfast the day before, he couldn't bring himself to fill his plate.

Over his hours trapped by the storm, he'd had time to think. And pray. And put his heart in alignment with his Maker. Somewhere in the darkest part of the night, he'd reached a conclusion, and he knew he wouldn't be able to eat or sleep or gather eggs until he'd gone to Dinah and asked her forgiveness for his cold treatment of her.

He took the time to see to the needs of his animals, providing them with fresh food and water. Although the wind had died, the still air was bitterly cold. His bare hands trembled, hindering him as he secured the chicken house door with a length of scrap lumber. He'd repair the broken hinge when he returned from town. As he pulled himself onto Ike's back, Sam and Gid pranced near Ike's feet and whined.

Amos gazed down at the hopeful pair and sighed. "You two are tired of being cooped up, aren't you?" They yipped in reply, as if they'd understood, and Amos released a light chuckle. "All right, then. You can come to town, too." He climbed down, located a long piece of twine, and fashioned loose collars at both ends, which he slipped around the dogs' necks. On Ike's back again with the middle of the twine draped across his lap, he said, "Let's go."

Sam and Gid trotted along on either side of Ike, ears flopping and tongues lolling, their breath forming little clouds they chased with their pointed noses. Their antics tempted Amos to watch them instead of the road, but Ike sometimes took a notion to form his own trail, so reluctantly he aimed his gaze ahead.

He reached the end of the lane, and just as he turned Ike onto the road, the twine lying over his thighs suddenly zipped to the left—Gideon pulling. Amos drew Ike to a stop before Gid managed to lift Sam onto the mule's back. He looked at Gid, who'd lowered his nose to the ground. No doubt he'd picked up the scent of some wild creature, but Amos didn't have time for the dog to hunt prey. "Gideon, come!"

With a soft whine Gideon lifted his head, but he held something clamped in his jaw. Amos scowled. Had the dog found a dead sparrow or a field mouse? Either way, he couldn't have his pet marching through town with a small corpse in his mouth.

"Drop it, Gid."

Gid whined again, his stubby tail offering a few hopeful wags.

Amos injected sternness in his tone. "Drop it."

His tail drooping, Gid released his prize. A rock hit the hard ground, bounced, then rolled against Ike's hoof. Amos stared in amazement. Sunlight sparkled on an amber band circling a brown stone. A familiar brown stone. The very one he'd kept for months on his mantel and then thrown from the porch.

A chill broke across his frame that had nothing to do with the temperature. Finding the rock again after his night of reckoning was like receiving a glimmer of hope. Although his hip protested, he slid down and reached for the rock. Gid tried to steal it first, but Amos gave the dog's snout a light nudge and curled his fist around the stone that brought to mind images of Dinah.

He closed his eyes briefly, the cold stone warming within his palm. "Thank You, Lord, for giving this to me again. I accept it as a sign of Your forgiveness for my act of condemnation." After slipping the rock into his pocket, he gave

Gid's neck a quick scratch of thank-you, then climbed onto Ike's back. With a
smile on his face, he set out again toward town.

Dinah

Dinah hummed "Bringing in the Sheaves" as she ran a soapy rag over the washbasin in one of the hotel rooms. She'd taken up Ruthie's habit in the hopes it
might make her miss her friend less, and she discovered humming cheery tunes
gave her heart an unexpected lift. Perhaps, she reflected as she shifted her attention to the painted water pitcher, Ruthie's sunny disposition was due in part to
her penchant for humming hymns.

"Bringing in the Sheaves" kept her company until she'd finished dusting,
sweeping, and scrubbing. She moved to the next room, switching her song to
"How Firm a Foundation" as she worked. Midway through cleaning, instead
of merely humming the tune, she began singing, softly at first and then with
increased volume, nearly unmindful of the change. By the time she reached the
fourth verse, she was singing at full lung and brandishing the feather duster
with gusto.

"'When through the deep waters I call thee to go, the rivers of woe shall
not thee overflow; for I will be with thee, thy troubles to bless, and sanctify to
thee thy deepest distress.'"

"Amen."

The softly uttered word, spoken with deep emotion, startled Dinah so
badly she dropped the duster. She spun toward the voice, then gave another jolt
when she realized who stood framed within the doorway. Pressing both hands
to her hammering heart, she stammered out, "A-Amos?"

A hesitant smile grew on his cold-reddened face, lighting his eyes with
both apprehension and tenderness. "Hello, Dinah. Mr. Irwin told me where to
find you. He said I could steal a few minutes of your time…if you don't see me
as an intrusion."

She almost laughed. Amos—an intrusion? Such a ridiculous concern. She shook her head, the intense beat of her pulse changing to a flutter of delight. "I don't."

The apprehension in his eyes faded, and his chest expanded as he drew in a full breath. He held it for a moment, then let out his air in a mighty whoosh. At the same time, his stiff bearing relaxed. He seemed to release a great burden. Witnessing the action, Dinah experienced the prick of empathetic tears.

She tucked the duster, handle side down, into her apron pocket and made her way toward him. Halfway across the floor, however, she stopped as snippets from their exchange on New Year's Eve crept through her memory. His words that night had stung like a whip's lash. The names he'd flung at her—harlot, trollop, one bearing stains—returned to pierce her soul. Then other names, titles she'd encountered in her nightly Bible reading, whispered through her aching heart—daughter, beloved, redeemed. The ugly references swept away as if whisked by God's duster. Her feet began moving again, carrying her within a few inches of Amos's waiting form.

She peered into his handsome, familiar, gentle face. She didn't know what had brought him here, but she thanked God for the opportunity to talk to him once more. And she prayed their conversation would be pleasant. She could accept a dissolution of their relationship if only they could end things with kind words rather than angry ones.

"Since Mr. Irwin approved my taking a break, let's step outside for a moment. The sun is shining through the window panes, and I don't hear wind rattling the shutters, so it's calm outside, yes?" She waited until he nodded, then added, "Good. Let's go to the porch, then. After last night's storm, I'd like to enjoy a moment of bright stillness." And outdoors, there'd be no curious gazes or listening ears tuned to their discussion.

He shifted aside in one clumsy half step to allow her passage. The thick carpet muffled their footsteps, but she sensed him close on her heels as she led him to the lobby. The entire distance she sent up silent prayers for God to prepare her heart for whatever Amos might say. *Your strength, my dear Father, endow me with Your strength...* She reached for the doorknob, but his hand shot out and closed over the crystal knob.

"Wait." He shrugged out of his jacket, and then slowly, carefully, with a touch so light he might have been bestowing a mantle of gossamer, he placed his jacket over her shoulders. His cheeks, already ruddy from the chill air, blazed even brighter. "It's cold outside."

She smiled her thanks, then allowed him to open the door for her. She moved to the edge of the porch and tasted the crisp, chill air. Sunlight shimmered through broken tree limbs, seeming even brighter and bolder than ever after yesterday's intense storm. A whine captured her attention, and she shifted her gaze to a swaybacked mule and two spotted dogs, all tied to a hitching ring by various reins.

A little gasp of surprise left her lips. She swung on Amos. "Did you bring Samson and Gideon to town?"

"Yes." He stood with his arms crossed over his chest. "And Jehoshaphat Isaac."

Dinah blinked, confused. Understanding bloomed, and she lifted one hand toward the old mule. "You named him Jehoshaphat?"

Amos offered a sheepish shrug. "I didn't. Someone else did. I just kept the name. But I mostly call him Ike."

Laughter bubbled in her chest. She'd thought Shadrach and Meshach odd names, but they couldn't possibly compare to Jehoshaphat. However, after having read the biblical stories about Shadrach, Meshach, and their friend Abednego, as well as ones about the man named Jehoshaphat who ruled over Judah in a godly manner, she decided the names weren't bad after all.

Swallowing a chortle, she gave the mule an approving nod. "I like it. Jehoshaphat had strong determination. That's a good trait for a mule, I would say."

"It's a good trait for anyone, I would say."

Amos spoke in a serious, subdued tone that dampened every vestige of Dinah's humor. Turning to face him, she tipped her head and braved a question. "Why did you come to see me today, Amos?"

Instead of answering, he limped toward her. She instinctively tensed at his approach, but she managed to stand still while he pushed his hand into one of the jacket pockets. He withdrew a rock, which he extended on his open palm.

She frowned. "What is it?"

"A rock."

She bounced her frown from the rock to his face. His answer was far from satisfactory. She'd recognized the object. She wanted to know why he brought it to her. Before she could formulate the question, he began to speak in a thready voice deep with emotion.

"I found it last summer, shortly after I met you right here on the porch of the Clifton." His gaze dropped to the multicolored stone, and he rotated his hand slightly from side to side, allowing the stone's imbedded minerals to capture the sunlight and send it back in glistening shards of white. "Its color reminded me of you. Of your brown hair with its threads of gold."

He raised his head sharply, his eyes seeming to examine the sides of her upswept hair. Dinah tugged his jacket more tightly closed at her throat, recalling how Mr. Sanger had focused on the waves of thick hair falling across her shoulders. But Mr. Sanger was gone, banished from town by the sheriff who warned him to stay away. This was Amos standing before her, a man who'd certainly inflicted pain with his angry words but who had never ogled her or touched her in a disrespectful way. She needn't worry.

"I kept it in my house. As a reminder of you."

Warmth spiraled through her. "Y-you did?"

"Yes. Until two Sundays after New Year's Eve."

Memories of New Year's Eve returned in a rush. Dinah hung her head as Amos continued, his fingers closing around the rock and clenching so tightly his knuckles glowed.

"On that day I picked it up, and I stepped out on my porch, and I threw the rock as far as I could." He drew his arm back as if preparing to throw it again. "I threw it in anger. In bitterness. In condemnation." He seemed to freeze for a moment, his arm poised, and then he sagged, his arm falling weakly to his side. "And I was wrong."

Startled, Dinah shifted her attention from his loosely held fist lying limp against his trouser leg to his face. Twin tears glistened in his eyes, brightening the deep-blue irises. She read contrition, sorrow, and—she stifled a gasp, hardly daring to believe it—even love shining from his eyes as he pinned her with his fervent gaze.

"I let my stubborn pride intrude. I acted just like the men who were ready to stone the woman caught in adultery, completely forgetting 'all have sinned, and come short of the glory of God.'" Still holding the rock, he lifted his hand, the movement so slow she didn't feel the need to flinch away. "We both made mistakes, Dinah, but God is faithful to forgive. He's forgiven me for my rash response and judgmental reaction." He offered her the rock, his callused fingertips providing a cradle for the glistening stone. "And now I ask you to forgive me for hurting you."

Dinah cupped his hand between hers and clung. Such sweet words—a request for forgiveness. Her reply poured out effortlessly. "I forgive you. And I beg the same of you. I intentionally hid pieces of my past from you. I'm sorry I wasn't honest. Will you forgive me?"

Even before he answered, she already knew what he'd say by the tenderness in his expression. Still, she gloried in his softly stated, "Yes."

For several minutes they stood smiling into each other's faces, his hand with the rock gripped between her palms. Cold hovered around them, dry snowflakes danced in little swirls on the painted porch boards, and from far in the distance, a train released a shrill whistle that echoed across the prairie. But as far as Dinah was concerned, nothing existed except Amos and her finding their peace again. She memorized the moment so she could thank God for every detail when she knelt for prayer that evening.

Then an odd noise intruded—a swoop of sound starting high and ending with a smack. Dinah gave a start and Amos laughed. One short, humor-filled snort of laughter. He tipped his head toward the hitching post. "That was Gid. He yawned."

She stared at Amos in amazement. "That was a yawn? It sounded like someone trying to learn to play the violin."

This time when Amos laughed, he threw back his head and let it roll with abandon. Dinah couldn't help but laugh, too. She skipped from the porch and crouched next to Gideon, smiling at the dog's mismatched eyes that blinked up at her with friendliness. "Are you bored, Gid, or merely sleepy?"

The dog responded by snatching the feather duster from her pocket and shaking it. Feathers flew and Dinah laughed again.

Amos hitched over, giving double hops on his good leg as he came. "Gideon, no!"

Gideon settled back on his haunches and looked in innocence at his master, the duster still clamped between his teeth. He made such a ridiculous sight that Dinah laughed even harder. And Amos joined her. She rose as he took a forward step, and when she turned, she found herself nose to chest with him. She lifted her face to look into his eyes, and something glimmering in the blue depths stilled her laughter. His chuckles ended, as well.

The train's whistle came again, closer this time, raising a whine from each of the dogs and causing Jehoshaphat Isaac to paw the ground in protest. But Dinah and Amos remained as still as a pair of porch posts, their eyes locked and their lips slightly parted, little wisps of their breath mingling between them. The ground beneath their feet began to tremble with the approach of the locomotive. The hotel door flew open and Mr. Irwin's voice bellowed, "Train's coming! Dining workers, get ready!" And still Amos and Dinah didn't move.

Not until the train screeched into the station and passengers began to cross the road to the hotel did Amos finally take one backward step away from Dinah. Although he hadn't been touching her, although she'd been standing on her own strength, his slight departure seemed to steal her ability to remain upright. Her knees went weak, and she placed her hand on Jehoshaphat's back to steady herself.

She was glad for the mule's presence when Amos spoke over the din of the invading crowd. If she hadn't had something to hold on to, she would have surely collapsed in a puddle on the hard ground in joyous surprise. Because he opened his mouth and said without an ounce of ceremony, "Dinah Hubley, will you wear my ring, and come summer will you be my bride?"

Chapter 45

June, 1884
Dinah

*D*inah, attired in her Calico Ball dress and clutching a fragrant bouquet of wildflowers, stood in the center of the attached gazebo on the Clifton Hotel's porch. Beside her, Amos stood tall and dapper in his familiar black suit. Before her, Preacher Mead held his Bible open on his hand and read from the thirteenth chapter of First Corinthians. All across the sunny lawn behind her, townspeople gathered with Amos's parents, brothers, and their families at the front of the small crowd.

A warm breeze, scented by the profusion of roses already blooming in the gardens, tossed the tendrils of hair escaping from her flower-adorned coronet of braids. A sideways glance confirmed Amos watched the dancing locks, and she was glad her hands were too occupied to tuck the strands behind her ears. Would she ever tire of Amos's adoring gaze?

In all her childhood imaginings, Dinah had never conjured a wedding day like this one, held on the porch of a Kansas hotel. She never envisioned a groom in a black wool suit, who suffered a fresh haircut that reached too high on the back of his neck and exposed a line of white where the sun hadn't kissed his skin with bronze. Her fanciful dreams had been filled with castles and gilt carriages, a prince in a snow-white uniform with gold epaulets on his shoulders and she in a billowing gown covered in layer upon layer of intricate lace. Her wedding day might lack the whimsical elements of a little girl's hopeful imagination, but it contained the most important feature—love.

The day was infused with love. From Mr. Irwin, who'd insisted on providing a sumptuous wedding feast in the ballroom, free of charge. From Ruthie and her family, who had assisted in planning every facet of the event. From Rueben, who'd traveled all the way from Chicago to stand in as Dinah's father. And mostly from Amos, whose tender, attentive gaze raised tremors of eagerness to speak the simple words—*I do*—that would bind her to him for all her living days.

Looking back, Dinah decided everything from Amos's straightforward proposal to this simple outdoor wedding was perfect. She no longer needed a fairy tale. Real life—God's amazing gift of this steadfast, honorable, big-hearted man—was so much better than any storybook account.

She forced aside her reflections to focus on Preacher Mead, whose voice, although at full volume, held a tenderness as he completed his reading. "'And now abideth faith, hope, charity, these three; but the greatest of these is charity.'" He closed his Bible and unfolded a slip of paper. Looking first at Amos, the minister said, "Amos, repeat after me…"

Dinah listened as Amos promised to love her, provide for her, support her in good times and bad for the rest of his earthly life. She marveled at the intensity in his dark-blue eyes, the sincerity in his tone. Oh yes, no prince could compare to the man God had chosen for her. When it came her time to speak her vows, her voice trembled, but Amos's tender smile encouraged her, and she finished on a strong note.

Preacher Mead turned to Amos. "Amos, do you take this woman to be your lawfully wedded wife?"

Not even a second of hesitation followed the question. Amos declared, "I do."

And then it was Dinah's turn to respond to Preacher Mead's query concerning her taking Amos as her husband. She replied through happy tears, "I do."

"The ring," Preacher Mead prompted Cale, who stood beside Amos with his skinny shoulders so squared he might have been a soldier on parade. The little boy dug in his pocket and withdrew a slim gold band. The minister took it and gave it to Amos.

Dinah passed her bouquet to Ruthie, who served as her attendant, then held her hand to Amos in readiness of him slipping the ring onto her finger. Although his callus-roughened fingers shook slightly, he managed to slide the band of gold past her knuckle where it nestled against the resized promise ring he'd given her for Christmas. The two were perfect together. Just as she and Amos were perfect together. She raised her beaming smile to him and found his dear face blurred by her veil of happy tears. But even through the watery sheen, she couldn't miss the happiness glowing in his eyes.

"Amos," Preacher Mead blared in a joyous tone, "you may kiss your bride!"

Heat flooded Dinah's cheeks as she tipped her face to her groom. Her eyes slid closed when his lips descended—warm, salty yet sweet, firm yet gentle. The kiss of a true prince. More tears rolled down Dinah's face as she received Amos's kiss with complete trust and the absence of any unpleasant recollections. She could have remained there forever, with his lips on hers, but Cale gave a whoop, and the townsfolk burst into laughter followed by thunderous applause, and Amos stepped away. But the promise in his eyes told her she could expect another kiss later. She nodded her approval.

Ruthie swept her into an exuberant hug, whispering in her ear, "Oh, Dinah, aren't you so glad you aren't a server? Isn't marriage to Amos so much better?"

Dinah couldn't agree more. From Ruthie's embrace she turned to Rueben. She gasped when he captured her in a hug so tight it stole her breath. He'd never touched her—not in all her growing-up years—yet receiving this hug from him seemed right somehow.

She rested her cheek against his broad chest. "Thank you for coming, Rueben. You're the only friend I ever had."

He pulled loose and his solemn gaze roved across the people crowding the lawn and surging onto the porch to offer congratulations. "It seems to me you've got lots of friends now." He cupped her face in his big hands and briefly touched his lips to her forehead. "That's what matters, Dinah—now. You've done good, made something of yourself just like I knew you could. I'm proud of you."

His words were something a father might say. Dinah's heart filled, and she rose up on tiptoe and kissed his cheek. Then she caught his hands. "I wish you didn't have to go. Chicago is so far away…"

An odd smile lifted one side of his mouth. "Well, Chicago's always been my home. But my little Dinah had the courage to start over somewhere new. It just might be you've inspired me to strike out for a new start, too. I noticed there's a little storefront for sale that could make a very nice café. Maybe I'll stick around and give that highfalutin hotel chef a little competition."

Dinah stared at him in wonder. But before she could question him, a warm, familiar hand touched the small of her back, and Amos's tender whisper reached her ear.

"The party is starting. Are you ready?"

She turned to tell him yes, but instead something else left her lips. "Can't we just go home?"

Amos drew back, surprise evident in his expression. "But the party…the food and music Mr. Irwin arranged. You don't want to stay and enjoy it?"

Dinah considered his question. All she really wanted was to go home with Amos. Her husband. Her God-chosen love. "I'd really rather just be with you."

An understanding smile broke across his face. "That's what I want, too."

Behind her, Rueben cleared his throat. "Um, Dinah?"

Both Dinah and Amos turned to him.

Rueben scratched his cheek in a sheepish gesture. "If you'll accept some uninvited advice, go to the party. It's in your honor. Amos's folks and other kin are there. The townspeople from where you're making your home are there. These people are your family and friends. Show 'em you appreciate them coming here today by spending some time with them. You'll have plenty of you-two time when the day is over."

Dinah consulted Amos with raised brows. He peered down at her, indecision thinning his lips. Then he nodded. "I think he's right, Dinah. We should go."

She sighed. "All right." She tipped her head and fluttered her lashes at him in a teasing manner. "But only for a little while. Yes?"

Rueben burst out laughing and clapped Amos on the shoulder. "This is what's known as compromising, boy, and if you learn to do it early, you'll have a lot fewer disagreements with your wife."

Amos showed Dinah he didn't mind compromising by bestowing a quick kiss on her smiling lips. Then the three of them joined the celebration taking place in the hotel's ballroom. Despite Dinah's initial desire to sneak out early, she had such fun talking and laughing and getting acquainted with Amos's mother and sisters-in-law, they stayed until all the townsfolk departed and Amos's family headed to their rooms. Mr. Irwin invited the two of them to enjoy supper in the dining room before leaving for the farm, but Amos politely declined with the excuse he needed to see to the animals.

So Dinah thanked her former boss for all he'd done to make their day a special one, hiding her smile at the man's flustered blush. And then she and Amos walked hand in hand to the carriage house where Jehoshaphat Isaac waited within the traces of a boxy delivery wagon—a wedding gift from Amos's family. Although at least twenty years old, the wagon wore a fresh coat of paint, compliments of the local wainwright. The man had also covered the springed seat with brown leather and inserted isinglass in the window openings, giving the conveyance a sparkling new appearance.

Amos paused beside the wagon, his gaze traveling over every inch of the wooden box painted a cheerful celery green. He touched one finger to the bold yellow letters proclaiming ACKERMAN FARM'S QUALITY EGGS & POULTRY on its side, the gesture almost reverent. "Do you know what this means, Dinah?"

She blew out a dainty breath, considering how much easier Amos's deliveries would now be. "It means you don't have to load your eggs in a child's wagon anymore."

"That, and even more." He faced her, his expression serious. "This tells me my father approves of my choice to raise chickens instead of growing wheat. For generations, first in Germany and then in America, the Ackermans have been wheat farmers. He was so disappointed when I left the family farm. But this…" He touched the wagon again. "This says what his words cannot. He approves."

Dinah's heart swelled. She stepped against Amos, wrapping her arms around his torso and clinging, reveling in the freedom to do so whenever she pleased because she was now his wife. "God is good."

Amos's arms closed around her. He rested his cheek on her hair for a moment before kissing the crown of her head once and then again. Setting her aside, he smiled into her face. "Mrs. Ackerman, are you ready to go home?"

"Home…" Dinah released the glorious word on a contented sigh. "Oh, yes."

Amos assisted her onto the high seat, then climbed up and settled himself close beside her. He took up the reins and gave a flick. "Giddyap there, Ike." The wagon lurched forward, the leather seat squeaking as their weight shifted. Dinah wrapped both arms around Amos's muscular upper arm and rested her cheek on his shoulder. He tipped his head to press his chin to her temple.

A clear blue sky served as their canopy as they rode through the early evening across the railroad tracks and out of town. Birdsong trilled from the treetops, the Kansas breeze carried the essence of musky soil and burgeoning plant life, and a yellow sun beamed its warmth as it slipped toward the horizon. Ike's hooves clip-clopped a steady beat, stirring dust that whirled in little wisps into the thick green growth alongside the road.

Dinah drew in a lungful of the unique summer perfume, savoring its essence. She hugged Amos's arm. "It's perfect."

"What is?"

She smiled up at him. "Everything."

Amos smiled, the corners of his eyes crinkling. "As you said, God is good."

Dinah tipped her face to receive his kiss on her eager lips, then settled her cheek on his shoulder again. Indeed, God was good.

*D*ear Reader,

   Thank you for visiting Florence, Kansas, and the Clifton Hotel. I rarely set a story in something other than a fictional community because I worry about getting the facts wrong. But I wanted my wannabe Harvey girl to come to the first hotel owned by the man credited with bringing culture to the West. (You can read more about Fred Harvey, his restaurants, and the Harvey girls at www.kshs.org.) Despite intensive research, I'm sure there are some places where whimsy has overridden fact. Partly because much of Florence's history records were lost in floods, and partly because I'm human. I hope historians with a close tie to Florence will forgive any discrepancies.

   This story, more than any other I've written, is close to my heart. Dinah is a fictional character, but unfortunately her experience is far too real. Statistics show that one in every five girls and one in every twenty boys will be sexually molested before they reach their eighteenth birthdays. Childhood sexual abuse steals a child's trust and innocence and creates tremendous scars that often haunt people well into their adult years. My heart breaks for those who struggle with relationships, who battle trust issues, who view themselves as unworthy, who use alcohol or drugs to numb the pain, who hide their feelings of shame beneath a mask of indifference or perfection or promiscuity because of someone else's selfish choice.

   Dinah found release from her burden of shame when she reached out in faith to the One who knows all and can heal all. I pray if you are struggling with the residual pain of childhood sexual abuse, you'll accept Ruthie's advice to Dinah: You shouldn't feel shameful over what someone else did. The shame isn't yours to carry. Give it to Jesus and walk in freedom.

   May God bless you abundantly as you journey with Him!
   Kim

ACKNOWLEDGMENTS

*A*s always, heartfelt appreciation to my family—*my husband, my parents, my children*—for your support and encouragement. I could not meet the challenges of this writing ministry without you!

My sincerest thanks to *Phoebe Janzen* from Florence, Kansas, who opened the Harvey House Museum for me and shared her wealth of knowledge about the first Harvey-owned hotel. Your passion for history and specifically the Harvey legacy is contagious. I'm glad you helped me catch the "bug."

Hugs to my *critique partners*. Every writer needs a cheer squad. I'm so grateful God blessed me with you.

Shannon and the fabulous team at WaterBrook, I marvel at your talents and abilities. Writing a book truly is a team effort, and I have been gifted abundantly by becoming a part of your team.

Finally, and most important, deepest gratitude and endless awe to *God.* Without Your healing touch, I would still be buried beneath the burden of shame, leaning on a cane, trying to earn my way to worthiness. Thank You for being my Healer, my Savior, my Enough. There is such joy in being whole. May any praise or glory be reflected directly back to You.

DISCUSSION QUESTIONS

1. Dinah was born and raised in a brothel. People in town viewed her as tainted and rejected her because of her connection to the Yellow Parrot. Was this a fair response? Do we sometimes make assumptions about people based on their associations? How can we be fair in our treatment of those who come from questionable home situations or backgrounds?

2. When Dinah agreed to meet the gentleman in the hotel room in exchange for money, her motives were good—she wanted the money to care for her mother. Her choice goes against the biblical admonition from 1 Corinthians 6:18 that instructs believers to flee from sexual immorality. Because Dinah wasn't a Christian when she went to the hotel, does that absolve her from responsibility for her decision? Why or why not?

3. Amos suffered an injury that resulted in a lifelong physical abnormality that left him feeling less worthy than his able-bodied brothers. Was his view of himself understandable? How would you have advised Amos? How can you help those you know who face physical challenges to feel capable and confident?

4. Dinah places great emphasis on becoming one of Mr. Harvey's servers. Why is this so important to her? Have you ever set a goal that proved to be out of reach? How did you handle the failure? Was Dinah's failure to become a server a loss or was it a victory? Why do you view it that way?

5. Ruthie wants to help her family financially and to honor her minister father by living according to God's Word. At the same time, she dreams of having her own family. How do her wants complement one another? How do they collide? How do Ruthie's desires change when she realizes she has put more focus on earthly relationships than on the one with her heavenly Father?

6. Dinah's treatment at the hands of the gentleman who used her for his pleasure leaves a mark that haunts her dreams and hinders her from formulating relationships. She holds the secret inside, fearing people's reaction if they discover the "dirtiness" of her soul. When did the secret lose its power? What brought about her healing from the past? What did Ruthie mean when she told Dinah she shouldn't feel guilty over what the gentleman had done? Do we sometimes carry responsibility for someone else's actions? How can we release a shame that isn't ours to bear?

7. Amos put great stock in building a successful chicken farm. Was he right to put so much focus on increasing his flock and making more money? Why or why not? How can we be certain the goals we set for ourselves are God-honoring rather than self-honoring?

Sometimes a secret must be kept for the truth to be revealed.

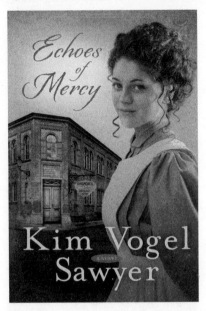

Echoes of Mercy follows investigator Caroline Lang into a Kansas chocolate factory where her resolve to end child labor involves keeping her true identity hidden. When she meets Oliver, who has also assumed an alias, her feelings for him challenge her to keep her secret and complete her calling.

Check out the e-exclusive prequel, *Just As I Am.*

Can one woman's fight for the poor and destitute lead to the love she has never known?

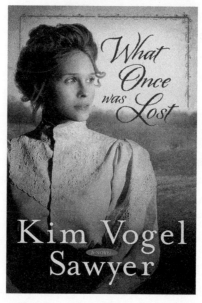

In *What Once Was Lost*, Kim Vogel Sawyer captivates readers with a hopeful romance set in a rural Kansas community in the late 1800s where a Mennonite woman and a bitter mill owner find that debilitating loneliness melts away through ministering to the needs of those around them.

Check out the e-exclusive prequel, *The Grace That Leads Us Home.*

Read excerpts from these books and more on
WaterBrookMultnomah.com!